CELTIC ENIGMA

PATRICK O'DONOVAN

Pen Press Publishers Ltd

First published in Great Britain
Pen Press Publishers Ltd
39-41 North Road
London N7 9DP

ISBN 1 904754 11 2

A catalogue record for this book is available
from the British Library

Printed and bound in Great Britain

Cover design by Jacqueline Abromeit
Geminivision

Contents

Acknowledgements
About the Author

Acknowledgements

I wish to thank those who encouraged me to undertake a task for which I had no previous experience. The assistance and support of my two sons, Ronan and Neil, helped me to persevere.

Above all, the patience and understanding of my wife, Catherine, who could be forgiven for often despairing of the fruition of this novel, are greatly appreciated.

About The Author

The childhood and adolescent years spent in the south-west corner of the Irish Republic conditioned Patrick O'Donovan for what transpired to be a varied and interesting career.

He complemented an agricultural science degree from University College Dublin in 1959 with a Master's and Doctorate in animal science from the United States, followed by four years of research work in Ireland.

In 1968 he began the first of many assignments with the Food and Agriculture Organization of the United Nations, culminating in his retirement at the end of 1996. He worked in research, training and extension in countries throughout Asia, Africa and both Central and South America. Doctor O'Donovan now lives with his wife, Catherine, in Dublin's south suburbs in the Irish Republic.

CHAPTER 1

Inistogue, County Kerry

'May the Divine assistance remain always with us...' Such were the words of curate Fr. Joseph Lynch as he rounded off the mass sermon on that cold and damp Sunday of November 2nd, 1952.

'Is he nearly finished?' moaned Seamus Dowling, perched on one knee in the last pew of the overcrowded church. The question, directed towards the dishevelled and weary man to his left, was met with the droll response: 'He finished fifteen minutes ago - his big problem is not knowing when to shut up.'

Everyone in this small rural village attended mass and in those heady days of the early 1950s, many were in dire need of assistance, be it of divine origin or otherwise, to lighten their daily poverty-induced burdens.

The village of Inistogue nestled at the foot of small undulating hills and the surrounding land was acidic, edging more and more towards peat through lack of drainage and lime. Decades of neglecting to apply fertilizers had stemmed partly from ignorance of its necessity but much more from sheer scarcity of money. The majority of farms within the parish of Inistogue had fewer than 40 acres: much of the income came from a nucleus of dairy cows whose milk yield had hardly changed for 50 years, plus the extra ready cash from selling dry stock. The carry-over of compulsory tillage from the war years meant that wheat, barley or oats, and in some cases an area of all three, were reluctantly grown on land ill-suited to the crops' needs. Pigs were used as scavengers, subsisting mainly on skimmed milk, a nutritious by-product of the whole milk delivered to the creamery for butter-making, since kitchen waste or meagre amounts of grain provided all too little energy.

The pigs consequently took several months over the customary six or seven to reach a saleable live weight of 200 pounds. Fowl such as hens, turkeys, geese and ducks, which relied heavily on farm waste, provided fresh eggs and meat.

It was on such a farm that Seamus Dowling had been born on March 16, 1924, the first of four sons and two daughters to Timothy and Julia Dowling. Seamus vividly recalled his Dad saying that he'd started celebrating the feast of St. Patrick one day early and it had continued almost uninterrupted till Easter. Seamus' birth confirmed not only his Dad's masculinity and his Mam's fertility but also ensured there was a healthy heir-apparent to carry on a farming tradition the Dowling family had long enjoyed in a poor but challenging part of the county.

The other sons, Tom, Paudie and Sean, arrived at almost yearly intervals, followed two years later by Marie and a further 18 months after that, by Eileen. The family size was small by local standards but more than could be supported on 28 statute acres with poor-quality grazing for only nine cows and their "followers".

Ever since Timothy Dowling had drawn his first breath in the wee hours of August 10th, 1881, he was destined to carry on the Dowling family tradition and reflect his Irishness even when there was scant reason to do so. He was the eldest of a large family of 12 (whose births had occurred with repetitive regularity), and his normal 16-hour work days were necessary to meet the most mundane needs of his brothers and sisters, all of whom would, in time, leave and settle in other parts of Ireland or, more ominously, emigrate.

Timothy's was an early life of hard work and drudgery, a role he shared with farmers throughout Ireland. Tenant farmers were in the midst of a renewed and aggressive struggle to carve out a better living from their small holdings and to secure improved terms from their English landlords. Timothy's relatives and neighbours were ever-mindful of the horrific eviction scenes that had been enacted during the 1845-47 famine years when, following the almost total destruction through blight of the staple Irish potato crop, tenant farmers were starving while large stocks of wheat, as rent payment, were being shipped to English landlords. Timothy often asked the question that so many others were to ask in the ensuing years: why had so many starved and died in the midst of plenty?

In the long and sustained Irish struggle for independence from England, spanning more than 800 years, nothing compared to the ravages of the famine, which had left an indelible mark on the Irish psyche and irrevocably damaged Irish-English relations. However long and hard Timothy worked on his meagre few acres, he was fighting a losing battle under a feudal system whereby the English landlord extracted a too large and iniquitous share of the farm's potential produce. Like so many of his contemporaries, he felt obliged to work - and fight if necessary - for a better and fairer deal whose benefits could be passed on to succeeding generations.

He made a good start by espousing all things Gaelic or Irish. He lived only a few miles from a *gaeltacht* area of Kerry where Irish was the only language spoken and understood. What better way to identify with and lay claim to one's country than by fostering and speaking a native tongue that both confused and exasperated the perceived oppressors. Timothy devoted his early years to learning Irish and quickly became fluent, which elevated him to a new and more influential position in the local hierarchy. His parents were devout practising Catholics and his own devotion to his faith never faltered through the years, partly because he constantly needed God's assistance but even more because his strong Catholicism distanced him from the Protestantism of the English.

Timothy was scarcely out of nappies when the Gaelic Athletic Association (G.A.A.) was founded in 1884. The G.A.A. encouraged national games of football and hurling (played with ash sticks or hurleys), which were the bedrock of future Irish sporting life. Playing these games was regarded as an explicit manifestation of Irish nationalism, compared to taking up what were perceived as English or "foreign" sports. From his early teens, Timothy played various grades of football for his Inistogue club and County Kerry which, because of its rapidly-developing success, had become known as the *Kingdom*.

But he took particular satisfaction from his political

endeavours to rid all Ireland of English domination. This mood was pervasive in his strong republican corner of the country where, despite numerous setbacks and repeated failures, there was a widely-held belief that most independence struggles eventually achieve some measure of success, even if much blood has to be shed in the process.

Timothy played a part in several liberation attempts, from his teenage years at the end of the 19th century until the independence of 26 of Ireland's 32 counties in December, 1921. His most cherished memories were of his valiant part in defending and holding the General Post Office (G.P.O.) in Dublin during the uprising of Easter week, 1916. After the rebels were outnumbered and out-gunned by the English, Timothy had managed to escape and live to fight other battles. A few years later the English had sent the Black and Tans to Ireland - newly-released and brutal prisoners with specific instructions to quell unruly elements among the natives This had led to some of the most bitter fighting over the next couple of years.

Yet Timothy remembered this period of his life with fond pleasure as well as pride and anger: for it was while being treated for gunshot wounds following a skirmish with a group of Black and Tans that he had met a young volunteer named Julia Moran who, in April 1923, had become his bride.

The independence treaty of December 1921 was seen by Timothy (and Eamon de Valera, whom he supported) as a sell-out to the English. The anti-treatyists vowed to continue the fight until all 32 counties were independent, and what followed was a very bloody civil war against the pro-treaty forces, led by Michael Collins, which culminated in Collins's death in his native County Cork in August, 1922.

The civil war brought nothing of substance except bitterness and animosity, even amongst relatives and close friends, yet it dominated every facet of Irish life for several decades. The end result was a new and independent Free State of 26 counties, which was subsequently to become a republic in 1949, and six northern counties where a two-thirds majority of predominantly Scottish and English settlers ensured that their land remained within the United Kingdom. Although the dust had temporarily settled on a land not totally at ease with itself, it was yet to rise and fall... and go on rising and falling before some semblance of stability, if not tranquillity, could be achieved.

Timothy Dowling had much to ponder on his wedding day. He was equally apprehensive about the likely political developments in his country as well as the daily challenges facing him and his bride in their new life together. Pressure to support his siblings had been largely responsible for him marrying at the late age of 42, but this was not at all unusual at the time. Nevertheless, he recognized that the flower of youth had passed him by and, should God bless them with a family, he would expect their children to maintain similar goals and standards to his own. But this was a matter for another day.

*

'If I had any control over my destiny,' mused Seamus Dowling one dark cold December morning in 1932, 'I would never elect to be the first-born.' Even then, about four months short of his ninth birthday, he had come to realise the enormous responsibilities placed on his very young shoulders, as he helped his father to make each day that little bit more productive than the last. Not that his brothers and sisters were standing idly by, but they all looked to Seamus for guidance and support.

Although Seamus and his Dad were at the forefront of farm management and decision-making, it was only through the combined help of all family members attending to many and varied seasonal jobs that a basic but simple livelihood could be eked out. Most of the food was fortunately farm-produced, for there was little or no ready cash. Each spring turf was hand-cut from a rented bog a few miles distant and dried through several handling operations during the summer months, before it was transported home, stacked and covered for the winter. It was acknowledged by shrewd local old-timers that turf operations were among the most difficult and back-breaking of farm jobs. But they were also among the most vital, for not only was turf the sole fuel for cooking, it also provided heat during the long cold winters of which Inistogue had more than its share.

The plight of the Dowlings and many other small farmers was not helped by the economic war between Ireland and England in the early 1930s. Instigated by the then Taoiseach (Prime Minister), Eamon de Valera, it was politically motivated as a means of putting greater pressure on and extracting extra concessions from Ireland's old adversary.

Seamus thought (though he was a little fearful of expressing it to his father): 'What has politics to do with selling our calves so that we can buy flour and other necessities?' It was all too complex and frustrating a subject for a young and energetic nine year old. Seamus witnessed his Dad slaughtering many of their young calves, rather than offering them for sale and export to England. Stories abounded (many too sad to repeat but some with more than a trace of humour) concerning the events of the time. One particular farmer had taken two young calves, in a horse-drawn cart with wooden side rails, to a monthly Friday market in a nearby town. Having sat nearby from 5 a.m. until 2 p.m. without receiving a bid that even bordered on respectability, the farmer decided to go to a bar for a drink. When he came out an hour later, he discovered there were five calves in his cart!

But it was not all doom and gloom in a county that, in the late 1920s and early 1930s, won four senior football All-Irelands in a row. While Timothy was now well past his playing days and his sons still too young to start, it did not exclude them from the annual September festivities signalling the championship season's end. The young Dowling boys had their own county idols, some not too distant from their native Inistogue, and all four played from their tender years, aspiring to greater heights.

At the outbreak of the second world war and the onset of their teenage years, thoughts began to drift ever so gradually to affairs of the heart. It was about this time that crossroads dancing reached peak popularity in County Kerry, providing a welcome respite from the farming routine. In the eyes of energetic youngsters, life indeed had much to offer.

The young Dowlings dreamt of future lives beyond the confines of their few acres and were greatly helped by their God-given gifts of good sense and intelligence. Some of their Dad's contemporaries had already landed good jobs in Dublin and a select few were ensconced in the upper echelons of the new government. It became a well-acknowledged fact that 'cute' Kerrymen occupied many of the most prestigious posts in Dublin's civil service. The significance of this was not lost on Timothy to whom, notwithstanding the daily need for male muscle power to 'keep his ship afloat', education was seen as an escape route for his children into a better life. Realising the role his eldest son Seamus would play in supporting the family, it did not displease Timothy unduly when Master Healy from the primary school hinted that Seamus's academic potential had distinct limitations, leaving the way clear for him to concentrate on farming. Seamus himself knew that, if successful, this would bring him satisfaction beyond belief, not only through providing for his brothers and sisters but, being a native by heart, it would spare himself the insecurity and heartbreak of seeking a living in a foreign country.

The start of the Second World War in September 1939 brought little respite. Timothy and Julia feared it could bring much more hardship and deprivation than the economic war they had luckily managed to come through. Then in stepped de Valera, offering a ray of hope by publicly declaring Ireland's neutrality. But Timothy and many of his kin remained unconvinced. 'What does this so-called neutrality mean,' they mused, 'when our young men must stand side-by-side with the English and French to fight the Germans? Will our economic woes be any different when the food rationing and shortages, that are already starting, become even more severe in the months - and possibly years - ahead?'

They were justified in being confused and intrigued by the Irish Government's stance on the war. Why should they join forces with the English, against whom they'd struggled for so long and still did, to fight the Germans, whose aspirations for global dominance threatened even more dire consequences? Timothy was consoled by his belief that the able-bodied men of

Inistogue and many parishes throughout Ireland had little independent say in the matter and were merely following the political decisions and directives of the time.

Training young men in the skills and rigours of impending war was essential and many Irishmen volunteered to become members of the Local Defence Forces (L.D.F.), with many branches scattered throughout the country. The older Dowling brothers, Seamus and Tom, joined the Inistogue branch, which held regular training sessions during the year plus more intensive two-week summer camps. Tough though the training was, both found it a refreshing change from the drudgery and monotonous routine of farm work. The summer camps, often near sandy beaches within earshot of towns, gave ample opportunities to soak up sunshine and admire the local talent by day and dance the weekend nights away. The brothers rigorously observed the training routine without having any idea as to its ultimate benefit or use. They possessed more than enough arms, equipment and know-how to shoot, and kill if necessary, but neither had the will or stomach to do so even in the most provocative of situations. Seamus and Tom prayed to the Lord to keep it so and silently acknowledged that the benefits of the non-military training would serve them well in the future.

As much by example as by word, Timothy and Julia instilled in their family a devout respect for the Catholic faith, an appreciation of all things Irish and, in a sluggish wartime economy, a need through appropriate education to pursue and attain important goals in life. In 1940s Ireland these were targets many were at liberty to dream about but relatively few were predisposed to achieve. Those who did make it were not always intellectually gifted but rather dynamic individuals who, supported at great sacrifice by their parents, worked extremely hard to realise their dreams. Fortunately, most of the Dowlings had their fair share of brains but it severely strained the family purse to educate them to the required levels. In the end, Timothy and Julia were thrilled and eternally grateful when the near-impossible became a reality.

Seamus later benefited from his three years of secondary school, the demands of farm work ruling out a continuation. Tom secured honours in his Leaving Certificate and went on to pursue his longtime ambition of studying electrical engineering at university. Paudie and Sean did their Leaving Certificate before going their separate ways, the former to join the civil service in Dublin and the adventurous Sean to sample the emigrant trail to London. As befitting young ladies of that time, both Marie and Eileen were lucky to attend secondary school for the full five years. Since university seldom beckoned for most girls, Marie took up a bank position in Dublin and Eileen became a draper's assistant in Inistogue. In the short space of five years the Dowling homestead experienced an outward movement and disruption, the effects of which would take many years to heal.

And so it was, as the late 1940s gradually gave way to the early 1950s, Timothy and Seamus were handling practically all that needed doing on the farm. Or, more correctly, Seamus did all the heavy chores and his Dad was always about to help with the lighter work. Tom was now working with a Dublin engineering firm and joined Paudie on weekend trips home when, in addition to summer holidays, they were able to give strategically-important farm assistance. It was altogether a team effort, with the girls contributing where necessary towards domestic work. The post-war food rationing was about to ease and many could now see a little light at the end of what for them had been a very dark tunnel. Timothy was entering his twilight years and often thanked the Lord his strong-bodied son was more than able to cope and, besides, his good neighbours were never found wanting in emergencies. They all chipped in for the big occasions like carting home the turf, saving the hay, picking the September-harvested potatoes and, above all, threshing the corn which, despite the hard and dusty work, was a social event to almost rival Thanksgiving festivities in the United States.

*

When the not entirely unexpected news finally broke, it still shocked not only Seamus's immediate family but most of the neighbours.

'I intend to marry Nora Relihan in October,' came the sudden outburst in front of his father and mother one fine July evening of 1954. They had just begun eating their 8 p.m. meal as was the norm after a heavy day's work saving hay, followed by the equally arduous hand-milking of the cows.

It took what seemed several minutes for either to react, much less respond, to such a weighty pronouncement. Then Timothy raised his head slowly and, with a gentle wave of his hand, said matter-of-factly, 'Er-ha what a hurry is there on you, aren't you still a very young man?' He said it as a way of neutralising the impact and gravity of what they had just heard. Both of them needed little reminding that, short of a family bereavement, there was nothing to so greatly disrupt family unity and togetherness than a marriage. The consequences were more far-reaching when a son brought his new bride to live under the same roof as his parents. There were numerous such instances in the neighbourhood and the early congenial relations often steadily waned and invariably turned for the worst.

In bed that night, before sleep came to his tired limbs, Timothy pondered many questions that would haunt him constantly over the coming weeks and months. Was Seamus really serious when naming an exact month for the wedding? Why the great urgency, a mere three months hence? If the wedding went ahead, how would it affect not only harmony within the home but, more importantly, all the family members' capacity to come and go as they pleased, as was their God-given right? Turning to Julia, who despite her obvious fatigue was still staring blankly heavenward, he said, 'As much as I hate the thought of Seamus's decision and its impact on the family, he is a mature 30-year-old and ought to know what's best for his own future.' It was a frank admission from a man whose own marriage had begun much later in life, and who was beginning to understand and appreciate the present trend towards an earlier liberation from parents' apron-strings.

Julia's concerns were of a different kind. For starters, she had hoped for a longer lead-up to her son's marriage, a sacrament deserving the utmost respect and preparation. Although his fiancee, Nora, came from a neighbouring parish just five miles distant, in 1950s Ireland, where transport and communications were rudimentary, this seemed almost a different country. And their courtship had run anything but smoothly. Since they'd first met six years ago, the intensity of their relationship had ebbed and flowed almost in rhythm with the daily tides. Most of the blame lay in Seamus' court. Despite the best intentions, his heavy workload had prevented him from keeping all their pre-arranged dates. And, because he relied totally on bicycle or pedal power, the winter rains and gales often saw him reach his destination late, if at all. Nora had interpreted all this as a lack of interest and affection, and it was the source of regular disagreements, fights, even occasional partings, cooling-off periods and reunions. Through it all, their love and affection endured and they finally realised that they wanted to spend their lives together. Seamus was later heard jokingly say it takes at least a decade to select a partner for marriage.

None of her friends were surprised that Julia had never seen the young lady who would share her house and help make daily decisions; the prospective groom was too shy and reluctant to arrange a face-to-face meeting. As in many rural, status-conscious areas, Julia was initially more concerned about Nora's background and upbringing, as she feared what neighbours might say if her future daughter-in-law came from a lower social class. Timothy's reminder that social rankings were an unpleasant legacy of English colonialism did little to soften her concern.

In fact, Nora Relihan was the eldest of a family of four boys and three girls and her father Tom owned only the half acre of land surrounding the family cottage. After leaving national school at the age of 14, he had started work on the nearby Michael McElligott farm. He was the sole breadwinner for his family and his initiative and hard work, coming from a lad with no farming knowledge and experience, had increased McElligott's income enormously. This did not skip the attention of the childless farmer and his wife, whose only heir-apparent was a distant grand-nephew, aged four. Michael McElligott, now entering his twilight years, had given Tom more and more responsibility in managing the farm, and compensated his efforts with liberal salary increments. He came to regard the young man as the son he would have dearly loved to father, and rumour had it that it was only a matter of time before Tom would be willed the farm outright. It might send shivers down the spines of Michael's distant relatives and cause the kind of infighting that only land disputes can provoke.

'Did you hear the good news about Seamus Dowling and the nice girl he'll marry and bring to our parish?' was what Julia overheard from two gossiping neighbours one morning as she sat at her window, writing a letter to her sister in the United States. The words soothed Julia's early morning nerves, which she was experiencing more and more as the wedding approached. She was inclined to rubbish most gossip but hoped for once this might be an exception. So, despite not having met or talked to her future daughter-in-law, she bragged effusively to her sister, saying that relatives and neighbours believed Nora would bring new energy and joy to the Dowling household. More from politeness than any real expectation she would attend, Julia invited her sister to the wedding; the chances of her coming over from America were virtually zero, so Julia could lavish praise on her daughter-in-law without suffering any future embarrassment. Sealing the envelope, she wondered what she might be tempted to write three or four years hence but quickly dispelled this thought from her mind.

Seamus was the butt of many jokes as the busy summer season progressed. For Sunday mass he made sure he didn't proceed beyond his customary last pew, to avoid public scrutiny, but on the rare Sundays he approached the rails to receive Holy Communion, wry smiles, sniggers and even guffaws from latecomers in the back pews caused him to blush profusely. Neighbours he met at the creamery milk delivery, turf saving and Sunday football club outings were more forthright with their remarks, preferring to spare his blushes, express delight and bestow encouragement for the important decisions he was making. As time passed, Seamus learned to become immune to the harsher vibes and get on with his life.

Without much thought for omen-conscious neighbours, the young couple had long earmarked October 13 for their wedding. The so-called unlucky thirteenth was commonly avoided for any major undertaking, especially a wedding. Timothy and Julia called Seamus to task, saying that, no matter how advanced preparations were, he should choose an alternative date. Also unsuitable was October 20, Inistogue's annual traditional fair day, when Timothy tried to sell his unwanted small livestock to generate ready cash for the long winter and to socialise with friends. In the end, everyone who mattered agreed to opt for October 27. A local comedian quipped that the new date would allow more time to recover from the ravages of fair day over-indulgence.

*

It was 17 minutes after eleven o'clock on that unusually sunny but slightly frosty October 27th morning when the parish priest, Father Jack Brosnan, shuffled to his feet in Inistogue's Catholic Church of the Divine Saviour. With the groom and bride seated comfortably in the front pew of the already crowded church and surrounded by their family, friends and neighbours, he carefully selected the right words and phrases for his sermon:

'I would like to extend a warm welcome to all present but especially to the relatives and friends of Seamus and Nora joining us for this joyous wedding ceremony. It is indeed an honour and privilege to be asked to officiate. Having been first curate and later parish priest in this area of Kerry for close on 20 years, I am in the happy position of knowing not only the couple's parents and relatives but many of their friends and neighbours gathered here.

'May I say at the outset that this is a marriage born out of affection and true love, which have survived through the good days - and a few bad days - of courtship. We now see a couple stronger and more devoted to each other than ever. This speaks volumes in the defence of longer than average courtships, as they better prepare couples for enduring and successful marriages. Both sets of parents are God-fearing and practising Catholics, steeped in proud Gaelic and republican values and hard-working beyond belief. How pleasant it is to witness the sound example of parents being followed by their children. Both Seamus and Nora have done so to the highest degree. It must be a source of pleasure and sense of achievement for the Dowling and McElligott parents to have so successfully raised their children through the difficult depression and war years.'

The service helped to put everyone at ease and encouraged members of each party to intermingle afterwards and get to know one another. As the young couple walked arm-in-arm down the aisle, to the admiration of the church's congregation, there was a general belief that they would carry on the proud ancestral traditions. One could sense, in the intermingling and exchange of greetings in the church grounds, the party had already begun and nobody would dare predict when it might all end.

As befitted the severe hardships of the time, the party itself was anything but lavish. Yet what little they had been able to afford made the enjoyment all the more intense. The priests had kindly consented to the use of the local parish hall for the wedding reception, thereby considerably reducing the cost. If the meal itself was very basic, everything else more than compensated. Youths in their teens and early 20s busily filled beer and stout glasses to the brim while Irish and Scotch whiskeys were relished by those with more sophisticated tastes. It was a merry group that was eventually assembled and seated by 4 p.m. for the wedding meal amid loud chatter and general bonhomie. Afterwards, the best man began to manage proceedings and asked for speeches from a few with distinctly slurred voices.

Now it was Timothy's turn. This was the moment he had feared most of all, and he felt more nervous than when defending the General Post Office (G.P.O.) in 1916 and gun-running in the subsequent civil war. His fear was born out of a lack of education, and a childhood dread of standing in front of so many people and expressing his innermost thoughts and feelings. But, this being no ordinary occasion, he summoned up his courage, rose to his feet, braced himself, and with a glazed look began to speak. He expressed himself passionately and philosophically about the past and looked optimistically to the future.

'I'm not a man for speeches so I'll keep this short. The Dowlings of Inistogue have lived on this small patch of land for at least 100 years. They struggled and managed to survive where others might have gone under. Times have been hard... yes, very hard... and over the years we have tried to make things a little better. Long before the famine came we knew the colonial power of England was the cause of our misfortune. The Dowlings did their best to rid the country of the illegal occupier and oppressor but we haven't fully succeeded. Generations of Dowlings have come and gone and continued the struggle for what we see as our God-given human rights. These simple rights were denied to my father's generation and much of my own as well. When Ireland succeeded in 1921 to win independence for 26 of the 32 counties, the job was unfinished. Those six northern counties, still ruled by England, are as much a part of Ireland as Inistogue is. Our Irish colleagues in the north suffer many of the same injustices today as we did before 1921. We must ask ourselves the question: should we not make the same effort to help our brethren in the north, who wish to shake off colonialism, as we ourselves did here up until 1921 so that they may become part of a united Ireland? I, like many others, sided with de Valera's forces after 1921 to free all of Ireland but, for reasons now clear to all, we did not succeed.'

Some of the seated guests shuffled nervously, sending a clear signal that the tone of Timothy's speech was too political for a wedding reception. He paused, composed himself and resumed: 'On this happy day let's not be concerned about the past but look with hope and confidence to the future. Julia and I are delighted that today our son has married into a strong Irish and republican family, the McElligotts. We wholeheartedly accept Nora into our household and, now that our own years on earth are limited, look forward to them upholding our family values and traditions. In endorsing what has already been said, we encourage them to follow the righteous path and to rear any children they may be blessed with in the true Irish Christian spirit and make this country a better and more prosperous place in which to live. God be with you in all future tasks you undertake together...' With tears welling up in his sad eyes, he looked momentarily towards the seated couple, took his seat next to Julia and grasped her hand in a nervous gesture of love and affection.

Attention now turned to the five-piece local band of self-taught musicians. They were setting up their equipment on a small stage at the top of the hall from where they would entertain everybody into the wee hours of the next morning. The youngsters, meanwhile, were seeing to it that nobody stayed thirsty by serving white-foamed pints of stout, delicately pulled from wooden kegs. A local middle-aged and quick-witted bachelor, Joe Moriarty, was first on the stage to sing his favourite 'The Rose of Tralee', but not before plenty of alcohol had banished his customary inhibitions. The revelry grew in strength until 2 a.m., then plateaued for two hours, and most of the guests were physically exhausted when the couple finally took their leave at 5 a.m.

Cock-crowing before dawn was particularly irritating to those who had just, a short while earlier, laid their weary limbs and groggy heads to rest. Many later remarked that few Inistogue cows were milked before midday and when they were, a few of the high yielders had shed some of their milk. But it was a small price to pay for such a rare event in this sleepy village. All agreed that it had been the wedding of the century and, despite the harsh times and lack of luxuries, everyone had enjoyed life's simple pleasures to the full. Those who drank more than they were accustomed to were hazy about things that had happened after midnight and lost out on all that was worth remembering.

It came as no surprise that the honeymoon was short and simple, with the newly-weds reappearing in Inistogue three days later. A neighbour jokingly said they must have just taken the bus to Limerick and back. Six months later it became clear there had been time for much more when Nora confided to friends that her first-born was expected in July. Timothy gave his usual wry smile on hearing the good news and was elated by the knowledge that the Dowling dynasty was being perpetuated. He was also pleased with the good working relationship within the new household, where the harmony and peace served as a model for others. Seamus realised that just now life was very good to him and he was determined to continue savouring every minute of it.

While the years 1956 and 1957 witnessed the Irish Republic steadily emerging from the post-war hardships to a time of improving economic growth, the politics of Northern Ireland once again began to raise their ugly head. There were a number of skirmishes in the north, sometimes aided and abetted by republicans in the south, which, under the guise of securing more justice for the Catholic minority, were in reality a covert attempt to work towards a united Ireland. The small number of southern republicans killed were regarded as martyrs and fomented interest among others in the republican cause. Exploiting the training he already had, Seamus felt duty-bound to assist in however modest a way and he found plenty of opportunities to do so. However, due to the strong action by the then de Valera government in charging and imprisoning offenders, this rather brief and disorganised campaign of intended liberation never really took firm root. But the peaceful decade that followed was merely a respite in the protracted struggle for freedom.

*

It was 10.30 p.m. on a Monday in late September, 1959 when the cavalcade reached the tiny square in Inistogue. Gardai were there to marshal the huge crowd of fans from all over the county of Kerry who had come to honour their footballers who, a day earlier at the national Croke Park Stadium in Dublin, had won yet another of their many All-Ireland titles. The convergence of so many on Inistogue was a tribute not only to its proud football tradition but, more importantly, to the fact that this year's captain and two other team members were native sons. Many in the huge crowd had made the long and arduous train journey to the game and, despite being the worse for wear, were in jubilant mood during the speechmaking and revelry. Many of the elders present, seeing that the county had a proud tradition and enjoyed extraordinary success, regarded a September trip to Dublin as a God-given right, if not annually then at least once every two or three years. The thrill of success and anticipation for the future of this brilliant team could easily be seen on their faces.

As the captain was concluding his speech to vast applause, a loud thud was heard in the crowd periphery. Those in the immediate vicinity either looked towards or rushed to the back of a stationary truck whence the sound came. Seamus Dowling was among the first to arrive, only to find, to his shock, that it was his father who had collapsed from a wooden plank used as a vantage point to better savour the excitement. The previous day Timothy had listened with intense excitement to every word of the radio commentary and now, in the wee hours of the next, the pressure of it all had finally taken effect.

At first glance it was obvious to Seamus that this was much more than a simple fainting spell or exhaustion. He loosened the only tie his Dad possessed, at the same time trying to get some response from him. Meanwhile, a small crowd had gathered, some to actively assist and others looked on with apprehension. Joe Moriarty rushed to collect his car and within minutes he and Seamus had Timothy comfortably stretched and supported on the back seat and on their way home. Meanwhile, another neighbour had phoned the local doctor and priest, who were to come forthwith to his house. The only words Seamus could extract from his father was a faint 'Please bring me home.'

As Dr Michael Egan, a long-time friend and confidant of Timothy's, was about to take his leave he ushered Julia into the rarely-used sitting room where he could discuss his diagnosis in privacy. He began by saying, 'Mrs Dowling, I am very sorry that Timothy fell ill so suddenly and unexpectedly at a time when he was enjoying his county team's success.' Julia knew that this was just a preamble and a way of settling her before delivering the real news, so she braced herself for what might follow.

Dr Egan hesitated, drew a deep breath and went on, 'I have been such a close friend of Timothy's for many years that I feel very unhappy saying what I am duty-bound to say. On my initial examination close to midnight, I hoped that he had suffered little more than a very mild stroke brought about by the excitement of the past couple of days.

'But further tests have revealed a condition which might have developed slowly but steadily over the past couple of years. As men age - and Timothy has just entered his 79th year - fat can accumulate in the arteries near the heart, which in time blocks off the vital blood supply to and from the heart. This condition is called "arteriosclerosis" and, while eventually there may well be an effective treatment or cure, I'm afraid there is little I can do now, especially for a man of Timothy's age. There are also signs that his heart muscles are weak, an added strain in pumping enough blood throughout his body. I note that Father Brosnan is here and, while I think there is no immediate need for great concern, this is a prudent step.

'I realise, Mrs Dowling, that your family is scattered, with three in Dublin and another in London. I suggest you notify them so that they can come to see their father before he gets too ill. You will, of course, ask me how long he is likely to live. In my profession I have long since refrained from second-guessing God's plans. Nobody can predict but in my professional opinion, I fear that, given his advancing years and frailty, we may be speaking in term of weeks instead of months.'

With that rather stark prognosis, the tears welled up in Julia's eyes and Doctor Egan, patting her arm gently and apologising for not being able to give better news, bade her farewell.

The days that followed hung heavily on the Dowling family as well as the whole neighbourhood, contrasting starkly with the recent euphoria of Kerry's victory. Word had gone out to members of the family away from home and they were expected within days. Meanwhile, Timothy's health improved a little to the point where he could recognise friends and neighbours before drifting in and out of bouts of sleep or semi-consciousness. Julia and Nora were steadfast in their support and it cemented further their already close relationship. They took turns staying up at night and made sure he was made as comfortable as possible.

Sean was the last to arrive home from London on Saturday evening to complete the family reunion. They had all seen their Dad individually but nobody stayed very long and they were able to exchange only a few words. As sometimes happens when a terminally ill patient knows all his family are present, Timothy called for Julia in the early hours of Sunday morning and told her how much better he had been feeling during the past couple of days. He continued to rally and regain a little of his strength before indicating his desire to see all his immediate family as a group.

Propped up by pillows and holding Julia's hand, Timothy, looking glazed and tired, began addressing them. 'I'm sorry my failing health prevents me from speaking to each of you separately. I would dearly love to, but unfortunately this must be simple and brief.' It was obvious in his contorted face that speaking even these few words required the maximum exertion. But after a brief pause he summoned enough courage to resume.

'Since my young days in Inistogue, I promised to work hard to make this small country of ours a better place to live. What's been achieved in my lifetime is certainly spectacular, both economically and politically. For so long during the depression and wartime food rationing, I was kept awake at night by hunger pangs, yet I still had to get up the next day to work long and hard all over again. But this shows man's perseverance and determination to survive, whatever the odds. Now, thank God, all of that is past and we can look to a much better future.

Seamus, just 15 years old when the war broke out, empathised with his Dad, as the referred - to hunger pangs also blighted his early manhood. Timothy confirmed that they had made great strides politically. He was born into an Ireland governed by a foreign power where there was no freedom to practise the Catholic faith or to make decisions to improve their economic wellbeing. Through their constant efforts, and at the expense of many human lives, they managed to win freedom and independence for 26 of the country's 32 counties. The Irish

Republic now has the liberty to plan and map its own future and, in the past decade or so, it has emerged from the economic doldrums with much better days to come.

Timothy now broached a subject that had irked him for years.

'In the northern six counties we've had far too little success. Not that we haven't tried, but time after time our best efforts have been frustrated by political uncertainty, and progress has been blocked by the reluctance of the British to lose a colony on its own doorstep. It's an issue so close to my heart that I dearly regret this same heart no longer has the strength to work towards the unification of Ireland. I only hope that my able-bodied sons - and in whatever capacity, my daughters - can work tirelessly towards achieving that cherished goal in their lifetimes. I now pass the torch to a new generation which must not be found wa-'

Timothy's strength was gone. He squeezed Julia's hand tightly, gasped for air, slumped back on his pillows, closed his tired eyes... and died.

In the difficult days that followed her husband's death, it was a consolation and comfort to Julia having all the family present and each played a part in the funeral arrangements. In tribute to Timothy's love of his national sport, the coffin was draped in the county's football colours of green and gold and many stars of his era came to pay their respects. Men who had fought with him in the 1916 rising and the civil war formed a guard of honour and neighbours remarked how proud Timothy would be if he could witness this show of appreciation. As many of these men were themselves elderly, it served as a reminder to the young generation of the enormous task that still lay ahead.

But life in Inistogue and, indeed, all of Ireland had to go forward. Who could predict the course of events? There were ominous signs of many twists and turns before any clear pattern would emerge

CHAPTER 2

Liscorley, County Down, Northern Ireland 1961

Amid the magnificent mountain and coastal scenery in the small town of Liscorley, little of note occurred to disrupt the day-to-day monotony and routine. But that was before September 1960, when the county footballers achieved a near miracle. Not only had Down won the Ulster provincial title but they had also captured the supreme award of an All-Ireland by beating none other than the mighty Kerry in Dublin's Central Stadium. Ever since the games had begun in the late 19th century several teams from the northern province had tried unsuccessfully to win an All-Ireland. Down's success, therefore, captured imaginations north and south of the partitioned country. And, according to shrewd judges, the manner of their win suggested that the same county could well have one or more other titles on the record books before the decade was out.

The proud team trainer, Shane McCabe, would never forget the pride and euphoria welling up within him as the superior strength and skill of his lads steadily gained the upper hand and dominated many of the second half exchanges. He later equated the feeling with what might await him in Heaven on meeting his Redeemer. Celebrations during the following days and weeks, firstly in Dublin and later all over the county, were indelibly etched in his memory. When calm finally descended on Liscorley, Shane confided to a friend, 'If I never accomplish anything else of importance in my lifetime, I will die happy.' It was a frank outpouring from an ambitious 31-year-old not easily given to spontaneous expression.

It was at the post-game dinner in a Dublin hotel that Shane first met Seamus Dowling, who had, the previous year, been elected to the Kerry Football Selection Committee. Seamus was most gracious in defeat and there was an early bond of friendship which neither then realised would grow and prosper and transcend any rivalry on the playing fields. Seamus was full of admiration for what this young man had done and knew he hadn't yet reached his full potential. Shane spoke with an accent Seamus could scarcely understand, admitting that Kerrymen had little of the Oxford intonation. The rapport and chemistry between these two men overrode any problems in mutual understanding.

In the spring of 1961 it was Kerry's turn to travel to Down for a league game that had much less at stake than the previous September All-Ireland. Meanwhile, Shane and Seamus's friendship had prospered on the strength of regular letters and more frequent phone calls. Shane wrote inviting Seamus to stay with him and his family that weekend and, if at all possible, to remain an extra few days so that he could show him some of the local sights. Just three years earlier Shane had married his Belfast-born fiancee Brenda and they were now proud parents of two sons, Jim, aged two, and six-month-old Liam.

Seamus was never normally absent from home for any length of time. How then could he explain where he was going to Nora? Or the name of the person he had befriended up north? Yet she had no reason to question his fidelity in marriage and initially had prepared to give him the benefit of the doubt. Then, as they sat together one evening eating supper, Seamus was very forthcoming.

'Nora, with the disappointment of Kerry losing last year's All-Ireland during my first year as one of the selectors, I'm afraid I was in no mood to describe everything that happened in Dublin.' This opening statement, or the manner in which it was phrased, served only to heighten her suspicion of a possible extra-marital affair. Just as she was about to pose a question, Seamus interrupted her and continued, 'As you know, I have trouble expressing myself clearly but, in case you judge me too harshly, I need to reassure you there's no other woman involved nor, as you well know, will there ever be.'

Having visibly relieved her of her anxiety, he was now able to proceed to tell his story. 'Our September visit to Dublin is regarded by many within the county as an unmitigated disaster football-wise. That subject has been aired over and over again so I won't bore you further. But it did, in my view, bring many successes. Until seven months ago I had no idea what Dublin city life was like, the atmosphere on a big match day, the hotel scene and the enlightening experience of competing against a team of men from the north-eastern part of Ireland. I had the good fortune to meet and socialise with the trainer of the winning team, hearing his points of view and appreciating the hard work he did under enormous pressure. We quickly became good friends, something that was beyond my wildest dreams. That good friend has invited me to stay with him during my weekend visit with the Kerry team and for a few extra days to see his part of the country.'

With Nora much more at ease and reassured about the real motive for his trip, Seamus decided to complete the business.

'I know, Nora, how inconvenient it will be for you to have all that extra work and responsibility while I'm away. But our neighbours will pitch in and help with the cows and I'll make advance arrangements for that. Dad often spoke about our fellow Irishmen and women up north but until recently I've had no chance to meet any. It's important we get to know them, understand how they live and be familiar with their problems and aspirations. Although we inhabit the same tiny part of this planet, we're poles apart. We seem to be so caught up in our daily farm chores we have hardly any time and energy for anything else; we're like horses blinkered on the race track, shutting out all interference and distractions. I would dearly love you to come with me, Nora, to share the experience but someone needs to take charge while I'm gone. I expect there'll be another chance sometime in the future.' Seamus was pleased that, apart from needing certain points clarified, Nora gave the green light to his plans. He had learned early in their marriage that the most effective way of stalling what could be head-on collisions was to sit down together and calmly discuss the main issues. Their marriage, as a consequence, had gone from strength to strength.

*

The McCabe family had its roots in County Cavan, not too far across the border in the Irish Republic. When Shane's father, Eoin, was a teenager in 1916, his native Cavan was no different from any other county in Ireland, north or south, in that it was ruled by the English. Like so many other youngsters, Eoin was imbued with the spirit of republicanism without ever really knowing what it all meant or what benefits might come from it. He was caught up in a nationalist frenzy that permeated the air he breathed and was the subject of conversation wherever he went. His one great regret was not being able to more actively assist during the 1916-1922 period of intense political turbulence but he often gave indirect and moral support. Many of his colleagues were adamant that he contributed much more than those in the heat of battle at Dublin's G.P.O.

The dire economic conditions and desperate struggle for survival pervading all the country were felt nowhere as acutely as in his small Cavan town. Each day brought its own set of new challenges. Being the eldest in a large family of ten, Eoin was the principal breadwinner, far surpassing the little his father gleaned from his daily labours on a large farm on the outskirts of town, which returned a very handsome profit, thus allowing its owner to lead a lifestyle which was the privilege of the very few. This was to sow seeds of mistrust, envy and hatred that only intensified with time.

Eoin had been obliged to leave school at the tender age of 14. With his poor education there were few jobs that could bring him little more than a pittance. His first was as a butcher's apprenticeship where he soon discovered that the leftovers from meat he cut and sorted by day were insufficient to quell the hunger pangs that kept him sleepless at night.

Then something extremely fortuitous changed his life. The butcher had a regular visit from a county Down-based cattle dealer named Ian McSorley, with whom Eoin was to work closely in receiving the beasts intended for slaughter. Ian was quick to observe Eoin's work ethic and dedication to duty.

One evening in late October, as daylight was waning, Ian unloaded two bullocks which Eoin penned at the rear of the shop, to be ready for slaughter early next morning. Noting a strange sadness in the boy's eyes, Ian posed a question he had long considered asking but had not had the chance to.

'Every time I come here you are working like a slave and virtually running the show. May I ask what is your weekly salary?'

Eoin immediately felt a burden being lifted from his shoulders. That somebody acknowledged and expressed concern for his labours was like panacea from Heaven. It so happened that Ian was at that time eagerly seeking an able and willing hand, not only for his cattle dealing but also to run his home farm near Liscorley, county Down. The seeds of Eoin's move were firmly sown on that October night and his first day's work for Ian was on the following December 1st, a day Eoin described as a new beginning after emerging from captivity.

Despite his own better prospects, there were early signs warning Eoin of an uneasy relationship between people within his new community. But at the age of 20 he was too inexperienced to determine just what it was and how it might affect him. He was happy to leave this question aside, at least for the time being, and to turn his attention to improving his economic wellbeing. Here, too, he knew that while his present job was an improvement over the previous, there were distinct limits to his advancement. As the years with Ian McSorley passed by, Eoin remained steadfast in his goal of earning enough money to get married and, if God so willed, of raising a family with whom he would share the rest of his days.

Reflecting nostalgically on his early years at Liscorley, Shane acknowledged that his parents Eoin and Maura had done everything that could possibly be expected of them. Michael was their first child, born in November 1928, followed by Shane in March 1930. Had the family been larger, Shane speculated whether he and his brother could have survived the terrible deprivations that daily confronted them. If the early 1930s had their own set of woes, the ominous dark clouds of impending war in Europe later that decade offered no respite. Shane took much comfort from his Dad's admission that he was giving his all to family needs and that worldwide economic recession was at the root of many of their difficulties. Eoin remarked more than once that the world at large was virtually powerless to stem the global ambitions of the fascist who had ruthlessly taken power in Germany.

If Shane and Michael's formative years were fraught with hardships, they also brought immense satisfaction and were full of the joys of youth. Emblazoned on their modest bedroom door was the slogan: 'Look at the world through the eyes of a child and see beauty.' For children yet unable to grasp or appreciate the significance of the events unfolding about them, it was as good a world as they could wish for and, besides, they had nothing to compare it with. Their friends attended the local school and they all played together on the streets and in the nearby park. Little did Shane and Michael realise then, but those same friends, who were not of their parents' choosing, were also not a representative sample of the community. While this was of little importance during their childhood, it would become a major concern with advancing maturity.

Eoin had long instilled in his two sons a sense of pride in their Catholic heritage and a desire to be successful in life. He knew from his own experience that, given the minority Catholic population and the disproportionate power wielded by the Protestant majority, Catholics needed to be well educated before they could hope to compete successfully for jobs and gain other rights normally taken for granted. His sons could best overcome the religious barriers and prejudices by doing exceptionally well at school and university, a route to a better life which, through unavoidable circumstances, had been denied to him. Michael and Shane needed little reminding of the tasks facing them and, with unstinting support from their parents' meagre resources, set specific goals for themselves.

Michael's future was simple and clear-cut. As early as ten years of age it was abundantly clear that he had little interest in the academic life. Although his mental ability was well up to the average, he was less than enthusiastic about subjects such as history, geography, Latin and maths, which appealed only to a particular type of student. Without any prior advice or consultation, he was convinced that his future depended solely on what his two God-given hands could achieve. He displayed a flare for most things mechanical, a trait readily noticed in a household where there were many desperately-needed repair and maintenance jobs. His Dad encouraged these jobs as they not only gave his son much-needed practical skills but saved scarce money for basic necessities. But Eoin always guarded against pushing Michael towards a career, however lucrative it might be, for which he showed insufficient enthusiasm.

The path Shane chose was of a far different kind. He took to his studies like a duck to water. It was not that he had a superhuman or even a much above average intellect; but he used to the maximum what God had given him. It was as if the Creator had forewarned him of impending challenges in a corner of his universe where equality was poorly dispersed. When he contemplated advanced study, it became clear that Shane's interests swayed heavily towards teaching. Such a career held considerable prestige at a time and place when few had the opportunity to follow it..

Shane was attracted to teaching because he intended to use his knowledge and training to lessen the tensions between the two communities in his province which professed different religions. Even if he was still too immature to grasp their full meaning and possible consequences, he knew that the present trends were distinctly unhealthy for a true democracy. He saw in the teaching profession a means of not only educating a larger proportion of his own Catholic community but also of reducing educational inequalities between Catholics and Protestants and thereby promoting greater understanding and harmony. At least these were his idealistic goals but he appreciated it might take many years of his and other people's efforts to make a significant impact.

He well remembered the day he had received the exciting news that he'd gained a place at teacher training college. His proud parents invited a number of his friends to the house where Maura had prepared what seemed a feast in those days. Eoin was not fond of speeches but on this occasion he'd recounted with pleasure what the family had achieved in a short space of time and looked with greater confidence to the future. Slowly but surely there was a new dawn emerging for the

McCabes and their hard work was beginning to pay off.

Shane had his share of guilt complexes right through his two-year teacher training course. While extremely happy with his academic progress, he was always conscious of not bearing his due share of the family's everyday burdens. Not only did he not earn any money but, more worrying, he was a drain on scarce funds. He lived as frugally as he could and used most of what he got for specific college needs. The fact that his parents never once begrudged him the necessary money was a source of comfort and convinced Shane of their loyal support. It encouraged him no end and propelled him along the path to success, as he eventually graduated with a good honours degree.

The 'real world' presented the usual adjustment problems for the 22-year-old Shane. But the start was made easier by his filling of a long-standing teaching vacancy in the local Liscorley primary school. He was happy to concentrate his energy on educating his own community and by living at home he was able to reduce expenses and assist his family in numerous ways. In the economic climate of the time, it was unquestionably the route to take and a necessary short term expedient. Only many years later, with the benefit of hindsight, was Shane able to identify what he would have done differently if he'd had more money. But he wished only to think positively and do all that was humanly possible to improve the lives of those about him.

Shane quickly appreciated that, along with the status and respect surrounding his teaching job, it also brought responsibilities and additional duties he had not bargained for. He revelled in being able to take young kids, especially those from impoverished homes, and monitor their progress and independence, which were directly associated with a good education. Through these young children he fully understood what his father meant when he referred to 'liberation through education'. Shane admired his father's noble and far-sighted view of the importance of education in the post-war era when there were so many other more pressing problems . Shane rapidly succeeded in the role of teacher but there were forces outside his control that were to limit his influence and impact.

Central to practically all school decisions was the imposing figure of Father Colm McKnight, Liscorley's parish priest for the past two years. While there was an elected committee to manage and oversee the primary school, few were in any doubt as to who wielded the real power. Shane was shocked by the virtual one-man-show but was too new and therefore slow to complain lest he was labelled a brash young teacher. He slowly accepted the status quo and worked within its confines, putting the interests of the school in first place. 'Is this our new young teacher?' was how Father McKnight greeted the headmaster during Shane's second week, glancing momentarily in Shane's direction. The fact that the priest had not bothered to approach Shane and greet him personally left a lasting poor impression: Shane knew Father McKnight's motive was to confirm who was in command and to highlight the newcomer's insignificant role in the school set-up. Having made his point, Father McKnight acknowledged Shane's presence during subsequent visits but maintained his distance and authority.

It was not in Shane's make-up to harbour grudges and he quickly banished the thought of his first 'skirmish' with Fr. McKnight from his mind. But there were nights during restless bouts of sleep when pangs of anxiety invaded his subconscious. He wondered aloud whether this was normal behaviour for a disciple of Christ in whom so many of his parishioners had placed their trust. More importantly, how would it impact on Shane's teaching and his commitment to student education and development? He was still too immature to judge whether the Catholic church had too great a role in school management and if it was conducive to delivering a balanced education. He was greatly surprised at how little influence parents had on the way their children were taught during their formative years. He was convinced this issue would become clearer after he had a few more years of experience and, in his plans for improvement, he would put it at the top of his priority list. He was to add many more before very long.

Unlike Shane, his older brother Michael had preferred from an early age to use his hands. Towards the end of primary school his term reports were on the up-and-up but, in spite of his parents' urgings to enter secondary school for at least two or three years, he had other plans. Being almost two years older than Shane, who at that time hadn't yet completed primary, Michael felt duty-bound to earn what little money he could to help his family. Having convinced himself that he was making the correct decision, he lost no time in seeking a job. His teacher, having noted Michael's interest and flair for most things mechanical, introduced him to a local garage owner and, as they entered Irvine's garage after school on a wet Thursday in June, his teacher greeted Mr. Irvine, saying, 'I have an energetic student whose love of cars and all their moving parts is very impressive. He'd welcome the opportunity to serve his apprenticeship with you.' This request took Mr. Irvine totally unawares but he promised that if Michael came to see him on Monday he would give him a definite answer.

When Michael appeared 15 minutes before the arranged hour of 8 o'clock, Mr. Irvine was reassured that he had made the correct decision the previous Thursday. If Michael had acquired advance knowledge of Mr. Irvine's strict adherence to punctuality, a vital ingredient in business success, then he had scored what could be classified as a first-minute goal. The boss was impressed with his demeanour and honesty but still had no idea of how he would shape up to the manual work. Irvine lost no time in explaining what the job entailed.

'Because we are still in the grip of our second major European war this half century, there are few cars on the road and servicing is still very much in its infancy. Much of my income comes from renting cars with a driver to locals in times of need or on special occasions. Assuming you're willing to learn driving skills and obtain a licence, I expect that your work will in due course be divided between that and the odd routine car servicing. If you approach the tasks with interest and enthusiasm, I reckon that the experience will serve you well throughout your adult life.'

It was a beginning that a young lad of 14, still unaware of the benefits of continuing education, could scarcely have imagined. He took to his work like a fish to water. If he was losing out on academic studies, he was gaining practical experience with each passing day, a 'commodity' in short supply and highly valued in

1940s Ireland. After just six months, Michael was familiar with basic driving skills and he was content to bide his time and get further experience before being eligible for a driving licence. Small though his weekly salary was, it lent vital assistance to his family at a time of great need.

The McCabe brothers remembered the golden years of the 1950s with great joy. The gloom of the post-war years and the lingering food rationing had ended, and it was a time when everyone looked not only with hope but with distinct confidence to the future. It resembled a reawakening after a long winter of discontent when the brighter and longer spring days bring smiles and new-found pleasantness to so many faces. Both Shane and Michael played regularly with Liscorley Gaelic football club around which much social life and camaraderie developed. The weekend dances were the focal points for meeting and socializing with members of the opposite sex, although neither was yet ready to enter into a long-term relationship. Shane used his extensive school teaching experience to deliver a better education to all children under his care. Meanwhile, Michael felt he might now have attained everything he had set out to achieve in his present job and was on the lookout for opportunities to advance his career. But both brothers felt a quiet satisfaction with the success that had so far come their way . Michael's summer weekends were busily spent driving local groups of supporters to football games within a radius of 20 miles. These were fun-filled occasions and netted him valuable additional overtime. He keenly looked forward to driving at local weddings, despite the long hours, as each one was sure to provide him with enough jokes and anecdotes to last six months, many of which were uttered in slurred tones. He preferred to dismiss as quickly as possible from his mind the memories of so many sad funerals when he had to transport grieving relatives and friends, most of whom he knew personally. All these added up to unforgettable experiences but Michael was beginning to show an inexplicable restlessness.

It was about this time that emigration from both the north and south of Ireland was gaining momentum. Michael had given the subject much thought in recent years but had never had the courage to develop it further. Then, in the early autumn of 1957, the lure of foreign soil finally gripped Michael. He and two of his friends, John McKeever and Peter O'Neill, had gone for a quiet Monday night drink in Liscorley's Nag's Head pub. With the summer over and the enveloping long winter nights looming, adventure needed little encouragement. Peter talked at length about how many from the province had emigrated over the past five years and how they were faring abroad. Some had since been home to relate their stories first hand. John agreed there were increasing opportunities in the English-colonized countries of Northern and Southern Rhodesia and in South Africa. The daily newspapers often ran advertisements seeking professionals and skilled manpower in these countries and, with the false courage of three pints of beer over as many hours, the young men decided to lose no further time in trying to secure emigration papers and jobs.

Luckily the entire operation proceeded at breakneck speed because of a fortuitous set of circumstances. Although some from the parish had earlier chosen Rhodesia, from where favourable reports were emerging, none of the three friends balked at the prospect of settling in South Africa when they were made attractive offers. It was a giant step into the virtual unknown but they agreed to give it their best shot. The jobs carried the additional benefit of free travel by sea, on condition that they remained in employment for the agreed three years. It was with tears in their eyes but much hope in their hearts that they sailed the first stage out of Dublin for Southampton on November 1st. The second and much longer voyage from Southampton would bring them to Capetown in time to celebrate their first Christmas in a remote land without the comfort of family and friends. But, once that annual landmark passed, there would surely be many positive things to look forward to in this exciting new country.

*

The first Sunday in March, 1961 saw the second meeting in six months of Kerry and Down footballers but this time only a league instead of a championship was at stake. It took place at Down's home venue and the All-Ireland champions of the previous September ran out easy winners against an under-strength Kerry side. Only 3,000 mostly host county supporters ventured forth to defy the bitterly cold east winds. On days such as this, everybody in the small crowd should have 'keen football enthusiast' emblazoned across his or her chest and receive free entry tickets for the next game. These were staunch supporters prepared to sacrifice their time and all-too-little cash for a sport they dearly loved.

Seamus Dowling had made his longest journey yet to realise a childhood dream. Much as he loved the game, football came second to the knowledge and experience he longed to share with his host family. He wanted to identify the similarities and differences between the two opposite corners of his country and, if possible, break down any ill-conceived and unjustified prejudices. He had few illusions about acquiring an in-depth understanding of the situation in a matter of days, much less coming up with any resolutions. But it was an exciting challenge to which he would devote his entire concentration and energy.

Seamus's most abiding first impressions were the extent to which the mountainous Inistogue terrain resembled County Down's. His school geography classes had taught him that Ireland's topography was saucer-like, with hills and small mountains scattered sparsely around the coastline and the flat, more fertile agricultural plane in the centre. Seeing it now first hand was effectively his first small geography practical. The landscape and scenery, however, were not his sole interest as he had much to do in too short a time. Shane had managed to get Monday and Tuesday off school, giving him time to show Seamus around more so that he could return home with a balanced view of life around Liscorley, a microcosm of northern Ireland. But Shane guarded against influencing his friend, preferring to let Seamus come to his own conclusions. He was sure it would be beneficial to both of them.

The lack of excitement in the football game was more than compensated for by the after-match buzz in the Nag's Head. Game or no game, there were rarely any spare seats in this popular pub and this evening, even standing room was in short supply. Shane was accompanied by his close friend Brian McNeill, whom he introduced to Seamus. By way of welcome, Brian shook Seamus's hand firmly but warmly, as if they were lifelong friends, and put him at ease before beginning to talk about life in and around Liscorley.

'I fully appreciate, Seamus, that you come from the opposite corner of this small island and, while there are similarities between the people and the way things are done, we differ in one fundamental respect. Culture sets us apart. The Celts, who settled in Wales, Scotland and Ireland, brought with them their unique culture and customs, which many hold dear.

'We still have many Scots and their descendants here', piped Shane 'and it hasn't improved the situation one bit. Are you suggesting we bring in more?' 'Nothing of the sort. I should stress that this occurred long before the north-eastern part - which we are extremely happy you have chosen to visit, by the way - was colonised and settled by the English. But, thank God, the era of colonialism is steadily disappearing. A good start has already been made in Africa and several other countries on that continent are either well advanced or in the final stages of throwing off their repressive shackles.

Shane reminded Seamus that for nearly the last 40 years, the south has been free to make its own decisions in a truly democratic way, a right denied to the minority one-third Catholic population here. Ever since the southern 26 counties became independent, we've drifted further away from a democratic society.

'While you're here,' Brian advised, Seamus, 'have a good look at the forces controlling and shaping this province. Ask yourself specific questions about the Catholic minority: how do their educational opportunities and career prospects compare with those of the Protestant majority? What percentage of all jobs do Catholics hold in government, business and higher education? Is there a fair allocation of acceptable housing and, more fundamentally, what role do Catholics play in running the province?'

Seamus was clearly taken aback by Brian's frank political views so, to lighten the mood, Brian asked cheerfully, 'Will it be another three pints of the black stuff?' and, without waiting for a response, proceeded to the bar counter to renew the order.

While he was gone, Shane and Seamus continued their chat.

'Brian's right, Seamus - we've never experienced real democracy and our two communities have become more and more polarised. The Catholic population's patience is wearing thin as they sense that peaceful means of protest are hardly having any impact on the Protestant majority's intransigent attitude to change.'

'Are you saying they should stop being peaceful?' asked Seamus.

'Well, violence has had its positive effects. There've been plenty of skirmishes, especially during 1956-58, when the south supported us against the Protestants. Yes, a few distinguished patriots died in the struggle but if strong Irish Government action hadn't imprisoned the ring-leaders, more progress might well have been made.

'It appears to me that there was little thought given to that part of the campaign', said Seamus. Brian confirmed that the whole effort was just badly-planned, haphazard and too short-lived to have any significant impact or force a change in attitude, much less edge closer towards equality and social justice. But it did serve notice that the silent minority won't remain silent for ever and what has happened is very likely a small ripple ahead of a very big wave.

In a matter of hours, aided by the mellowing taste of Guinness, Seamus was already beginning to get a feel for the complexities of life in the province and would surely be better informed with time. Though he had often heard his late Dad talk about injustice and the need to fight on in support of his northern compatriots, he still kept an open mind. He wasn't entirely convinced his father had had a clear insight into the deep-seated causes of the strife; he suspected Timothy had been, to a certain extent, caught up in an Inistogue tidal wave of republicanism seeking a just cause. How he wished his Dad could be here now, to see for himself and form his own ideas, as Seamus was doing. He concluded that much of the misunderstanding and strife was born out of ignorance or an unwillingness to see the other side's point of view. There was a golden chance in front of him now to correct this. However, he must be cautious not to let his Catholic upbringing prejudice his ideas.

When the three finally emerged from the Nag's Head near midnight, the March easterly wind had subsided but the temperature had dropped to a few degrees below the frost line.

'Shall we finish our chat at my house over an Irish coffee?' enquired Shane. 'That'll also give us a chance to work out what Seamus should visit and see in this area.'

The very thought of a hot alcoholic drink was enticement enough for Brian on this cold night. But he was equally keen to ensure that Seamus should witness the lifestyles of the Protestant and Catholic communities, though both he and Shane were adamant that they would not encourage Seamus to see things that might tilt him in favour of one community over the other.

It was midway through their first drink that Brian agreed to accompany them during the first two days. Seamus, with the benefit of hindsight, insisted on meeting and talking to as many people as possible in order to have a large and representative sample.

'We have far too many people in the south claiming to be experts on Northern Ireland,' he said, 'yet most don't even have enough information to support what they say,' said Seamus. 'It'll only be through a better understanding of everyone's views and feelings, backed up by an effective dialogue between the two communities, that the problems can be solved.'

It would be an important first step but Seamus had misgivings about how tangible and long-lasting progress could be achieved.

Seamus was unprepared for what he experienced over the next two days. His visits covered a good cross section of agricultural, business and cultural life and he wasn't slow to pose questions, even if they bordered on the delicate and sensitive. As he spoke with a strong Kerry brogue, few were left in any doubt about his origin and motives, particularly those of the

Protestant affiliation. After little more than a half day, a distinct pattern had emerged which was repeated over and over again. Shane and Brian were always on hand to lend assistance and to clarify complex problems.

Shane's wife, Brenda, had prepared a sumptuous dinner in Seamus's honour for the eve of his departure, and a few close friends of Shane and Brian also came. The meal was accompanied by copious supplies of drink. In the pre-dinner get-together, Seamus summarised what he had observed and posed more questions than there were answers.

'It seems to me that the core issue relates to fair or proportional representation in all aspects of Northern Ireland life. You don't need to be a mathematician to identify the inequalities in the existing system of Government. With a Catholic population of one-third, shouldn't we expect to find this proportion in key Government and other important positions? True, Catholics can be found in increasing numbers in the more menial jobs, earning far less for work that Protestants are loathe to do. Yet shouldn't a Catholic have the same right to a good education, decent housing and the opportunity to control his or her own destiny?'

It was obvious to Shane and Brian that the shrewd Kerryman had grasped the core problems in the province but, before he could expound further, was called to take his position at the dinner table.

After Shane had said grace and proposed a toast to Seamus, he continued: 'Scarcely six months ago Seamus and I were virtual strangers until a major sporting event brought us together. The rivalries of sport are one thing and the bonds of friendship another. All of us in Liscorley have been honoured to have him with us for the past few days and, while, sadly, he leaves us tomorrow, we'll fondly remember him. He has helped to highlight how little we know about the cultural differences within this small island of ours. We must firstly get better acquainted north and south before we can learn to more effectively help one another.'

Shane then went on to talk about how world - and particularly English - colonialism was proving to be a modern day disaster at the very heart of the Irish problem. Even if there was a slim justification for colonising underdeveloped countries in the seventeenth and eighteenth centuries, he argued, pending their slow economic progress, there was absolutely none in Ireland. The more diffuse nature of English occupation in the south had enabled the independence movement there to unloosen the shackles a little earlier, but the entrenched mentality in the northern province had stifled all attempts at change - until now. Had equality of justice been meted out fairly to all our citizens, urged Shane, the need for reform would have been less pressing.

'Does anyone here know of a country where coloniser and colonised live in harmony with equal rights and privileges for all?' he concluded.

After the meal was over, they all retired to the sitting room with more drinks. Sitting comfortably near a warm turf fire rekindled for Seamus memories of peat-rich Inistogue and brought out the best in him.

'Firstly,' he began, 'I would like to sincerely thank my gracious hosts, Shane and Brenda, for a great weekend and a marvellous experience and education. This visit has exceeded my wildest expectations, opened up a brand new world, laid bare many questions and enigmas and unearthed problems for which I have all-too-few solutions. But being aware of the problems is a positive and significant first step and I'm wiser and better for it. Nobody is naive enough to pretend that the solutions will be easy but I can give you the benefit of my experience.

'Our own struggle against colonialism and repression in the south was long and arduous and we're still smarting from it. The Dowlings and freedom-fighting are synonymous. It started several generations ago and my own father continued the tradition in his indomitable way. The Irish, like the Chinese, possess an extraordinary capacity to endure suffering and mistreatment, which reached crisis point during the famine years of 1845-47. They have long believed that this struggle should run its full course, in the faint hope that gradual concessions will be granted which might ultimately result in full democracy and civil rights. Sadly, for us, this peaceful means ended in failure, and it was sustained and prolonged armed resistance that eventually brought us our independence in 1921.'

Brian, who had been waiting patiently for the opportunity to air his views, now began. 'Having Seamus with us for these couple of days has given us the rare treat of exchanging ideas and suggestions from widely different perspectives. We can really benefit from more of the same. The quality of patience Seamus referred to is getting scarcer by the day in this province. If we accept everything without reservation, however unjust or barbaric, we are fools. It is only when stiff resistance and civil disobedience remind those in authority of the urgent need for reform that some progress can be expected. The passive resistance of the past must make way for an active resistance of the future, though its severity will have to be gauged and adjusted according to need and the results on the ground.'

Brian paused and looked around him. Seeing he had a captive audience, he continued: 'The republican movement is fast gaining momentum and will be a force to be reckoned with before the end of this decade. Although the authorities outwardly belittle its aims and make light of its potential threat, they spare no effort in infiltrating its ranks - a real indication of how serious their concern is. We have the energy and capacity for a long struggle, such as the guerrilla warfare that proved so effective in Vietnam during the last decade. A small province like ours may not be able to stand up to the military might of the United Kingdom but it can wreak havoc disproportionate to its size. What happened in Vietnam kindled hope for many small nations and is a stark reminder to big powers not to underrate the resolve of the oppressed.'

Soon the whole room was buzzing with animated conversation. There was much comparing of political struggles. Just as north and south Vietnam had joined forces to oust the French, argued one man, so too could similar parts of Ireland support one another to gain independence.

Then Brian raised a hand for silence. 'My friends, it is in this context that Seamus' visit is so timely and relevant. However hard we try, our efforts will have little impact without help from the south. It is for this reason that republican or liberation movements are proceeding simultaneously on both sides of the divide. The great contribution made by the Dowlings of Inistogue to secure southern independence 40 years ago will need to be repeated many-fold before people here can breath freely. We have learned from Seamus that the fire which burned so brightly in the 1920s is now in conflagration for our noble cause. We urge them not to be found wanting and, while the sacrifices will undoubtedly be monumental, the pay-off will be equally rewarding.'

It was well past 2 a.m. when Brian took his leave and, en route home, felt the chill morning air seep into his very bones. Were these March winds originating in far-off Siberia, the forerunner of still more evil omens from this poorly-understood region? He pushed the thought quickly from his mind, concentrating instead on what future strategy he would develop with Seamus and Shane at their meeting later that morning before Seamus' return home. Brian had established a good rapport with Seamus and was confident that they could work constructively together. He felt that they might have just fashioned the first link in a long chain of north-south co-operation and he was grateful that Shane had been the cement in the mortar. He wondered why there had been so little previous contact between the two diverse parts of the country. Was there a reluctance by those in the south to get involved in a province that was of little concern to them? Were they too complacent, preferring to enjoy the fruits of their own hard-won freedom? Did too many, realising that the task of liberating Britain's nearest colony in its own back garden was too difficult and complex, choose simply to remain aloof? His mind boggled and his body shivered as he escaped from the harsh outdoors to the warmer confines of his small apartment.

Early meetings after late nights call for strict personal discipline. Brian was back at Shane's house by 8 a.m. and the three friends worked out implementation procedures, a mechanism to coordinate activities between north and south as well as a continuous information exchange. As it was the first effort of its kind, there were bound to be 'teething problems' but if everyone concerned worked to their potential, considerable success would undoubtedly ensue.

Shane, by way of concluding the meeting, and Seamus's trip, stressed how invigorating an experience the past few days had been for him. Not only had he been able to renew a valued friendship started the previous September but Seamus, Brian and he had also managed to sow the seeds of a new north-south co-operation which would hopefully grow steadily and prosper. There was no better or more opportune time, all three agreed, to harness the resources of Catholics within the country to work, and if necessary fight, for justice and equality, to give the Catholic population the rights and freedom it deserved.

The long-term aim was to secure the long overdue unification of the northern six counties with the southern 26 to form a 32-county republic.

'Should we not be masters of our own destiny or at least have a significant say in it?' demanded Shane. 'The process of decolonisation is very much alive in many countries; we must ensure we don't get left behind. The path to freedom and independence is bound to be a long and possibly bloody one, as the English are unlikely to let go easily. This is further complicated by the reluctance of the Protestant majority to sever its long-standing and loyal ties with England and to have any dealings with the republic, much less join in a 32-county republic. On the surface, the task is well-nigh impossible but that should not distract us from our goal which, in many people's eyes, is a very just and noble one.'

Seamus nodded, adding that the south's struggle for freedom had differed greatly from the north's in that the 99 percent plus Catholic population had been steadfast in their resolve to gain independence, and had persevered. Difficult though it was, there had been fewer problems and complications. Here in the north, the views of the Catholic minority had little leverage against the Protestant majority.

'In my honest opinion,' he continued, 'you can only do so much on your own. You'll reach a point where, however hard you try, success won't come your way without outside assistance and support. We in the south can provide some, if not all, of what you need. We've also learned that patience and passive resistance have their limitations and, when they aren't respected or heeded, there should be a transition to full action. It seems to me you're nearing or have already reached that stage. Although we partially achieved our ambition, republicans are still ready to complete the task, to help their northern brothers gain freedom, leading to full unification. That was much in evidence about four years ago when a few well-known patriots lost their lives following incursions into northern counties. The republican movement is firmly in place both north and south of the artificial divide and what we need to do is to strengthen it and, more importantly, to coordinate our activities.'

For all three huddled in the sitting room of Shane's house that morning, there was a mutual understanding of the issues confronting northern Ireland and the course of action they would promote and pursue. It was to usher in a new and more troublesome period in Irish politics, a gamble which brought with it all the associated risks and bloodshed. Starting from a rather small base, it grew steadily with the passing years into a state from which it would be difficult to retreat - even if the majority willed it. None of the three could have foreseen that morning that the tiny fire they had kindled might one day blaze out of control, engulfing and destroying the lives of many.

Seamus took his leave after pledging his allegiance to the cause and vowing to muster up and organise support in his native county. As the train took him on the first leg of his return journey from Belfast to Dublin, he eyed the green fertile fields as they flashed by. Naturally, strange thoughts filtered through his mind. Is this the land occupied by foreign settlers to which access is denied to the native Irish? What price could or should be paid to wrest it from the perceived oppressors? No matter how powerful the colonisers, they had no God-given right to seize land not rightfully theirs? Yet did not the might of the occupier reign supreme? Was there any effective mechanism whereby small oppressed nations could form an alliance and speak with one voice calling out for justice and equality? Seamus watched the animals in the fields and pondered on the natural world, where dominance of the large over the small and weak was also in evidence.

He slept the final hour of the second stage and then saw Inistogue peering gradually through the mist. It was nice to be back on home soil once again where freedom was taken for granted, but he thanked the Lord for giving him the chance to experience life beyond the border. He was a better man for having seen it and, before too much longer, he would do all in his power to meet his Liscorley commitments. It was too early to say what shape and form this might take as urgent farm matters now had to take precedence. Nora, meanwhile, greeted him with open arms and joyfully announced that she had been confirmed pregnant with what was to be their third child. What more perfect ending to an already glorious long weekend could he have anticipated?

CHAPTER 3

Northern Ireland 1969-1972

For all the youth privileged to experience the decade of the 1960s in Ireland, it was an exhilarating time to be alive. The years of deprivation and sacrifice had given way to hope and the first inklings of modest prosperity. Emigration was much lower than in the late 1950s and there were early signs that the Irish Republic's economic recovery programmes were taking root. In both parts of Ireland most of the decade was one of peace and stability but the final two years in the north were to usher in a new era of disquiet and conflict.

The silence was abruptly broken during a Presbyterian Sunday service in a small County Antrim church in March 1969. The Reverend Trevor McMichael rose and, with few preliminaries, began his unexpected tirade: 'Each of you present is chosen by God to do his bidding. You come here today in the clear knowledge that your brand of Protestantism is the right and only path towards eternal salvation. You must treasure this fact every moment of your short lives on earth. More importantly, you must tenaciously preserve it in the face of evil forces.'

Many in the large congregation were regular attenders and had on occasion been chastised for failing to adhere more closely to the Holy Scripture. This usually came in the form of a mild rebuke for deviating from the recognized norms of Christian behaviour. But nothing could have prepared them for what was to be fired in their direction today. Reverend McMichael took a deep breath and then resumed: 'The evil forces I refer to are all around us and represented by half a million Catholics in our midst. Their centre of rule is Rome from where the supreme commander, the Pope, reigns over a vast empire dispensing rules and regulations and pronouncing judgment on those failing to conform. The Catholic population is outpacing ours and, unless we do something soon, our very existence is insecure. For this reason, we must consider a war declared against Catholic supremacy. Not only must we do everything within our God-given powers to stem the spread of Catholicism, we should also reinforce our political structures to ensure that Protestant rule succeeds and continues. I know I can count on your support for this noble cause to which we must devote all our energy so that future generations may reap the rewards.'

There was shuffling and elbowing in the crowded seats as the ferocity of the remarks reached a crescendo. Later, as friends mingled and chatted outside the church, generously supported by donations, there was a general air of embarrassment. Although many thought and felt as Reverend McMichael did, few would even mutter in private, much less speak openly, about the religious rights and superiority of any particular community. The questions that ran through their minds on that brisk March morning were as follows: What had suddenly provoked the minister to speak out so forcefully and bluntly? Was this to be just the beginning of many more Sundays of venomous attacks? Would the shock waves reach the Vatican walls and precipitate a public response from the Pope? What would be the international reaction and repercussions? Would this spontaneous outrage by a Protestant clergyman reopen old wounds and foment a new era of strife between the two religious communities? Above all, should not each Protestant church-goer now seriously question his faith and trust in a church and minister espousing religious bigotry and superiority?

Shane McCabe could scarcely believe his eyes when he read the front page headline in Monday's newspaper as he was preparing for his 9.30 a.m. class. Later, he could not recall imparting any coherent messages or instruction to his students during the entire day. When he returned home that evening he found Brian McNeill waiting for him with more than a look of anxiety on his face.

'Have you read today's paper?'

Shane nodded. As soon as he had eaten what was for him a light dinner, they both retired to the quieter confines of the sitting room. Sitting upright at the edge of the sofa, Brian remarked: 'When the long and sad history of Northern Ireland is eventually written, as I'm sure it will be, yesterday will surely be a watershed. It will be described as a day when relations between the two religions soured beyond belief. For any clergyman, of any denomination, to utter such bigotry and profanities from the pulpit is inexcusable. If a layman had done it, he'd be publicly castigated. One of the fundamental principles of Christian belief is surely to love your neighbour as you would yourself. Yesterday, Reverend McMichael eschewed this doctrine and, instead (as would be expected from a man of the cloth) of helping to encourage and consolidate relations between the two faiths, he drove a very deep wedge between them. He sowed a poisonous seed of hatred and discontent which can only grow to lethal proportions in the years and decades ahead.'

Shane agreed. 'You're right, Brian. There's no denying that yesterday's outrage was an unmitigated disgrace at a national and international level. It damaged our psyche and image in the eyes of the world and repair, if it happens at all, will take many years. But it's not all bad. McMichael's remarks don't represent the views of the entire Protestant community - remember, they came from a single individual, clergyman though he may be. The question we need to ask ourselves is: what percentage of Protestants actually share the minister's beliefs? No doubt he has some faithful followers who may well be less extreme. We must keep an open mind and not react too hastily. It would do little to heal the wounds that already exist.'

Just then, Brenda called Shane and Brian for tea and scones before she got the children ready for bed. Jim, the eldest, was born in 1959, followed by Liam in 1960, Frank in 1962, Jane in 1963 and Eileen in 1965. Sitting down at the kitchen table, Brian greeted all the children in turn, giving special hugs to the two little girls. 'What a lovely family you have, Shane, and such a caring mother in Brenda. There are times when I rue staying single, especially when I see all your kids growing up happily together. But, on the positive side, it means I can devote more time to the cause and help to make this province a better place to live. Looking at your children, I see more hope for their future, simply because they'll be less tolerant of the injustices meted out to our generation. We can only prepare and guide them as best we can; the rest is in their hands.'

Brenda retired to bed at 10 p.m., bidding goodnight to Brian, whereupon he and Shane repaired to the sitting room. When seated comfortably, Brian began, 'Up until yesterday, there were four decades of what you could describe as accommodation between Protestants and Catholics. Of course we had our differences but, for all intents and purposes, they remained beneath the surface. It took just 30 minutes of Reverend McMichael's harangue to irrevocably change all that. Now we have a future of uncertainty which Catholics are ill-prepared for. The coming few weeks and months will be crucial, a time to gauge the reactions and possible repercussions. If there's little effect, then normal life as we know it can continue. However, if it leads to civil strife and unrest, then Catholics must be prepared to defend themselves and perhaps even take the fight to their adversaries. In brief, we must be ready to face a possible future of discontent.'

Both Shane and Brian knew the history of the republican movement. It may have had its ups and downs but the fire was never fully extinguished. Now the words of Reverend McMichael had provided the fuel to rekindle it anew and perhaps even cause it to rage out of control. Brian had been an active republican a decade earlier and, although their achievements had fallen far short of their goals, there was, he believed, enough spirit and justification to continue.

'If we stand up for ourselves, Shane, you and I can look every Englishman in the face and unashamedly demand what is rightfully ours. But will he listen or take heed? Oh no... and it's that very stubbornness that has lent a springboard to republicans, not only massively increasing their numbers but imbuing them with a greater resolve to continue and intensify their struggle. As in the past, Shane, I know I can count on your support and others throughout the province. And we mustn't forget our good friends in the south and, in this regard, Seamus Dowling's visit in 1961 established a link that we will now reactivate and promote. Without the active support and participation of our southern colleagues, the chances of significant progress are very slim. No time must be lost as the events of yesterday give the matter some urgency.'

It was a quarter after midnight when Shane stood up, giving a gentle hint that the present session should be brought to a close. They both agreed that, in view of yesterday's events ushering in disturbing times, they should meet with others from Liscorley at regular intervals.

'I'm delighted you showed your concern and made the effort to come,' said Shane. 'There are obviously some important issues to be addressed.'

'Looks like I may have converted you to my republican way of thinking,' smiled Brian, 'and we'll need every able-bodied man in Liscorley to face up to his responsibilities and put his shoulder to the wheel. Just as well Reverend McMichael presented us with an excuse to raise our war effort to a higher level.'

With that, Brian stepped into the frosty night air and evaporated into the darkness.

*

Until the advent of more advanced dairy technology, there was no other event in the agricultural sector which captivated rural Ireland so forcibly than the daily trek to the local creamery. Its main purpose was to process, mainly into butter (and to a lesser extent cheese), milk from the cow herds, ranging from a few in poorer households to many in the more affluent ones. Immediately after the morning milking, ponies, donkeys and in some cases horses were yoked to carts which were used to transport the churns filled with the daily milk. Right up until the late 1970s, when modern technology took over, it was a sight to behold with many or most of the farmers from a particular parish descending on the local village's (or town's) creamery depot. Although the monthly-issued cheque for milk had to meet most of the family's needs, the creamery run involved much more. On the return journey skimmed milk was transported as well as concentrate livestock feeds and a variety of human foods. Apart from the business and everything else, a trek to the creamery was a social occasion *par excellence*, an opportunity to discuss with neighbours and friends recent happenings both near and far and how these might impinge on their daily lives.

Much passed through Seamus Dowling's mind as he urged his pony along the narrow country by-road on that Monday morning in early October, 1970. On the lighter side he was rejoicing over yesterday's narrow win by Inistogue footballers in the county semi-final and it was certain that, during the queue at the creamery, he would have ample opportunity in the company of neighbours to relive the game almost kick by kick. That longed-for pleasure would be somewhat tempered by the increasingly disturbing news emerging by the day from Northern Ireland, something Seamus was prepared to dispel from his mind for a little longer. As he reached the creamery he discovered there were 14 other carts in front of him and men were huddled in groups in animated discourse.

'Here's the right man to answer all those difficult questions' said Joe Moriarty, on seeing Seamus approach. Joe was in the midst of a half dozen farmers debating who deserved to be nominated 'man of the match' and, more importantly, what changes were required for the final two weeks hence against more formidable opponents.

'The first is a simple matter and the second will have to wait for the committee's decision next week,' blurted out Seamus. Then, noticing a large bandage on Michael O'Grady's right hand but not liking to approach him personally, he asked Joe what had happened.

'Well, that's a long and "delicate" question indeed,' began Joe, 'but I'll try to be as brief as possible. I need scarcely remind you that the same Michael is a very keen supporter (and has been for 25 years) of the Inistogue football club. So keen, in fact, that during important games he gets so excited that he virtually loses control. Not that he's harmful or abusive to the opponents' supporters, no... no, far from it. Yesterday, in the dying moments just before Inistogue scored a goal to win the game, he was standing behind a barbed wire fence and exhorting his team to a superhuman effort. Every time an Inistogue player won a ball he pounded his fist against the fence, oblivious to the fact that the offending barbs were severely cutting his hand. At the end of the match he was rushed to the local doctor, who inserted several stitches. Henceforth, nobody should be in any doubt as to how good a supporter Michael is!'

Seamus burst out laughing. 'If he stays as he is, we may well lose him completely before the second round of next year's championship!'

No sooner had Seamus and Joe delivered their milk than the festering clouds unleashed their moisture.

'As the remainder of the day is unlikely to be good for much,' said Seamus, 'what would you say to a couple of relaxing drinks?'

'It's without doubt the best suggestion I've heard so far today,' replied Joe.

As they entered Denis Greany's pub they could easily overhear the gay laughter and intense discussions and within minutes they were immersed in a group of six. When the dissection of the previous day's game was complete, thoughts naturally turned to non-sporting news.

'I don't like the look of things up north,' said Michael O'Grady. 'I'm feeling sorry for myself, having so stupidly cut my hand, but how do you suppose our northern friends react to the way they're unjustly treated, incurring far more severe injuries in the pursuit of rights too long denied them?'

'All over this island of ours we talk too much and do too little,' piped up Joe, 'and the sooner we swing into action the better.'

'Having won our own independence, admittedly at a great cost in human suffering, we shouldn't rest on our laurels and forget others' said Seamus. 'Inistogue is the core republican area of the county and, while the movement is up and running, we must accelerate and intensify our efforts.'

If the cheers and chorus were anything to go by, there was

unanimous agreement on this last point.

The sky had cleared as Seamus and Joe emerged from Greanys at 3 p.m., having said all their farewells. They untied their two ponies, which had waited patiently for their masters, and set off, one after the other, on the homeward run. Seamus was in full voice up front singing verses of 'The Rose of Tralee' with rhythmical shouts of approval from Joe. As they parted company near home, the effects of the alcohol were beginning to take their toll and they braced themselves for the reception, cooler than the beer they had drunk, which was sure to be waiting for them from their wives.

*

'Most of the decade, not only in Northern Ireland but world-wide, ushered in a new period of hope and prosperity,' proclaimed Brian McNeill nostalgically to a party of friends as the final minutes of 1969 were celebrated with aplomb. 'What we are now witnessing is loosely referred to as the "civil rights" movement, but it is much more than that.'

Shane McCabe, listening intently and buoyed by the start of another year and decade, was in more up-beat mood. Shane explained that in the year just ended, something unprecedented occurred in the north-eastern part of Ireland, Ulster. Catholics began to demonstrate, gaining momentum with each passing month, for the basic rights that are taken for granted in practically all liberal democracies worldwide. On the positive side, it must be regarded as a major victory. The authorities are just beginning to recognise and accept that Catholics have never enjoyed, compared to their Protestant brethren, fair and equal rights to government representation, employment, housing, education and, in brief, their due share of the "national cake". The marches and demonstrations highlighted the chasm between the existing and what should be everyone's civil or human rights. From that perspective, the year was an unmitigated success.

Far from their minds on that auspicious night was the scale and intensity of things to come. When the force behind civil rights came in the person of a young female activist, Helen Quinn from the neighbouring town of Dunfoyle, it not only mesmerised but threw down the gauntlet to all the male chauvinists. From early childhood right through her teens, Helen had absorbed all that was happening around her, vowing that when maturity dawned she would play her part in ensuring that the rights of Catholics, in their broadest sense, got due recognition. She had few illusions about the scale of the task but was determined not to be found wanting in what had been, up to now, a male domain. Now, at only 20 years old, she had already, during the past six months, sent out preliminary signals through mass meetings and speeches that she and her supporters were no longer willing to tolerate injustices.

Had tolerance, she often wondered, been an accident or inherited through her Catholic lineage? As the years unfolded it became more and more obvious that the latter was the case. How could she and her Catholic friends not be afforded the same rights and opportunities to advance in life, privileges so unstintingly granted to her Protestant counterparts? Why should religion or one's personal beliefs be a passport to success? Was it a fairer system in the U.S. where, as she remembered from her school history lessons, the Constitution guaranteed equal rights to all citizens, irrespective of race, colour and creed? These were some of the questions that had caused her many hours of wakefulnesss and anguish. But, rather than taking the fight to the enemy, she was determined to take the moral high ground, opting instead for a path of peaceful demonstrations and alerting the Government to the blatant inequalities.

At the Catholic school Helen had attended, she'd made many friends with whom she socialised, to the exclusion of people outside the school. It only became clear to her in her teens that this was a sheltered existence and, despite the fact that two-thirds of the population were Protestant, she knew barely any of them. She had pondered the practicality and usefulness of segregated schools simply on religious grounds. It was in her view the earliest 'strike' at dividing people, which continued at every stage thereafter. Reflecting on Reverend McMichael's

54

outburst, she wondered whether it might not yet prove to be a blessing in disguise, for it had highlighted the Protestants' dislike and mistrust of Catholics and, more importantly, their fear that the Catholic community might acquire more than the paucity of rights they currently enjoyed. It had also inspired Catholics to seek more of what they justly deserved, and the civil rights movement was gaining momentum, getting not only national but also international publicity which could only help the Catholic cause. Though people in far-off Balouchistan or Patagonia might have heretofore been unaware that Ireland was a divided country, they would in future know that Northern Ireland existed and democratic rights were not equally apportioned to Protestants and Catholics.

Previous civil rights demonstrations were rather low-key compared with what was planned for February 23rd. Helen, who chaired the Liscorley-Dunfoyle organising committee, saw to it that nothing was left to chance - save, perhaps, as had occurred previously, an unpredictable intrusion by the security forces. This was something she preferred not to worry about as there was precious little she could do to prevent it. The plan was to start the march at Liscorley's village centre at 3 p.m., proceed to Dunfoyle and then northwards through several other villages and small towns before the final stop and speeches at Northchester's city square. Each participant was to prepare and display a banner calling for more equitable civil rights for the Catholic minority. The final speeches were scheduled to begin at 8 p.m. and, all going well, the whole proceedings could be brought to a close shortly after 9.30 p.m.

The snow that had fallen earlier that morning of the 23rd did little to dampen the enthusiasm of those congregating in Liscorley where Helen both welcomed them and explained the *modus operandi*. She stressed that today's march and demonstration, as previously, must above all else be peaceful. In this manner we shall demonstrate without rancour the justice of our cause and hope to elicit an appropriate response from the government. It's appreciated that we inevitably have in our midst republicans for whom restraint may be difficult, but rest assured that at this juncture provocation has no worthwhile place. Our march may, of course, be impeded or interrupted by security forces but we should remain cool and not give way to anger. You will be given further instructions from time to time and, meanwhile, may success attend all our efforts towards a more just society.

It all began as a lighthearted show of solidarity with 150 people of mixed ages steadily leaving the outskirts of Liscorley. Felix O'Kane was one of three septuagenarians for whom this event was the realisation of a lifetime dream. As a teenager, when the abortive 1916 rising had temporarily shattered hopes of a southern republic, Felix had been at the forefront of attempts to wrest the whole of Ireland from British supremacy, only to be utterly disappointed with the 1921 treaty whereby the north remained within the United Kingdom. Felix wasn't a man given to impetuosity and bided his time over the next half century: as a God-fearing Catholic he was convinced that his Creator would sooner rather than later bring His all-foreseeing justice to bear. Hadn't he, Felix, done more than his share to bring it about? Here today at the head of the march, he was a man rejuvenated with a new sense of purpose and direction, believing that freedom with equality might after all come within his lifetime.

Helen's supporters at Dunfoyle had swelled the number to 500, many of the young men being not only in awe of her political acumen but staunch admirers of her youthful vivacity and sexual attractiveness. They pushed macho tendencies to one side at the prospect of long-term and more lasting gains. Helen was for them the symbol of the new emerging Ireland which would soon seek its own destiny in a fast-changing world. Despite her warning against overt shows of republicanism, there were at least ten to 20 percent of this most recent influx born and reared with an imbued dislike of what they perceived as their Protestant oppressors, a trait which invariably gave way in their teenage years to various acts of physical expression, a euphemism for terrorist attacks in extreme cases. More and more joined in the villages and towns en route, swelling to some 4,000 at the outskirts of Northchester as the frosty air chilled the last of the daylight hours.

It was here that an incident occurred which would shape the future of maintaining peace in the province. Whether it was due to the increasing fatigue and restlessness of the marchers or triggered by an unwelcoming presence of security police strategically lining both sides of the route, nobody can say with certainty. What is beyond doubt is that the nerves of opposing forces became frayed beyond repair and a skirmish was waiting to happen. Several youths hurled profanities at police, followed by stones, bricks and whatever other physical objects conveniently came to hand. The police on this occasion exercised restraint, a commodity which would in future become ever more scarce. The fracas lasted but 30 minutes but was to usher in a new and more unsavoury era of confrontation. Fortunately, apart from some minor bruises and cuts, the marchers were able to proceed virtually unscathed to their rendezvous at the city square.

As the crowd mingled and shuffled, Helen Quinn appeared on the podium. She explained that it was her duty and pleasure to welcome them to this unprecedented event in the long history of Ulster. Today they'd struck a blow (in the metaphorical sense!) for the future of this province. What they'd ventured would have been unthinkable a mere decade ago. As her imposing female figure and good looks caught the attention of the young men, there were shouts of approval and wolf-whistles. Sensing that there was no shortage of support, she elaborated. 'Apart from one unsavoury incident, this demonstration for the cause of civil rights for all citizens has gone according to plan. This is just a beginning and you must not flinch from your purpose. The question of civil rights is the most important issue and, once this is improved or changed, most other problems will be resolved. Nobody in a truly democratic country can justifiably be denied these basic rights and, as long as we campaign on this issue, our feet are on a very solid foundation. We can point to many grave injustices and our task must be to set these right. Let nobody present be under any illusion about the enormity of the job ahead but I ask you most sincerely for your full support and co-operation.'

'This is a peaceful campaign and it should not be confused

with republicanism. There is no place for the rush of blood as seen earlier this evening. By this peaceful approach, far more can be achieved than was gained this past century through the barrel of a gun. However, to be effective, we need the involvement and support of as many people as we can muster. From this historic beginning, let us go forth and achieve what we have unjustly been denied for far, far too long.'

As she left the podium, the loud and long applause rent the chill night air, intermingled with guffaws, whistles and cat-calls. Not only had her leadership been fully vindicated, but there were scores of male admirers ready to share something more intimate than a cold podium with her.

There were speeches of lesser import from the other committee members, mostly reiterating Helen's sentiments. It was patently obvious that she was the brains and strength and would command the respect and loyalty of those around her. As the crowd dissipated, Brian McNeill was heard uttering in hushed tones to Shane McCabe, 'You should never underestimate the firmness of purpose and charisma of the female psyche. This night has filled me with more hope and optimism than was ever engendered by even our ablest male politicians.'

They both quickened their step in anticipation of better things to come.

*

It was 6 a.m. on an early March morning when Michael McCabe awakened to the sounds of singing birds and increasing traffic, at his home in the northern suburbs of Johannesburg. As he breakfasted, the eastern morning sun lit up his spacious dining room, a sun which shone with virtual regularity for practically all of the 365 days of each year. This and the evening twilight hour were precious moments for Michael, having a character which could only be described as uniquely African and savoured by foreigners. In arranging his work schedule, he noted with asterisks the urgency of writing that same evening to Shane, a letter that was long-promised but unavoidably

58

postponed because of a backlog of work during the first two months of the year. The nostalgia surrounding Saint Patrick's day, now only ten days away, gave him the much-needed impetus.

235 Edenvale Road, Alexandra,
Johannesburg
March 7, 1971

Dear Shane,

There are so many good reasons for feeling happy that I decided it was a good time to send you my news, observations and prognosis for the future. The first is the easiest and I will begin with my own personal up-date.

Ever since setting foot on South African soil in December, 1957, success has accompanied my every movement. Having as a firm foundation my earlier Liscorley experience in the car business, I gradually developed this line further to the stage where now I own and run my own garage and car dealership right in downtown Johannesburg. The first few years of establishment and adjustment to the new environment and modus operandi weren't easy but, now at 42 years of age, my life could scarcely be better. I've never harboured the ambition to be a millionaire, nor will I ever be, but financial independence has brought many comforts and a very pleasant lifestyle.

As you already know, my greatest stroke of fortune some ten years ago was in meeting and marrying my wife Jennifer Ashley, a native of Brighton in England. Our two children, Jonathan, 8, and Sarah, 6, keep us busy and enthralled. They look forward to one day meeting all their Irish relatives in what is increasing being termed a 'troubled land'.

My two good friends who emigrated here with me, John McKeever and Peter O'Neill, carved out distinctly different niches for themselves. For ever the gourmet enthusiast, John trained as a chef followed by another course in hotel management and is presently enjoying the fruits of his labour in an assistant managerial role at a five-star Capetown hotel. Peter was employed in a number of jobs during the first five years before settling for the long-term position of bus driver. His daily route passes my garage entrance and the daytime perfunctory salutes are regularly followed by nightly social get-togethers. About once a month John manages to escape from his Capetown hotel duties to join us for a weekend rendezvous in Johannesburg

My observations and views of my adopted country are profound and long-reaching and in all justice require more time and space than can be given here. But, it is my right and duty to treat them briefly since there is an uncanny similarity between the situation here and in Northern Ireland. Common to both is the overriding and oppressive colonial system. Let me hastily preface that the major economic and technological developments would never have occurred in the absence of colonialism, but economic without social and human advancement for all citizens can only precipitate an inevitable time-bomb.

African-style colonialism suffered serious setbacks in the late 1950s and 60s with many countries winning their rightful independence. Those who had once held power were in the minority and, despite their superior military might, were fighting a losing battle against the less well-equipped but more numerous and motivated native black communities. While in truth I am a member of the so-called minority elite, and enjoying the economic fruits, my inner being and conscience tell me this is unreal and transitory. So many other white South Africans feel the same but are reluctant to acknowledge it even in private, much less to even hint it in public.

It is not so much a question of nationalism and independence as the more mundane and everyday issues of civil liberties and rights. In my own garage more than 95% of business is with the less than 20% white minority, and it shows no signs of changing. Segregated schools predetermine who gets a decent education and can go on to command responsible positions in society, not to mention governmental roles. Black people are denied access to many hotels, cinemas, buses and even toilets. Yes, they are readily sought after for the most menial of tasks at fractional rates of pay. From the outset the system appeared strange and I felt uncomfortable working within it. To their credit, the blacks for so long displayed an unusual tolerance and forbearance but, as you can sense internationally, there is now serious disquiet brooding. It is not so much a matter of if but when significant changes will occur.

A concrete example will interest you. One evening last month, on my way home from work, I stopped at my local golf club for a drink. I saw a sea of white faces save for one black man perched on a high stool at the corner of the bar. Since he appeared to be unaccompanied and lonely, I decided to sit next to him and engage him in conversation. After the initial shock of a white man trying to befriend him had subsided, talk began to flow freely. It transpired that he was the manager of a freight company and obviously had succeeded well in business. He did not play golf but for the past seven years had enjoyed pavilion status, giving him the privilege to use the bar and other facilities. He told me in all sincerity that he stops one or two evenings each week for a drink or two on his way home. On enquiring if any whites had ever conversed with him, apart from the cursory greeting, the reply was a firm and definitive no. *He poured out his heart to explain as calmly and unobtrusively as possible how it was the first time a white person had talked to him at length over the seven years. I can only assure you that the incident rent my heart and I wondered how human relations could be allowed to reach such a 'low.' It reinforced my long-held belief that, above all else in this country, skin colour determines the extent to which you can succeed and integrate into society. My friends, John and Peter - and indeed thousands of others - can cite you many other incidents but I should instead stress that this intolerable situation has a very limited lifespan.*

The reason for my optimism is well founded. Even with all the military might of the minority ruling class, it can scarcely indefinitely control the majority. The injustices meted out to them will increasingly reach propaganda proportions throughout the rest of the world. This will reach new heights when continually beamed into so many homes, which now have TV sets. Had the ruling white class relented gradually over the last few decades, giving more and more rights to blacks and appeasing their anger, the clamour for change would not have been as intense. But now it will come with greater strength and ferocity. This latter is to be feared (although inevitable) as there is a grave danger that the economic gains, built-up over a century, could be destroyed or not maintained at the same level. In other words, we look to the maturity and farsightedness of those entrusted with power to preserve what is good while guaranteeing a fairer society. My educated guess is that this type of society will materialise far in advance of similar changes in Northern Ireland.

England is loath to easily give up its Northern Ireland colony so conveniently situated at its own back door. The fact that two-thirds of the population are on its side makes the task none the easier for the Catholic one-third. Here skin colour pre-determines what side of the fence you are on but in an all-white community there is no such facility. Until the quite recent start-up of hostilities, few people in the world were aware there was a 'separate' Northern Ireland, much less that there was an uneasy peace about to disintegrate. Just as in South Africa, the situation will never be quite the same again, which can only favour the Catholics' aspirations. The inequalities will be exposed and publicised as never before and, as you appreciate so well, it will be a long uphill battle in trying to rectify them. My optimism for South Africa extends to my native sod but I'm afraid I may well be down under growing daisies before a lasting solution and peace come to my homeland.

The freedom movement that has ignited African countries over a decade ago began the putsch against colonialism and the 'pockets' still remaining need solutions. Time and world opinion are on our side and we must continue the struggle. We must begin by ridding our societies of injustices and, should independence and unification come in its wake, they will be God-sent bonuses. Also in Ireland, we must recognise and preserve the gains of the past (giving due credit as appropriate), and ensure that the transition is peaceful and blood-free so as to develop a future working climate devoid of rancour and recriminations.

We will monitor the changes in our respective countries which are experiencing many similar 'teething' problems. Should all continue to go well with my business, I envisage having a long-promised holiday in Liscorley within the next few years.
Love and best wishes to you, Brenda and all the family,

Michael

*

It was a wet and dreary Sunday morning in late January, 1972 when the civil rights marchers reached the outskirts of Cloonbridge. The city had attained notoriety in the late 17th century for having stubbornly defended itself against invading forces and the still-pocked perimeter walls testify to the historical bravery of its citizens. Located in the western part of Northern Ireland, close to the border with the Republic, it contained an uneasy mixture of those either loyal to the English crown or strong supporters of reunification with the Republic. Furthermore, the city had proven to be a focal point for cross-border gun-running, with tension and security causing great concern for the authorities.

Tension and security reached new highs as the marchers edged ever more closely towards the city centre. The smaller protests during previous months in towns and rural areas went virtually unreported. They, however, served notice that unless something was done towards meeting their demands, a stronger show of force could be expected. Helen Quinn, in charge of all the planning and preparations, convinced herself that she was leaving very little to chance and felt exhilarated by the massive turnout on this dull January day. What she couldn't plan for or guard against was the level of discipline among her supporters and, if that deviated excessively from the norm, the likely retaliation which would come from the security forces. It was something that now, as tension escalated over the last 500 yards, came to the forefront of her mind. She momentarily upbraided herself for allowing things to reach this dangerous state but managed to convince herself that she was willing to accept the consequences, come what may. After all, it was high time to strike a significant blow for civil rights and she, plus most of her supporters, were fully convinced of the justice of their cause.

As the crowd fanned out into the square preparing to listen to the speeches, several shots rang out. Security police chased youngsters who held in their hands nothing more lethal than stones, pieces of bricks, wood fragments and whatever else they could easily find. Nobody will ever know what goaded the police into action or what prompted them to overreact as they did. They obviously sensed that serious clashes between marchers and police were imminent and wanted to nip in the bud any possible trouble. Further shots were fired at 15-30 second intervals and a number of those fleeing fell to the ground. Pandemonium reigned, with the shrieks of pain from the injured being followed by ambulances with sirens converging on the square. The entire saga lasted no longer than five minutes but it took a heavy toll of human suffering and anguish. When the dust settled some 13 people lay dead and a further 35 had various degrees of injuries, a few critical.

Father Colm McKnight was one of those in the vanguard of relief assistance, his of the spiritual variety. His presence was truly a quirk of fate: after attending a monthly meeting of the clergy, he had been strolling to the square to meet some of his own Liscorley parishioners. Nothing could have prepared him for what he was about to witness.

Just as he was administering the last rites to the first victim, Father McKnight enquired if the man had any last wish to make. In words scarcely audible, the dying man said, 'Please tell my parents not to worry on my behalf. My big regret is that I am dying not having fired a shot in the name of freedom. I hope those to follow, who will fire many shots, will one day enjoy the fruits of our long-sought liberation.' With tears welling up in his eyes, the priest watched the young man's breath ebbing away before attending in turn to the rest of the critically injured. He thanked God for having granted him the opportunity to be present to dispense so much spiritual 'medicine' within so short a time.

The crowd that day was an unstable mixture of largely peaceful demonstrators infiltrated by a small number of republicans with wider aspirations who felt that the pace of developments was well below par. It provided a forum to air their grievances and bring them to the attention of the international community, a vital first step in trying to muster up enough support for their perceived legitimate cause. But the response from the police was far beyond what they could ever have anticipated.

Among the marchers were a select few from the Inistogue branch of the IRA, including Seamus Dowling and Joe Moriarty. Seamus had contacted Shane McCabe who kept him informed of the preparations and scheduling of events. Excusing himself from the early stages of the march, because of the lead-up to the busy cow-calving season, Seamus left him in no doubt of his intended presence before the finale at Cloonbridge. 'This will be an opportunity no true Irishman can afford to miss,' he confided to Shane. Seamus and his colleagues joined the march two miles from the city, just as tensions were about to spill over. They edged their way discreetly into the outer layer of the onward flow and were soon in the centre of the large throng.

With the ambulance sirens still blaring and intermittently illuminating sections of the square, Seamus ran to help a young lady who lay prostrate with a blood-stained sleeve. Removing his jacket, he placed it beneath her head and positioned her face upwards. He immediately took a white handkerchief from his pocket, applied a tourniquet and cleaned the smeared blood. Even a fleeting glance was enough to convince him that she was a girl of striking beauty and he guessed she was about 20 years of age. On feeling a little more composed she enquired, 'Where am I, what's happening and who are you?' Seamus, as calmly as possible, explained that during the final minutes of the march to Cloonbridge skirmishes had erupted with police who felt obliged to calm proceedings by randomly firing into the crowd, with inevitable consequences. 'As for your final question, my name is Seamus Dowling and I hail from Inistogue in County Kerry, reassuring you that more than just the people of Ulster are behind you in your quest for justice.'

Helen then said it was more the shock rather than the superficial arm injury that bothered her. 'After a bullet ricocheted off the ground and struck my arm, I intuitively fell face downwards to avoid any further injuries.'

'You acted wisely like a seasoned campaigner,' replied Seamus, 'and I'll now take you away from this danger zone.'

As the moans and groans of injured people still pierced the low-hanging dark clouds, Seamus stooped to lend an arm to the injured Helen. Just then he heard a shout from behind.

'Where are you taking my lovely girl friend, Dowling?'

Seamus turned to discover it was Shane McCabe accompanied by Brian McNeill. After Helen reassured them that she was not seriously injured, there were the usual warm greetings and embraces. 'I know a small quiet pub we can go to attend to Helen's wound and talk,' said Shane. There was not even a hint of disapproval and within five minutes they were entering the petite cosy lounge of the Royal Oak at the corner of Grosvener Street.

The barman was quick in delivering first aid to Helen, after which they relaxed and reminisced about what had just taken place.

Seamus noted 'that today marked a watershed in relations between England and the whole of Ireland. It tested, in the most delicate way possible, England's readiness to allow a greater say to the Catholics of Ulster in running their affairs. Even a peaceful protest has met with the sternest of resistance; I dread to think what their response would be if we'd taken a more militant course of action. However, we must learn from today's events and use it as a guide in future campaigns.'

'What occurred today will further poison relations with our larger neighbour,' voiced Shane, to which there was unanimous assent. 'But let us refrain from doing anything in haste and we can only benefit from the favourable international support, which is bound to be forthcoming.'

'What initially may appear to be negative, can in the long term turn to our advantage' said Helen, whose humour was now distinctly more up-beat. 'We could justifiably feel very incensed, and the wrongdoings will eventually be exposed, but we must act rationally at all times - that's the main code of conduct within the civil rights movement.'

Brian McNeill was less accommodating. 'Down through history, patience and subservience have achieved nothing and, after today's experience, we must keep all our options open and be ready to use those which will help us achieve our objective.'

The group was obviously split between the two camps. This did not detract from the conviviality and bonhomie which were eased gradually into high gear by the accelerating force of alcohol.

Yet despite differences in viewpoints and means to an end, here was a small nucleus of dedicated Irish people who would reach cell and even tissue proportions as the months and years elapsed. It was both an exciting as well as a dangerous time in Irish politics and nobody here present was willing to miss either. When at a late night hour they went their separate ways, the one certainty remained that political forces would bring them to work - and die, if necessary - together again, in the pursuit of their goals.

CHAPTER 4

Libya - 1981

It smacks of a fairytale. A country of about 675,000 square miles, one quarter the size of the U.S., whose northern edge hugs the Mediterranean, has 99% of its surface area occupied by the Saharan plateau or a veritable desert. There are no permanent rivers: the many *wadis* (dry river beds) are filled by flash floods during the rains, only to be reduced to a trickle in the long dry season. Annual rainfall declines and is more variable as you proceed inland from the coast. Libya's capital city is Tripoli and the second biggest, Benghazi, has between ten and 15 inches of rain yearly. Deep in the Sahara it is common to have 200 consecutive rain-free days in a year and semi-desert conditions prevail when rainfall is less than six inches. Although there are underground water reserves, these are difficult and expensive to develop. The arid dry climate is worsened by the *ghibli*, a hot and dry wind blowing from the south several times during the year. It all adds up to an inhospitable environment.

Under the Ottoman Empire from the early 16th century, the Italians invaded Libya in 1911 and continued their occupation throughout the First World War. The 1922 fascist Italian government started a programme of total occupation and colonisation and this succeeded along the coastal strip, including Tripoli, but resistance continued in the east, led by Omar Al-Mukhtar, until he was arrested and executed in 1931. In 1935 the Italian fascist, Benito Mussolini, launched his ambitious programme of 'demographic colonisation', under which 150,000 Italian settlers were located in Libya and comprised almost 20% of the total population at the start of World War II. At the war's end in 1945, the country was underpopulated, impoverished and deeply divided along economic, political and religious lines. In December 1951, the pro-British King Idris I was appointed and he declared Libyan independence. Although Libya became a member of the Arab League in 1953 and refused British forces landing rights for the 1956 Suez Canal expedition, its policy generally was strongly pro-Western.

One of the most strategic and fiercest phases of World War II was contested in north Africa, most notably the Libyan desert. Here the Nazi army under Rommel was pitted against the might of the western allies in the 1942-43 campaign. With the allied push northwards to capture and destroy the enemy's fuel storage tanks at Tobruk near the east Libyan coastline, there was destruction and carnage in its wake. That it succeeded signalled a turning point in the war and the beginning of the downward slide in German fortunes.

Abdul Majid Al-Mahdi experienced first-hand many of the atrocities that devastated his native country. Born in May 1908 not far from where the bloodiest battles occurred, he could remember as a young child the horror news reports and stories of the First World War which tore Europe apart. Little did he then anticipate a second such catastrophe causing more pain and affecting many of his own friends and neighbours. Until 1942 he had worked at any jobs which brought him the simplest and most basic food and little else, and had always served foreign masters. Devoid of skills, he worked mostly in agriculture and often found peace and contentment as a shepherd, bringing him small but definite fringe benefits that eased the late night hunger pangs. But his life was in great need of a new direction.

The Libyan desert war of 1942 had, despite the upheaval and atrocities, a curious beneficial spin-off effect for Abdul Majid. Before and during the advance on Tobruk there were logistical problems in getting much-needed food and other vital supplies to the front lines. Local knowledge, Arabic skills and, above all else, a readiness to operate under the cover of darkness were within Abdul Majid's capacity. And those in need were only too willing to pay well for the service. Often with only the aid of a camel he risked his life edging ever more closely towards enemy fire to ensure that allied troops were better fed and battle-hardy. He often mused about how much he had earned: in just six months he had pocketed more than ever before and, perhaps, ever would again in his entire life. He knew that once the fighting stopped he would revert to his old job of shepherding but for now he was happy to bask temporarily in the glory of his long-denied but rapid success.

As all this was happening something equally momentous occurred. On a hot September afternoon in 1942, Abdul Majid's wife, Fatima, gave birth to their sixth child, a son named Mohammad. As the cannons roared and gunfire lit up the night sky further north, little did baby Mohammad appreciate what was unfolding all around him. Many of his enemies later remarked that the sound of gunfire signalled his arrival in this world and was destined never to leave him. Abdul Majid was ecstatic at the prospect of his young son one day growing up in a Libya free of war and oppression and ready to take its rightful place among the powerful and independent countries of the world.

The war years passed and even after King Idris came to power in 1951 economic development still continued at a very slow pace. Then in 1959 Libya emerged from the poverty trap and dependence on international assistance and income from the rental of U.S. and British air bases, to an oil-rich monarchy. Oil was discovered in both Tripolitania and Cyrenaica within easy reach of the Mediterranean sea coast and Libya would never be the same again. Such were the projected vast oil reserves that economic expansion surged on the back of increased government programmes and expenditure, leading to a rise in economic living standards. As one shrewd observer remarked: 'Libya suddenly changed from its dependence on camels to almost total reliance on automobiles.' It also ushered in the most difficult period in the country's history: how to manage and best utilise this new-found wealth for the maximum benefit of all of its citizens.

Mohammad spent his childhood and adolescent years in close association with his father, doing their daily chores together, and the elder's influence on the youngster's active and inquisitive mind led to a father-son rapport and understanding of great significance. The youth saw in his father's difficult life many of the injustices born of colonialism and oppression and he became determined to do everything within his power to support causes domestically and abroad to remove this awful curse. His incisive mind convinced him he stood the best chance of effecting changes by assuming a position of power and the army was an important stepping stone. When his father suddenly fell ill and died in 1963, Mohammad was already a young private. Looking with obvious pride on his handsome son, Abdul's dying wish had been that Mohammad would devote all his energy to making Libya a country where all its people could work in freedom and dignity and command due respect of all other nations.

Once his grief had waned, Mohammad lost no time in fulfilling his father's wish that was also very dear to his own heart. He rapidly worked his way up the military hierarchy, becoming a colonel in 1967. Scarcely two years later, on September 1st 1969, he and a small group of army officers deposed the king and declared Libya a republic. The new regime led by Mohammad was strongly pro-Arabic, devoutly Muslim and quickly severed the monarchy's close ties with the U.S. and Britain. Strong government policies followed, including a push for higher oil prices and a controlling share of oil income, from 51% Libyan to outright nationalisation. Although Arab unity was high on the priority list, a less than enthusiastic response from some other Arab countries stifled progress. Nothing, perhaps, was closer to Mohammad's heart than the sad plight of the Palestinians, scattered far and wide, and in search of a homeland. He promised support for revolutionary and guerrilla organisations in Africa and the Middle East, an issue dangerously provoking certain western governments threatened by such groups.

Libya, under the new leadership of Md. Al-Mahdi, continued to introduce changes and innovations during the 1970s and early 80s. In March 1977, the General People's Congress (Libya's quasi-legislature) announced that the country was to be renamed The People's Socialist Libyan Arab

Jamahiriyah (signifying 'government through the masses'). In the early 1980s, however, a decrease in the world demand and price for oil was beginning to thwart Al-Mahdi's regional influence. Nevertheless, he had ample resources to pursue the main goals he set himself and firmly believed in. His next moves were awaited with apprehension and trepidation by most countries, particularly those in the western hemisphere.

*

Ever since the inauguration of 1969, preparations for the annual September 1st festivities were meticulously planned and executed. Those in power, spearheaded by Md. Al-Mahdi, spared no effort to remind the Libyan masses of how the 1969 revolution drastically changed life for the average person and this annual gathering was essentially convened to confirm this. Not that many Libyans were overly concerned about matters political but rather how to grapple with the fast evolving changes brought by socialism.

The crowd thronging the large square (Maidan Ashuhada) in downtown Tripoli on that warm September day in 1981 had representatives from far afield. The organising committee, through its network of so-called volunteers, ensured that all who possibly could come were present. Those who by their absence might be perceived as being anti-establishment reluctantly showed up. A fleet of buses and trucks, laid on free of charge, eased the transport problems of rural people. The large crowds had converged on the square since shortly after daybreak and a few of the elderly were heard remarking that not since the onslaught on Tobruk were so many advancing bodies seen in one area. The scene was all the more impressive and colourful by the numerous placards and billboards proclaiming the achievements of the revolution and, above all, its leader. His photograph was proudly displayed on each placard, showing a man dressed in his native white robe and seemingly at one both with his surroundings and all those present.

Five minutes before the scheduled starting time of 11 a.m. there was the usual flurry of security activity beside the large raised podium at the square's northern end. This was the site of every major gathering since the revolution and today was yet another. Then, as he appeared in his flowing white robe, with body guards fore and aft, key handpicked supporters in front of the podium and facing the crowd gave the signal to start the applause. The emotions and frenzy that were unleashed, accompanied by incessant wild cheering, were carried on the Mediterranean waves half way to Malta. After some semblance of normality was restored, the chairman called on the local *mullah* or holy man to recite a prayer from the Koran during which all showed extreme reverence and respect. It was then the turn of their leader Mohammad, who rose slowly to his feet, again amid loud and sustained applause, looked out over the sprawling masses and began what was to be an impassioned speech.

'My comrades and fellow citizens, I will begin by thanking you for coming here today in such large numbers. Since I first addressed you at this very spot 12 years ago to the day, great changes have transformed our world and no country more drastically than our own. Have you noticed how many new cars, trucks and buses ply our streets and countryside, the proliferation of large supermarkets with food, clothing and electrical appliances from various world countries, the huge growth in employment and a better overall standard of living? For too long we wallowed in poverty, unaware of the enormous oil wealth beneath the soil we daily walk upon. Our socialist government, with foreign technical assistance, developed the oil industry for the benefit of each and every one of you. Had our government not pressed for the justified oil price increase in the early 1970s, supported by other friendly Arab countries, we would have only a fraction of the wealth there is today.

'Our system of government as depicted in the country's new name follows socialist lines, not the extreme socialism or communism of the Soviet Union but a milder version better suited to our needs. The challenge facing us from the start was how best to use the increasing proceeds from oil but I can assure you we have more than measured up to the task. Though we are now overly dependent on a foreign labour pool, this will either be reduced or cease entirely once we have a technically skilled labour force ourselves. Education and training are long term in nature but our targets are being met. In spite of a trend for reduced oil prices, we have enough money for the foreseeable future to keep both our domestic as well as foreign programmes running smoothly.

'My government lost no time since assuming power to declare our firm commitment to foreign policy. We are fiercely determined to support and assist oppressed and disadvantaged countries and people and this is truly an enormous task. Obviously, we have to be selective and a few issues are receiving priority. A subject very dear to me, and I know to all here present, is the Palestinians' right to their own homeland, a right denied to them since the 1948 unjust creation of the state of Israel. We are doing all within our power to assist in righting this blatant injustice and abuse of human rights but there is much ... much more to be done. We will not rest peacefully until there is a fair and lasting solution.

'Until the eruption of fresh disturbances in Northern Ireland in 1969, just before my own inauguration on September 1st of that year, I was ignorant of the fact that the north eastern corner of Ireland was still part of the United Kingdom. I made a firm inaugural pledge from this very podium that my government would help the nationalists rid themselves of the shackles of colonialism. Since then we have supported them with weapons and trained members of the up-front fighting force i.e. the Irish Republican Army (I.R.A.). There is yet no sign of British willingness to loosen its grip on its nearest colony but we must continue our steadfast support for such a deserving cause.

'Our ties with Ireland stretch far beyond the military role as economic links are growing by the year. Most likely the beef you will eat after leaving here had its origin in the Irish Republic and there are several other agricultural products from that small country to be found on our supermarket shelves. Irish companies are assisting us to develop various sectors of our own agriculture and we have regular visits from Irish government representatives. Both countries are beneficiaries of these areas of mutual cooperation.

'Finally, I reserve my strongest remarks for the most powerful and technologically advanced nation on this earth, the United States of America. Let me begin by saying we have the greatest respect and admiration for their scientific discoveries and innovations, including putting a man on the moon shortly before I first addressed you in 1969. We owe much to their technicians, and those from other countries, for developing our oil resources and we presently have many U.S. personnel on our soil. We bear no grudges against the average American but have great reservations about their foreign policy. Our major concern centres around their massive military support, presently amounting to billions of dollars, for the Israelis, ensuring that our Palestinian brothers can never be strong enough to regain the land that is rightfully theirs. But weapons and power alone will not defy a displaced people willing to continue the struggle for as long as it takes. We give refuge in Tripoli to many Palestinians and our government will make their cause a top priority.'

It was these last remarks that elicited the loudest and most sustained applause, after which the large crowd began to shuffle and move slowly from the square. They were reminded, if it was indeed necessary, of the thrust of the government's programmes at home and abroad.

What no one could possibly predict, however, were the consequences and fallout of such programmes. For now, fresher on the minds of the disbanding masses was the thought of juicy Irish beef that would satisfy the hunger pangs that had slowly built up over the past three hours.

*

The Libyan Arab Airlines plane was 50 minutes late leaving London's Heathrow airport bound for Tripoli on a grey and cloudy morning in February, 1981. It was a great tribute to airport authorities that they could keep the delay to this very minimum. Incoming flights from some snowbound U.S. cities were behind schedule and the queue of planes preparing to descend had caused severe congestion. For inexperienced flyer

Jim McCabe, in a window seat in row eight of economy class, the late departure went virtually unnoticed and, judging by his nervous demeanour, he might have felt happier escaping his claustrophobic surroundings and returning to Liscorley. He quickly banished any thoughts of backtracking and reminded himself that, during the early morning connecting shuttle flight from Belfast, he had been imbued with excitement and adventure.

As the plane taxied in the queue for takeoff, the pilot announced he expected to be airborne within ten minutes. With a furtive glance at passengers on board, Jim reckoned that between one-third and one-half were Libyans, perhaps another third were British and the remainder were a hotchpotch of other races. To Jim's left in an aisle seat was a young lady in her early 20s like himself, with an English gentleman of 40-something seated between. The girl appeared to be speaking with a southern Irish accent but he would explore it more fully after takeoff. After engaging the Englishman in conversation, Jim discovered he was a roughneck named Geoffrey Palmer heading for a month-on-month-off stint in the Zaltan oilfields in Libya's Surt basin, situated about 200 kilometres southwest of Benghazi in Cyrenaica province.

Jim firmly grasped the armrest of his seat as the plane cleared the runway and began its steep ascent. This was due partly to his nervousness of flying and also to an apprehensiveness of the unknown into which he would soon plunge himself. Before he had boarded the plane that morning in Belfast, with his father Shane and mother Brenda at his side, he'd had serious doubts about the wisdom of his undertaking. And, although both were heartbroken to see him leave, they realised it was a mission he firmly believed in, carrying on the previous good work of Shane and his colleagues. Now almost 22 years of age and the eldest son, Jim sensed that although he had fully trained as a primary school teacher, he needed to take time out and do something entirely different. How different, he wasn't yet in a position to say.

Jim, Geoffrey and the girl chatted for a while, until Geoffrey said, 'Seeing you two appear to have common interests, I'll gladly change to the window seat and allow you to sit together.'

Jim was delighted and thanked him profusely. He immediately shook the young lady's hand and introduced himself. The name McCabe clearly rang a bell from way back when and her eyes displayed a mixture of astonishment and delight.

'I can't believe it,' she said, 'because since I was knee high I remember my Dad talking in glowing terms about the McCabes of Liscorley and the wonderful friendship nurtured through football over the years.' Then she went on to explain that she was Deirdre Dowling, second child and eldest daughter of Seamus and Nora Dowling from Inistogue, Co. Kerry. Jim likewise was unable to conceal his delight at not only meeting an Irish girl but also a close friend of his own family.

Now that they were at ease with each other, Jim said their chance meeting was a cause for celebration and enquired what Deirdre liked to drink. Obviously she was more attuned to the customs and practices of her soon-to-be host country, for she said, 'Much as I'd love one, I'm afraid that Libya, being a strict Muslim country, doesn't allow alcohol consumption - and that includes aboard its national carrier!'

Jim was disappointed and for a while regretted not flying with British Caledonian, as he could have done. But they both soon agreed that had he taken this latter option and celebrated gaily on board, he would have incurred the greatest hangover - and longest recovery period - he'd ever experienced.

The plane had long reached its full cruising altitude of 33,000 feet and the mixture of male stewards and female stewardesses were preparing to serve the meal. A stewardess enquired whether they wished to have lamb or cous-cous. Jim rarely ate sheep meat but, when told that the second was a traditional north African dish, he opted for the first and decided to postpone his culinary exploration for at least a few weeks. Deirdre advanced Jim's education a step further by pointing out that the head scarf worn by the stewardess reflected a standard Islamic religious custom and, in more reserved rural areas of Libya, most females from the age of puberty revealed nothing more than a small part of their faces, often just the eyes. At first

Jim thought this was just Deirdre's way of warning him to keep his distance, but it proved 100 percent correct after their arrival in Tripoli.

Both Jim and Deirdre were a little uneasy about discussing their plans. Deirdre began, 'About three months ago there was an advertisement in a London newspaper looking for teachers for an Oil Company International School in Tripoli. Seemingly, it was established to service the educational needs of children of international personnel stationed in Libya. Little did I think when I replied to it that I'd be called for an interview and later offered a job. So, here I am on my first trip abroad and en route to a country I know hardlly anything about.'

'Well, from what you've already said, your knowledge is 200 percent more than mine,' replied Jim.

Deirdre continued, 'The recruiting agency assured me that accommodation provided will be within walking distance of the school. According to what I've heard from a friend of a friend who worked in Libya, demand for housing far outstrips supply due to the oil bonanza so I'm understandably a bit worried about the exact situation.'

Jim had many more reasons to feel anxious. At the start of his teens, he'd accompanied his father Shane on a civil rights march that had culminated in the massacre of some innocent civilians in Northchester Square on January 30, 1972. The quasi-barbaric incidents on that day had both traumatised and goaded him to action. Like his father before him, he felt duty-bound to be a motivator for change and had become increasingly active in Liscorley's branch of the I.R.A. He vowed not to let republicanism impede his priority goal of a decent education and had graduated from the primary teacher's training college in June 1980, just two months short of his 21st birthday. Having a platform from which he could later launch his career, he decided to devote a few years of his young life to the most noble cause of helping his disadvantaged fellow countrymen achieve justice and equality.

Word filtered through to I.R.A. branches throughout Ireland of Libya's altruistic offer of assistance, a pledge repeated annually on national day by Mohammad Al-Madhi.

During the mid to late 1970s selected young men completed six months specialised training in the use of weapons, a supply of which had illegally found their way into the republic and onwards to the north. Jim was now one of another group on a similar mission but had no information about the others or whether they had already arrived in Libya. His link between obscurity and salvation following his arrival at Tripoli airport hinged on a firm promise from his Liscorley branch that a reliable official would meet him, bearing his emblazoned name on a banner, and would take care of the rest. Not having a single word of Arabic, in case of an emergency, only heightened Jim's isolation and apprehension.

As he mulled over all the uncertainties, Deirdre awoke from a brief nap, turned to Jim and asked, 'Are you taking up a teaching position as well?'

Taken aback and unprepared, Jim coughed twice to win valuable time before stating within earshot of Geoffrey, 'Yes, I've got a six month assignment to teach English.' Then, to cover up his blatant lie, he replied 'As soon as I get established, I'll tell you more about it.'

The plane had now begun its descent and you could clearly see the blue foam-tipped Mediterranean waves gently lapping the mostly brown Libyan coastline. The pilot announced to his crew that there was just five minutes to landing. Approaching the runway and looking at the strange vista on both sides of the plane, Deirdre turned to Jim and mused, 'Does it ever rain in this part of the world?'

It was an immense cultural shock . On entering Tripoli airport's large new arrival hall, which was festooned with colourful banners proclaiming in Arabic the achievements of the revolution and the socialist doctrines governing people's daily lives, Jim looked askance at Deirdre whom he was helping with hand luggage and remarked, 'Whatever your concerns about rain, my first impression is that the number of the weaker sex is minimal.'

As they walked side by side down the wide marble stairs to the baggage carousels, the high ceilings and sparsely-furnished arrival hall echoed to the frenzied rush of arriving passengers and the crying of sleep-deprived children. Deirdre struggled to hurriedly fill out a landing card until Jim procured one from a bench in both Arabic and English. Apart from the women among the arrivals, there wasn't one other female to be seen. The baggage was off-loaded in stages and it was at least one hour before Jim and Deirdre could proceed with their laden trolleys towards passport control and customs. The long queue and scrutinous checking of passports and luggage meant that it was almost another hour before the ordeal was complete.

Jim felt a load lifting from his heart. Turning to Deirdre he said, 'The customs official asked me two questions in broken English: what was my nationality and did I have any alcohol in my luggage? On seeing my Irish passport he stopped short of opening my suitcase. Not knowing in advance about liquor restrictions, I'd put a bottle of whiskey at the bottom of the case wrapped in a pullover, not in an attempt to hide it but to ensure it arrived in one piece.'

'Your Irishness may have saved you a lengthy prison sentence - the usual penalty for such a breach of their Islamic code,' whispered Deirdre. 'Having to visit you in prison is something I can do without during these first few weeks.'

Jim promised her that, since the whiskey was now virtually worth its weight in gold, he would save it for a future occasion when they could both share and enjoy every dram of it.

Before they reached the automatic doors they saw a lady and gentleman waiting on the opposite side, each bearing a placard clearly showing in Arabic and English the names Deirdre Dowling and Jim McCabe. The relief on their faces showed instantly. Deirdre was met by the assistant principal of the school, an American in her late 40s accompanied by a driver. After introductions and a brief conversation, Deirdre left with her escort after Jim had promised to contact her at the school within a week or two. Greeting Jim was a moustached erect gentleman in military garb and sunglasses. He shook Jim's hand firmly, if not warmly, and said in halting English, 'On behalf of our great leader, I welcome you to the People's Socialist Libyan Arab Jamahiriyah and hope you will have a pleasant stay in our friendly country.' The country's name was more than a mouthful for Jim to grasp and assimilate and considered his host to be more businesslike than friendly. The driver arrived shortly after and steered his trolley of luggage towards a car at the far corner of the airport's parking lot. Before long the car with its three passengers sped quickly northwards on the wide 20 kilometre motorway leading to Tripoli's city centre. Signs and names in Arabic flashed by and, with the minimum of conversation and the alien environment, the first pangs of homesickness engulfed Jim. But then it was his first trip to a foreign country and he willed himself patience before coming to any hasty conclusions.

*

'Mornings are almost as dark here as in Ireland,' noted Jim as he awakened to the daybreak call to prayer from the nearby mosque in downtown Tripoli. Not remotely familiar with the religious customs, the wailing high-pitched Arabic intonations over a loudspeaker perched high on the mosque's minaret sounded to Jim more like a person in distress. Switching on his low-wattage bedside light and glancing at his watch told him it was only 06. 14 a.m., so there was still time to catch up on lost sleep before appearing for breakfast at the pre-arranged time of 08.30 a.m. He was staying at a smallish hotel, the Arabic name of which eluded him, and had been given little information other than that he would meet with others and be briefed after breakfast. So far, everything had hit him as shockingly as a high pressure cold shower on a warm body and he was convinced the worst was yet to come.

There was an eerie silence as Jim entered the hotel's spacious dining room a few minutes after 08.30 a.m. Is their timekeeping on a par with back home, he wondered? All the tables were set with white tablecloths and there were no waiters in sight except one heading for the table with a single seated guest. With just a quick glance Jim reckoned he could well be a fellow countryman and, in order to have some company, decided to request his permission to join him at table. A nod of agreement came forthwith. A friendly 'good morning' confirmed that the man hailed from the Republic of Ireland. Extending his hand and shaking Jim's, he said, 'With an accent like yours, you can only be from that idyllic north eastern part of Ireland', to which Jim replied positively. Jim took a seat opposite at the four-place table and began, 'My name's Jim McCabe from Liscorley, County Down and I'm delighted to meet an Irishman the first morning after my arrival.' He was yet to discover that several others would appear in various capacities before many days or weeks elapsed. The man introduced himself as Declan Horan from County Tipperary, with no reference to the precise location. The waiter had just taken their order for breakfast but, judging by his slow gait, there would be ample time for discussion before any food arrived.

Declan continued, 'Let there be no pretence between us in a country where you'll find an abundance of it.. A few days before your arrival I heard there was another Irishman due to join our ranks. I assume you've come to bolster our small group of Irishmen, from both north and south, seeking military training in the art of guerrilla warfare so that we can more readily make all of Ireland one political entity.'

An expression of relief washed over Jim's face at finding what appeared to be a forthright and honest comrade, a word that was increasingly flouted in this socialist country. With the first barrier between them broken, Jim responded, 'Yes, the purpose of my mission is precisely as you described it and I look forward to an interesting and productive six months among friends.' After 30 minutes of jovial conversation and the gastric juices beginning to flow freely, the waiter's arrival with fried eggs, toast and tea was never more appreciated.

During breakfast some others entered and took seats at scattered tables. Again Jim was amazed there was not a single female among them. Declan sensed his unease and felt obliged to brief and forewarn him. 'I must stress the cultural differences which you should keep at the forefront of your mind at all times. The behavioural code for Moslems is quite distinct and merits respect; to do otherwise is both insensitive and discourteous. This hotel in a city where rooms are scarce and at a premium is reserved by the government for training foreign nationals to

81

further their political aspirations. You ought to be careful how
you behave and what you say to the multi-ethnic people you
meet. Furthermore, as in all socialist countries there's a covert
but very effective information gathering network and to avoid
trouble a person must respect the adage that 'the walls have
ears.'

The waiter was now approaching to clear the table and it was
almost 09.25 a.m. 'You'll receive further instructions from the
behind-doors briefing - we're off there now.'

On the narrow corridor Jim was greeted by a Libyan with
whom he would remain in close contact for the next six months.
'My name is Abdullah Rashid and, being chief of the training
programme, I would like to welcome you and will be your host
while in Libya. There are many of your countrymen here, some
of whom you will meet shortly, and you should feel at home.'
With a wave of his hand he ushered the others into a small dimly-
lit room where 21 others were moving to take up their seats.
From only a cursory glance he reckoned that four or six of those
might well be Irish, an estimate he was soon able to confirm. Jim
took a seat next to Declan in the front row just before Abdullah
rose to address them from the podium.

'I welcome you all to our third six-month training session of
the 1980s. Our great leader, Mohammad, would have
addressed you personally hadn't urgent international business
instead occupied him. He sends warm greetings and intends to
meet each of you during the coming weeks, a strong vindication
of his interest in and commitment to the work he so generously
supports. Palestinians and Irish account for more than half of
those here present with a smaller number representative of
equally-deserving causes: our Moslem brothers in the Sudan,
those seeking an independent Spanish Sahara, racial injustices
in South Africa and the horrible civil war in Angola, are but
some examples of where our attention is concentrated.

'If your stay here can advance or improve the situation in
your own country, it is work well done. We greatly believe in on-
the-job training, sharing our own experiences of how minority
groups can manoeuvre to wrest power from oppressive and
unjust regimes. Unfortunately, this often involves what the west

regards as unlawful tactics but do minorities have any alternative? The lives of a few must occasionally be sacrificed for the benefit of the masses. Any of you too squeamish to countenance this philosophy is in the wrong place.' Jim shuffled nervously and wondered whether he could measure up to the task. 'Although I am personally responsible for the overall training, each group has its own leader. Let's finish this briefing and disband for a tea break designed to get you acquainted and begin lasting friendships.'

With Declan doing the introductions it was a strange mix of foreigners who in turn shook Jim's hand. He had a vague idea from his school's religious instruction classes and Sunday mass sermons that Palestine was part of the Holy Land where Jesus Christ had ministered. As he sipped his tea he suddenly realised he was now face-to-face with young men from that sacred land and he was temporarily uplifted. But it wasn't until he met his own countrymen that the all-pervasive homesickness began to lift. He hoped to work with one or more of them but there was no guarantee of this. When the social half hour interlude ended and cars pulled up in front of the hotel, Jim, Declan and two others were ushered in to the first. Jim was pleased to be joined by Abdullah, whose presence emphasised his mission's importance, and a fellow Irishman named Vincent Tuohy. Vincent hailed from county Cork and spoke with a lilting accent so difficult to understand that it only compounded his communication problems.

For a young man from Northern Ireland where road traffic laws and rules are strictly adhered to, he wondered if any existed here. From the time the driver catapulted the car from the kerbside its occupants' lives were at serious risk. His speed was reckless on city streets full of pedestrians roaming virtually at will. It appeared to be a contest in which drivers competed for control of crowded thoroughfares and almost continuously honked horns to clear obstructions - both metallic and human! Jim likened it to an outdoor carnival of bumper cars he nostalgically remembered from his youth, except for the much greater potential loss of human life. He was surprised at the large number of damaged and dented cars and how few people bothered to repair them. It was yet another aspect of the cultural shock that he could not easily comprehend.

On reaching the eastern suburbs of Tripoli Abdullah took on the tour guide role, something he customarily did for each newcomer. 'Since independence Libya has devoted much of its energy and resources to education and research. On our left is an agricultural institute engaged in soil, plant and animal research. Less than a kilometre further to our right, we will pass the University of Tripoli where students in many faculties will chart our future progress and development. At present, we have international assistance with equipment and professional manpower helping us achieve our goals. Our leader, Mohammad, regularly visits the University to teach the principles and ideas contained in his green book. If we continue driving due east for about 12 hours, with the blue Mediterranean just to our left, we will reach what many people regard as Libya's loveliest and second largest city, Benghazi. But that's for another time as today our journey takes only 45 minutes.'

Jim remembers passing a village, which when translated to him from Arabic meant *Tajoura*, where a few large state-run dairy Friesian herds and a milk processing plant dotted the sandy landscape. About five kilometres further on, the driver turned right on to what appeared to be a private and recently tarmacked wide road, in contrast to the narrower and less well maintained main road . Abdullah quickly sensed Jim's surprise and tried to put him at ease. 'Because of our leader's immense devotion to this project, he has spared no resources to make it a success and you will learn more about it during your six months of training.' What stunned Jim were the layers of armed security guards positioned along the entrance road leading to the portals of the camp proper around which was a very high fortified wall. A thought occurred to him: does it take more ingenuity, cunning and firepower to penetrate the security and defences here than to take over the U.S.'s gold reserves at Fort Knox?

Matching the intense security on the outside was the code of secrecy within. At the inauguration ceremony participants were bound under oath not to divulge to anyone, particularly other internationals working in Libya, the purpose of their stay or the nature of their work. Not that any of these measures were essential: the scale and effectiveness of Libya's information-gathering network was little short of the best and any leaked messages were easily traced to the source and the transgressors duly punished. Jim's clandestine activities with the I.R.A. were in the little league compared to what he now faced but he was willing to abide by the ground rules. He stood to gain valuable experience that he was later prepared to apply to good effect in Northern Ireland. Right now, he preferred not to ponder the consequences but Abdullah's warning of the need to sacrifice some lives for the benefit of the masses might yet return to haunt him.

*

The rented villa's location posing as St. Patrick's Catholic Church was simply idyllic, perched on a hilly west Tripoli suburban street overlooking the Mediterranean. With the influx of foreigners following the oil boom of the early 1970s, the Vatican hierarchy couldn't overlook the spiritual needs of the sizeable Catholic community, many of whom were Irish and Maltese citizens. In a country where the Moslem faith was devoutly practised and protected, the Government publicly admitted to tolerance of religious minorities. But for obvious reasons there should be no open or showy displays of devotion to Christianity that might send the wrong signal to the casual passers-by. Therefore, by way of subtle camouflage St. Patrick's purposefully retained all the characteristics of a villa and few of a church.

Because of the rather inadequate directions to the church that Jim had received at the hotel, he spent extra time probing nearby streets until he hit upon a fellow Irishman heading in the same direction. It was St Patrick's Day, March 17th, an important date for not only Irish people the world over but those with just thin - or threadbare - connections to Ireland. They entered the church just as the Maltese priest began his sermon and they took seats at the rear to avoid drawing unnecessary attention to their late arrival. Of the nearly full congregation, Jim reckoned that about half were Irish. His gaze rested on a nice dark-haired girl seated in the third pew from the front and, without being able to swear under oath, he was confident it was Deirdre Dowling. He would conjure up an excuse as to why he hadn't contacted her before now but the trauma of settling in should more than suffice. He concentrated little on the rest of the lengthy sermon or what followed and begged God's forgiveness for allowing a girl's presence to distract him from his religious duties.

It was a routine after-mass practice for the crowd to have tea and a light snack on the church's rear veranda with an imposing sea view. After Jim was introduced to several Irish and his initial discomfort with strangers was beginning to dissipate, he went to Deirdre whom he spotted conversing with a small group nearby. 'Deirdre! Great to see you again - forgive me for not getting in touch with you earlier. Excuses mean little but when you hear mine there should be no hard feelings.'

'Are they the self-same canned explanations Irishmen often give when their interest in a member of the opposite sex wanes?' enquired Deirdre. It was not the time for bickering and Jim wished he could show his affection in a more tangible way but that must wait its turn. Deidre explained that two U.S. national teacher friends and herself had rented a villa within walking distance of the Oil Company School. 'As luck would have it, and to honour our National Saint, we're hosting a party at our place tonight and we'd be delighted if you can come. Here is a map showing where our villa is, two blocks from the school, right turn and our villa is second on the left.'

Jim couldn't conceal his delight at having an opportunity to enjoy his first St. Patrick's night on foreign soil. 'I'm thrilled with the invitation and, as promised, I have a bottle of Irish whiskey to share with you.'

Deirdre interrupted, 'Best not in public - that bottle can be saved for another time. I must leave now to start all the preparations - look forward to seeing you any time after 9 p.m. this evening.' In an instant she was gone but the after-mass interlude was something Jim would remember and savour for a long time.

Social gatherings in Tripoli were discreetly arranged, taking care to draw the least attention and to reduce noise and revelry. Not that Libyans were anti-social but it was assumed that fundamental to the enjoyment of foreigners was the use - and often abuse - of alcohol, a behavioural pattern alien to a good Moslem's code of conduct. While theoretically anyone caught with alcohol in his/her possession or under its influence was liable to imprisonment, there was a practical realisation by the 'powers that be' that moderate consumption was all right. It was a tacit acknowledgement of the foreigners' contribution to Libya's development, using oil as the springboard, and the authorities reluctantly tolerated this small misdemeanour. En route by taxi from his city hotel to the western edge it occurred to Jim that, since he'd landed in Tripoli five weeks earlier, he hadn't tasted alcohol - a near five-year record for him. The taxi driver had the street address written in Arabic on a piece of paper, arranged through the hotel reception, and the number of times he consulted it suggested he might be new to his job. After he circled several times and enquired of locals he gravitated to a narrow street where there were numerous cars parked higgledy-piggledy on both sides and Jim knew he had arrived.

When Jim entered the high-ceilinged brightly-lit entrance hall he realised this was his ideal orientation to the foreigners' social mecca and an essential focal point. The Irish here hadn't had the opportunity to honour St. Patrick in daytime parades as at home but were prepared to compensate this evening. With background Irish music as a welcome soother, it was 'virtual reality' Ireland within the four walls. Deirdre in her colourful green dress quickly greeted Jim and eased him into enjoying the evening by introducing him to several of the guests. He sipped from a large glass what looked to be normal beer, but tasted only remotely like it. It was to be his first of many evenings drinking home-made Libyan beer, made from ingredients and under conditions not entirely suited to this skilled operation. He felt relieved when one seasoned drinker convinced him it would taste like normal beer after five or six pints.

Just as Ernest Hemmingway once remarked about Monte Carlo that there were 'many shady characters in a sunny place', it struck Jim before too long that it might equally apply to the present assembly. He noted that some were drinking a colourless liquid which they called 'flash', so named perhaps because of the rapidity of getting drunk after imbibing small to moderate quantities of this almost 100 percent pure alcohol. Or in the hands of an amateur it could be a lethal potion, if the methyl instead of the ethyl alcoholic fraction was distilled. Jim's fears were allayed when by chance he spoke to a friendly and open Irishman who unabashedly claimed to be the producer and supplier of 'flash' to most of Tripoli's foreigners. He could stand over its purity and prime quality and, in the 15 years he'd been in business, there hadn't been a single complaint. He stressed that due to its illegality he lived on his nerves and was always just one step ahead of the law, keeping his underground back garden operation well camouflaged. A fellow countryman was less fortunate and ended up behind bars and what saved him from a similar fate more than once were a few Libyan friends in high places. Jim did his preliminary sums and reckoned that at a 'flash' going rate of U.S $60 per bottle, he was likely speaking to a millionaire once or twice over. To evade the police, the man made 'flash' deliveries by various routes and means and at odd hours. Was there something in the Irish psyche that courted risks and danger? At least he was well compensated for his efforts; Jim thought of all the I.R.A. men and women who risked, and sometimes lost, their lives without getting even a penny in return.

The conversation intensified with the rising blood alcohol levels, which could not exceed the established limits for orderly driving and behaviour on Tripoli's late night streets. Jim bumped into Geoffrey Palmer ready for a month's leave after a hot, gruelling seven-day week stint in the desert. 'How nice to see you, Jim, had rather expected to find you here and made enquiries of Irish friends of your possible whereabouts.'

'Had I not accidentally met this morning that nice Irish girl who sat next to me on the plane, tonight's wonderful experience would have eluded me,' said Jim. There was just the usual small talk, Jim feeling a little apprehensive in case he was quizzed about the nature of his work. Jim was fully aware of how efficient an information-gathering system the British had, especially in matters relating to the I.R.A., and from rumours and reports the Irish in Libya were being constantly monitored for republican leanings. The fact that in many jobs British outnumbered the Irish by at least four to one made this task a little easier. Jim intuitively was on his guard, sensing that trust among foreigners in Libya was a scarce enough commodity. Although many were legitimately employed, some were there to benefit from the oil bonanza and the fall-out therefrom. As one experienced campaigner remarked in trying to keep on the right side of the law: 'It doesn't pay to be crooked, but there is a distinct advantage in being a little *bent*.'

What Jim saw continually at his Tajoura training camp was confirmed at tonight's festivities. The centrally planned Libyan economy suffered from many cracks which only huge amounts of oil revenue kept from sundering. The large food supermarkets were awash with products for only a short time after consignments were received, being snatched up rapidly by the high purchasing power of its citizens, and there could be days or weeks of scarcity thereafter. Inadequate forward planning and poor management were at the very heart of many daily problems. Locals seemed unperturbed about queuing for basic food items, something foreigners believed from films they had seen to epitomise the war years. But Jim knew that there was nothing he could do to change things and anyhow he was here for vastly different reasons.

With the singsong of mainly Irish ballads in full swing and the musical accompaniment coming from the talented few, it was entertainment at its very best. It gave Jim the opportunity he'd been seeking all night and he immediately approached Deirdre and asked her to dance.

Within minutes several couples took to the floor for just a few dances before the party broke up around 2 a.m. After all, tomorrow was a working day and it was already several hours after Libyans had gone to sleep. Taking advantage of the slower tempo, Jim saw fit to thank Deirdre for the wonderful night and granting him a glimpse of the Tripoli he scarcely knew existed. She stopped short of enquiring how his work was going, preferring to defer this to a later date. Fortunately, he had the privilege of a second dance during which Deirdre accepted his invitation for a date on Thursday week.

'Since Friday's our rest day, there will no pressure on getting home early,' said Jim. With that, the music came to an end and, after the final discussions and farewells, the crowd began to disperse and move away quietly in their cars. An Irish friend, of two hours standing, gladly obliged in dropping Jim at his downtown hotel. How little he could do unnoticed struck Jim forcibly next day. On returning from work, Abdullah was able to tell him what time he left the hotel, where he went and when he returned. Being his superior and mentor, Jim decided the less he said the better but the thought of somebody breathing down his neck was not only alien to him but gnawed at his democratic rights. Above all, he felt uncomfortable that a seemingly unobtrusive intelligence gathering network should uncover so much about a person's private life.

Of more immediate concern was his approaching date with Deirdre and what he could do to give the wrong 'scent' to his would-be followers. The very thought of Deirdre evoked mental images of her natural beauty, outgoing disposition and zest for living, traits for which he was prepared to sacrifice much. Living with danger was increasingly becoming part of his life and, when it came to affairs of the heart, he was determined to compromise little.

*

Male omnipresence was tiresome every single working day. When it was briefly interrupted by only the occasional woman with practically all her face covered by a dark veil, Jim began to question the moral ethics of it all. Even though it was only five weeks since his arrival, it seemed more like a long drawn-out year. It was Deirdre who first alerted him to the strict Moslem code governing relations between the sexes. He would be forever in her debt as once or twice he might unknowingly have broken the rules, and had to face the attendant repercussions.

Second time round he needed no directions to the spacious villa that only a week earlier had reverberated to the sounds and echoes of Ireland. The gate guard verified his credentials before admitting him to the front door where Deirdre effusively welcomed him. 'I forewarned the guard about your arrival and time as he knows from years of experience that any slip-up in this delicate issue means immediate dismissal.'

'Am I to assume, then, that you're well protected from unwelcome intruders?' joked Jim. Deirdre's appearance in a lovely low-cut sleeveless dress suggested that not only was she attaching great importance to this evening but the likelihood of her venturing on to the streets was virtually nil.

'Sharon and Cathy went to Benghazi for the weekend,' she smiled, 'and since night life in Tripoli isn't very exciting, I figured you might prefer to watch a video here. Besides, we have plenty to discuss and catching-up to do.'

After the harsh realities of previous weeks, her suggestions couldn't be closer to Jim's heart. Before going any further he removed a present from a small bag he had carefully protected and camouflaged en route. 'To celebrate our first date, I've brought you that whiskey.' This elicited a hearty smile from Deirdre and a friendly peck of appreciation on Jim's right cheek.

Deirdre offered and poured Jim a welcoming drink, a hefty glass of 12-year-old Jameson whiskey given to her by the school principal. She knew he had his own contacts, often receiving gifts from satisfied appreciative parents, and did not query its source. Sitting next to Jim, and raising her own glass containing a stiff gin and tonic, she invited him to drink a toast to Ireland and to the peaceful reunification of that divided country. Until Jim knew better, he wondered whether it was the strong Dowling republicanism he was hearing. While the alcohol seeped through their blood, they discussed the early impressions of their host country, essentially comparing them to what they enjoyed back home.

Well into their second drink, Deirdre confirmed she had prepared a simple dish of Irish stew and proceeded to heat it on the kitchen's gas stove. Soon they were seated at the dining room table enjoying wholesome and nutritious food. Jim paid tribute to her culinary ability, confessing that even the sumptuous dishes prepared by his own Mam came second to what he had just eaten. 'Being the eldest girl in our family, and my Mam often helping with farm work, forced me into sharpening my kitchen skills,' said Deirdre.

It was 30 minutes later, when sitting on a sofa and drinking Irish coffees, that Jim finally broached the subject that he had kept in abeyance for too long - the nature of his work in Libya. 'I've something to tell you, Deirdre. On the plane, within earshot of an English gentleman, I purposely lied to you, saying that I was taking up a teaching position. Yes, I am a fully qualified and trained teacher and perhaps that's what I should be doing. However, coming from Northern Ireland where minority Catholic rights are ignored, and from a family with a strong republican tradition, I feel duty-bound, for a few years at least, to try and improve conditions for my less-privileged fellow citizens. The path of peaceful co-existence and *status quo* is exhausted and we must increasingly take up arms to achieve our goals. In doing so, we're only too well aware that lives will be lost but, unfortunately, there's no alternative. I should stress that my decision was not taken lightly.

'Since we need training and experience in guerrilla warfare, an area in which Libya is recognised to be well advanced, our Liscorley I.R.A. branch rightly accepted Libya's offer of assistance. I'm just one of many Irish, from several I.R.A. branches, availing of this training right now. Obviously, we must keep this secret or its effectiveness will be greatly reduced or nullified. There are far too many Englishmen in our midst only too willing and ready to pass on information. I apologise for not being more open and forthcoming to you but I'm confident you fully understand and are ready to forgive me.'

Understanding and forgiving came easily to Deirdre. 'I'm a member of the Dowling family of Inistogue in County Kerry,' began Deirdre, 'whose roots in republicanism could hardly be deeper. My grandfather's dying wish was for the tradition to be upheld and I must say my Dad and brothers, through

Inistogue's I.R.A. branch, are not found wanting. On more than one occasion they risked their lives, and continue to do so, in an Ireland becoming more dangerous both north and south of the infamous border. Our house, particularly for the female members, was constantly at risk and an unsafe place to live. I looked forward to the completion of my teacher training and a chance to travel far from my roots, at least to get a breather for a few years. Then, luckily, this Libyan position was advertised and I was offered a contract. Little did I realise I'd agreed to work in a country whose reputation for militant tactics differ little from those of the I.R.A. But I like my challenging and interesting job of teaching expatriate children, most of whose parents are in responsible positions assisting in the development of oil, agriculture and other sectors of the economy.'

Jim felt a strange queasiness envelop him. Here was a staunch republican attempting to befriend a young lass whose dislike of militancy had just been laid bare. It came to him as a great shock but he decided to bide his time and not act hastily or rashly. It was most important now that she didn't look too unfavourably on what he was doing and try to interfere. Had his lying about teaching shattered her confidence and was it likely to affect future relations? He prayed it hadn't because even at this early stage he had a deep respect for her independent views and convictions. Besides, he was developing a real affection for her, and he wanted to do nothing that might seriously jeopardise it.

Sitting close to her now he felt the urge to tangibly display his emotions but was the time right? A moment later, standing and ready to leave, he extended his hand to thank her for the wonderful evening. As they touched, there was a mutual desire to edge closer and within seconds they were in a warm embrace. When they broke, Jim looked her straight in the eye and said, 'We may have differing views about our country's woes but promise me you won't allow them to hijack our friendship.'

Misty-eyed, she replied, 'Let me sleep on that.' After agreeing to contact each other soon, Jim took his leave and returned to the hotel.

The next week dragged as never before, with the routine and monotony compounding Jim's anxiety. It was 08.30 p.m. the following Wednesday, as Jim and a few friends were midway through their dinner in the hotel dining room, when the receptionist announced through the intercom that there was a telephone call for him. He sprang to his feet and within seconds was lifting the telephone.

It was Deidre. 'Hi, Jim, sorry to disturb you at mealtime but I have something important to tell you.' When he expressed his delight at receiving her call, she continued: 'You remember the last night I expressed my concern about military action in Northern Ireland? Well, since then, I've agonised over the matter and now see things more as you do. You influenced me into thinking that perhaps you're right. I respect and admire your unselfish decision to put your own career on hold for the benefit of others. As far as I can, I'll assist and support you in your efforts but I fully intend to see my teaching contract through in Tripoli.'

Jim was at pains to hide his elation. 'Jim...Jim, are you still there? Your bottle of hard-won Irish whiskey is now almost 13 years old and, when you come next time, it will provide us with the energy and momentum to chart a rescue package for your beleaguered province.'

Jim was stunned at Deirdre's quick turnabout but the decision was entirely hers. He preferred not to consider whether he had even remotely influenced her. He felt on top of the world just now and, with God's help, he might just be able to stay close to the summit.

CHAPTER 5

Russia - 1984

It was a move born of ceaseless frustration. Ever since the Conservative Government assumed power in Britain in December 1979, the battle lines were drawn between it and the I.R.A. And not without good reason. The decade of the 1970s was marred by some of the most horrendous atrocities in Northern Ireland's tortured history for which blame and counterblame were hurled from all sides. The entrenched attitudes created mistrust and foreboded several years of tension before any signs of *detente* might be reached. Many shrewd political judges were united in their view that only a near miracle could unravel the impasse.

But the first woman Prime Minister in Britain's long history was no great believer in miracles. In her inaugural speech on a chill December morning, Margaret Thatcher left nobody in any doubt about her stance on Northern Ireland. It was obvious from the tone of her remarks that increasing I.R.A. terrorism of recent years not only hardened her attitude but strengthened her resolve to stamp out terrorist activities. She knew in her heart it wasn't easy but, being the "iron lady" she purported to be, she was prepared to do her utmost. It was a task from which she certainly would not - and as time ensued *could not*, - flinch. For its part, the I.R.A. was even more stubborn and intransigent. Neither side being unwilling to give an inch only heightened the frustration and anger.

From her assumption of power until late 1984 was a showdown period. It began with the I.R.A., out of sheer frustration at the lack of progress, resorting to hunger strikes among its prison inmates, hoping the tactic might win practical concessions. Margaret Thatcher was unrelenting, allowing one prisoner to die unceremoniously. Others were to take up the cause, only to quit while there was still some, though faint, semblance of life. It soon became clear to the I.R.A. that this particular battle was lost but, as throughout previous generations, the war would continue on many and diverse fronts.

Libya's ever-increasing training of and support for I.R.A. activists were a constant irritant to the Thatcherite government. Libya's unsavoury influence was strongly felt throughout Europe and even beyond. In recent months Libyan arms shipments routed through various European ports were intercepted on the high seas, some close to the Irish coastline and destined for the I.R.A. Libyan nationals and their accomplices in western Europe had targeted American and British bases and night clubs, in an overt display of anti-western feeling and an implicit show of support for I.R.A. terrorism. Only weeks earlier Libyan staff within their London embassy fired at whom they perceived to be anti-Al-Mahdi opponents on the street outside, accidentally killing a young English police woman. It signalled a low point in British-Libyan relations and caused a diplomatic break between the two countries. British intelligence uncovered plans to attack key European airports and airlines aligned to western countries, especially the U.S. and Britain. It was a time of heightened tension and high alert plus vigilance across many ports and airports.

The year 1984 proved to be a watershed in republican strategy. The Libyan connection had, despite increasing anti-terrorist pressure from the west, served its purpose and it would continue supporting the liberation struggle in many less transparent ways. Nobody was prepared or in a hurry to turn one's back on such a staunch ally. But the signs, nevertheless, were ominous. Growing discontent at what was perceived as Libya's terrorist and belligerent stance might, sooner rather then later, force western countries to take military action against it. And it would likely result in severing Libya's economic and diplomatic ties with the west and leaving the I.R.A. effectively isolated. But, the I.R.A. hadn't yet given even the slightest consideration to what assistance the world's second superpower, the Soviet Union, might be willing to offer.

The credit for nurturing contacts with the Soviet Union lay entirely with Gerald Dowling, eldest son of Seamus, rapidly taking over a responsibility long shouldered by his Dad. The idea arose more out of desperation at the lack of progress rather than any extreme affection for communist ideology. He went to Denis Greany's bar on a balmy August evening, with the last of the season's hay just saved, more than ready to wash down and disinfect with Guinness the day's inhalation of hay seed and dust. His thoughts developed in parallel with his gradually increasing blood alcohol levels. When Joe Moriarty arrived an hour later, he had a crystallized plan which might be in the Soviet Union's best interest to support.

'I've seldom seen you in such contemplative mood this beautiful August evening,' greeted Joe, knowing it was worth a drink or two. With two full pints in front of them within minutes, Gerald lost no time in explaining what the I.R.A.'s future strategy ought to be. 'I'll give you a brief outline as the details can be decided upon at an Army Council committee meeting. You could say it all came to me in a midnight dream.'

'What unusual dreams you're prone to,' remarked Joe!

'Our hard work wooing support from the west and, more importantly, the net benefits fall well short of expectations,' continued Gerald. 'Have European countries and the United States, apart from the empty rhetoric and feigned shock at brutal killings, helped in any tangible way? The answer must certainly be *no,* so why should we persevere down this fruitless path? Had the Good Lord bestowed on Northern Ireland only a fraction of the Middle East's oil wealth, I can unreservedly say we'd have a queue of countries only too willing to assist. Yes, my good friend Joe, you may not fully understand international politics but that's what's at work here. Besides, despite the U.S.'s concern about the importance of the Irish-American vote, it is unwilling to do anything which might be seen as interfering with the external policy of Britain, an age-old staunch ally. We are now at a crossroads and choosing the next route could irreversibly change the course of Northern Ireland's history.'

'But, can you realistically and safely do business with communists?' Joe enquired.

Gerald prefaced his proposed strategy by emphatically stating he was never a firm believer in communism. Since he was knee-high, he vividly remember his Dad tell stories - and some passed down from his Dad - describing the vast improvement in the lot of the masses after the communists gained power in the Soviet Union. Whilst the principles of communism, working towards a better life for the majority, looks near perfect on paper, it falls miserably short in practice. Seems nobody took account of the importance of incentives, either cash or otherwise, to boost productivity. However well the needs of the masses are met, would-be dissenters are often meted out sentences incompatible with the severity of the crimes, including hard labour and banishment to remote cold and sparsely-populated regions. But it is for entirely different reasons the I.R.A. identifies a need to rendezvous with communists.

Both Gerald and Joe agreed on the core issue. As far as the U.S. and Britain are concerned, nothing goads them to a more rapid response than the mere suggestion of communists intruding in their own sphere of influence, or Northern Ireland in this particular instance. Representations should be made to the Soviet Union, explain in whatever detail necessary the injustices of the present situation and determine if/how they may be able to assist. Nobody should have any illusions about what the Soviet Union can do but the possibility needs to be explored. Even if nothing concrete emerges, news of the rapprochement with the Soviets will send shock waves through both the U.S.'s and Britain's houses of parliament. In other words, in these heady days of "cold war" diplomacy, we will simultaneously extend a carrot to the Soviets and wield a big stick in front of our erstwhile western friends. Wonder, what will be the U.S.'s and Britain's reaction to the very thought, much less the actual presence, of Soviet troops in such a strategic location as Northern Ireland?' Neither was qualified to respond definitively but the smile of satisfaction on both their faces leaving Greany's bar in the wee hours suggested that a drastically fresh approach was now well overdue.

The timing of Gerald's novel idea couldn't be better as the

next scheduled I.R.A.'s Army Council meeting was in Dublin the following week. He quickly telephoned its members saying he had what might be interpreted as a radical proposal to be aired and discussed at the plenary session before taking a final decision at the follow-on committee meeting. His message sent a ray of anticipation to all those who had long yearned for a change of direction. Gerald knew it needed all his debating and persuasive powers to win a majority because of the considerable reluctance to do business with a communist superpower, still viewed with a degree of suspicion.

After chairman Jim McCabe called upon Gerald to speak, he dispensed with many of the preliminaries, preferring to go straight to the subject. 'Most of you will agree that after 15 years of hard work our policies and programmes are not succeeding. We are all aware of the Cold War between capitalist and communist ideologies: seeing we have long wooed support from countries in the former camp, with limited or no success, is it now high time for a new beginning?' There was a restlessness but muted silence among the audience. 'What I propose has more of a psychological than a tactical dimension. In other words, we ought to take advantage of the Cold War for our own selfish benefit, because at this stage we have no reasonable or sensible alternative. The key word is to "explore" what assistance the Soviet Union can provide but this is a far cry from accepting it. Then we can blackmail our traditional capitalist allies: unless they can fast-forward our aspirations, we'll accept help from their archrival, the Soviet Union. I can assure you this is a thought few so-called exponents of democracy will relish.'

His audience stared with open mouths and hushed silence at what first seemed an utter profanity. After Gerald elaborated by responding to difficult questions, on the rationale behind his ideas and the likely benefits, there were far fewer dissenters. When it came to a show of hands at the end of the meeting, those in favour were massively in the majority. The exploratory element, instead of a definite commitment, made for easier acceptance. At the committee meeting immediately thereafter elation filled the air, buoyed by what these new tactics could produce. Gerald sought and received an assurance that he wasn't to be held accountable for any misadventures or even disasters in its execution.

Before the meeting ended a plan of action with schedules was drawn up. A delegation would visit Russia six weeks hence which allowed ample time to make discreet contacts and finalise arrangements. They were confident that, once the nature and purpose of the visit was leaked, Russian officials would process visas promptly, minimising the normal lengthy bureaucratic delays. Members of the delegation were equally divided between the northern and southern camps: Jim, Liam and Jane McCabe from Liscorley, Gerald and Deirdre (recently returned from Libya) Dowling from Inistogue and Vincent Tuohy, senior member of the Cork I.R.A. branch. Duties with a heavy work load were apportioned to each and two progress report meetings were scheduled. 'We are about to enter the realm of the unknown and mysterious' warned Gerald, 'but as a small nation we must take the initiative to extract the maximum from the biggest irrespective of ideology.' After years of fruitless endeavour, nobody was in any mind to disagree.

*

From the departure lounge of London's Heathrow airport, where all six of them had met from earlier incoming flights from Ireland, Jim McCabe saw the tail-end of the incoming Aeroflot turboprop plane hit the runway with a series of bumps causing smoke to belch into the early afternoon sky. 'That certainly doesn't impress me,' was his casual but concerned remark. It was this selfsame plane that was to take them on their outward journey to Moscow. Jim, the moderately-experienced traveller among a group of virtual novices, took care not to increase the anxiety of his already nervous companions. The announcement 30 minutes later did not surprise him, 'due to a technical problem with the aircraft, we regret to report there will be a one hour delay in the departure of Flight SU 203 to Moscow.' He tried to hide his innermost fear of the plane not being air-worthy and chose instead to engage his colleagues in friendly banter. He succeeded admirably and they finally boarded almost two hours late. Gerald's earlier warning of entering 'the realm of the unknown' began to ring true.

For all their initial fears, the plane's faultless take-off and gradual ascent helped to set them at ease. It was transient, however, in that in its attempt to reach full altitude an inordinate vibration engulfed the aircraft. The 'fasten seat belt' illuminated sign only heightened the anxiety of the timid. Deirdre leaned towards Jim and whispered 'there was none of this vibration on my maiden flights to and from Libya.' Jim dismissed it lightly explaining that this was an older plane and, perhaps, was less well maintained. The meal served up an hour later was cold and unappetising and they all wondered if it was a foretaste of what awaited them on the ground. The rest of the time was punctuated by bouts of dozings and awakenings until the pilot's message in halted English announced they were but 30 minutes from Moscow's Sheremetyevo international airport and he was beginning his descent.

Jane McCabe, less than one month away from her twenty-first birthday, occupied a window seat next to Vincent Tuohy whose strong Cork accent she found difficult to 'decipher.' Turning to Vincent as the plane taxied from its remote landing site to the airport terminal, she enquired what the bold letters displayed on the building's facade meant. 'That is written in the Russian alphabet my knowledge of which is virtually zero. Unless we have good interpreters, the next ten days will be full of nightmares,' replied Vincent. It was the first sense of fear and isolation that Jane experienced but she was convinced it was just one of many yet to quickly follow. Undaunted, Vincent was not the person to allow a foreign language to stifle his progress. Smiling affectionately at Jane, he joked: 'I struggled to learn two words in Russian, *dah* (yes) and *niet* (no). Will need to answer so many questions, I reckon these two words can keep me out of trouble.' Jane wondered whether it was this innate ability Corkonians possessed to survive in difficult situations - and enjoy it - which set them apart from most other counties of the republic.

Visitors and tourists were unable to choose hotel accommodation or travel to whatever part of the Soviet Union they so wished as these were centrally controlled and administered. It made very good economic sense because the 'real' cost, paid for in hard currencies which the ordinary Soviet could only dream of acquiring, was several times what a native was obliged to pay. And that amount was outside the reach of most. Central control was indeed politically motivated. By limiting the scope for foreigners to travel - and even then under strict supervision - it reduced the risk of top security information being leaked to the west, so important to the arms' race and "cold war" politics. In short, any would-be visitors paid a high price for the privilege and what they saw and experienced was so selected and controlled that it often left them more confused than enlightened.

The communist portraits and slogans in the arrivals' hall were reminiscent of Tripoli airport. A novice might be forgiven for believing that communism offered the only way forward and the evils of capitalism should be avoided at all costs. The nervous Irish group slowly inched their way towards a passport control booth piled high with forms and papers of all sorts. 'At this rate of progress we may not finish here before daybreak,' said a tired and frustrated Vincent, also worried about his yet-to-be -collected luggage. Then a Soviet man appeared near the booth brandishing a board on which were six illegibly-scrawled names. He first spoke to the passport control official who bade the six to come forward, sidestepping the lengthy queue. It was a welcome relief for tired bodies even if the favouritism shown belied the egalitarian principles of communism.

Extending his hand to each in turn, he upstaged the passport control officer saying 'My name is Vladimir Markov from the Politburo and I am charged with taking care of all your needs during your stay in the U.S.S.R.' Without further ado, he rapidly processed and stamped the six passports, all the while engaging the official in friendly conversation. Glancing at the long queue, Jim McCabe noted not only weariness and impatience but frustration and anger at the preferential treatment. He wondered if this favourable introduction was a sign of even better things to follow.

There was plenty of activity at the baggage reclaim carousel.

Coming from a country where labour was scarce and expensive, there was no shortage here. Luggage was off-loaded in several instalments and there was nothing that even politburo staff could do to expedite operations. When the suitcases eventually appeared, Vladimir motioned to his assistant/driver to load them on to two waiting trolleys and to proceed towards customs. Giving the senior customs officer a beguiling smile and distracting him with friendly banter eased Vladimir through without question. After all, his was an easily-recognizable face in these hallowed precincts. Now with virtually all formalities completed and everyone assembled in the airport's main hall, he relaxed momentarily and spoke English not too far removed from the Oxford dialect. 'It is with pleasure I welcome each of you to the Soviet Union where I trust you will have an enjoyable stay. Firstly, I will accompany you to your downtown Moscow hotel, the Metropol, where you will find all you need. For those of you interested in ballet, the world-renowned Bolshoi theatre is within a stone's throw. I will come to collect you tomorrow morning about 9 a.m. Then you will meet with senior officials and discuss the programme we have drawn up for you.'

The minibus was parked conveniently just in front of the airport's exit door, a prime location in the large car park. Driver Gennady, a diminutive weather-beaten man in his late forties, lost no time in loading the baggage, placing what there was room for in the lower compartment and the remainder on the exterior luggage rack. As they sped towards the city, Vladimir, from his vantage seat beside the driver, pointed out some of the key buildings and attractions. Because of the accumulated travel fatigue, his words were poorly assimilated. What struck Jim McCabe forcibly were the relatively few other cars on the streets and how shabby and old these were but it wasn't the time or place to comment to his host.

'You may have guessed that we are now approaching downtown Moscow and we will soon be at your hotel.'

'And not a minute too soon,' whispered Vincent to Jane seated next to him. There were two porters willing to grab each suitcase, raising concern that they should be tipped with roubles not yet at their disposal. Or would pounds or dollars be the preferred currency? After all had registered at the hotel reception, filling the requisite forms and leaving their passports for later scrutiny and validation by the police, Vladimir was ready to take his leave. 'For those of you still having the energy, there is a bar on the upper floor where alcoholic and soft drinks are served. I should emphasise, however, you must pay with hard currency. Enjoy the rest of the evening and will see you at nine.'

They were assigned six rooms with a street view on the second floor. Gerald Dowling was intrigued with the stout lady seated on a wooden stool and operating the elevator. What an interesting occupation he mused, passing the same point almost one thousand times each day. The less mobile lady seated midway in the corridor of their floor was the eyes and ears of her surroundings, ever aware of who came and went. He reckoned she was a vital information and security link to hotel authorities and beyond to national level. But group leader Jim McCabe had more urgent business on his mind just now. In the privacy of his hotel room (unless it was "bugged", something he dared not contemplate) he held a short meeting to develop plans and strategies in advance of tomorrow's high-level talks. He stressed the importance of not conceding too much before the Soviets' real intentions became clear. 'I realise all of you are weary so, responding to Vladimir's idea, I suggest we relax with our first Russian 'pick-me-up' drink in the upstairs bar.'

It was pure coincidence that the second record played after entering the bar was the traditional Irish ballad - long since internationalized- 'Danny Boy.' It brought tears to tired eyes and evoked strong national pride. About one-third of the seats were occupied, almost entirely by a wide spread of foreigners, and the favourite melodies from the east to the west were being aired. Jim, in his own erudite manner, said that their immediate surroundings was a microcosm of the capitalist world in a communist setting. That point was reinforced when a waiter appeared requesting the equivalent of U.S.$18 for the six drinks, all whether alcoholic or soft commanding the same unit price. The waiter left them in no doubt that cash dollars was the preferred form of payment. Jim, being the leader that he was and heeding advance warning to bring some 'green-backs,' settled the bill promptly. The waiter's face lit up on receiving a two dollar tip, thanked them graciously and resumed his duties with a rare spring in his step. 'I'm glad we had just the one drink, as we need all our wits about us in the morning' said Liam McCabe who was slightly in awe of his older brother. Deirdre Dowling, fresh from her Libyan experience, was more confident and up-beat and suggested there was everything to gain and nothing to lose. 'We must remember the famous words of that once great leader and proponent of western democracy, President John Fitzgerald Kennedy': "Never negotiate out of fear - but do not fear to negotiate". Before the forthcoming talks with the Soviets are completed, Jim was quietly confident that these prophetic words would stand him in good stead.

*

Speaking through an interpreter, President Yuri Chernov extended a warm welcome to the Irish delegation meeting him in his plush office at 09.30 hours. Vladimir did the introductions after Jim McCabe and Gerald Dowling took the top two seats. Deirdre Dowling and Jane McCabe sat poised with pens and notepads to jointly record the proceedings. Liam McCabe and Vincent Tuohy were content playing astute observer roles. The President's personal secretary and support staff attended as was the norm.

'There is one very important item of news I must firstly bring to your attention,' began the President. 'Only very late last evening my Chief of Intelligence reported to me a disturbing fact. As we know, much to our own cost, the British Intelligence Service misses few good opportunities. In your transit through London and boarding the Moscow-bound plane, they were alerted to your visit here. Since most, if not all, of your names and I.R.A activities are known to them, they have a special interest in your movements and motives. Word was speedily passed to Moscow. Of course, we are also on our guard and we will do everything to deceive and thwart them. In this time of espionage and counter-espionage, we have handled more intricate issues so, other than being aware and careful, I suggest you do not worry unduly.'

Having dispensed with the preliminaries, he continued. 'This is a historic and unique occasion which should lead to a mutually beneficial outcome for our two countries. Many historians say we do not learn from past mistakes nor try to redress them, a comment which few will dispute. All of you are too young to remember that two of Hitler's big blunders of the Second World War involved our two countries. After violating a non-aggression treaty with the Soviet Union, his military invasion got him bogged down in a war he could not win and from which he could not honourably extricate himself. His second more subtle but, perhaps, no less profound error stemmed from his lack of success in dealing with the Irish question. Ironically, it was centuries of British repression which 'steeled' your then Prime Minister de Valera into not cooperating actively with his neighbouring enemy. Hitler realised that an alliance with Ireland that even fell well short of military occupation - his ideal or ultimate goal - was crucial to his objective of global domination. Perhaps it was this world dimension to Hitler's strategy, and his vision of national boundaries crumpling, that prevented de Valera from conceding more to the Germans. Had Ireland done otherwise, the world today would be totally different.'

Now more than 40 years on the Soviet Union regards Northern Ireland as equally important to its vital interests and markedly at variance with Hitler's. Whereas the German dictator sought to conquer countries and use/abuse its peoples for his own selfish national advancement, the Soviet Union aims to spread and promote socialism (not mentioning the harsher word, communism) which guarantees the more equitable distribution of a country's wealth for the maximum benefit of all its citizens. The great original 'thinkers' Marx and Engels experienced the evils of capitalism, or most of the wealth remaining in the hands of the few, and their tireless work was eventually rewarded with the birth of socialism under Lenin in 1917 .'

The President stated that long before the I.R.A. approached them, they took a keen interest in Northern Ireland and marvelled at its resilience to prolonged and incessant colonialism. Just as Hitler considered Ireland to be a vital stepping stone to his North Atlantic conquests, the Soviet Union saw its northern province as opening up a window to our archrival capitalist enemy, the United States. Furthermore, the Soviets can embarrass England by their influence or presence on her own virtual back door. You might say this is an opportunity that until now was beyond our wildest expectations. Seeing that it is much closer to reality, let's work towards making it mutually beneficial.

The Soviet Union is broadly aware of the I.R.A.'s objectives and tactics in trying to wrest freedom from the British colonisers and oppressors. In principle, it has the capacity and willingness to support the I.R.A. in this noble and just endeavour but there is a need to discuss and work out the nature and extent of this assistance. Any moves jointly pursued must bring relatively quick results and hasten the end of this long-drawn-out struggle. The Soviet Union, for its part, will not fail in its commitments. Obviously, it will look for certain favours in return and the President personally undertook to participate in final discussions on this subject before the delegation's departure. The Irish looked warily at the President's suggestion of 'favours' and wondered if these were beyond their capacity to deliver. After a slight pause, perhaps to gauge his audience's reaction, the President checked his watch to see what time remained before his next appointment and began his concluding remarks.

'I asked my staff to give their full attention to drawing up a comprehensive programme of visits which can be altered if you so wish. Vladimir will be with you as often and as long as you decide. Although his knowledge of English is acceptable, I am assigning an interpreter to help with technical issues and to relieve him of the very heavy work load. Driver Gennady will see to all your transport and incidental needs. During the coming days I would like you to witness first hand, whenever possible, the great achievements of the Soviet Union the fruits of which will be enjoyed long into the next millennium. There is ample allotted time within the programme for sightseeing and social events. I want to ease your minds on a financial matter: I apologise for failing to advise you in advance but our Government will take care of all your hotel and other expenses and I have given strict instructions to Vladimir to pay special attention to this. Finally, on the eve of your departure we shall hold wrap-up meetings, followed by a farewell dinner. May I wish you a very productive and enjoyable stay and look forward to meeting you again next week.' Jim McCabe had less than 60 seconds to extend his thanks, on behalf of the group, before the next delegation of three men and a woman entered his office.

An hour later, they were having a mid-morning snack in the Metropol hotel's main lobby when Vladimir explained some of the procedural arrangements. He advised where meals should be taken and signed for at the hotel. He provided coupons to be used when situations warranted their eating elsewhere. Then he enquired if a copy of the programme in front of each of them needed modification. Jim, speaking on behalf of the other five, commended all involved in its preparation and said, although leisure and tourism accounted for more than anticipated, they would honour it to the letter. After all, they were novices as far as Soviet history and culture were concerned, a remark which elicited a wry smile from Vladimir. 'We left this afternoon and evening free to do what you please as we reckoned you may want to rest and become familiar with your surroundings. You may take a walk and view the sights within the immediate vicinity of the hotel. You must have your passports with you at all times as the police regularly ask foreigners to confirm their identities, a normal security procedure.' After ten minutes of answering questions on a variety of local interest, Vladimir took his leave and promised to collect them from the hotel at 09.00 hours next morning. Judging from his pallid complexion, he was drained and likely to benefit immensely from a good rest.

Shedding capitalist tendencies, however temporarily, was not easy. At the souvenir shop in the hotel lobby, where the group explored and browsed, was an array of Soviet-made and imported products. They were taken aback to discover that, like in the upstairs bar, these must be paid for in foreign currency at greatly inflated prices. Jim explained privately that the Soviet

Union was in great need of convertible currency to fund their extensive national development and research programmes and the income from foreigners was vital to sustain these. Having purchased postcards to impress friends in Ireland and other countries, Deirdre approached an attendant to enquire about stamps and postage rates and was met with a sharp retort 'It is a capitalist trick to charge according to country as communist countries have the same postage rate for all parts of the world.' The curt reply briefly stunned Deirdre but she finished her business meekly, not wishing to involve herself in controversy. She noted that three attendants or saleswomen were, in one way or another, involved in this simple transaction. Jane clarified the anomaly by saying 'now you can clearly see why the communists have no trouble in guaranteeing full employment.'

By this time their six passports were returned to the hotel reception from where they retrieved them with great relief. The police working within the Ministry of the Interior had done their duty and found everything in order. They were once again legal citizens of a country with a democratically elected government prepared to honour their rights. Until proven otherwise, they still harboured doubts about what privileges their host government was willing to grant its citizens but that required further exploration. Jim called for a brief meeting within the private confines of his own room, to hear early views and to assign individual tasks. 'Each has the duty, by keeping his/her eyes and ears open, to glean as much information as possible on which we can base realistic conclusions and decisions. To do this well within the short time available will demand all our skill and intuition.' It epitomised the seriousness Jim brought to all his undertaken jobs and he expected much the same from others. His deputy, Gerald Dowling, was no less enthusiastic and he was satisfied they had a team more than capable to do the job. Jim closed the meeting by saying 'Seizing Vladimir's wise suggestion, we will take a walk and get our first impressions of Moscow.'

It was an experience none of them was to forget quickly. What they already saw were the hallowed halls of the ornate Presidential quarters and the hotel's elegance. Organized state level visits often 'sheltered' guests from getting a balanced impression of life for the average person, seeing only what they are allowed to see. Vincent, the ever practical campaigner, was quick to stress that the best barometer of a government's achievement is the living standard of its people. As they walked from the hotel he silently thanked Vladimir for giving them the freedom, in a country where freedom is a scarce enough commodity, to judge this for themselves.

With Jim as leader, they strolled leisurely observing the buildings and the people going about their daily lives. Liam noted the rather sombre mood in the streets and of the people passing them by. 'When we learn more there may be very good reasons for the lack of cheer,' remarked Gerald. They were now approaching a large apartment complex only a few blocks to the rear of the hotel and the stark contrast was incomprehensible. A mere glance from the outside revealed decades of poor maintenance and even shoddy construction in the first instance. An elderly couple had just entered and were about to climb the steps to an upper floor apartment, carrying what looked to be a sparse supply of groceries and vegetables. Their clothes showed signs of several years of constant wear and of a fashion or style long since abandoned in the west. A good three-quarter century of hard work and duress was etched on their weary faces. At the hallway entrance, paint peeled from the dark walls and electrical wires dangled menacingly. All six moved away in horror. Liam, trying to lighten proceedings, remarked that a paint salesman was the most attractive business opportunity in this area. But Vincent was quick to respond: 'Given the little money they have for the more basic needs, such as food and clothing, you would be bankrupt in no time.'

Vladimir arrived at 09.15 next morning and they awaited him in the hotel lobby. Apologising for his lack of punctuality, he suggested they take ten to 15 minutes to overview the programme. Of the eight days remaining, five were earmarked for business and discussions and the remaining three days for sightseeing and cultural treats. With no dissenting voices, he warned them about the secrecy surrounding their impending inspection of key military installations. 'We want to alert you to the military might of our socialist republics and to determine what aspects and components might best serve your own needs. Once this is clarified, you will receive training in operating the equipment. Of course, we will place particular emphasis on guerrilla warfare, something that has special relevance to your own struggle. Our President has given me the *carte blanche* to reveal to you our most up-to-date weaponry, even some of which is still at the research stage. Such is the importance he attaches to your mission. But, in return, he is at liberty to exact a high price for any obvious breach of this trust. At the final meetings, he will brief you on specific favours he may seek from you.'

For today's series of visits a three-car convoy proceeded firstly past the large Rossiya hotel, and along the highway leading towards Minsk. Seated next to the chauffeur in the first was Leonid Zyuganov, a senior officer in charge of armaments in the Ministry of Defence and the Irish delegation was divided between the two remaining cars. About 40 kilometres out of Moscow the lead car turned right on to what seemed a freshly tarmacked road which ended, almost 500 metres on, at the large gate of a high-walled compound. Jim McCabe thought for one moment he was entering Libya's terrorist training camp near the village of Tajoura, so similar were the two in design and appearance. Did Libya's Al-Mahdi learn from his more experienced *comrade* up north? It took only a brief exchange of words between the chief security guard and Leonid before the three cars were waved past the entrance to the visitors' reserved parking area.

The central meeting room had more communication facilities than were required today. From his seat at the head of the rectangular table, Leonid, being the technical expert who had greatly helped arms development to its present high status, was eager to dispense with the usual preliminaries. 'It is my pleasant duty and privilege to welcome you and, acceding to President Chernov's specific instructions, I will give you an overview of our position *vis-a-vis* our western capitalist adversaries. We were first in space exploration (you will have heard from your elders the name, Yuri Gagarin), have maintained our advantage ever since and have no intention of relinquishing it.' Irish heads turned in anticipation of still more propaganda whereupon he got down to the business on hand.

'My job for the remainder of this morning has three components. You will see a twenty minute film on the subject of arms production in the Soviet Union. I will spend a further 30 minutes clarifying and supplementing what you saw while the last hour is devoted to questions and engaging in discussion. In the afternoon, Vladimir will give you an extensive tour of the facilities.' The morning's programme was very impressive and Leonid worked hard to convince them of the Soviet Union's superior military strength. What they saw in the afternoon was a practical display of a sample of it. Deirdre and Jane were in awe of it all, hoping that in their lifetime neither of the two superpowers would be provoked into any unilateral action which could spell the end of the human race. It was a thought too horrific to contemplate. Was it morally correct to seek support from a country which itself, at a whim, had the wherewithal to conquer and destroy all others? In the wider context the answer must surely be *no*, but help towards an independent and united Ireland must certainly be within its remit.

The other military establishments they later saw were virtual carbon copies of the first. Having identified their needs and preferences, there was limited time for organized and systematic training in the proper use of the equipment . Jim was quick to admit that the range and variety boggled the mind but that in itself was not all bad. In the discussions still taking place there was ample time to sift the grain from the chaff. Besides, at the final series of discussions with the President, the views of all could be sifted and crystallized into a meaningful package of military support. To achieve this within the short time span was a daunting challenge.

*

A day-long tour of Moscow and its environs was unquestionably the highlight. True to their communist tradition the Soviets did their utmost to convince foreigners that their system of government did the *most* for the *most* people and today was no exception. Jim had earlier indicated to Vladimir his preference for joining a regularly-scheduled tour, instead of being granted any special or privileged treatment, and his wish was honoured. Jim knew this would give them a more balanced view, an opportunity to mix with other nationalities and get their views and reactions and allow extra time to evaluate what was on display. The 40 seater bus was already half full when it collected the six Irish and another four from the Metropol hotel at 09.10 a.m. Complete with a young lady tour guide proficient in several languages, it made two other pick-ups before the official tour began.

Starting with Russian (it was scarcely necessary as she was the only 'representative'), she effortlessly covered the other common languages. Welcoming aboard the almost capacity load of 38 passengers, she started with basic information and statistics. 'The Soviet Union, of which the Russian Republic is by far the largest, consists of 15 different republics and is the world's largest country, comprising a sixth of the earth's surface. It is made up of more than one hundred nationalities, from Russians numbering almost 150 millions down to the smallest (Negidals) with only about 500. The Russian Republic alone covers 11 different time zones, with Moscow as its capital. Moscow (or *Moskva* in Russian) *oblast*, or administrative region, has an area of 18,000 square miles circling the city. The 300 metre high Klim-Dmitrov Ridge runs east-west just north of Moscow. South of the ridge is the wide plain of the Oka and its principal tributary, the Moskva, on which Moscow stands, with a population in excess of eight million.' Gerald Dowling was heard to exclaim 'Jaysus, that's almost three times more than is in our little republic.'

The bus was approaching Red Square, a primary tourist attraction, when the guide provided some background. 'The central showpiece here is the Kremlin, or the seat of the Russian government. In medieval Russia, a Kremlin (or formerly *Kremnik*) was a central fortress, usually situated at a strategic location along a river and separated from the rest of the city by a wooden (later replaced by brick or stone) wall with ramparts, towers and a moat. Many Russian cities were built around Kremlins which also had palaces, cathedrals, ammunition stores and governmental offices. Moscow's Kremlin, originally built in the 12th century and altered several times, has an architecture (Byzantine, Baroque and classical) reflecting its long history. It was used as the seat of Russian government until the early 18th century and again after the 1917 revolution. The Kremlin is triangular-shaped, faces Red Square to the east, has four gates and a *postern* (back gate) which hides a secret passage to the Moscow river.'

Before the guide got round to pointing out what is a 'must' for foreign visitors Jane McCabe pre-empted her remarks by asking, as they stood in the centre of Red Square, 'what are all those people queuing for?' 'I was about to mention the second (some might regard it as the first) biggest attraction in Red Square and that is the tomb of our founding father, Lenin, who won independence and established our communist state in 1917. His embalmed body is there for all the world to behold. As the queue can take one or two hours to file by, I suggest you come another day to witness this unique spectacle.' She pointed out St. Basil's cathedral, across the square from the Kremlin, and many high rise buildings in what could be described as Moscow's epicentre and often revealed to the outside world.

Looping around the city's landmarks the bus then proceeded along a road at the edge of the Moscow river towards the university. It was here the guide saw fit to unleash some of her most powerful propaganda. 'We in the Soviet Union have the best and most affordable educational system in the world. It is in fact free for anybody wishing to attend.' An American, near the rear of the bus, said to his friend seated next to him 'Would you please ask her what is a graduate's starting salary on leaving the university.' It certainly would be several times less than in the U.S. but nobody dared ask. Nor were many too interested as the bus took their tired bodies back to their respective hotels.

Two days later the Irish were escorted on a pre-arranged air trip to Russia's second largest city, Leningrad (formerly St Petersburg). Russians by no means exaggerate in claiming this to be their jewel. Where the Neva river empties into the gulf of Finland, Leningrad is elegantly poised on its southern estuary. When the Soviet Union's role in the second world war is ever discussed, all Soviets - and many others as well - salute with pride the citizens of Leningrad. Surrounded and besieged by the best that Hitler could throw against them, they fought and resisted against such terrible odds where others might easily have capitulated. It was a marathon siege with the eventual triumph of the besieged at an enormous human cost, but was an inspiration to troops fighting on various other western, North African and Pacific fronts.

But it wasn't war or resistance that preoccupied Irish minds on this particular visit. They were content to savour the history, culture, buildings and scenery. On the third bus stop they honed in on the world famous Hermitage museum where the magnificent paintings would take your breath away. Vincent was rudely made aware of these priceless treasures: one of the many female guards scattered throughout rebuked him for innocently trying to touch one of the frames. The short stay of two hours was sufficient only to scratch the surface (pardon the pun!) of such an extensive exhibit. Other stops were made at the monument to Peter the Great, Peter and Paul Fortress and Kirov stadium before making a suburban visit to the elegant and ornate Winter Palace. On the return journey to Moscow, they were unanimous in their view that Leningrad was an educational and stimulating experience. Jim enquired whether this might be enough of the official sightseeing to which Gerald replied: 'Call it what you will, official or otherwise, I'll be content if I get a 30-second peep at Lenin reposing in Red Square.' How could anyone dare turn down this inviting prospect?

*

Rat-a-tat... rat-a-tat-tat.

'Who's there?'

'It's Jim, I want to have a word with you at this quiet hour.' Deirdre peeped through the tiny hole in the centre of her bedroom door to confirm that it was indeed Jim and not a feigned intruder. 'Make sure the lady guard is not watching and enter quietly.' Little did she know how meticulously Jim had timed his visit for 22:30 hours when there was a 15-minute gap between the departure of one guard and the arrival of the next for the lengthy night shift. He was aware of how sensitive the Soviets were to two or more people, irrespective of the sexes, meeting secretly lest there be any intent to plot against the regime, sometimes raised to the level of an obsession. Was there an obsession of a gentler kind in the offing? Apart from the brief admiring glances during the course of their daily work, this was the first chance to relax in each other's company since landing at Sheremetyevo airport.

Jim remarked how ironic it was that their first real opportunity to chat freely was in a Moscow hotel room where privacy was rarely taken for granted. In the upstairs bar on the evening of their arrival, Jim recalled an American tourist relating how his suitcase had been secretly opened and inspected after he had left his room. They even managed to close it without any noticeable damage to the locks and the ruffled contents was the only suggestion of tampering. Were the Americans paranoid about Soviet espionage or did they purposely bug foreigners' rooms? If so, Deirdre was satisfied that I.R.A. guests of the government might not be on the priority list or did they really trust anybody, least of all their own citizens seeking a better life? She was hopeful that the smiling Irishman sitting next to her on a slightly uncomfortable sofa could be trusted, especially concerning matters of the heart.

'Do you find many similarities between Libya and here,' Deirdre enquired. Jim admitted that the harsh brand of communism was a far cry from the milder Libyan socialism. 'My first impressions - hope this room is not bugged - are that Al-Mahdi was clever enough to choose what's best in communism and to reject those aspects unsuited to his particular situation. I think you will agree there are two fundamental differences: there is greater personal freedom in Libya and the per capita income is considerably higher, only a part of which can be attributed to oil wealth.' Deirdre had little reason to disagree citing as confirmation the gregariousness of

Libyans and their ability to buy consumer products from the many well-stocked supermarkets. 'All except alcohol' intoned Jim 'but that was for strictly religious reasons.' One item that is neither scarce nor expensive in the Soviet Union is their locally-produced vodka. Jim unscrewed the cap from a bottle he had brought from his room, filled two glasses and raised his own in toast. 'However well we can relate to our Soviet hosts, I hope that henceforth our relationship will continue and prosper.' For Deirdre who still harboured doubts, it was Jim's first real effort at expressing his innermost feelings in meaningful and reassuring words.

Buoyed by this latest sentiment, it was Deirdre's turn to respond. 'Following my three-year Libyan contract my parents were most anxious I'd accept a teaching post in Kerry not too far from Inistogue. But my time in Tripoli changed me in ways I could never have foreseen. I suppose you could say my horizons have broadened (become "internationalized"), in no small measure due to the people of many nationalities and races with whom I had the good fortune to come in contact. And Libya certainly has that kind of varied and unique mix. It was an experience and education no money can buy.' She almost inadvertently let it slip that, had she not travelled to Libya, the young man she is increasingly growing to respect and love wouldn't have entered her life .... but she took a deep breath before continuing.

'Luckily, a few months before my contract expired, I applied for a teaching position in Dublin's north side and, to my surprise, they made me an offer which was too attractive to ignore. My instinct told me my best chance of smoothly settling back into Irish customs and mores lay in working in a big city and Dublin was an obvious choice. After the Libyan experience I could, perhaps, settle in any one of most world capitals. My parents, who rarely travel outside Inistogue, consider Dublin to be light years away but I'll try to see them at least once every four to six weeks.' Jim, laying his hand on her bare shoulder, reminded her that their relationship was at the stage where they should meet more regularly. He silently thanked the Lord that she chose Dublin, less than a two hour drive from Liscorley.

She quickly admitted that her Dublin contract was on a month to month basis. 'I needed time to readjust and had no intention, at least for the first year, of committing myself indefinitely. It leaves my options open which suits me fine. It begs the question as to whether I can continue to play the dual role of teacher and part time I.R.A. collaborator. My ten days here is charged to leave I haven't yet earned and this is unsustainable in the long term. I can appreciate why you made the bold and firm decision to put your career on hold, as there was no alternative given your full time I.R.A. involvement.'

'I will do all I can to help you,' said Jim. 'If you have no objection, I intend exploring the possibility of finding you a job as close as possible to Liscorley. You may consider it selfish of me to want you near but isn't love supposed to be selfish? Forget about the *cliche* of absence making the heart grow fonder, as it has severed more friendships than it has sustained. As best an Irishman can reveal his feelings, which reputedly falls well short of international standards, my life has changed irrevocably since God brought the two of us together. I appreciate I have been less forthright than is justified but let me make immediate amends. You may not be aware that I worked behind the scenes to have you as a member of our Soviet mission (not that you didn't fully deserve it in your own right) in order that the spark between us might develop into a brilliant flame. You have given my life a new meaning and purpose and my big hope is that it's not one-sided.'

'Not a bad attempt for someone wary of open expression,' joked Deirdre, with obvious delight at what she had just heard. Snuggling closer and wrapping her right arm around Jim's waist, she kissed him tenderly before withdrawing and saying, 'Just to prove it's not one-sided. Not only are Irishmen reluctant to say what they feel but their female counterparts do little to help, in that they respond poorly to positive vibes. Coming from Inistogue's small village community where the word sex, not to mention any open expression of it, is frowned upon, we can expect only gradual improvements. But the reverend clergymen, who for so long instilled fear in us of any wrongdoing, are now themselves being accused and paying the price for their own sordid and bizarre misdemeanours.'

'We'll have one final vodka' said Jim, not hiding his delight at how well everything had gone between them. Holding Deirdre in a firm but warm embrace, he showered her with passionate kisses which he wished could go on forever. He knew well that anything so good could not last too long but he would savour each and every second. 'I can't express in words, Deirdre, what a thrilling and delightful experience this whole night has been and all the credit goes to you. How interested do you suppose the Soviets will be in our conversation, if they were able to tape it and feed it through to KGB headquarters?' Of more immediate concern to Jim was how he could evade the security guard's prying eyes as he sneaked his way back to his bedroom. He also worried slightly for the guard's safety, lest his welled-up testosterone laced with the power of four vodkas might be too difficult to contain.

*

President Yuri Chernov, while appearing affable and hospitable to those he meets, has also the reputation of driving a hard bargain when it comes to promoting the political aspirations of the Soviet Union. And at no time since assuming power was it so vitally important to take a firm stand. He needed little reminding there were groups and forces, particularly among the young and educated, clamouring for greater individual freedom and a move towards a more open society. But Yuri Chernov's belief in and dedication to communist principles were even stronger now than when he first swore his allegiance during his late teens. He saw in the Irish mission his greatest opportunity to score what might well be the most telling success of his unspectacular presidency.

As the clock ticked past 10 a.m. on the penultimate morning, President Chernov chaired the final meeting in the ornate committee room, with the usual advisers and aides in attendance. He dealt with the niceties and preliminaries within a matter of two or three minutes, eager to get on with the important discussions and negotiations. 'Although Vladimir has continually briefed me on progress, which in his view was very satisfactory, I would like to have your own personal appraisal.' Jim nervously rearranged the individual sheets of paper in front of him, on which were scribbled numerous notes, before acting as spokesman.

'It is my pleasant duty, on behalf of all our mission members, to firstly thank you, Mr. President, for inviting us to the Soviet Union and for affording us unstinting support and warm hospitality. We were mesmerised and overwhelmed by the extent and variety of your arms stockpile. It will not surprise you to hear that our biggest problem is to decide what is best suited to our own needs. Those following the long tortuous course of Irish history, including your own active interest Mr. President, are well aware that our past success against the British was dogged time and again by our drastically inferior fire-power. We have learned from our mistakes and are determined to bridge the yawning gap. Even should the Soviet Union lay what's needed at our disposal, our biggest challenge lies in getting arms into Northern Ireland undetected, as hostile forces in England and north and south of the Irish border are on high alert. Only too often in the past have our best efforts been frustrated.'

Sensing Jim's inability to arrange his thoughts coherently, President Chernov availed of the early opportunity to present his long-pondered ideas and strategy. 'From my limited knowledge of recent Irish history, geographic location has worked to your own disadvantage, as the mighty power of England is within a stone's throw of your own shores. Just two years ago we witnessed the hazardous and costly war England fought against the tiny and insignificant Falkland islands with few inhabitants. If it was prepared to muster up such manpower and armaments to engage in a far flung war, I suggest that they will make even a greater sacrifice to preserve the *status quo* near home.' It was an admission all too familiar and painful to the Irish ears cocked attentively.

'In my honest and humble opinion there are two plausible courses of action. The first is the continuation, albeit more extensively and aggressively, of the policy of arms supply to the I.R.A. It will raise the tempo of the entire conflict from the ongoing low key guerrilla tactics to one where, short of outright success, you will exact concessions in the long run which might now appear unthinkable.' He knew that it was the less attractive option, in terms of possible results and strategic advantage to the Soviet Union, but would be of considerable interest to his guests.

'The second option brings greater risks but, on the positive side, could end sooner than expected this war between neighbours. My somewhat radical proposal is that a significant number of Soviet troops fight side by side with the Irish which will raise the level and intensity of the conflict. Initially, this ought to be done clandestinely, gradually increasing the amount of arms and troop numbers. But, the latter stages will call for significant but tactical sea and air strikes on selected targets. I realise that this will not only raise England's involvement, something we are ready to embrace, but there is an even bigger danger of our foremost adversary, the U.S.A., being drawn in. The latter will have mixed feelings in that, while welcoming the prospect of all Ireland reunification, it cannot stand idly by when the feared communist tentacles are gripping its eastern but distant neighbour. For this operation to achieve the desired results, it must have the tacit if not outright support of the Irish government which is favourably disposed to an united Ireland. I look to you my Irish friends (almost mistakenly said *comrades*) to win over key government ministers. The job will not be easy but, without some support, field operations will be fraught with danger.' He paused briefly before getting to the 'what's in it for me' topic.

'I make no secret of the Soviet Union's intentions of gaining a foothold in Ireland where our policy of spreading communism worldwide can take root. In other words, it is a partnership agreement whereby in return for Irish liberation the Soviet Union will have favoured status, the extent and details of which are still subject to negotiation and mutual agreement. In my humble opinion, without the Soviet Union's assistance, being a rival super-power to the U.S.A., Ireland's reunification will still be but a cherished dream 30 years hence. Similar to business conglomerates, the chances of small countries going it alone are becoming all too rare. We are ready to help you with a national issue of supreme importance, something in which the U.S.A. is extremely reluctant to involve itself .'

The second Soviet option took the Irish by surprise and needed a lot of digesting.

'We will continue to accept arms,' began Jim, 'and these will likely need to be increased in the next year or two. As for the second, I and members of my group can't give you a definitive response just now since it involves national policy over which we have little or no control. Your proposal, Mr. President, is both novel and radical but then the complex Irish problem calls for a drastically fresh approach. I personally feel it has much merit and we will give it serious and full consideration. We promise to give you a decision within the next couple of days.'

Early that same afternoon Gerald, accompanied by Vincent and Jane, realised his ambition by visiting Lenin's tomb beside the Kremlin wall in Red Square. He was later able to boast to his Inistogue friends about the unique experience. They lost little time in getting back to the hotel as Jim had scheduled a wrap-up meeting for 4 p.m. Not only had he intended discussing developments of this morning's meeting but, if at all possible, preparing in draft format a reply for the President, to be later finalised and sent officially. His most optimistic forecast was this can be done within 24 hours of their departure from Sheremetyevo airport tomorrow morning at 10:30 a.m.

The number of distinguished Soviets attending that evening's farewell dinner conveyed a message of high expectations. At the head table President Chernov was flanked by three Irish on each side but he conversed mostly (through an interpreter) with Jim. It was neither the time nor place to discuss politics but rather to engage in friendly banter so as to set everyone at ease. After all, there was a lighter and jovial side to Soviet life and the President was at pains to convey this to his guests. Vincent was unimpressed, having earlier remarked that under communism practically everything was rationed: he was heard to say 'they have rationed the food, they have rationed the fun but, try though they may, they have yet been unable to ration the fu--ing.' The impressive population growth suggested there is an element of truth in the latter. After the usual post-dinner speeches, the conviviality was brought to a close but not before the exchange of Soviet-style bearhugs and embraces that brought blushes to the cheeks of Deirdre and Jane.

Soon after next morning's plane approached cruising altitude, leaving the city of Moscow bathing in the early sun, Jim removed from his briefcase the original draft reply the group worked on for two hours the previous afternoon. From his window seat in row ten he glanced furtively to his immediate left to find Gerald in dozing mode and it left Jim free to proof-read and make minor alterations to the draft. There was a broad consensus on keeping the reply brief and to the point and Jim's editing enforced this rigidly, being no great believer in tiresome waffle. He finished it just as one of the stewardesses arrived serving pre-lunch drinks from a trolley, the noise of which awakened Gerald. They ordered two straight whiskies with dashes of ice and, as they savoured the first sips, Jim checked one or two points with Gerald before agreeing the final text.

Dear President Chernov,

Reiterating my remarks at the farewell dinner, I thank you most sincerely, on my own behalf and the entire group, for the wonderful hospitality and cooperation unstintingly given by so many of your staff during our recent visit. It was an invaluable experience we will treasure for many a day. We wish to convey our special appreciation to Mr. Vladimir Markov who worked long and hard, both before and during our stay, to ensure that nothing of the organisation and management was left to chance. Your own attention, Mr President, plus your excellent advice and suggestions gave us more food for thought than we could ever have imagined, for which we'll always be in your debt.

Our group lost no time in studying and appraising all that we saw and heard and, as promised, arrived at a decision within 24 hours of our departure. This doesn't imply it was done in haste but only after painstaking hours of deliberation did we come to an agreement. Given the vagaries of international mail, I hope this reaches you within the next week or ten days.

Our foreseen strategy for continuing co-operation between our two countries has two distinct time-frames. The first short-term one is to request your agreement and assistance to bolster our arsenal of weapons without which our programme has no direction or meaning. The plan is to make everyday life so uncomfortable for the British that, short of engaging in open war, they will be forced to make major concessions. We'll make no effort to conceal the source of our new-found strength (not that their security services need any information) as it will ultimately work to our advantage. Your scale of involvement will not merit British retaliatory action and, fearing further escalation, may grant concessions which in normal circumstances they are unprepared to do. But this is largely speculative and, if the plan fails, the second option must be invoked.

This calls for the full military might of the Soviet Union, a move, Mr. President, you are not reluctant to undertake. Nor are we, if we are left with no viable alternative. We are prepared to give the first every chance of success - at least for the next two years - monitoring progress as we go and postponing a decision on phase two until the final three months. In other words, a tactical war is being waged and we are hopeful it will yield the desired results. As you well know, Mr. President, there is no certainty when it comes to predicting the likely course or outcome of any armed struggle and it calls for the utmost patience and dogged perseverance. I cannot be more specific and can only give you a general outline which will likely need periodic modification. Assuming we agree on this proposal, we can look forward to a harmonious working relationship.

I propose to appoint my second in command, Gerald Dowling, as liaison officer working closely with Vladimir Markov, whose principal duty is organizing and coordinating military supplies. Gerald will be well supported by other staff and I'll have a personal interest and involvement in all major decisions relating to our joint operations. I foresee regular visits to the Soviet Union to strengthen the links already established.

I trust you will find our strategy and proposals acceptable and we are anxious to have them operational without undue delay.

Yours sincerely,
Jim McCabe

The "fasten seat belt" sign illuminated the overhead panel just as Jim finished the final draft. Never at ease with phraseology, the small exercise took him much .. much longer than anticipated. After a very smooth landing in perfect visibility, the plane taxied to Aeroflot's normal slot from where they walked via the "tunnel" along what seemed a very long trudge towards passport control. Jim was the first to present his passport whereupon the clerk checked his credentials against records kept in a "black book" reserved for key I.R.A. suspects. Jim's heart almost stopped when he ushered him and his five companions into a nearby office where a senior officer awaited them. The Soviet warning of being tailed by British security officials now became patently clear. The interrogation was harsh and protracted with all hand luggage thoroughly checked. The senior officer was confident he had the right people and was eager to extract the maximum information, either confiscating or copying the relevant papers.

As they made their way down the escalator to recover their baggage, Deirdre wondered aloud if their very successful mission had now been rendered worthless at the very last gasp. 'Look at all the incriminating evidence they have to convict us,' remarked Liam. 'We were extremely foolish in the first instance to travel via London where all the prying eyes left us with little chance,' piped Jane. Vincent regretted that the key document, their response to President Chernov, was now in enemy hands and spelt their disaster. But Jim was more sanguine . 'Whether it was Divine Providence or otherwise, when I finished the draft reply on the plane just before landing I instinctively folded it neatly and placed it inside my left sock. Fearing the worst, I knew that, save an exhaustive body search, our war of liberation would continue.' Jumping with glee, Vincent was ecstatic saying 'what a clever tactic from a County Down man - do you, by any chance, have any relations in County Cork?'

CHAPTER 6
Syria - 1986

Quirks of fate played an important role. Any suggestion only a few years earlier of Syria being a likely player in Ireland's destiny was certainly remote. But then few could have foreseen the rapidly unfolding events. Just about the mid-1980s tensions between Libya and the United States were stretched to almost breaking point. The U.S. and Britain irately pointed accusing fingers towards Libya after a series of terrorist bombings throughout Europe had targeted their forces and recreation centres. Airports' security was on high alert after two attacks and threats of several more. Britain saw good reason to align itself firmly with the U.S., as memories were still raw of the shoot-out near the Libyan embassy in London, causing the death of a young policewoman and forcing Britain to sever diplomatic ties. Countries in the so-called western alliance, perceived as defenders of democracy and the rule of law, knew that appropriate action must be taken against the aggressor but were unsure of its nature and scale.

The answer was swiftly provided by the then U.S. President much of whose earlier career was devoted to movies in which guns were often unsparingly used. The day of reckoning finally came in mid-April 1986 when, operating from British bases, U.S. war planes selectively but severely bombed key targets in Tripoli during the pre-dawn hours. Among these was President Al-Mahdi's residence from where he luckily escaped with only minor injuries. Relations with Libya hit a new low and seemed likely to continue. Furthermore, Libya's actions and behaviour would henceforth be closely monitored, particularly by the U.S. and Britain. The I.R.A.'s "love affair" with Libya had reached a watershed and the omens suggested it was time 'to come in from the cold.' Not that it signalled the end of the friendly and mutual cooperation but a scaling down of military hardware, something that could be easily detected and appropriately punished.

Syria's sympathy for Ireland's independence struggle was rooted in the former's historic past. It was part of the Ottoman Empire until the end of the First World War and a 1920 League of Nations mandate permitted French forces to occupy Syria. Nationalists declared an independent republic in September 1941 and the French troops relinquished power in January 1944, paving the way for Syria's full independence on April 12, 1946. Syria and Egypt merged in February 1958, forming the United Arab Republic (U.A.R.), but a 1961 military coup in Syria reinstated its independent status. The decade of the 1960s saw the increasing influence of Kemal Siddique as leader of the Ba'ath Socialist Party. He became Prime Minister in November 1970 and within months took over as President, a position he held until his death in 1999.

The hopes and aspirations of Syria and Libya were indeed very similar. Only slightly more than a year of Al-Mahdi taking power in Libya his "eastern star", Kemal Siddique, took supreme command in Syria. Not only did their Arabic heritage and Moslem religion bind the two leaders but they both espoused the same brand of socialism which was then infiltrating many countries, including some in east Africa. But, unquestionably, it was the Palestinian issue that cemented their true friendship. Kemal had given shelter to many Palestinians and increasing numbers were finding homes and employment in Libya. They were equally vociferous in soliciting international support for a Palestinian homeland.

Not that relations between the two countries was always amicable. It was at arms' length during the 1960s and most of the 1970s. Finally, there was a "thaw" accelerated by Al-Madhi's historic visit to Syria in October 1980 when all past differences were set aside. The two powerful socialists pledged support for a new era of friendship and cooperation. It was hailed in the media as a "marriage across the sea" - or the broad blue expanses of the Mediterranean! It ushered in what was to become many unbroken years of *bonhomie*. It irked the west that two countries, often labelled with the terrorist tag, should end up such staunch allies.

The 'fall-out' from this close alliance worked to the I.R.A.'s advantage. When the heat came on Libya in mid-1986, following the bombing of Tripoli and the close surveillance of its subsequent actions, it was Al-Madhi who made personal representation to President Siddique. Seated cross-legged in his tent on the outskirts of Tripoli, with an Irish delegation in front of him, he spoke at length over the international telephone line that for once worked without crackling or interruption. It took a few minutes to dispense with the usual friendly salutations and enquiries about the well-being of so many friends and acquaintances before getting down to the real business, spoken in fluent Arabic.

Al-Mahdi briefed his friend on the background to the Irish problem, of an oppressed Northern Ireland minority rather similar to what the Palestinians were suffering at the hands of the Israelis. He acknowledged that the plight of the Palestinians, being deprived of a homeland, was considerably worse but the Irish too had the right to freedom and to chart their own destiny. They could learn from their Palestinian colleagues about the type of warfare which had brought them many successes but were still short of their eventual target. He proposed that lines of support and cooperation, up to now firmly based in Libya, should henceforth be largely on Syrian soil. This was sweet music to Siddique's ears who had long yearned for a greater share of the terrorism-promotion stakes and had often envied Al-Mahdi's lead role.

The proposal of *rapprochement* with Syria was further strengthened following decisions taken at an I.R.A. Army Council meeting in Dublin during July 1986. It was specially convened to consider the implications of the new leadership in the Soviet Union calling for a more open and questioning society, moving steadily from the closed and secretive years of communist repression. This change of direction also spelt the virtual death knell of the strategy already worked out during the Irish delegation's 1984 visit. There was general disappointment at how political developments can influence long term plans but most delegates were essentially upbeat. These changes were long overdue and they were confident of still being able to count on the Soviet Union's continuing support.

One thing was clear. The I.R.A. could rely on the assistance, be it military hardware or of the token variety, of all three countries i.e. viz Libya, Russia and Syria. Circumstances would dictate what each could contribute but all were one hundred percent committed. Unquestionably, I.R.A. personnel can learn from the tactics which achieved so much for the Palestinians in their long struggle against their Israeli archrivals.

*

It was approaching 10 a.m. on October 23rd when, under a clear blue sky and a temperature in the high 20s, a small group of UNIFIL (United Nations Interim Forces in Lebanon) peacekeeping troops began their daily patrol in southern Lebanon. It was a disparate mix of nationalities, with Dutch, Belgians, Swedes, Canadian and Irish working under the common United Nations banner. Their central role in this war-torn area of south Lebanon was to preserve the peace between the Israelis and the Hizbullah-supported Palestinians where there were many attacks and counterattacks during the past four years. The use of Lebanese territory from which to attack northern Israel was an effective Arab ploy but the Israelis were having none of it. Among the Irish was a 23-year-old volunteer, Paul Dowling, from Inistogue in county Kerry. His thoughts this morning, and indeed every morning of his four month stay, dwelt on his native village he knew and loved so well. As he anxiously listened to the sound of gunfire coming from a nearby hill, he wondered why he was predestined to come to this strange and troubled land.

One thing was indeed certain. Not an ounce of planning went into Paul Dowling's childhood years to groom him for what he was to experience later. Growing up as the youngest of four brought him early concessions and favours but these soon melted. He hated being labelled "the pet" long after little favouritism was shown him.. Gerald's long absences from farm work to attend to his I.R.A. duties obliged Paul to take on adult chores well before he was ready or able. But "unable" was one word he refused to admit to, often keeping pace with Gerald at jobs demanding more brawn than brains. Intuitively he knew that as long as God guaranteed him his strength, he would eke out a respectable living for himself.

His first, and what transpired to be his only, career guidance experience came in the autumn of 1978 when not yet quite 16 years old. The Principal of the local secondary school came to present his parents, Seamus and Nora, with Paul's Intermediate Certificate exam results. His demeanour and sombre mood spoke volumes as he asked to see them in private. Paul had failed all but two subjects and the signs were ominous: an academic career was inappropriate but there were plenty of opportunities for him to use his hands.

Despite the unfavourable news, the Principal was accorded the same respect and hospitality generally reserved for the clergy. After he was treated to tea and cake in the infrequently-used parlour, he summarised his views before the anxious couple.

'Let me begin by stressing that as far as hard work and conduct are concerned, Paul's record is exemplary. It was clear from a very early stage that he lacked the concentration to study long and hard and this is reflected in his below average results. However, I am confident he will succeed in whatever he finally decides to pursue in life and we all have an obligation to give him the best guidance and support. From discussions I've had with him and observing his extra-curricular activities, he seems to have a keen interest in an army career. I realise you may have more lofty ambitions for your youngest but the training and discipline associated with the army are second to none. Whatever your long-term goals may be, I strongly recommend he spends one or two years in the army, something which will stand him in good stead for the rest of his life.'

The word 'army' conjured up ignoble images for Seamus

and the thought of his youngest son devoting his tender years to a dangerous profession initially made him feel queasy. But on further reflection, pent-up pride began to surface. If, during the course of duty, Paul preserved the already strong Dowling republicanism, what greater joy could this bring him and the family? Nora's views were, as ever, neither sought nor heeded.

Shortly before leaving, the Principal invited Paul to join them to hear his own ideas and to ensure that there was unanimous agreement. 'Rest assured I will give all the necessary assistance to set you on the right track and get you established.' Seamus thanked him profusely for not only what he had done for Paul, but all his children down through the years.

Paul took readily to army life. He steadily moved up the ranks and, instead of espousing republicanism that his father hoped for, he pursued a role of preserving peace as opposed to fomenting war. His exemplary behaviour was not lost on his superiors and, to his great delight on a beautiful morning in June 1986, he received a letter offering him a six month post on a UN-sponsored Irish peacekeeping force in southern Lebanon. Without taking time to find out where Lebanon precisely was on this planet, or why it was a priority hot spot, he replied positively and was later informed they were leaving Dublin on June 21st for Damascus, Syria, headquarters of UNIFIL's peacekeeping operations for all of Lebanon. It left Paul just ten days to prepare himself for one of the most exciting and danger-filled periods of his entire life.

Although having little free time before departure, he spent much of it acquainting himself with the new culture and traditions that differed greatly from what he had already experienced. He recalled his Dad relating stories to him in his pre-teen years about the violent clashes between Palestinians and Jews leading up to the 1948 creation of the Jewish state as we know it today. Widespread persecution and massacre of Jews under Hitler's Second World War tyranny aroused international sentiment favouring their return to Israel after many centuries of exile . The numbers trekking homeward exceeded all expectations increasing the already high tensions between Arabs and Jews competing for an all too small area of impoverished and rain-deprived land. Some of the stories his Dad told him, of the British trying to defuse bombs and prevent carnage on a massive scale, were later to haunt him and caused nightmares during his pre-waking hours.

One story was especially poignant. During his Dad's elementary school years he befriended an orphan child and classmate named Michael whose notoriously rowdy behaviour merited the schoolteacher's harshest punishment. But his Dad intuitively knew it was the absence of real family love, and not bad breeding *per se*, that caused him to act in this way. They were good friends until both left school in 1938, and within a few years, Michael left to work in England. In war-ravaged Europe there were few letters sent to relatives and friends, least of all from orphans trying to eke out an existence in a foreign country. More than a decade elapsed without anybody in Inistogue ever hearing what became of poor Michael. Then about 1950 the sad story of Michael rather mysteriously took shape. Soon after reaching England he enlisted and served five years in the army before being sent to Palestine in early 1947. War office records reveal that Michael met his tragic end one year later when trying unsuccessfully to defuse a bomb in one of Jerusalem's narrow streets. Paul remembered weeping profusely on hearing this sad story. He had every reason to wonder whether he was now tempting fate, volunteering to keep peace in this still volatile part of the world.

At the briefing session the day before departure the thirty-two-strong Irish contingent were reminded of their duties and responsibilities. The army's Chief of Staff was at the same time blunt and reassuring. 'Each of you was chosen to do what most knowledgeable people regard as impossible: to maintain some semblance of peace in one of the world's most troublesome regions. The risks cannot be underestimated. Several of the first Irish group of volunteers, serving with the United Nations in the Congo in 1960, returned home in wooden boxes. That unfortunate setback did not deter our resolve or belief in a just cause and ever since, when called upon to do so, we placed young Irish lives in many conflict areas throughout the world. But veterans of such missions can reassure you of the immense payback and sense of accomplishment. For every volunteer sacrificing his life, thousands of others were saved from bloody and often senseless conflicts. If you are prepared to embrace the challenge then there can be few other more personally rewarding and satisfying experiences. I ask you to exert due care and remember, on and off duty, each of you is an ambassador for your country. My thoughts and prayers, and those of the whole of Ireland, go with you.'

Their departure from Dublin airport was for Paul a morning of mixed emotions, the sad farewells to close relatives and friends tinged with the excitement of a brand new adventure. The first leg of the journey took them to Frankfurt from where they boarded a Lufthansa flight bound for Damascus. Paul's first brush with the Arabic language and customs was a handful for a young Kerryman but these did not unduly faze him. The airport's flashing neon lights extended a warm welcome in both Arabic and English and he was determined to relish the experience. Three Irish army officers were on hand to give them a Gaelic *cead mile failte* (a hundred thousand welcomes) and whisked them by bus to UNIFIL's headquarters north of the city centre. For the next few days of orientation they were all treated royally with evening parties that lasted well past midnight, making it seem a home away from home. It eased them into a term of duty that each knew was to become harder by the day but nobody was in any hurry to get started.

And now four months into their six-month term all thirty-two Irish soldiers were unscathed. A few had occasional near misses with rifle fire exchanges but they kept a safe distance from real danger. And this routine patrol of October 23 proved to be no different. Paul reckoned that if the Israelis and Hizbullah-backed Palestinians wanted to become engaged in a head-to-head shoot-out, there is little his unit could do. Were they a viable deterrent or were they simply supervising at arm's length a guerrilla war destined to continue? Their minds were fortunately in positive mode, a vital ingredient for survival as well as job satisfaction. Soon their routine patrol was over and later that afternoon they would travel by road to Damascus where next day they were to join all their colleagues in the celebration of United Nations Day, an event that had been religiously observed since the Organisation's founding some 41 years previously. From recent correspondence from home Paul was aware of a pending visit from an I.R.A. delegation concerning which he was both excited and apprehensive. He was certain the Dowling family was represented and looked forward to catching up on home news. He had little interest in the I.R.A.'s programmes which were diametrically opposed to his own peacekeeping initiatives.

It was early afternoon when the convoy of Landrovers started the interesting and scenic trip to Damascus. Although it was Paul's fourth such journey this was special and an experience he later relived many times over. As the other vehicles were loaded first, it remained only for the last Landrover and its driver Ismail to collect Paul who occupied the front passenger seat. A shy and placid Ismail had on numerous previous occasions driven Paul and others on surveillance missions but he had always been reticent about himself and his background. Now in Paul's company, with no Arabic-speaking witnesses they can be so wary of, his shyness slowly dissolved and he became more talkative. The convoy first headed northwards until reaching the wide Beirut-Damascus highway from where it turned right and proceeded due eastwards.

After covering just a few miles of the journey Ismail unloaded some of his pent-up thoughts and emotions which heretofore he couldn't muster up the courage to do. 'Well, Mr Dowling (as he regularly and politely addressed him), I have worked with you all these months without revealing anything about myself. It may surprise you to hear that my roots are in Palestine, the country where I was born in 1946 but whence I am long since estranged. Following the illegal and unjust creation of the Jewish state in May 1948, my father and many Palestinians found it increasingly unsafe to live in a country to which we rightly belonged but had precious few rights. In the summer of 1949 all my family, my father, mother, my two older brothers and myself, left our native town of Nablus for an uncertain future. Taking with us only the clothes we stood up in, we trekked for weeks through hostile terrain until reaching the south-west border of Syria and onwards to Damascus where we were warmly received as, indeed, were many thousands of Palestinians. Damascus is our home ever since and, though we are still a people in exile, we are hoping for the virtual impossible - of one day returning to our native land.' Paul recalled the song 'The Impossible Dream' but there was too real an empathy developing between him and his driver to even mention this delicate analogy.

One of the most obvious signs that Ismail was living on his nerves could be gauged from the numerous cigarettes he had lit since setting out, some smoked in their entirety but several others discarded after fewer than half a dozen puffs. He lit yet another now before continuing: 'Let me try to explain to you, Mr Dowling, the emotional upheaval and trauma associated with severing connections with the country of your birth. When my father took the painful decision to leave Palestine, he realised there was no going back for himself or any of his family unless, of course, there is a separate and independent Palestinian state established. When the reality of statelessness hits you, I cannot describe the homesickness and emptiness that envelopes you. My father related to me many bedtime tales of his early life and escapades in Nablus. Before I was eight years old, I already had a vivid mental picture of what the town looked like and the customs and traditions which meant so much to him.

'He kept his promise to one day show me the town of my birth. With the assistance of a close friend Karim in Damascus, who had his own car, this was a treat my father reserved for my tenth birthday. Just before daybreak the three of us set out from Damascus and headed due south-west. I had no idea of our route or destination but I clearly remember my father telling Karim to proceed towards the Golan Heights, which at the time meant nothing to me but later became such a strategic and disputed area between Jews and Syrians. From a high vantage point on the Golan my father, in the clear late morning sun, pointed towards the beautiful town of Nablus on the distant dry plain below. With his hand trembling and tears welling-up he could scarcely finish what he wanted most to achieve. He identified the various buildings which were once the cornerstone of his life and wondered what changes the years had brought. It was for both of us a nostalgic trip down memory lane. Turning to me he said: "My mission is now complete and I can die happily, knowing that you will pursue the Palestinian cause and one day return to where you drew your first breath."

'Ironically, my father died of a severe heart attack on June 15, 1967, a matter of days after the Israelis captured the Golan Heights in the bitter Six-Day war. Many close friends are firmly convinced that the seizure of Golan was the principal cause of my father's untimely death.'

They had already taken the right turning and covered five miles heading eastwards on the Beirut-Damascus road. Paul's immediate reaction was one of sorrow and pity and was awestruck at the resiliency of a race bent on survival at all costs. But then on further reflection Paul considered this to be the natural instinct of any people threatened by extinction, a prospect increasingly facing the Palestinians. He tried to console Ismail and to reassure him that international public opinion was on their side and sooner rather than later there ought to be a just solution to this anomaly. This was Paul's private opinion since, as a member of an UN peacekeeping force, he is obliged to be strictly non-partisan.

Lighting yet another cigarette and turning towards Paul, he continued. 'From what I've seen on TV and read in the papers, you in Ireland have your own problems. One thing that never ceases to amaze me is why England should have any involvement in Ireland. The Africans have all but freed themselves from the oppressive yoke of colonialism and why has it persisted for so long within a shout of England's borders?' Paul gave him a brief synopsis and history of Northern Ireland up to the present impasse and informed him it takes much longer than the duration of the road trip to Damascus to give him the complete story.

'There is so much for you to see in this ancient land of Syria' Ismail boasted. 'As I drive we are passing through some of the most historic and holy sites of the Middle East. There is a small village within a 45 minute drive of Damascus, which nestles at the foot of a mountain, where its inhabitants speak Aramaic, the language Jesus Christ used to communicate with the native people. To sit in that little village takes you back in time to when the spiritual side of life was all that mattered. Fortunately, numerous generations of Aramaeans were sheltered from the contaminating influences of the outer world and still have a very simple and rustic means of existence. Of course, you Christians regard Jesus as the Son of God while we Moslems look upon Him as a Prophet comparable to our own great Prophet Mohammad.'

'There are so many attractions that your short stay of six months will allow you witness only a fraction of it. I could take you to the coastal region, where the Phoenicians originated, and see where the first alphabet was developed. Dotted along a stretch of Syria, starting at the coast, are several crusader castles which Europeans used as fortresses in their middle ages' treks to and from the Holy Land. The name of Saint Paul is closely associated with Damascus where he stayed more than once.' Whatever about the pomp of Saint Paul's entry to Damascus, Paul knew from the houses flitting by on either side that he too, in a far less ceremonious way, was approaching that same city. On his left was the Sheraton hotel following which Ismail exited the main road and headed past yet another hotel, the Marriott, which was close to UNIFIL's headquarters.

It occurred to Paul that here was a driver, with little formal education, from whom he had learned so much in the space of a few hours. He needed time, however, to "ruminate" on some of the issues Ismail raised. In the event of confrontations between Palestinians and Israelis, could he maintain a neutral peacekeeping stance as he was obliged to do? He remembered going to local football games in his youth, with no allegiance to either side, and ended up fiercely supporting one. Had he now by association, or perhaps empathy, warmed to the Palestinians and their cause? As if Ismail was reading his thoughts, he remarked: 'There is no doubt our two peoples share similar problems but you can cherish the fact that you were never banished from your homeland.' It was a heart-rending statement that haunted Paul for years to come. When Ismail stopped the Land Rover in front of UNIFIL's headquarters, Paul's Irish friends who had already arrived were there to greet him. One of them rushed towards Paul, exclaiming: 'I just saw a copy of the programme for tomorrow's UN Day's celebrations, and it promises to make you homesick many times over. The secret information he purposely withheld from Paul was bound to bring him nostalgia of a far different kind during the next 24 hours.

*

'Before you have a shower to wash away the journey's dust, I have a few unexpected guests you will be delighted to meet,' said the UN's Irish commander to Paul. He took a seat obviously fatigued after the long road trip, when a door opened and in stepped his older brother Gerald followed by Liam McCabe and Vincent Tuohy. It was the refreshing tonic he had wished for over the previous four months but there was no better time than the present to savour it. Gerald's repeated embraces restored his self-esteem and composure and the mere sight of Vincent with all his quips and good humour enlivened his spirit. 'We came to bring you home,' joked Liam in his sharp northern accent which contrasted markedly with Vincent's Corkonian twang. Trying to conceal his excitement, Paul disappeared for fifteen minutes to wash and clean-up but not before he arranged a welcoming drink for them in the comfortable sitting room. For all but Vincent it was a cultural shock for which they were poorly prepared. The previous evening at sundown Gerald heard over the nearby mosque's loudspeakers the universal call to prayer and was both startled and curious, enquiring if this was a war alert from their less friendly neighbours. Their education was yet incomplete.

When Paul returned Gerald gave him a large package containing his favourite foods from home. On hearing that it contained sausages, Paul extended Gerald's education further by whispering that any food products containing even a whiff of pork were considered unclean and unacceptable to Moslems. But if kept strictly for himself he'd enjoy the culinary experience. Paul went on to explain he could get a wide array of foods in the UN's commissary but not specific Irish treats. As for booze at low duty-free prices Paul reckoned he was in a position to be permanently inebriated, if he were so inclined. At this stage his visitors had taken two hefty drinks which brought flushes to their cheeks. Paul then suggested they retire to the UN's own restaurant within the building where he could hear all the latest developments from home. Also, if the happy reunion ended with somebody showing the signs of excess alcohol, he was well hidden from the outside public gaze.

When they reached the restaurant it was almost 9 p.m. and the last meals were being served. They took a table for four in a quiet corner and there were about 20 others dining. Paul first greeted several at other tables with whom he was on first name terms. They then requested a drink and the waiter took their orders. Gerald said it was easy to tell alcohol was cheap, the way that large measures of spirits were doled out. In Liam's opinion the high duty on drink in Ireland not only benefited the poorer sectors of society but was an effective means of keeping those prone from drifting steadily into alcoholism. Vincent was supportive of drinking in moderation saying it helped to sort out difficult problems and, besides, how many were saved from the ravages of more acute addictions now cancerously eroding our society?

Impatient for home news Paul enquired about his Dad and Mam, living up to the high regard in which he was held as the youngest member of the family. 'Our Mam is as active as ever,' replied Gerald, 'but Dad is beginning to show all of his 62 years. Never a man to shy away from heavy farm jobs, he is increasingly leaving these to anybody younger and stronger in sight and, unfortunately, I am within his near vision. It was seldom a problem for me to be away for several days or even a couple of weeks but I fear this may be my last trip abroad without calling on a neighbour to help. Hardly a day goes by without him mentioning your name. He says he feels proud of you as a trained soldier doing what you can to right the injustices in such a sacred part of the world. But his heart has always been, and will continue to be, closer to home problems and particularly Northern Ireland. I suppose, whether he fully appreciates it or not, he is locally perceived as upholding the strong republican ideals espoused by his late Dad. You might say we not only inherit the physical genes of our ancestors but their beliefs and behavioural patterns are also passed on.'

They had finished their starters, and awaited their main dish, when Paul enquired about his sisters Deirdre and Joan. Gerald responded 'knowing that Liam and Vincent have more than a passing interest gives me pleasure to speak at some length. Joan is her vibrant self and never in awe of her older sister. You will be glad to hear that Deirdre's romance with Liam's brother, Jim, has reached a new level. From a small beginning, the relationship took hold during their visit to the Soviet Union where they discovered that the sharing of common republican principles helped to cement their love for each other. It took little of Jim's persuasive powers to get her to move from Dublin and take up another teaching post within five miles of Liscorley. My Dad is pleased and confident it will before too long result in a happy marriage between members of two strong republican families. Those who happen to see them together vouch for the strong chemical bond between them.'

Gerald paused briefly while the waiter placed the main dishes on the table and then resumed. 'There is another pair whose relationship is steadily gaining momentum but of which little is said..' Looking in Vincent's direction to gauge his reaction, he continued. 'It took their stay in the Soviet Union - and more specifically their shared interest in seeing Lenin's embalmed body in Moscow's Red Square - to sow the seeds of Vincent's friendship with Jane McCabe. Being a 'cute Corkman,' he is loath to give much information away, even to his close friends. He shrugs off the constant teasing about his ill-judgement in selecting a girl friend at the other extreme corner of Ireland from his native Cork. He could benefit from Jim McCabe's advice on how to bridge the distance divide between them.' Vincent's only well-considered comment was 'we will make sure that business brings us together frequently and, from there, we will let affairs of the heart take their natural course.'

Before they finished their desserts, accompanied by a favourite liqueur, the conversation turned to politics. Paul who was too busy on the Israeli-Lebanese front for the past four months and ill-informed of recent home events, asked for an update. There were few more qualified than Gerald to expand. He confirmed that the I.R.A. had reached a watershed in its long and bitter struggle. It can be truthfully said that, at no time in the past 17 years, has it experienced such an unfortunate set of reverses. It was dealt a mortal blow earlier this year with the combined decision of the United States and Britain to attack Libya (and more specifically Tripoli) with devastating consequences, not only for the targeted country but for the I.R.A.'s future hopes and aspirations. Henceforth, Libya's support for terrorism will be closely monitored to the point where it will effectively cease altogether. Fortunately, for us some of Libya's vast oil wealth can still be channelled to the I.R.A., not directly from Libya but through a third party which happens to be a close ally i.e. Syria. It is for this reason Vincent, Liam and myself are here to explore and promote this promising future avenue of cooperation.

'And what about your rapprochement with the communists?' enquired Paul.

'Not much luck there.' said Gerald, 'because recent political changes in the Soviet Union are working to our great disadvantage, undoing practically all of the progress achieved during our overtures to them two years ago. While the decline of communism, leading to more openness and accountability, is long overdue, it wrecks the foundation of the communists' original motive for involvement. With the Soviet Union's desire to spread communism westwards no longer a priority, so too will be their lack of interest and support for the I.R.A. It was a political trump card we withheld from playing until the going got tough but that is now dead and buried. We are not yet sure if or to what extent we can count on the support of the new political leaders.

It was now Vincent's turn for a share of the bad news. He mentioned the major setback to the I.R.A.'s recent operations caused by Britain's improved information-gathering network.

Its lifeblood has long been the illicit importation of arms, largely by sea from Libya and often transshipped via different European ports, and this is faltering. Where large quantities of arms and money are involved, there are bound to be informers cashing in. Strike rates over recent months have irreparably damaged progress, not only losing arms but having some key men arrested and imprisoned. British authorities must be deluded into thinking that Libya continues to supply arms while at the same time cultivating and promoting the Syrian axis. Sebacks never broke the I.R.A., only strengthened its resolve to find viable alternatives.

Within the close confines of the restaurant corner, and in whispers barely audible, Gerald revealed some of the I.R.A.'s most closely guarded secrets and the basis of their campaign strategy over the next few years. At a recent Army Council meeting, a decision was taken to pursue the war on two fronts, which is guaranteed to do the maximum amount of damage. Bombs and the threats of bombs will be intensified both in Northern Ireland and strategic targets in Britain. The I.R.A. already came close in Brighton when only a miracle saved many key Conservative Party members from extermination. Earlier it took terrorism to Westminster's car park and assassinated an important political figure. While the I.R.A. doesn't condone murder for murder's sake, there is little short of it that will instill urgency and bring the results and concessions it desperately needs. It is sad to have to admit that small nations like Ireland have no alternative when under the yoke of a strong colonial power.

Paul was appalled at what he had just heard but knew that the opinions of junior family members were often neither requested nor respected. Nor did he feel it was the time or place to comment now. What he clearly knew was that the experiences of the past four months influenced his mind and his views in a way he never once imagined. Guilt complexes were a constant reality. As he daily preserved peace within earshot of two hostile forces, he wondered where his real loyalty belonged. At this very point in time there were hostilities of a different kind within his own country where lives were also under threat. It seemed ironic he should be serving abroad when his own country desperately needed him. But was there anything new in this? He vividly recalls his father and uncles describing the great feats of Irishmen in the American Civil War and the First World War, times when at home men were involved in a protracted struggle against Britain. He put it down to one of the many contradictions in Irish society for which he and many others couldn't offer a plausible explanation. Sensing it was futile to allow Gerald's political emotions to rise higher at this late hour, Paul suggested they retire for the night and be well rested for the following day's events. The weary look on all their faces guaranteed the unanimous adoption of the proposal.

Although the annual UN Day of October 24th wasn't an official holiday, it was an opportunity for outposted staff to travel to Damascus for all the right reasons. Firstly, there was a meeting to review work progress, identify and discuss problems and to plan ahead while those far from the city used the occasion to purchase food and beverages from the well-stocked commissary. The grand finale was reserved for the evening hours. This year the formal dinner was taking place in the plush and ornate setting of the Sheraton Hotel. In addition to all UN employees there was a broad spectrum of invitees, from senior Government officials to representatives of the various embassies plus international staff working in various capacities. It was a night to commemorate the forty-first anniversary of the UN's founding, to inform those present of its role both globally and within Syria and to say thanks to all who helped to make it possible. It was a publicity and marketing strategy all too rarely used to highlight the UN's achievements throughout the globe.

It was a spectacle Gerald was to recall for years to come and he, Vincent and Liam were there as Paul's guests. As the large embassy cars, brandishing their national flags, pulled up in front of the hotel, the immaculately attired guests alighted and entered through the automatic doors to the spacious foyer. Gerald was overheard saying to Liam that not since President Kennedy's funeral had he seen such splendour and elegance. What he had then seen on TV, he was now witnessing first hand in the flesh. He was enjoying the experience as, back in

Inistogue, it was a totally different world. There was a palpable buzz during the pre-dinner drinks followed by near silence at the meal when they busily satisfied their healthy appetites. Then as the coffee was served, it was time for speechmaking. Though there was sure to be much repetition after the first speaker, all the guests were happy to accept it as a *fait accompli* and to get a comprehensive briefing about the UN's laudable work and achievements.

It was followed by an informal session when guests mingled and discussed a wide range of topics. Paul introduced his three visitors to an American working with aid projects whom Paul had met on a previous visit to Damascus. After the pleasantries were dispensed with, the conversation turned to politics. The American, in his broad Texan drawl, remarked, 'I understand you have your own problems in Ireland, of which I must admit I know virtually nothing. Is Northern Ireland a separate country from where y'all come from?' Gerald momentarily raised his eyes heavenward in an expression of disbelief at how insular some person could be. Then he began to give a brief and simple synopsis of a situation he felt even the uninitiated could grasp. Armed with this information, the American was able to draw parallels which both amazed and enlightened the four Irishmen.

'The longer you live the more you certainly learn, assuming Alzheimers doesn't take an early hold,' began the American. 'I can scarcely believe that what I heard pertains to the late twentieth century. You are aware how various European countries, the French and British in particular, tried to wrest some of our own country from us. It required our stiffest resistance to win the day, the Boston tea party being an example of how we warded off the best efforts of the British. The French made their big push in the south and their influence is still strong in Louisiana. The British taking Northern Ireland is very similar to say the Germans occupying my own state of Texas. They can then refuse to recognize Ronald Reagan as their President but instead remain loyal to the Federal Republic of Germany. How long do you suppose this untenable situation would be tolerated? Our history suggests it would be an overnight wonder that would surely disappear soon after dawn. We were fortunate in that the majority threw out the less powerful, the reverse of which, as I interpret it, applies in your case. That should not deter you from trying to remedy a twentieth century anomaly. Take heart from the sad American experience that no matter how much we committed to Vietnam, in terms of manpower and weaponry, we ultimately were to lose out to a guerrilla movement with an inordinate long term belief in itself. Much of what I've seen on TV leads me to believe that the I.R.A. is little different.' It was the type of reassurance seldom meted out to the I.R.A. and it brought copious smiles and warm handshakes before they exited the hotel.

It was now only a little after ten o'clock, about the time when most residents of Damascus retired for the night. But this being Thursday meant that next day was the Moslem rest day when the most devout visit a mosque to pray. For the four Irishmen it was still early, Liam reminding them that, were they in Ireland, there was plenty of time to begin their usual trek to the city's bright lights. Damascus not being able to deliver some of their home delights, they instead decided to return to the UN guest house and have a couple of drinks. Gerald didn't yet have the chance of one to one discussions with Paul to which he intended devoting some of Friday's free time as well as a leisurely tour of Damascus' ancient sites. He managed to conceal his anxiety about the important string of appointments scheduled for Saturday, the first day of the Moslem working week. He and his two colleagues needed to call on their best tactical skills in order to bring about a much-needed turn of fortune. The fresh but bad news from home, received on their return to the guest house, guaranteed to make next week's deliberations all the more difficult.

*

He was born on Syria's coastal region and reputed to have some of the characteristics of a lion. Previous wars against the Israelis had left physical and, even more significant, mental scars from which Syria had never fully recovered. Israel's 1967 seizure of the Golan Heights added insult to injury and, without its return, there was little hope of reconciliation. It showed on President Kemal Siddique's drawn face as he took his seat at 10 a.m. in the ornate room of his palace, the appointed time and place to meet his three Irish visitors. As a boy he had been aware of the Israeli threat to his country, in the army he did his utmost to suppress and contain it and now as statesman he had to swallow his pride and negotiate as best he could. He was known to strike a hard bargain and some went as far as to say that his deep resentment of his arch-rival stood in the way of any satisfactory settlement. He tried to banish local troubles from his mind and get on with today's tasks. The immaculately dressed mustachioed gentleman sat, as was his custom, in a sideways position and looked somewhat askance at his three guests before the interpreter coughed briefly to relieve the tension.

With a faint trace of a smile the President began 'It is my pleasant duty to welcome you to Syria for what I hope will be the start of a worthwhile understanding and wholehearted cooperation between us, in our mutual thrust for fairness and justice. Thanks to the medium of television, in addition to several briefings I've had from President Al-Madhi of Libya, I am reasonably well informed of the Northern Ireland question. You may not yet be aware of the recent setback for the I.R.A. which was reported in this morning's TV news, of the interception just off the Irish coast of two cargo ships laden with weapons. The prime suspects were arrested and will be charged. It could not come at a worse time for our deliberations here today.'

Gerald silently cursed recent advances in media technology that allowed President Siddique access to news that was confidentially given to them only hours earlier. He felt he needed all his strength and ingenuity to play down the consequences of this reverse in front of his most promising benefactor. Smiling, Gerald responded 'Firstly, Mr. President, I would like to thank you for inviting us to Syria to commence what I trust will be a future of mutual understanding, respect and support. Let me hasten to respond to your remark about arms' seizure. Yes, we are disappointed with its scale and timing but we in the I.R.A. are accustomed to temporary mishaps in our long term strategy. We gain experience and a renewed energy to continue, stemming from a firm belief in the justice we pursue. What has just happened shouldn't in any way influence or alter our goals.' President Siddique looked admiringly towards Gerald, with a hint of a smirk, as if to say: this man certainly knows what he wants and is determined to get it. The resoluteness of Gerald's statements and his overall demeanour convinced the President that here was a man he could easily do business with and would be worthy of his support. There was a strange empathy beginning to develop between these two strong characters.

Again it was President Siddique's turn. 'I need hardly remind you of the similarities between our own PLO and your I.R.A. concerning goals and tactics, largely of the guerrilla and terrorist kind. Our struggle began in 1948, considerably later than yours, but we both have precious little to show for it. Results, however, must not be judged in years but in decades and even a century, if the patience does not wear thin. We can learn from each other, refining our strategy and tactics to suit the local conditions. Three years ago we *upped the anti* and took our war to a new level. You may remember our daring attack in Beirut when a suicide bomber drove a tank through the main gate of an American marine compound, killing almost three hundred young men. It shocked the world and got headline news. There are many others of the Moslem faith ready to lay down their lives for the benefit of the masses. Some will regard these acts as cowardly but the people carrying them out are courageous in the extreme. They do so in the knowledge that all other viable options have been exhausted. Only very angry men subjected to long-term injustices will behave in this way.'

'You have many brave men in the I.R.A. similarly motivated. Your Catholic beliefs, however, can be a restraining influence, falling short of the fatalism spurring on Moslems as exemplified in the Beirut attack. We do not condone such atrocities which often punish the innocent but what is the alternative to publicise our cause? Syria is now labelled a terrorist state and so-called western democracies are ready to punish us for our crimes. Our citizens have to undergo long and meticulous scrutiny when travelling through European and U.S. airports, regarding all of them as terrorists. Should they spend as much time trying to remove the root causes of terrorism, they would soon discover these men and women to be more law-abiding than their own people. We ought to learn from the human health field in that proper disease diagnosis coupled with administering the right medicines is the only just way forward. In both Northern Ireland and throughout much of the Arab world we are growing tired of ceaseless medications which aggravate rather than cure our basic complaints.'

Gerald, while sharing all of the President's sentiments, was anxious to steer the conversation along Northern Ireland's trajectory. At the same time he sensed the President was trying to exorcize the feelings of rancour and hurt that plagued him for years and he had no wish to hijack these. Was a man so seething with rage at Israel's wrongdoings the correct choice to broker an agreement or did it warrant a more moderate stance? The President seemingly was in power for the long haul and all concerned had no choice but to deal with him and humour him the best they could. Gerald became very aware of this and, with less fire coming through the President's words, considered it opportune to interject a little bit of Irish banter.

'There is a saying in Ireland that whatever remote corner of the world you visit, you are likely to find a few first, and many more second and third, generation Irish people. Not all were success stories but many enriched the societies into which they were fully integrated. Since 1948 the Palestinians too have wandered far from their homeland, leaving an indelible imprint on those lives they touched. We share equally difficult problems and hopes of a better tomorrow with one salient difference. Irish people can, if and when they choose, elect to return home, a right, unfortunately, denied to the Palestinians. The world at large, with very few notable exceptions, fully supports the Palestinians' right to their own country.' This last remark epitomised all that President Siddique had ever worked for and brought a smile of satisfaction that only emphasized his greying moustache. Gerald knew he struck the right chord and what they were to discuss and agree upon from here on in was made all the easier.

The President, now looking more composed, continued 'We in the Government of Syria are in accord with Md. Al-Madhi of Libya that Northern Ireland's liberation war should enter a new and more aggressive phase. In essence, it highlights the very poor return to date for all the resources expended and the heavy human casualties. We must henceforth take the war to the oppressors, striking at the very heart of key establishments both in Northern Ireland and Britain. There were some successes already but these were too few, small scale and poorly planned and executed. We are thinking in terms of the Beirut attack, a mere 100 kilometres from where I now speak. Look at the Vietnamese example. There they had first to wreck the economy and the very fabric of the country before ironically they could declare it a success. Later they were happy to rebuild their country from the ashes in the knowledge they were simultaneously restoring their freedom and pride. While I do not advocate a 'scorched earth' approach, it should be a restricted version of it, so severely damaging your enemy's capacity to retaliate that, in the long run, they will be forced to quit.'

Liam gave a sceptical glance at Vincent and whispered 'I have my doubts. If it was so simple, why has the 15,000 strong Syrian force in Lebanon failed to even dent Israeli strongholds?' Paul's briefing of only two days before, about the battlefront positions and progress, had not escaped Liam's attentive ears. It was now time for the President to get down to specifics.

'With Libya providing the money, Syria will meet its responsibility for all arms purchases and shipment. Always wary of the threat of arms seizure en route, we will use all the tactics and guile within our powers to ensure not only safe delivery to its destination but effective deployment. It will entail decoys to distract authorities from the real transport routes and the tacit cooperation of certain high-ranking staff working at your ports. Rather than shipping large quantities of weapons over a short period, which is impractical and risky given the strict surveillance operations, we will concentrate on a gradual delivery and stockpiling at strategic and secure locations within Ireland both north and south. I should emphasize that for maximum impact it is necessary to have a smaller but significant proportion of the arms stored south of the Northern Ireland border for cross-border attacks and harassment. From my reading of your internal politics, this will be easy with so many I.R.A. sympathisers only too willing and able to get involved. Of the total amount of money allocated, up to one third is identified for payments to those making the operations work. Put simply, there is little point spending on arms which either get waylaid in transit or discovered in storage. Syria's support for the PLO has never wavered and, if we apply a similar strategy, there is even greater scope for advancing Irish freedom and reunification than at any time in the past. I invite you while here to have a good look at the Syrian defence organisation and *modus operandi* and its links with and assistance to the PLO.'

'To highlight the importance I attach to your mission, I am taking steps to appoint the Assistant Chief of the Armed Forces to be with you for the rest of this week, until your scheduled departure on Thursday. He is seated to my right and his name is Naji Ahmed. Not only has he prepared an interesting itinerary for you but at great pains made sure you will not leave without an understanding and appreciation of Syrian culture and traditions. Business trips are interspersed with an overview of our historic and tourist sites and an opportunity to meet with members of rural communities. Naji will later give you details of the programme which you may alter, if necessary, to suit your specific needs and interests. I have set aside time to meet you again before departure to hear your views and comments and crystallise future plans and programmes. Meanwhile, you may have questions to raise at this juncture.'

The smile of obvious satisfaction on Gerald's face spoke volumes. 'Mr. President, in my humble opinion you have represented our interests fully and admirably. You, obviously, took a personal interest in our mission and spent much of your precious time assisting us. We are entirely at your disposal and I have no doubt that what's arranged will meet our needs. I'm glad there is a wrap-up meeting scheduled because by then there should be much more to discuss. Meanwhile, we are grateful for your valued help and look forward to an interesting and productive week under Mr. Ahmed's guidance.'

After the President said his farewells, he started attending to the numerous daily visitors to whom he gave much of his time. Mr. Ahmed took the three Irishmen aside and suggested they go to his office to discuss the detailed programme. The rest of Saturday was devoted to meetings with senior personnel in the Ministry of Defence in Damascus to learn of its overall organisation and, more importantly, the varied field operations. Mr. Ahmed reminded them that tomorrow morning, like most work mornings in the Moslem world, would have a 7:30 start but was pleased to state that work would finish at the regular time of 2:30 p.m. For Gerald accustomed to rise at home before 6 a.m., this came as little surprise. Liam cynically remarked that in Ireland this is regarded as a half day's work but he wasn't complaining.

Back at the UN guest house it was Paul's last night before returning to his southern Lebanese base and the final chance to meet informally with Gerald. Ever since his arrival in Damascus two days earlier he yearned for a one-to-one with his older brother. It was as much to do with politics as to hear in more detail about Inistogue's innermost secrets or small village gossip. Before the two had finished the preliminaries Paul interjected 'If there is one thing above all else Syria and Lebanon did, they enabled me to rationalise my political thinking. In Inistogue, I was blinkered not only from the outside world but even the townlands and villages all about. There was little scope for independent thought and action or to mix with other races and creeds, facilities which are ever present here. This allows me the liberty to be introspective and to question many of the things I've too readily taken for granted.'

The expression on Gerald's face did not hide his fear of what might come next, before Paul continued 'We tend to follow like sheep, imitating and even trying to outdo what our parents achieved. This can have many advantages for one's personal advancement in life but can be counterproductive or even catastrophic in the political arena. Look at our own country and the northern problem. We have tunnel vision in trying to resolve it, with guns and more guns seen as the only option. For more than 20 years of my life I was blind to this fact - or prevented from seeing it - but it took much less than the four months I am here for the penny to drop. It is too long and controversial a subject for the short time we have together but, seeing our family's long tradition in republicanism, we of the current generation ought to ask ourselves some hard questions.'

It was these questions Gerald had kept well locked to the back of his mind for too long, refusing to entertain them, and it was unlikely anything his young brother now said would influence him. Awestruck by Paul's brief confession, he was in no mind and had little time to debate the issues. Gerald then wrapped up their meeting on a personal note. 'Every day that passes all our family are concerned for your safety and wellbeing and we hope you will return fit and healthy in two months time. Our father, in particular, is very proud of your noble work, knowing you are helping to maintain peace without his full knowledge or appreciation of the underlying causes of the conflict. About the time you return to your Lebanese post in the morning, we will begin our tour of duty in Syria. Take care of yourself.' Both struggled to hold back the tears as they warmly embraced and then parted close to the midnight hour.

*

'Because Syria is such a big country and your time here is short we must combine air with road travel' said Naji to his three Irish guests as the pilot taxied his six seater plane to the take-off runway of Damascus airport, located south-east of the city. Once airborne and circling Damascus before heading due northwards, Naji proudly briefed them about what is reputed to be one of the oldest cities on this planet. The turbulence unsettling the passengers' stomachs distracted their attention but as the plane reached its cruising altitude their anxieties dissipated. None of the Irish were yet ready, however, for Naji's early morning offer of coke and sandwiches.

They first flew over the city of Homs and were heading

towards the old city of Hamah. Naji pointed to the vast areas with enough water, resulting from a combination of moderate rains and river irrigation. Immediately below was one of Syria's three sugar cane factories, with its visible smokestacks, which contributed to the country's sugar self-sufficiency. But with a rapidly growing population of sweeter tastes it may soon be necessary to start importing. One of the highlights of their subsequent car tour of Hamah was a stop at the site of an old water wheel. As Naji explained, the ingenuity of man, even in pre-Christian times, knew no bounds. The large wooden wheel which was partially immersed in the river water - and rotated by its power - was able to continuously extract small quantities of water with each revolution and considerable amounts during 24 hours. It was a simple but effective way of harnessing water for all the communities' needs, from the varied domestic to crop and fruit irrigation. Coming from a country where water was an embarrassment, it wasn't easy for the Irish to appreciate its significance. However, they marvelled at how important a role each precious drop of water played in this largely arid country.

It was business as usual the following morning with an inspection tour of one of Syria's large military establishments near Hamah. It was here many of the troops were trained before serving their term of duty in Lebanon. Equally important was the strong Palestinian contingent receiving tuition and practicals in guerrilla warfare, a programme in which the President took a personal interest. In an introductory talk from the group leader, he outlined the components of the austere training programme, the methodology of applying what they had learned and their successes and achievements. There followed an intense exchange of views and a question and answer session, all the while comparing the Palestinian approach to the I.R.A.'s strategies and tactics. Notwithstanding the similarities, all agreed there was plenty of scope for learning from each other. Vincent was very impressed with the intelligence and enthusiasm of the Palestinians, confirming what he had read of being one of the most progressive minorities among the Arab people.

With the afternoon sun beaming into their eyes, but the car's air conditioning keeping them comfortably cool within, they sped along the highway leading to the Mediterranean coastal cities of Tartous and Latakia. Naji was quick to remind them it was in this area the Syrian President grew up and it was now a fast developing tourist resort. At various times he pointed to a number of reasonably well-preserved hilltop-sited castles which had also aroused his guests' curiosity. He explained that these were monuments to the 12th Century Crusaders, serving as defensive ramparts in their treks to and from the Holy Land. While in western eyes these Crusaders were perceived as preserving Christianity, the Arabs at closer range saw much more of their ulterior motives such as plunder and material gain. Or was the good intention of many hijacked by the greedy desires of the few? Strolling subsequently along the Mediterranean beach in the late afternoon sun helped to dispel thoughts of any religious bigotry.

During that evening's flight to Aleppo the old city walls, resplendent in the setting sun, captivated the visitors. Naji explained that Aleppo (or *Halab* in Arabic, meaning *white*) derives its name from the soft limestone used to construct most of the buildings. In the second millennium BC the city was under successive Hittite and Egyptian rule, the Persians were in control from the 6th to the 4th century BC and it was assimilated into the Roman empire in the 1st century BC. It was under Byzantine influence until conquered by the Arabs in 637 and from 1516 until the end of the First World War it was part of the Ottoman empire. Walking through the crowded alleyways of the city's extensive *bazaar* or *suk* in the fading light was an experience to captivate and enthral any westerner. The cacophony of sounds and the array of smells, both pleasant fragrances and others less so, were guaranteed to linger long after the night had passed. Here traders both big and small, rich and almost destitute vied with one another to sell to the strolling customers anything from expensive silk carpets to cheap mundane household items needed for day-to-day survival. It was a display of smart and crafty Arab trading, a business they had refined and perfected over the centuries.

On the southern approach to the city of Aleppo, after

leaving the hill of *Tal Hadya* on the right, is a narrow but tarmacadamed road not readily visible to the unobservant. The first thing likely to perk the attention is the heavy security presence both day and night. It was on the third morning of this upcountry run that their government car ground to a halt at the entrance, to establish their credentials, before proceeding to the main building 500 metres further on. Upon entering, Naji introduced his guests to the commanding officer who invited them to the visitors centre for a video presentation and talk. It was all handled with the usual Arab politeness and courtesy but with more than a hint of top secrecy.

Standing in front of the select group, the commanding officer began 'This is the second (the first is near Damascus) high security military training centre which is rather special. Two factors set it apart from the usual run of the mill. We cater to not only national but international needs and, secondly, we specialise in training terrorists who can advance the cause of freedom in their respective parts of the world. Only Libya in the Arab world has the equivalent level of technology and sophistication. That we can get involved is due largely to Libya's financial backing and you are aware of that country's support for just causes. After completing our discussions we will demonstrate the practical work and you are invited to participate. I understand you are available for the remainder of today.' It was a long and tiresome day for everybody but it opened Irish eyes to all that's sinister and bizarre about terrorism and the motives of those who engage in it. The Irishmen came away wondering whether the end justified the means and, if so, it must be a very worthwhile "end" indeed.

Only a few hours of the next day was devoted to business. Later their plane took them due eastwards and then slightly south to the city of Al-Raqqah delicately poised on the banks of the Euphrates river. Looking out on this expansive river, Naji explained. 'It rises north of Erzurum in eastern Turkey traversing its southern region before entering Syria and flowing southeastward across the eastern part of the country and it continues through Iraq. So many lives in these three countries depend on the water within its banks and any serious diminution of its supply can spell disaster along its course. It is Syria's lifeblood but, although there is a tacit agreement between our neighbours for its rational use, being second in the queue often works to our disadvantage. In times of greater need, such as during each dry season of the year, Turkey can siphon off more than its share. Even worse, Turkey has started constructing dams to irrigate vast tracts of its southern region and when these are completed within ten years we may be reduced to a trickle.' Countries fought wars over water in the past and there was every likelihood these would increase further. Within an hour's plane journey from where they now stood was the Iraqi frontier, a country already into its sixth year of a bitter and bloody war over water rights with its normally friendly neighbour Iran.

The next and final day of their upcountry run was devoted entirely to leisure. It proved to be so good and exciting that Gerald was later to describe it as 'keeping the good wine until last.' It began with an early morning visit to the ancient city of Palmyra in the Syrian desert. Palmyra is the Greek and Latin for Tadmor, the pre-Semitic name still in use today. Stone inscriptions reveal the existence of Palmyra and its inhabitants as early as the 19th century BC. A road built through the city in the 3rd century BC made it an important east-west trade route which, two centuries later, was of international significance. Under the Roman empire for most of the first three centuries AD, leaving an indelible mark on the architecture and the well-preserved ruins now in full view of the visitors, the city later came under Moslem domination during the 7th century. The Palmyrenes spoke Aramaean and exchanged goods with India, by way of the Persian Gulf, and with cities on the Nile river and Rome. To walk between the Roman columns on this clear sunny morning was to savour an unique experience. The feats of man, or rather thousands of poorly paid or even slaves working in unison, were nothing short of heroic, putting in place massive stone slabs and columns all by hand. The sense of awe and bewilderment, not only surrounding the physical achievements against such massive odds but the bizarre mix of cultures and traditions, was the stuff of fairytales. Liam interpreted the historic developments by saying that from as early as several centuries BC the quest for racial supremacy was uppermost in the mind of *homo sapiens*. He said it as if to absolve himself, if need be, from carrying the Northern Ireland struggle into the 21st century AD.

Surrounding Palmyra was an extensive semi-desert and desert region with annual rainfall ranging from less than four inches to virtually zero. It was home to nomadic tribes existing on the products of their livestock, mainly sheep, goats and camels. To do so, and to exploit the better available grazing in different areas throughout the year, they periodically moved all their meagre belongings, using camels for transport, pitching tents at each stop. Meat from their animals, slaughtered rustically as and when needed, and a variety of milk products such as cheeses and yoghurts comprised most of their daily sustenance. It is a way of life as old as Syrian civilisation itself - practised throughout the Middle East and Africa - and is almost tamper-proof. The efforts of so many Governments to change nomadic habits, in favour of the greater efficiencies accruing to settled communities, have been fruitless. As one learned observer remarked 'I agree with the advantages of settling nomads but *who* is going to do it,' emphasising the centuries of frustrating attempts. Whether it should ever have been tried, in the first instance, is a moot point.

It was shortly after 4 p.m., and the end of their routine daily *siesta,* when Naji ushered his three visitors into a nomadic tent about 50 miles due north of Palmyra. It had previously been arranged through the local agricultural officer, well known to the community and who entered a couple of steps behind Naji. Much to the surprise of the apprehensive Irishmen, the welcome was as warm as it was stomach-filling. After the minutes-long embraces and ear-to-ear smiles that spoke volumes for their relaxed and worry-free life styles, all were invited to be seated cross-legged on the floor supported only by cushions. Seated in circle format around trays full of locally-made food, prepared by the women who kept their distance in true Moslem fashion, it was Arab hospitality at its simplest but very best. The several blood-related families conversed loudly and uninhibitedly. But were there strong hints of the effects of centuries of inbreeding, recessive genes throwing up a variety of malformations among the young?

Here was a way of life rooted in the past but carrying many exemplary messages of what the future should be all about. None among the large group could be regarded as being well fed, in terms of quantity and quality, and each had to work hard to eke out a subsistence not knowing what the next day would bring. Yet they would be grossly insulted should their distinguished guests decline to eat a good proportion of the little they had for themselves. They might be toil-worn and spent from long hours under the desert sun but the weariness brought a satisfaction and stress-free demeanour absent from western societies laden with the burden of keeping pace with the Jones.' It beggars the question whether those with the least worldly possessions are the most contented and happy. Vincent was intrigued with the seasonal movements, dictated by the animals' feed supply. He said that Ireland's unique minority of travelling people opted less for open country, preferring roadsides and scavenged sites from mostly unwilling donors within cities and large towns. He was full of admiration for his hosts and the unobtrusive way they gained the most from the little they had. The experience and memories were to linger for the rest of his life.

*

The major shock to the Irish psyche was reserved for the eve of their departure. With Naji as tour guide, he escorted them through selected suburbs of Damascus reeking with Palestinians in block after block of shabby and sometimes derelict and overcrowded apartments. He hastened to stress that the exodus from Palestine which began in 1948 was the single greatest human tragedy of the twentieth century, depriving a people of their rightful homeland. 'Syria was first among neighbouring states to grant them refugee status, housing them in large numbers with very limited resources, providing education and helping them find whatever jobs could be secured in an already overcrowded labour market. The pain and hurt of not being able to return home is poorly understood and appreciated, particularly in western countries. Your own country, perhaps, may be the one exception as your people experience many similar problems.' Isn't that the very reason, thought Liam, we are here in the first instance.

The enormity and complexity of the problems facing the Palestinians weren't easy for the casual visitor to comprehend and assimilate. Just as in Northern Ireland they were born out of one of the two communities having fewer rights to education, jobs, housing and so many other things normally taken for granted in other countries. Such inequality breeds mistrust, leads to frustration and anger and a long term commitment to right the serious wrongs. But, as in Northern Ireland, the rival communities profess different religious beliefs. Ironically, here at the virtual epicentre of Christianity, where Jesus Christ spent his public life and performed many miracles, it is odious to witness a protracted guerrilla war being waged that rivals or even surpasses all other wars. There are many imponderables in life and this must surely rank very high on the list. Gerald Dowling was moved by the injustices manifested in these Palestinian-inhabited apartments but could not afford to be unduly distracted from the purpose which first attracted him to Syria.

The wrap-up meeting with President Siddique the next morning brought few surprises. During the first ten minutes he talked more of Syria's problems *vis-a-vis* the Palestinian issue than anything of direct interest to his listeners. It took a brief interjection by Gerald to break the impasse. 'I am conscious of how precious your time is and would like to waste as little as possible of it by summarising our findings and discussing future lines of cooperation.' The broad smile on Gerald's face belied his impatience and helped to relax the President and hone him in on matters of immediate concern. 'Mr Ahmed did a first rate job in not only attending to the business end but in showing us much of which Syria can be justly proud. Syria is often accused of being a terrorist state but, judging from what I have witnessed, you are doing nothing more than trying to attract international concern for problems that have festered for too long.' It was sweet music to the President's ear and, after Gerald had given a full account of what they saw, it brought a reciprocal and effusive response.

'We are kindred spirits in our fight against oppression and the pursuit of fairness,' began the President. 'The fact that the PLO's activities transcend national boundaries, and have the backing of all Arab-speaking countries, legitimise their standing. You may have the advantage in economic development but the PLO has the edge over the I.R.A. in both the type and scale of its operations. By combining our efforts we can exceed the sum of what each can do alone, in a synergistic thrust forward. Going side-by-side with Syria's active material support must be an interchange of personnel between the PLO and the I.R.A., enhancing the performance and effectiveness of each. I am instructing my Chief of Staff of the army to establish and develop this link and to identify areas of future involvement. At any given time I envisage a healthy core of I.R.A. men in Syria and Lebanon and an equal PLO representation in Northern Ireland, once false documents and other details are sorted out.'

'You have rightly upped the bombings in recent months and our increased weaponry will help to intensify it further. Let not the discovery of one or two caches of arms, as occurred recently, deter you. As the Palestinians have demonstrated in Lebanon, let not the loss of a few lives turn you off course. As far as the next few years are concerned, our supply of arms plus logistical support will raise Northern Ireland's war games to a menacing level, to a make or break intensity.' These were fearsome words from a man noted for a strong personality and a penchant for belligerence. Was it now possible that President Siddique could, if he were to do what he promised, achieve success for Northern Ireland, something he was consistently frustrated in doing for the Palestinians? Or was he attempting to prove, to those who actually cared, that he could go one better than his good friend, Libyan President Md. Al-Madhi?

The stakes were now higher than ever before. The three Irishmen returned home more hopeful than any time in the past. When it came to depending on help from an outside source, whose motives for doing so weren't altogether clear, there was bound to be some degree of scepticism. Gerald was adamant that the single most crucial need was to receive enough arms on time and these should be landed ashore without detection by the security forces. He was far less enthusiastic about taking Palestinians on board to help with internal operations and felt confident of convincing President Siddique that this was not necessary. Foremost on their three satisfied minds was to pursue long-sought independence and, as far as pay-back time to the Syrians was concerned - and the form it might take -, these were matters they could comfortably postpone to another day.

CHAPTER 7
Ireland (North and South) - 1987

Seamus Dowling's birthday celebrations on March 16 were now low-key affairs and a far cry from the revelry of previous such nights. Long gone was the camaraderie and merriment that continued for days and nights on end. It was as if each passing year gradually eroded his own and friends' appetites for celebrations and mirrored Seamus' slower pace and zest for life. It was all too obvious at his last month's 63rd, opting for a quiet evening at home with his family and very few friends. Looking back, he had much to be thankful for and only minor regrets.

He always knew his devoted wife Nora contributed much more than she ever received credit for, a general failing among Irish husbands. What was it in the Irish psyche that prevented fathers from acknowledging the enormous role of mothers? This was too complex for Seamus to ponder, much less to unravel, but he had started working on it. In many small ways he was conveying messages to Nora that a decade ago he hadn't even contemplated. A friendly nod of approval after her all-too-rare visit to the hairdresser and an odd bunch of flowers for special occasions greatly boosted her ego and self-esteem. As their sex lives showed signs of waning, their relationship took on an openness and freshness they hadn't previously experienced. All four of their children were fully grown and mature and were expected to 'leave the nest' within the next five years.

'With his able-bodied son Gerald always at his beck and call, he had long since envisaged easing out of farm work soon after his 60th birthday. Not that he withdrew entirely but each of the last three years saw him take on less and less of the heavy work, reluctantly admitting to his own muscular limitations. He never complained about releasing Gerald for republican duties, while completing all that had to be done, but he could not indefinitely display this unabashed enthusiasm. Just as he had failed Nora, he hadn't fully recognized Gerald's often superhuman efforts in carrying out two jobs. Even though his Dad didn't tell him directly (perhaps, he will get around to it one day), Gerald was intuitively aware of his father's pride in his republican ideals and the sacrifices he was making. Gerald's single wish was that these efforts would yield tangible results, if not in his Dad's lifetime then certainly in his own.

Seamus was grateful to all his Inistogue friends on whose assistance he had heavily relied over many years. It was an odd quirk in his genetic make-up that he couldn't muster up the courage to tell them personally. Must it wait, he mused, until they are in their death beds when they can no longer hear the showers of praise cascading on to their cold, numb and unreceptive bodies? Wouldn't one ounce of gratitude in their living years extend a little their time on earth? If people were equally willing to laud achievements as to chastise misdeeds, then our world would be a far better and friendlier place.

No such thoughts preoccupied bachelor Joe Moriarty when he took his fireside seat opposite Seamus on that late April evening, as he had done once or twice weekly for the past 40 odd years. From his small cottage a few hundred yards away he was the eyes and ears for all that moved and spluttered in the neighbourhood. He entered the open back door to Seamus' house as if it were his own, not looking left or right to recognise or greet anyone, until he was seated with the daily newspaper he rarely saw the need to purchase. He then nodded in Seamus' direction as if to win approval for his presence, something he never once formally did. Nor did Seamus ever dare request it. There was a rapport and understanding between them often missing in close relatives. Without the genetic bonds, they were brothers for all intents and purposes.

There was a Joe Moriarty-like character in hundreds of villages throughout Ireland. Although he didn't progress beyond the seventh grade of primary school, he had wisdom and an I.Q. guaranteeing him almost unlimited success. His mind was free and uncluttered of the problems driving others to near distraction and he was able to rationalise issues at his own leisurely pace. He was involved in practically everything of note that happened in Inistogue - both good and bad - and had virtual mayoral status. Seamus both admired and envied him.

His advice was regularly sought on many issues and the clarity of his replies stunned the more learned. He had an uncanny ability to accurately forecast the following day's weather from what to the casual observer were obscure sky colourings and cloud formations. For animals and humans alike, he could diagnose the causes of obscure diseases and illnesses and suggest simple yet effective remedies concocted from ingredients in everyday use. His humanitarian role included helping neighbouring farmers, particularly during the peak summer work period. His good deeds also saw many of the villagers safely into the next world, helping to manually open and close their graves and lessening the grief of their loved ones.

On the question of politics and Northern Ireland, Joe could never be motivated and excited to the degree Seamus would have liked. But he was favourably disposed to an United Ireland and whatever tactics were needed to achieve it. He often said so in Seamus' presence, not out of any strong conviction but as a show of support for Seamus' republican ideals. Within the confidential atmosphere of his own house, Seamus expressed his misgivings about Paul's army role and his attitude towards Northern Ireland. 'Somewhat like having a son becoming a priest, I was overjoyed at Paul's decision to take up an army career. I thought that in some small way my youngest son could advance the cause in which all true Irishmen believe. His tour of duty in Lebanon inexplicably changed all that. Within days of his emotional homecoming, he informed me that his army life will be devoted to preserving peace and not fomenting war. I hear he may soon be off to some other world trouble spot. Yes, it is a great disappointment and let down and he brings shame not only to his family but the entire village. I am sorry to burden you Joe with this bad news but I know that, as always, I can confide in you.'

Joe knew better than to say something that might only fuel an already hot fire. He tried to reassure Seamus that Paul was always an exemplary son and his actions should not be misinterpreted as a blatant defiance of his father's wishes. 'Young men of today have their independent views and desires and these ought to be respected. In ten years from now you may well look on Paul's stance in a completely different light.' Seamus hoped he would still be around ten years hence and the faint smile beginning to appear on his face confirmed that his agitation was subsiding and he was becoming more at ease with himself.

'Hasn't Deirdre taken a fancy to a young Northener' enquired Joe, as if to change Seamus' mood to a more positive mode? It was a subject alien to Joe's heart due to his limited interest in and knowledge of relationships. 'Few things in my life give me greater satisfaction than Deirdre's love affair. She knew what she wanted from day one and I understand it grows in intensity by the day. Our family and the McCabes have for long been close friends and their accidental first meeting is the stuff of fairytales. Jim McCabe is a true republican and it took all his charm to bring Deirdre to his way of thinking. Now their emotions and ideals are interlocked.' Joe was in awe of the strong feeling Seamus infused into each spoken word. Seamus radiated happiness and Joe was eager to receive as much as possible of the "fallout".

Seamus was equally satisfied with his continuing good friendship with Shane McCabe, which by now had stood the test of more than a quarter of a century. Shane's most recent letter of two weeks ago was full of 1960 reminiscences of a keenly-contested football game between their respective counties of Down and Kerry that first brought them together. He confessed to being still football crazy in spite of Down's slump in achievements since the late 1960s. It contrasted with Kerry's spectacular four All-Ireland wins from 1978 to 1981 but he appreciated that such feats were taken for granted within the "Kingdom". Irish football was what cemented their national aspirations and the results were of secondary importance. Shane was fully aware of Jim's growing affection for Deirdre and was excited at the prospect of it bringing the two families still closer. He used his limited diplomatic skills to allow the relationship proceed without undue parental interference.

Irrespective of its outcome, the forces keeping Shane and Seamus close friends would become even stronger for the remaining healthy years God was prepared to grant them.

If political progress could keep pace with the building of friendships, Seamus would be a far happier man. In his short life he witnessed fleeting rays of hope obliterated by numerous disappointments which slowly eroded the patience and endurance of countless brave men and women. That was after attempting and testing a wide variety of strategies. After a quarter century of his life and energy, had he and his associates advanced one iota the cause to which they all subscribed? It was a thought he intuitively knew ought not occupy the remotest corner of his mind, lest it dampen his will to continue. But, wasn't it time to realistically appraise progress and, as a consequence, exploit the positives?

He engaged Joe Moriarty's attention as he finished the sport pages of the weekly "Kerryman" newspaper. Seamus went on to describe how difficult it was to continue on an optimistic vein, given the repeated set-backs. But then has anyone read or heard about a republican movement enjoying an easy passage to independence? Without a firm belief in being able and willing to pick oneself up from the ashes and try ... and try again, there is little hope indeed. Not that there hasn't been enough ashes and destruction of buildings and human life. There is, unfortunately, no viable alternative to proceeding along this route. Like constantly dripping water wearing a stone, so too will undying persistence slowly but surely break the will of longtime oppressors. If Seamus bothered to look sideways, he would see from Joe's rueful smile he wasn't entirely convinced.

'Well, have we taken the correct course of action, then?' Joe wondered.

Seamus rushed to continue, questioning whether they had taken enough time to evaluate the merits and impact of foreign assistance. Few Irish people have doubted Libya's willingness to support liberation movements and the I.R.A. is extremely grateful to the regime for its continuous aid during testing times. But, the international community regard this type of assistance as exceeding the bounds of decency, often resulting in the deaths of too many innocent people. International surveillance on Libya prised the I.R.A. away from this hitherto staunch ally. However, there is hope that Libya's funds now being channelled through Syria will maintain the momentum. He considered it unfortunate that the change of political thinking in the Soviet Union reduced the scale of assistance and may even put its future in jeopardy.

Joe, the political novice, was determined to air his own unbiased views. 'I am always suspicious of large and powerful countries purporting to help small nations, often under a range of disguises. The questions we need to ask are: how much material support is forthcoming, to what extent does it advance the cause for which it is intended and what strings are attached or pay-back demanded? There is little given free in this world, even when it comes from a country so wealthy it scarcely dents its resources. The donor has a stranglehold on the recipient from which it is impossible to extricate itself. That is to express it in extreme tones but the reality is not very different. My humble experience is that, if you cannot achieve your goal with your own sweat and blood, you should not rely heavily on others to do it for you. Or, should we compromise our political freedom by accepting sometimes poor quality or even obsolete equipment from the Soviet Union? We want to make sure we do not end up losing more than we stand to gain.'

As it was steadily approaching midnight, Joe was not only sleepy but realised that, however true Seamus' pronouncements were, his limited education and political experience prevented him from continuing an intelligent discussion. Besides, Nora's entry to monitor the quality of the turf fire provided the gentlest of hints that Joe might just be outstaying his welcome. Even for a man who had virtual permanent tenancy rights, he hated to be seen abusing them. With fewer farewell statements than greetings on his arrival, Joe took his usual leave and was quickly absorbed into the midnight darkness.

The thirty minutes around midnight came to be regarded by Seamus and Nora as the 'quality half hour' when only the two of them occupied the fireside chairs, with the dying embers radiating a gentle heat. It all began no differently tonight as they had done throughout the many nights of their long marriage. It was the private 30 minutes for recounting the ups and downs of the day and the family's progress, adventures and problems.

There was an openness and frankness displayed in recent sessions signalling a coming of age in their relationship that was long overdue. Nora pushed her chair closer to Seamus to remind him that no word of what she had to say ought to be lost. It was Nora's way of saying there were issues she wanted to discuss forthwith.

'While we should thank the Lord for many blessings, a couple of matters worry me,' began Nora. 'Deirdre's letters deal at length with her romance with Jim McCabe and, more significantly, her growing involvement in the republican movement. She never harboured strong nationalist ideals but Jim's influence lured her in that direction. Her teaching profession now takes second place to the sinister role of bomb-maker and terrorist. She says this is a part-time activity at weekends but I know it goes far beyond that. When I hear almost daily TV and radio reports of terrorist attacks in the north, my heart stops until I hear the names of those involved. At night, I lay sleepless, often hours on end, thinking of what might happen, only to be reassured by her later phone call saying she survived another nerve-racking ordeal.'

Seamus, in one of his rare gestures of affection, put his right arm around Nora, gently pulled her towards him and kissed her warmly. 'Promise me you will stop worrying about Deirdre who is able to take good care of herself.' He could not conceal his pride for what Deirdre was doing in her own small way to further the cause of Irish unification. He wasn't convinced his few words and mild expression of his love for Nora lessened her fear or increased her chances of more restful sleep.

*

Authorities in Damascus were reluctant to give reasons for their inaction. This ran counter to their overt show of enthusiasm for assisting during the mission's visit. Once again, the onus fell on Gerald to decipher and make sense of the confusing rumours, innuendos and occasional statements originating at lower levels of the eastern administration. The message, when it finally surfaced, came as little surprise. President Siddique remained steadfast to his assertion that, without the active involvement of experienced and battle-hardened Palestinians, the hardware they were ready to supply to the I.R.A. could not be used to maximum effect. Gerald's immediate reaction was mildly hostile. 'Was the President unaware of or blind to the magnificent achievements of the I.R.A.'s striking force? Had he been too busy to watch on his TV screen repeated acts of heroism rivalling those of the most experienced Palestinians?.' Incensed though he initially was, he appreciated that "beggars can't be choosers" and, when the dust settled, he must explain as calmly and diplomatically as he could why they ought to reach a compromise on his farsighted proposal.

In the management hierarchy strictly adhered to in Arab culture, Gerald was convinced that the letter he addressed to Naji Ahmad, Assistant Chief of Syria's Armed Forces, would end up on President Siddique's desk to await a final decision. He, therefore, couched his statements in diplomatic phraseology of which he had little experience. He tempered his unwillingness to involve Palestinians with a few conciliatory statements. 'This is not to say we are unwilling to accept the help of Palestinians under any circumstances. We fully recognise our joint efforts will bring about a more speedy resolution but the logistical problems associated with foreign troop participation is beyond my own powers and all in the I.R.A's administration. We fully respect and appreciate your genuine enthusiasm to give maximum support and, should conditions change or the going gets tougher, we will consider all possible options including your own excellent idea at an opportune time.'

Although unaware when writing it, the last sentence proved to be decisive in coaxing the President to relent. It contained two appealing aspects. Praising the President's original and novel idea did much to boost his already healthy *ego* while leaving the door ajar for possible future troop involvement eased his anxiety, an important "face-saving" gesture. Gerald was stunned at how speedily action then took place. Once the green light was given by the President, orders filtered down the line in true Arab fashion and unblocked all the previous obstacles.

It meant dispatching more arms and ammunition than the I.R.A. was initially able to accept and deploy. There was an urgent meeting of senior staff to draw up plans which were rigidly enforced. Foremost among the priorities was reactivating the network of receiving agents and spies both in Britain and mainland Europe. The scaling down of activities over the past year meant that a once well-functioning set-up required reorganizing. With the stepped-up weaponry from Syria, the final years of the 1980s witnessed a bombing campaign the scale and intensity of which wasn't heretofore seen. It was as if all involved felt it was a make or break situation, throwing whatever was available at the old enemy. Even if only a fraction of the arms was successfully deployed, it could wreak untoward havoc on the opposition's capacity to contain it. But this was precisely the I.R.A.'s intention from the very start and now Syria's generosity gave it the best chance yet of realising it.

There was little need to convince Northern Ireland republicans, as history had repeatedly shown, that however hard they try they cannot fully succeed without the help of their like-minded southerners. Weapons and ammunition can more easily be stored and hidden on the southern side of the border, away from the prying eyes of northern security forces, but within agonizingly close range of British military targets. It was these cross-border incursions that proved so effective in inflicting maximum damage in the past. Emanating from within the Irish Republic, there was little the British could do to stem the flow except to complain to the Irish Government that its gardai were not vigilant enough. That was a well-recognized understatement since the Irish police forces were often perceived to 'look the other way' when it came to apprehending political activists. The artificial border is regarded as a semi-permeable membrane which, through the process of osmosis, allows the selective movement of troops, and their accompanying arms, in either direction as politically expedient. Republicans 'milked' it to the utmost.

As new mostly-underground arms stores were created south

of the border, it called for more I.R.A. recruits from southern counties to man important positions. Vincent Tuohy needed little persuasion to become involved. Not only was he now an experienced and senior officer but he welcomed the opportunity of meeting and working with Liam McCabe whom he had not seen since visiting the Soviet Union together three years ago. Although reluctant to admit it, there was the additional prospect of resuming his relationship with Jane McCabe and nurturing it beyond its rather "cold" and informal Soviet beginning. He did not minimize the risks in cross-border gun-running and engaging in the biggest operation yet against the British forces and their perceived Northern Ireland accomplices. His imminent move northwards both excited and scared him.

Vincent's reunion with Liam was cordial but businesslike. After a week's adjustment they both realised there was little time and place for leisure and socialising amid the increasing hostilities and confrontations. They were members of a large team of volunteers ready and willing to sacrifice much - even their very lives - to achieve their ultimate goal of a free and independent Ireland, embracing all 32 counties. They knew the odds were stacked against them in the short term but, like many generations of their ancestors, patience and perseverance would sustain them and, hopefully, win out in the end. What was different about this new phase of the war was its waging on three distinct fronts i.e. Northern Ireland, England and the European continent. Vincent and Liam were determined to win as many battles as possible in a war that had all the hallmarks of being destructive and bloody.

For the first few weeks, in a house less than a mile from the border, they stayed with the McCracken family, passionately sympathetic to republicanism. Although God hadn't blessed Michael and Mary McCracken with any children of their own, families who could were able to rely on the McCrackens to help their children achieve their utmost for the Irish liberation movement. Ever since the renewed war against the British commenced in 1969 Michael McCracken, then an able-bodied man of 31 years, often stared death in the face in numerous skirmishes with British troops on the northern side of the border. On his small 35 acre farm, scarcely able to support his wife and himself, he erected sheds and later underground bunkers to store arms and ammunition to seriously threaten his northern enemies. Recent Syrian importations were likely to tax even further his limited storage facilities. He was but one of several scattered along the southern edge of the border on whom British intelligence was keeping a very close eye. But knowing full well who the troublemakers were did not give the British the licence to cross the border in search and destroy missions, a constant source of annoyance and frustration. Now Michael, on the threshold of his 50th birthday, was beginning to show his age, less able for the rigours of war but an ideal mentor and adviser to those who could. The timing of Vincent's and Liam's visit, therefore, could hardly have been better.

Michael was one of a select band of cunning "foxes" who had learned through the sheer agony of sleepless nights on the run, injuries and gunshot wounds, hospitalisation and even periodic imprisonment, the heavy human toll of a cross-border clandestine guerrilla war. At the same time, it was slowly but surely proving to be Britain's "Achilles heel", just as the border between north and south Vietnam had been for the Americans and their allies. But, in contrast to the North Vietnamese pushing southwards, he felt with a mixture of hope and confidence that the southern Irish would one day move northwards and reunite once and for all the whole island of Ireland which was their God-given right. He lost no time in briefing Vincent and Liam, treating them as eager and courageous sons he himself never had, on the various routes to the north, the identified targets, the *modus operandi*, the risks associated with various terrorist attacks and the escape paths to recognized safe havens. With good advance planning and proper execution, he advised them, they too might live to celebrate their 50th birthday, an encouragement that only slightly impressed the two virtual novices.

It took less than three weeks for these young men to experience the bloodshed and horror that up to now was alien to them. In the company of three senior I.R.A. militia, they took a lead role in planting and detonating a concealed bomb placed in the centre of a country road just ten miles south-west of Northchester city. They had advance information about a routine patrol of eight British troops in a military jeep shortly before 10 p.m. Vincent, on the receipt of up-front advice from Liam, pressed the remote control button with split-second timing to send all eight to an untimely and horrific death. Liam has memories, he later wished he never had, of initial screams of anguish followed by wails for help. Those who died instantly were the lucky ones compared to three unfortunates who vainly struggled for 30 agonising minutes before dying where they lay. As Vincent and Liam made their getaway, the carnage and bloodshed of this initial escapade was certain to haunt them for many years to come. Their immediate concern was to retreat as quickly and unobstrusively as possible to a safe hiding place, away from the security forces who must surely be in hot pursuit. As terror and fear enveloped them, causing a numbness in their feet and stalling progress, they both wished the ground beneath them opened and gave them refuge.

Strange how the perpetrators of dreadful crimes possess an uncanny ability to escape, receive protection from the law and re-emerge later to start all over again. The artificial border, therefore, between southern and northern Ireland, dreaded and despised though it may be by republicans, gave many of these same people a buffer against seizure and sentencing. Vincent and Liam fell within this category. Through a number of so-called "safe houses", strategically located away from the scene of the crime, they spent some time in each and after seven days made their way back undetected to Michael McCracken's house. The pangs of remorse weighed heavily on their shoulders for several days and it took all of Michael's experience and cajoling to get them back on track. 'Remember it is a job and a duty like any other,' he admonished them, which was cold comfort to their troubled minds. As Michael had foreseen, this initial raw confrontation with death steeled them for even greater atrocities to come. During the following year Vincent and Liam were in the vanguard of several other attacks, only marginally escaping injury and even death on more than one occasion. They were but two of many I.R.A. activists who were striking fear and heartbreak into Northern Ireland's community at this time.

Hitting English targets and bringing the war to the enemy's own doorstep was what the I.R.A. long felt would bring about major concessions and a speedier resolution. The hitherto piecemeal approach was having limited effect but, now awash with Syrian-provided weaponry, the time was right for taking the war to a higher level. The network was already in place and required only supreme command orders to unleash timely but devastating blows. They were heartened by small periodic past successes. Any organisation that comes within inches of assassinating a "sitting" British Prime Minister deserves to be taken seriously. Tighter security would likely exclude a repeat occurrence but they were prepared to damage the very heart of the English Establishment. It required only a small number of the large Irish population in Britain and they concentrated on recruiting the unemployed and those disillusioned with their lot. There were many to choose from and the starting date was only a month behind that of Northern Ireland.

Because it coincided with the start of winter when farm work was less, Gerald Dowling was able to lead the operations around London, the main focus of attention in England. He arrived when everything was in an advance state of preparedness and his first major task was to restrain them from acting irrationally. To keep the British on high alert and to continually harass and even embarrass them, Gerald tried to streamline operations so that there was one attack, however small, every two weeks. No sooner did they recover from one than another greatly heightened the tension. In time, the frustrated British people would pressurize the Government into more speedily solving the Northern Ireland problem, the terms of which might invariably favour the I.R.A. Or would it only strengthen British resolve to resist and fight back and to deny the I.R.A. what easily might have been granted to them in the first instance? It was a gamble Gerald and others were willing to take.

The 'war on England' continued unabated through a winter of discontent. It began in London with small bombs being detonated at random locations, causing substantial damage to buildings but, apart from minor injuries, there were no deaths. These served as a warning of what could follow. It did not take the I.R.A. long to raise the siege and target VIP's and politicians, culminating in abortive attempts on the lives of Westminster parliamentarians and even the Prime Minister at 10 Downing Street. It was about as far as they could go. So thought most, but not the indefatigable Gerald. He was encouraged and honoured by a letter he received the previous day from Naji Ahmad, Assistant Chief of Syria's Armed Forces and endorsed at the highest level by President Siddique. He began by saying:

'Both the President and myself have watched with interest the progress of events in Northern Ireland, and more recently throughout England. May I compliment you and all your colleagues on the successful strikes against the enemy. In my humble opinion you have achieved more in the past six months than the entire previous six years. I say this, not to boast about the kind and power of the arms we gave you, but to recognize how effectively you used them. You have the British Government seriously worried and, should you be able to maintain the momentum at this level for another six months, you will force them into making decisions that can only be to your great advantage. Sooner, rather than later, their patience and will to persevere must be seriously stretched.'

It was the last paragraph, however, that raised imponderables for Gerald. 'The offer we made earlier, which was then unacceptable to you, still holds - that's to send a limited number of "crack" Syrian troops to add muscle and guerrilla warfare experience to your own men. I firmly believe the coming months will be crucial and working together we can finish the job. You must also be heartened by the insignificant seizures of in-bound arms which enhance your already healthy stockpile. I appreciate the difficulties and sensitivities surrounding the involvement of foreign personnel but, should you find a way to surmount these, we stand ready to help in any way possible.'

With many pressing problems on Gerald's mind, he hastily stuffed the letter into his inside pocket. He knew it called for another diplomatic non-acceptance reply, when he could find the time, and he should couch his response so as not to offend his very generous benefactor. Progress with his English operations were better than he could have imagined and he would do nothing that might damage that. Among his friends, Gerald acquired a reputation of having a keen insight into the strengths and sensitivities of Arab culture and found it easy to do business with them. He was confident of being able to address their objectives and concerns without jeopardising the I.R.A's military successes.

But the I.R.A.'s most valuable trump-card and propaganda coup were reserved for the European mainland. For all the atrocities in Northern Ireland over the previous 18 years, only a small percentage of Europeans, and far fewer on other continents, were remotely aware of the underlying problems precipitating hostilities in the first instance. An informed public is best positioned to judge for itself, to identify where the injustices exist and to row in with the cause of the disadvantaged. The Palestinians' plight is publicised worldwide, and understood to varying degrees, and it has attracted considerable sympathy and invoked calls for concrete action. Why should the I.R.A.'s cause be any different?

Jim McCabe, for one, was convinced it shouldn't but steps to correct it were neither straightforward nor simple. Choosing to work in a country far from home against culture and language barriers wasn't easy and the correct personnel and backup support needed to be put in place. Although he had long contemplated taking the war to Europe, it took all of his energy to bring it to fruition six months after the Northern Ireland and English campaigns. He would have liked to lead the operation himself but his home duties demanded all his time. He was lucky and privileged to have Helen Quinn, an experienced worker since the early days of the civil rights protests, take up the gauntlet and agree to be in charge of a small select group operating from a secret German hide-out. Ignoring the risk of being accused of nepotism, he had no hesitation in appointing his young brother Frank to be an active participant. Frank specialised in languages (with emphasis on German and French) during his university degree course and was ideally suited to the role. Even his physique and manner were Germanic and he was soon to face his stiffest test.

Their stay in Germany was of fixed duration and specific in purpose. 'We will be in and out of Germany within three months,' declared Helen to her seven compatriots before leaving Dublin airport on a flight bound for Frankfurt. She described her plan to them at last week's meeting. 'Our objective is clearcut: to attack a British military base near Cologne in Germany where troops are serving with NATO, causing significant material damage to property and possible injury or even deaths. For the first two months we will get acquainted with the terrain, gather information about the base and its detailed operations over 24 hours, monitor troop manoeuvres and movements and slowly gain their confidence. This last duty will be coordinated by Frank McCabe, because of his language expertise, and is, perhaps, the most important component: looking and speaking like a German will not arouse the expected suspicion among the British, who are ever on the alert for would-be I.R.A. infiltrators. Not only must Frank gain access to the base, he must mingle with the British at off-duty locations such as bars and night clubs.'

'The remaining six of you will prepare and later plant the seeds of destruction. You will secretly conceal a bomb just inside the base's perimeter wall from where an underground wire goes under the wall to a remote control devise in a secure location. On Wednesday of the 10th week this bomb will be detonated to coincide with the troops' scheduled manoeuvres, as per Frank's insider knowledge and with the expected devastation. A week later, in a selected bar or night club, a time bomb will explode wreaking havoc and killing some of those present. Then, the hard work for us begins, to get quickly and invisibly on our escape routes home. We'll have many dress rehearsals covering each and every facet of the operation. I must alert you to the risks involved but your courage and dedication will see you through. Good luck and May God protect you.'

Her years of rigorous apprenticeship in Northern Ireland had taught Helen not only to adequately plan for major tasks but to do her utmost to complete them successfully. She was equally committed to this latest German assignment and marshalled her forces as no man could. The successes were also as she had predicted. The bomb exploded within the base at precisely 12:01 p.m., killing four young men and seriously injuring another sixteen, six of whom were later to die in hospital. It caused havoc and mayhem in an area usually renowned for its tranquillity. In a country harbouring many foreigners and organisations of different beliefs and persuasions, nobody was quick to point an accusing finger. Nor would the I.R.A. admit responsibility in advance of completing the job. The second shock one week later, as the dust settled and some semblance of normality returned, was more than anybody could bear.

The explosion occurred at 11:30 p.m. in a bar frequented by British soldiers and a mere two kilometres from the base. It was timed to go off when, with the drinks flowing freely and everyone in jovial mood, few would have noticed anything suspicious lying about. The two Irishmen, who thirty minutes earlier had finished their drinks at a corner table, made sure to conceal the small brown paper package behind an out-of-sight coat rack. Though appearing to behave normally, they chose the corner location for two reasons - to be out of full view and to be able to leave unnoticed through the side door. This they did at 11 p.m. sharp, giving them enough time to reach a safe haven within 30 minutes. Ten men were blown apart by this latest atrocity and another 12 were gravely injured, with the final casualty count reaching 15. One of the greatest manhunts in German history was set in motion.

Next day's international papers carried the grim statistics of the carnage and harped back to the previous week's casualties. Without the I.R.A.'s spontaneous admission of guilt, German security had accumulated sufficient evidence of its responsibility but further hard facts were needed. It was the type of publicity the I.R.A. had long craved for and which lured them to Germany. It was another significant *coup* for Helen Quinn and her dedicated band. They thought more in terms of the results and less of the human tragedy and suffering.

They took the slow route homeward, opting for various

means of transport and trying to conceal their real identities. Helen visualised Gerald's delight at what they had done and, perhaps, he could convince the Syrians that the I.R.A. was capable of going it alone. Taking all three fronts into consideration it was the I.R.A.'s best year and the only question remaining was could it stay the distance and finish the task?

Amid the euphoria, there was but one 'sting in the tail.' A spot check on the homeward run revealed that Frank McCabe was absent. In the security clampdown, had he been arrested and imprisoned? Doing all the upfront information gathering and posing as a native German exposed him more than the others and could have speeded his arrest. Helen was decidedly upbeat: 'we achieved far more than we set out to do, seven returned unscathed and I firmly believe Frank McCabe will somehow wriggle his way back to the fold.'

*

Jim McCabe's work over the past two years became an obsession. He couldn't help nostalgically reflecting on his leisurely six hour days as a young teacher in Liscorley when, after his 3 p.m. finish, he could if so inclined complete another six to eight hours of work before bedtime. Getting indefinite leave from teaching and joining the republican movement saw a gradual but steady erosion of his free time and an upward surge in his responsibilities. Not that he felt totally unhappy with his lot but he would appreciate a more respectable balance between work and leisure. Now that the guerrilla war was raging furiously, it was unlikely he could get much of the latter for the foreseeable future.

Three years ago, at the age of 25, he'd decided to leave the family home and invest in his future. With a small down-payment, and the major cost mortgaged over 30 years, he purchased a three-bedroomed bungalow on the northern edge of Liscorley just three kilometres from his old home. Like most parents, Shane and Brenda were sad to see him go but respected his wish to be independent and to plan and run his own life. After all, he was within "shouting distance". He settled quickly and arranged the house as only a bachelor would, calling on his Mam's help once a month to straighten the mess. This, she said, she would willingly do as long as the good Lord spared her.

Jim converted the smallest of the three bedrooms into an office where he did all his work, when not on outdoor duty. In hindsight, it was a bad decision as it committed him to more work hours than he otherwise would. Now approaching midnight and at the end of a 16 hour day, he sat at his desk and pondered this and several other issues crossing his mind. He was pleased how his hard work brought better than expected results and was more optimistic now than he ever had been, especially with the successful strikes in England and Germany. The question that remained was, how much better can it get?

One thing he needed to improve was his relationship with Deirdre Dowling whom he might easily be accused of taking for granted. More than six years elapsed since they first met and, while there were no serious intentions by either party during the first few years, it took on a new meaning when Deirdre started teaching close to Liscorley. It was an opportunity contrived by Jim and readily grasped by Deirdre. He fondly remembers the gleam in her eye when he suggested the move and life wasn't the same since. Formal dates were fewer than normal, something that was outside their control, but there was a quality to their social contacts that more than compensated. Jim's duties often took him by the school where Deirdre taught and he would stop briefly to greet her and see if everything was going as expected. At times when Deirdre was busy with classes, he made a point of not disturbing her. Instead, he would leave a note which always ended with the endearment 'I love you, Jim xxx'. He genuinely felt it, was aware that words came easily and had a limited time span and that Deirdre would soon need clarification about their future.

Deirdre could be excused for discreetly trying to expedite things. She was now 29 years old, some 14 months older than Jim, and much of the past six years had passed her by. A few of her close friends had married before they were 25. Not quite 23 years of age when she met Jim, she too once harboured the ambition of following in her friends' footsteps. She took care not to be seen to pressurize Jim as that could send the wrong signal and cause a permanent break. She made up her mind to be patient, intuitively knowing he cared for and loved her. Why is it, she mused, girls cannot be equal partners in a relationship or will we have to wait another century before this much-needed change takes place?

She was happy with the way her career was developing. She always regarded teaching as a vocation, somewhat akin to nursing, not selfishly considering oneself but the educational and welfare needs of others. In her short number of years in the profession it gave her immense satisfaction to witness the success of school-leavers, often progressing to be leaders and innovators in society. Through various means such as letters or casual meetings on the streets or in supermarkets, her morale was uplifted by words of praise from former pupils whose success in life was partly attributed to her superior teaching skills. It was the type of encouragement that propelled her along when the going occasionally became tougher than normal. She never wished to do anything else but teach and had a burning desire to continue doing so as long as her body and mind allowed her.

The monotony that was beginning to creep into Jim's daily routine exacted a heavy toll. He was no longer having the continuous support of his parents and he neglected to eat regularly and benefit from nutritionally-balanced meals. He not only admitted to missing his Mam's good cooking but the stability and peace of mind that come from knowing your parents are at every beck and call. Moreover, the eerie silence that greeted him on returning from field duty confirmed the loneliness of a bachelor's existence. Despite being fatigued at this post-midnight hour and before he wrapped up the long-drawn-out office work, he decided to take a few extra minutes to plan and sow the seeds of a better future. In retrospect, it was short term quality work that was to change his life irrevocably.

No longer was he to take Deirdre for granted or deny her the long overdue attention. To put words into practice he will go to her school tomorrow, not during the working hours when she is inundated with children's demands but, when classes are just finished. This will give ample time to discuss at length and set many things straight. He was sure Deirdre understood the reasons why they saw far too little of each other in the past six months for which they both shared the blame. Instead of attending to republican duties over the following weekend, he might suggest they both keep it free and go somewhere together. It was something Jim often considered doing but baulked at the prospect of Deirdre's refusal, considering it brash of him and having undertones of intimacy. But did they not know each other sufficiently well now and wasn't it high time they openly expressed their feelings?

It came far easier than he expected. On arriving at Deirdre's school 15 minutes after her final class and all the children had scattered, he found her in the classroom tidying all the papers and ensuring everything was neatly in place. He could hardly have arrived at a more opportune moment. 'Now I am convinced teachers get paid half enough for all the jobs they do' was his opening remark. The very sight of Jim, not to mention his morale-boosting statement, provided the spark for Deirdre to run towards him, wrap her tender arms around him and shower him with kisses to which he responded equally affectionately. They stood there for several minutes, locked in each other's arms, more reminiscent of teenage lovers rather than mature adults. It smacked of long-separated loved ones reuniting after having had too few opportunities to express their love. The sense of urgency with which they embraced revealed they were more than prepared to make up for lost time.

Without too much coaxing Deirdre accepted his invitation to an early informal meal in a local restaurant. It gave them the chance to catch up with events of several weeks, to discuss their schedules so as to allow more time together and, if possible, determine each other's interest in and commitment to a continuing relationship. It was soon clear, to all who wished to notice, there was a *rapport* and chemistry between them that was not only to grow but race ahead as no one predicted. It was as if, in this rustic eating house, they had an appetite both for the food soon to be served and the love they were yet to experience. 'We were foolish to neglect our social engagements because of our heavy work loads,' began Jim, 'and we must ensure it doesn't recur.' Deirdre's broad smile and nod of approval needed no words to reassure him. She interjected 'apart from my regular duty on Saturdays, I am free for the remainder of the weekend and one or two nights during the week,' giving Jim ample scope to respond positively. He was more than forthcoming 'let's promise that henceforth we'll meet every Saturday evening and at least once mid-week.' It was a commitment that both realised came far too late but they were determined to look forward rather than backward.

Jim later reflected pleasurably on how he made all the right moves on that night. He confessed openly to Deirdre of his earlier shortcomings, bared his heart and soul about his feelings and love for her and resolved to make amends. Deirdre needed little convincing. All these years, more from what Jim said than done, she had guessed his positive intentions. According to her innocent judgment he fell within a category of Irishmen prepared to let things slip and never in a rush to express his true feelings to a member of the opposite sex. Once it is recognised and understood there are few problems and many happy marriages stem from this obscure and weak foundation. Just now Jim's mind was focusing on this self-same route to happiness.

Two weeks later Jim did his utmost to ensure their Saturday evening together was a date to remember. Before then he had a lot of work and soul-searching to do. He was satisfied Deirdre was the girl with whom he wanted to spend the rest of his life and he was hopeful if not confident she felt likewise. They were pretty sure there wouldn't be any objection from their respective parents which was a major advantage. The common republican bond copperfastened that. Jim knew he was moving in the right direction but there would surely be many twists and turns along the way.

For their mid-week date, Jim took Deirdre to her local cinema where a Hollywood movie was showing. From previews he had seen, he was ready to forego his own preference and opt for one of Deirdre's feminine favourites. The central theme was a love story in which the two protagonists had their differences before ending on a happy note. Later over coffee he found the overall mood and atmosphere congenial to broach a question he had long pondered but could never muster up the courage to ask. Across a small table, bedecked with only the flickering flame of a tiny candle, he placed his hand on Deirdre's, looked straight into her lovely blue eyes and posed the question, 'My loving Deirdre, will you marry me?'

She stared and remained silent for another five seconds as if in a trance, which seemed like an eternity to Jim, before her face broke into a radiant smile and she could not contain her emotion. Then, to the amazement and obvious delight of a dozen others nearby, she jumped from her seat, ran to Jim and threw her arms wantonly around him. 'I will, I will, I will!' she squealed with delight, after which they passionately kissed in full view of the small audience. It was a fun-filled evening which dissipated doubts and dissolved any artificial barriers which might hitherto have existed between them.

Both of them moved about in a virtual daze for the next couple of days, neither divulging the good news to anyone. On the evening of the third day, when Jim arrived home to find his mother struggling to finish his monthly house cleaning, he ran to her and gave the warmest embrace he could manage. Then, holding her at arms' length and giving her a loving smile as only a son can, he motioned her to a seat. Sitting on the sofa, with one arm around her, he began. 'Mam, I cannot thank you enough for all you have done for me down through the years. I must honestly confess I am ashamed to be still depending upon you when I should be independent and self-reliant. Look at the way you have laboured today to keep my house from looking like a pigsty! You must surely think it is high time I did something about it. Well, I can emphatically say that very recently I took the first steps along a route which will lessen your burden within the next year or two. In brief, I intend to get married. The words brought tears of joy to Brenda's eyes and she couldn't wait to break the wonderful news to Shane.

But it was their date on the following Saturday that proved to be the high point. Jim wanted to keep it low key until the right moment. He had arranged to collect her at 7 p.m. and bring her to his favourite "watering hole", the Nag's Head, in Liscorley. There would surely be many of his friends in the bar later that evening but he could select a quiet corner away from the raucous crowds that usually descended on the premises. He could easily secure a table in a section cordoned off for serving food and out of earshot of the noisy masses. It wasn't the ideal *ambience* but one that combined reasonable quality food with pleasant conviviality. There was little better to be found in the small town of Liscorley and, besides, Jim was more at ease here. He was on first name terms with all the staff and he was assured of the best attention and service. This was vindicated when he was quickly ushered to a remote corner where they were able to enjoy the warmth and comfort of a blazing log fire.

Before ordering food Jim asked Deirdre if she would like to have wine, something he had never done before and which suggested this may be no ordinary occasion. While reluctant to admit it and showing no outward signs, it was Jim's way of calming his nerves and that of his loved one and to be comfortable in each other's company. Sipping the first glasses of wine into empty stomachs helped the process immensely after which they enjoyed the best food that could be found in the *a la carte* menu. After they had partaken of starter and main course dishes, with exotic names neither could fully decipher, they relaxed for ten minutes before ordering sumptuous helpings of high-energy desserts, guaranteed to trigger heart attacks among the over 50s This was washed down by numerous cups of coffee interlaced with two 'shots' of strong liqueur. Jim felt so satiated he was delighted he could afford to eat like this only once every twelve months.

Some of the weight gained at the table was soon lost on the nearby dance floor. The four piece local band played Irish ballads and folk music every Friday and Saturday night on an elevated stage at one end of the lounge. It generally had a captive audience and this night was no different. As Jim and Deirdre waltzed fluidly they were greeted by numerous well-wishers, many of whom were observant enough to notice a sparkling diamond engagement ring on her finger. She was reluctant to admit that it was scarcely one hour ago Jim had bestowed on her this precious gift. Having had her previous consent to marriage made it only a little easier for Jim. He waited until the second liqueur had steadied his nervous hands before placing the glitzy ring on her tender white finger, with no commotion and publicity. By way of apology for not moving faster, Jim said, 'My slowness during the first half of our relationship is more than compensated by the speed of the past six weeks.' Deirdre got what she had always wanted and, for now, she did not contemplate or need any apologies. She was beside herself with excitement and exhilaration.

The second last dance of the night was a slow waltz and an ideal opportunity for a newly-engaged couple to nestle closer and whisper loving endearments. Placing his two arms around her waist, he pulled her closer allowing Deirdre to rest her head on his left shoulder. The closeness of Deirdre's soft bosom against his muscular chest caused Jim's heart to race a little, sending urges to other parts of his body he tried desperately to subdue. It was as if both of them were in seventh Heaven, with neither wishing it to end abruptly. During the dinner Jim told her about how he had furnished his new home to his liking, with his Mam at his beck and call, and reminded her she had yet to see it. Would now be the appropriate time to invite her and could he risk a refusal? He was pleasantly surprised when his casual question of 'what about coming with me to see my new house' was met with her quick positive response 'I was wondering when you would invite me.' Just before the band wrapped up the night's proceedings to the strains of the National Anthem, Jim thanked Deirdre for a wonderful night, the memories of which would forever linger.

They tiptoed their way into the house shortly after midnight hoping the prying eyes of a nosey neighbour would not notice. If Brenda hadn't cleaned a few days before, the house would have been in a greater mess. Jim forewarned her as they entered telling her to disregard the bachelor look and general disorganisation. It was far better than Deirdre anticipated and, besides, there were far more important things on her mind. She struggled with her thoughts while Jim prepared coffee in the kitchen. Had she acceded too readily to his invitation and how should she react if he asked her to stay the night? On their engagement night, a refusal might reveal a coldness and lack of affection. An all-too-ready acceptance could give the impression of being 'free and easy,' something she certainly wasn't. She need not have worried as Jim was just as eager to declare his intentions.

Minutes later when seated side by side on a comfortable couch sipping coffee, Jim put his arm affectionately around Deirdre to comfort and reassure her. 'To put the records straight,' he began, 'I had no ulterior motive, Deirdre, in inviting you to my house. In these days of so much free love and promiscuity, you can be excused for feeling anxious and concerned. Much as I would like to make love to you, I fervently wish we can see our way to postpone this until we are legally husband and wife. I hope you decide to stay and you have your own room and bed. This may not be easy for either of us, Deirdre, but it will be a real test of our love and affection for each other.' The sense of relief and happiness showed instantly on her face, saying 'with those words, you have no idea how close you came to echoing my own wishes and sentiments.' It was a victory for understanding and respect.

Often when finishing office work late at night, Jim listened to his favourite taped music which brought a certain peace and tranquillity. He now switched it on and hoped Deirdre had a similar appreciation. He would keep it at low volume with background airs that facilitated, but not stifled, conversation. With the speakers strategically placed and the sound quality excellent, the music wafted across the room and he switched off a light to make the atmosphere even more congenial. In his few casual romances before meeting Deirdre he had never seriously considered letting them continue beyond a few months. Was he then too immature and unprepared for long term friendships or was he not attracted sufficiently to any of them? Not being able to reset his chronological clock, he would never be one hundred percent sure. But he had no regrets. Looking to the uncertain future, there were few things he could confidently predict, save one. This beautiful girl seated next to him will one day be his wife. In Deirdre he had found the perfect companion and, as far as he could tell, they were perfectly compatible. More from Deirdre's manner and behaviour, than what she said, he sensed it was mutual. He felt perfectly happy and at ease and should he ask for anything more?

From the way Deirdre nestled closer to Jim implied her needs may not yet be fully met. She got to her feet, pulled Jim from the couch and begged him for a couple of dances. These were some of their favourite tunes to which they could sing along. She loved how well he did all the different dances and taught her the intricate steps which she still had to improve upon. While in his arms she knew she was protected and sheltered and wondered would it be always so. The events of the past six weeks had overtaken her but she wasn't complaining because at no time that she could recall had she been so happy and fulfilled. It must be "love", a word so bandied about and of which she knew very little. What she did know was her life had changed irrevocably for the better and she would do all within her powers to keep it on course.

They sat once again, falling into each other's arms as a wave of exhaustion came over them. The music had stopped and an eerie silence descended. Jim rested his head on one arm of the couch and gently pulled Deirdre towards him, causing her to press her soft bosom against his muscular chest. It triggered hormonal flows and arousal as they had not previously experienced and it showed on their faces. Then Jim, slowly and gently without a murmur of disapproval, undid the front three buttons of Deirdre's blouse, inserted his hand between her soft and full boobs and fondled them lovingly, inducing an audible purr of satisfaction. With a little of Jim's encouragement, she unbuttoned his shirt and stroked every muscle of his chest, shoulders and tummy, sending shivers of arousal, bordering on lust, through every sinew of his body. How she would love to explore further but would either be able to pull back from a precipice they were fast approaching? Jim was also in the throes of exceeding his limits, shifting his hands from her breast to the buttocks and soft inner thighs, moves that equally pleased and distressed her. He knew he should stop but did he have the willpower and strength? A fleeting thought crossing his mind worked like magic. As he had promised Deirdre, he wouldn't sacrifice the love and trust they had carefully nurtured for the sake of a moment's pleasure. They had won a victory of sorts, crossing the first of what promised to be many hurdles in a lifelong togetherness.

*

He had a strong interest in records and calculations. There were almost 11,000 sunsets to the west of Table Mountain and Cape Province since Michael McCabe, brother of Shane and uncle of Jim, first landed in South Africa on December 15, 1957. In less than a month's time, he'd be celebrating 30 wonderful years in his adopted country. Through establishing and running his own car sales and servicing, he amassed a good deal of wealth and was enjoying the fruits of his success. Not in a brash and ostentatious way because he always stood ready to assist just and needy causes and was fiercely on the side of the poor and downtrodden. In today's South Africa he could continuously work on these latter aspects from dawn to midnight without denting the overall need but he was loath to give up. He easily saw the time-bomb that was South Africa, which festered for so long, that was certain to detonate within the next few years.

But in his lovely north Johannesburg home this sunny, summer November morn, Michael's thoughts and concerns were almost 7,000 miles further north, in his native Ulster. His business had already prospered when Northern Ireland's violence started in 1969. Hard to imagine how much progress he himself made in the past eighteen years and so little in his beleaguered province. Were they going backwards instead of forwards? Nobody could say for sure. Almost every other day of his working life somebody stopped by his office enquiring about the cause of the fighting, especially after devastating bomb explosions. He countered by saying it was so complex and involved he needed almost an entire day to explain it. What greatly struck him were the varying levels of information, or more appropriately misinformation, about the real situation. If the world at large knew the true reasons, he felt sure public opinion would be massively on the side of the nationalists.

Syria's increased supply of more sophisticated weapons in the past year moved the war to a new and dangerous level, to what appears to be a make or break situation. The stakes were never higher. Continuous bloodshed will only steel the resolve of the British Government to meet force with superior retaliatory strikes. It is splitting the entire Irish nation between the few espousing violence and the masses dearly wishing to see an end to it. It is even infecting and polarizing families which could have repercussions reminiscent of the 1922-23 civil war in the Irish Republic. I remember my late father describe to me the many sad tales of that civil war, contested between the protagonists of a 26 county Irish Republic that exists today and those determined to continue fighting until the entire 32 counties became free and independent. The six northern counties are still but a dream so have we learned much over the past 65 years?

Michael then gazed at a letter which lay in front of him, received a few days ago from a man named Paul Dowling. Although he had never met the young gentleman, the name somehow rang a bell. In Jim McCabe's letter to Michael of a few months ago, he was ecstatic about his romance with Deirdre Dowling and what the future held for both of them. He mentioned how Deirdre's baby brother Paul had recently completed a UN-sponsored peacekeeping assignment in Lebanon and, after a short break, was now engaged in similar-type work in Cyprus. How Paul managed to get Michael's address is a well-guarded secret and he resorted to writing only after the situation became desperate. He saw in Michael not only a man who had a broad understanding of politics, and by implication rational views of Northern Ireland's problems, but also someone who might be willing and ready to influence the minds and hearts of the McCabe and Dowling families. Key members of both families were caught up in a political liberation struggle from which they couldn't easily extricate themselves. If Michael talked sense to his brother Shane and his family, then he might indirectly influence the Dowlings. It was bound to be harder than it seemed but there was nothing to be lost in trying.

Michael realised he owed it not only to Paul but all Irish people to reply in a factual, constructive and sincere manner.

235 Edenvale Road, Alexandra,
Johannesburg

November 23, 1987

Dear Paul,

Your letter of November 10th shows a maturity and knowledge of Northern Ireland's problems and complexities well beyond your years. As I know, living for a time abroad gives you the rare opportunity to look objectively at your own country, to analyse and prioritise the problems and come up with realistic solutions. Above all else, in mixing and socialising with people from many other countries you acquire an understanding and appreciation of their culture and customs that give them that certain uniqueness. Irrespective of race, colour or creed, you soon learn they have the same likes and dislikes, are governed by laudable codes of conduct, are ready to help in times of need and have no aggressive or imperialistic tendencies.

We are kindred spirits in our views and analysis of Northern Ireland. You are rightly worried about the increasing scale of violence, the unnecessary bloodshed and loss of life, many of them innocent, and the fading hope for a just and peaceful solution. The longer the atrocities continue, so will the search for peace be more difficult and complex. I agree that we can play our part, however small, to lessen the violence that is tearing the province apart. We must start within our own families and lead by example. What is fundamentally important is to change the way people think and are motivated. We must peer into their minds and hearts.

Had I not emigrated 30 years ago, I might now think and act just like my brother Shane and nephew Jim - and your father Seamus and brother Gerald. We are to a great extent products of our environment, conditioned and influenced by the behaviour of those around us. We have a similar aspiration, to achieve a free and independent 32-county Ireland, and fundamentally agree on the means to attain it. The die-hard republican few who believe the minority will prevail by force are blind to harsh realities and the events of world history.

In Ireland there is a common fallacy that all English people are bad, not evil per se but responsible in one way or another for all the disasters that befell Ireland while under the imperialistic English yoke. It is only partly true and applies also to the small minority in government who control our destiny. To tarnish all with the same brush is a travesty of justice. We tend to forget that well in excess of 99% of the British have no objection to an united Ireland and some would actively promote it. I married my Brighton-born wife, Jennifer, for her good looks and pleasant personality but I later discovered she was avidly pro-Irish not, I might hastily add, out of any sense of loyalty to her husband but driven by a code of democratic principles. We must not harbour grudges against the majority of a nation who had no say or influence on how the Ireland of yesteryear was ruled and mistreated. In brief, we must be mature enough to forgive, if not entirely forget.

In early 1970, shortly after the resumption of fighting, a small group attending our local Catholic church decided to do something small but constructive. On two successive Sundays during the 11 o'clock mass, four people (one from each part of Ireland, one from England and another from Scotland) went in succession to the altar and recited prayers for peace in Northern Ireland. Each in his own carefully-chosen words pleaded with God to restore calm to an area that was rapidly careering out of control. Highly significant was the fact that all four were of different religious affiliations, only one being Catholic. It did not prevent them, as it certainly would in Northern Ireland, from briefly transcending their own specific beliefs to join hands with others for the common good. You might say the prayers fell on deaf ears but that misses the point. The very same religions are practised separately in Northern Ireland but could you ever visualise the same gesture of magnanimity being manifested there? Their reluctance to move away from established entrenched positions and embrace change only stifles progress.

Having worked in other countries, you will have been heartened by the way Irish people generally are warmly received and liked. You and I, as well as millions worldwide, feel justifiably proud of being Irish, except on rare occasions. The exceptions are when I.R.A. bombs, planted and detonated by so-called Irish freedom fighters, kill and maim people, many of whom are innocent by-standers including young children. During the 1970s, when an I.R.A. bomb destroyed part of an English midland city, I happened to be standing outside my office when the news was reported on the radio. When a passer-by asked a man filling his car with gasoline who he thought was responsible, the man replied, 'Don't you know well it's those f---ing Irish once again.' At that precise moment my shame was such I wished the ground would open and 'devour' me. Foreigners abroad are judged from a small sample, which is taken to represent the whole country, and any aberrant behaviour reflects badly. There is no cause so just and compelling that it must sacrifice the innocent.

There are many parallels between Northern Ireland and South Africa, with one notable exception. Here, Blacks outnumber Whites by about four to one. It's the majority Black population who are discriminated against in important areas such as education, jobs, housing and policing. But their day of salvation is fast approaching. They will gain their freedom and independence, as other African countries did much earlier, through the power of the masses. They are buoyed by a wave of international outrage at maintaining the status quo for so long and an inordinate desire of the black population for change. The last bastion of colonialism in the southern tip of Africa will soon crumble.

Northern Ireland's Catholics seeking independence are very much in the minority, accounting for only one third of the total population, and this proves to be their Achilles heel. In clamouring for equality in much similar areas as South African Blacks, they have considerably less leverage and bargaining power. But they must begin to make inroads. It is outrageous we still have segregated schools which only sharpens the divide between Catholics and Protestants. Children of different Faiths, who are denied the opportunity of playing and socialising with one another, are understandably filled with mistrust and even hatred.

Less-educated Catholic children invariably drift into inferior-paid jobs, can afford only lower grade housing, all of which perpetuates discontent, animosity towards their fellow Protestants and a bitter struggle for equality. Removing the obstacles to a fairer society must be seen as the first important step following which, slowly but surely, tensions will ease and lead gradually towards equal opportunities for all. Like so many aspects of Irish society, we can clearly identify the problems but the solutions come all too slowly.

Paul, you have experienced first-hand the violent exchanges between the Israelis and the Palestinians, a long-drawn-out war with religious connotations and no end in sight. What has always appalled me is why Jesus Christ would allow such atrocities to occur and intensify in a sacred region of the world where he once travelled and preached to his chosen people. Perhaps, nowhere else in the world over such a long time span have repeated acts of bestiality and carnage fomented so much mistrust and deep-seated hatred. The Palestinians, driven from their homeland and fanned out across the globe, depend for survival on the generosity of the host Governments, often doing menial jobs and living in poor houses and even shacks. You must have noted many similarities to the Northern Ireland situation but you will undoubtedly agree that at least some light looms for us, even if the shortening tunnel is still very hazy.

The I.R.A. has long since driven home its point through guns, bullets and bombs. How long more must it persist? The needed reform and changes are well documented and aired. It's now time for a more conciliatory approach. Granted, there is a yawning gulf between what the I.R.A. demands and the British plus Northern Ireland's Unionists are prepared to concede. Yet, each single step taken to reduce the divide must be perceived as a blow struck for democracy. It will be a long and arduous road but no longer and harder than the route guns have taken us until now. In a new and fresh environment, where weapons or the threat of force no longer exist, dialogue and compromise will prevail. It will take considerable patience and persuasion, though, to convince all concerned it is the correct path to follow.

Now, I want to address your expressed concerns. You are rightly worried about your deteriorating relationship with your father and, while I can readily understand his motives, he is too selfish and narrow-minded. Like his ancestors, he is a slave to his genetic make-up and heritage, opting to continue fighting with all his God-given strength wherever and whenever he senses any British influence or involvement in Ireland. To suggest you can win him over to your way of thinking is to misguide you and I have no intention of recommending it, knowing how difficult it is to 'teach old dogs new tricks.' I'm not even sure we can convince the younger men committed to violence to see the evil of their ways and be governed by reason instead of blind passion. If there is to be success, we must look to the youth who need our full moral support. It is a gargantuan task.

For you to continue doing your excellent work, and remain on good terms with your Dad, you should lead by example. Do not attempt to get into convoluted discussions on the merits or otherwise of the approach to the Northern Ireland problem and your own views are not for general airing. By your work and example you are sending a strong message, to all who care and are wise enough to listen, about what means most to you in life and how you are well on the way towards achieving it. Those of your ilk will admire and respect you and, even those who don't subscribe to your views and work, will be awestruck and silently moved by your belief and devotion.

Your Dad, too, cannot fail to be impressed and proud of his son and it's only his own pride and misjudged beliefs prevent him from expressing his true feelings. Yes, you ought to stand a safe distance from your Dad, continue being polite and courteous and help him as only a loving son can, in the knowledge that he is not fully responsible for all his actions. Ultimately, you will be the winner in the quiet unobtrusive way you want it to happen.

I will concentrate my efforts on Jim McCabe to whom I'll write within a matter of days. I've two good reasons for doing so. During my last visit to Liscorley three years ago, we got to know each other well and, although we steered away from political issues, I found him pleasant and understanding. The second, and perhaps more important, reason is because of his friendship with and recent engagement to your beautiful sister, Deirdre . By working on Jim McCabe he hopefully will in turn influence the Dowling family to scale down their republican activities. I cannot guarantee success but it may be possible to get them to see things more as you and I do and I'll be happy with even a 30 - 50% success rate. I appreciate it will be difficult for you, being the "baby" of the family, to win the attention and respect in order to extract significant concessions. But, with the two of us working in harmony, we could get the expected results.

As I have now a reliable and experienced manager to run my business, I expect to have more free time to spend as I wish. I plan to holiday in Northern Ireland next summer and, instead of the customary two weeks, may stay for up to six weeks. By then you will likely have finished your Cypriot assignment and, if so, I look forward to meeting you and discussing further the issues raised in your letter. I understand there are a number of active peace groups with whom we may be able to cooperate. Meanwhile, I will write to inform you of Jim McCabe's response to my letter.

Remember that keeping the peace can sometimes be more dangerous than waging war and you have shown remarkable courage. Now, you should concentrate your efforts on doing likewise at home. We owe it to Ireland's silent majority. Long overdue is the need to replace Ireland's old-style politics with the new.

Yours sincerely,

Michael McCabe

CHAPTER 8
Northern Ireland - 1988

Contrary to popular belief, fortune doesn't always favour the brave. Was it a school myth intended to rid youngsters of their shyness and harden them for the rigours and sometimes brutality of the real world? How many well-respected proverbs were flawed or failed to stand up to even simple tests? But, they provided standards to aspire to and helped to promote acceptable codes of behaviour.

No proverb, no matter how often repeated, could bring any relief to Frank McCabe for the plight in which he now found himself. Before engaging in any I.R.A. terrorist operations, he always pondered and evaluated the possible consequences. What he feared most was what had just befell him, being captured by security police and waiting an uncertain fate. Like many other Irish patriots whom he admired and respected, he'd prefer to die a martyr rather than suffer long term interrogation, incarceration and possible torture in an effort to extract the names of his accomplices. He was still on German soil but the protracted negotiations were still continuing as to whether and when he might be extradited to England. The pain and uncertainty had begun to play on his mind.

What nagged him most of all was the feeling of having been used as a guinea pig or scapegoat. Had the mission's leader, Helen Quinn, contrived to assign him the most dangerous role, citing his German proficiency as the reason? In hindsight, he was convinced she had while she and her colleagues were at a safe distance when disaster struck. Or was he just downright unfortunate to be apprehended? He decided to dispel all thoughts of what might have been and instead deal with reality. As the first rays of the rising sun pierced the darkness of his prison cell, like they did for months on end now, they signalled the start of yet another long day of routine and boredom. But, he would take each day, one at a time, hoping and praying there would soon be an end to it all.

Frank reflected on all that had happened since that fateful second bomb explosion in a German bar. Although he had pre-arranged to meet up with the other seven members thirty minutes later, circumstances dictated otherwise. Nobody factored in the confusion and mayhem within a five kilometre radius of the scene and, more importantly, the scale and intensity of the security operations. These made it well-nigh impossible for Frank to reach the arranged meeting point on time. This, perhaps, was a blessing in disguise because an escaping small group of people would almost certainly arouse police suspicion, leading to their capture and arrest. It gave Frank the breathing space he desperately needed but was he on borrowed time and would the net eventually close in on him?

It was a lonely and frightening first 24 hours until he moved away from the densely-populated area which was surely being finely-combed. Learning from his limited Northern Ireland experience, he knew he could safeguard his escape route by lying low during the day and moving stealthily at night. Acting beyond his years, he reckoned two changes to how he looked and behaved would greatly lessen his chances of being detected. Firstly, he let nature take its course and grew a beard and he tried to copy the German dress code and conceal his identity further by wearing a cap. Secondly, he vowed to communicate orally as little as possible because, despite his German language skills, his Northern Ireland brogue could easily break through and incriminate him. Obtaining the small amounts of food for survival was another concern but he bought infrequently and then from small shops, rather than large supermarkets, to minimise his exposure. Even with all precautions in place, he knew he was merely reducing and not eliminating the possibility of arrest.

Sleep was rarely planned or restful. His in-built compass steered him in a north-westerly direction which, if he followed it strictly, would eventually lead him to the Dutch border. For some inexplicable reason, he would feel more at ease among the

Dutch and, perhaps, could arrange a safe passage home. But, that prospect still seemed light years away. Meanwhile, he relied for sleep on remote haysheds, preferably with no evidence of nearby human habitation. He sought out each hay- or straw-filled shed well before daybreak, became ensconced in a quiet corner and was fast asleep before sunrise. Only in situations where it was perfectly safe to leave unnoticed before darkness set in, did he do so. It was a dull and lonely existence and he prayed constantly it would soon pass. One of the greatest risks to secrecy and personal safety in using haysheds was the threat from vicious dogs. After one or two close calls, Frank never failed to do his advance surveillance and homework.

Human contact nearly landed him in trouble on a few occasions. The first of these came when he sought refuge in a hayshed about a mile beyond a small village. All appeared eerie and quiet as he strode towards his rustic abode at 5 a.m., sporadically using the dim light from a small torch to guide him along. He hadn't reckoned with the early hours many German farmers start work. A less than friendly *Guten Morgen* both greeted and startled him when he was less than twenty metres from the shed. Frank responded magnificently, stating in his best-phrased German that he was on his way to a nearby farm where he was on a six months work experience contract. The farmer's sceptical look of dismissal said it all.

His second brush with danger could have been very pleasant in different circumstances. It came from an attractive German blonde *fraulein* in her twenties, an assistant in a small grocery store where he was purchasing his basic foods. She appeared to be intrigued with his accent and pronunciation of certain German words. Frank figured from her smile and demeanour, and her enquiry about where he lived locally, that she was moving 'in the fast lane' of establishing a friendship. He used his best diplomacy to dampen her interest and make a safe retreat. It was when he moved outside the store and looked furtively backwards that fear enveloped him. She had quickly lifted and was dialling the phone with a display of urgency. Had it suddenly dawned on her that Frank was implicated in the recent bombings and decided to phone the police? Frank took no chances and vanished into thin air with all the speed he could muster.

But it was the third encounter that ensured his capture was inevitable. He had nobody to blame but himself as a lack of foresight and lapse of concentration precipitated the ordeal. Had he briefly thrown caution to the wind at the most vulnerable stage? The accents he overheard during the previous few hours indicated he may be near the Dutch border where the German language was gradually weakening, or so it seemed to the non-expert. His haste in trying to confirm or refute it proved to be his undoing. As daylight was about to give way to dusk under a clear sky, Frank nonchalantly enquired from a passer-by how far he was from the Dutch border. The young and obliging gentleman explained it was merely 15 kilometres away or less than 15 minutes by car. When Frank thanked him and took his leave, he overheard the gentleman saying to a friend 'Doesn't he resemble the man for whose capture the German police are offering a reward?' It brought a spring to Frank's step, realising that prying eyes were upon him and he was no longer safe. With attractive money up front to secure his capture, time was running out for him.

Try though he did to be extra cautious from here on, the odds were stacked against him. He later was to discover that it was only during the previous three days, in the absence of any success to date, that a cash reward was offered for any worthwhile information which might lead to his arrest. He now felt like a scared hare in front of a chasing pack of greyhounds.

What was, perhaps, most frustrating was his closeness to the Dutch border without any real hope of getting across. Could he take one last big gamble to cross *incognito* but, with such German surveillance near and at the border, his chances were virtually nil. There were also risks in biding his time as the search intensity moved to a higher gear.

When it did come two days later, it was done with German speed and precision. It happened during the pre-dawn hours when he least expected it, in a remote hilly area straddling the German-Dutch border. As darkness set in the previous evening he sought out and settled in a small hayshed from where he could reach before daybreak the unmarked and unpoliced border just one kilometre away, and onwards to what he regarded as virtual freedom. But he hadn't reckoned with Erik Otte's insatiable appetite for obtaining 200,000 German marks without shedding even one drop of sweat. For a man long unemployed, and little interest in seeking work, he couldn't believe his luck. He followed all of Frank's movements since sighting him 24 hours earlier. Once he entered the hayshed for the night, he notified the local police who surrounded the area with all the protection and necessary firepower. Frank saw neither the dawn nor crossed the border but was arrested without struggle or protest within one hour of taking refuge.

The early morning sunshine rays entering his cell, in this high security prison within a shout of the Dutch frontier, reminded him of childhood summer days when he frolicked about the green fields of Liscorley, enjoying the very freedom he was now woefully deprived. He bore no grudges against the German authorities now detaining him who were simply doing their duty. He knew mainland Europeans were sympathetic to Irish reunification and Germany, itself a divided country, secretly longed to embrace once again all its people. He knew that British pressure would come for his extradition to England or Northern Ireland and Germany, a close military and NATO ally, could find it difficult to refuse. He shuddered with fear of the fate that awaited him in England, where they were ready to wreak vengeance for the loss of so many innocent British lives.

During the six weeks since the bombings he hadn't the opportunity or time to contact any of his relatives back home who must be distraught over his whereabouts and wellbeing. If newspaper and TV publicity concerning his capture and imprisonment has any positive spin-off, it will reassure his parents he is still alive, if not yet out of danger. None of his family was known to give up easily and the best chance for his own survival might be to do likewise. For nights on end he dreamt of being home in Liscorley among his relatives and friends. The big task ahead of him now was to do all within his power to turn transitory dreams into permanent reality.

*

It was a year of an unprecedented number of attacks across the length and breath of Northern Ireland. Syria's regular consultation with Libya's Al-Madhi ensured there was no let-up in the arms supply. Britain accused Al-Madhi of actively supporting the bombings in Germany but, with no hard evidence to backup its claims, it was empty rhetoric. President Siddique, either directly or through his aides, was in weekly contact with the I.R.A. to gauge progress and to discuss alternative strategies that could shorten the war. While Syria's assistance for the Palestinians' resumed *intifada* attacks on Israel demanded much of his attention, it was not the time to short-change the I.R.A. Were it not for Gerald Dowling's astute diplomacy, President Siddique would have hundreds of Syrians and Palestinians actively engaged in the ground war. Gerald, using his own brand of propaganda of exaggerating the actual successes, managed to curtail his expansionist *ego*.

President Siddique craved one major success abroad that would help to camouflage losses nearer home. For the past six years his Syrian forces had occupied Lebanon, ostensibly as peacekeepers but more covertly helping the Palestinians and their militant allies to harass and terrorise the Israelis from their Lebanese bases. He was painfully aware of European (including Irish) peacekeeping soldiers risking their lives to prevent outright war. Many calls for Syrian troop withdrawal were ignored despite their presence exacerbating an already tense situation. Syria could not pull back without abandoning its allies, weakening its commitment to take on the Israelis and, above all else, "losing face" among its Arab neighbours. It was an intractable problem which had no easy solution.

He secretly envied Al-Madhi's high international profile in assisting terrorist and liberation groups and wanted 'a slice of the action' to bolster his own image. He could be excused for trying to 'fast forward' and accelerate the liberation struggle in Northern Ireland. But was he too impetuous and irrational in dealing with a culture and complexity of problems he knew little about and unlikely ever would? Only Gerald's best efforts kept him at arm's length and from making monumental errors. So far it worked perfectly and, if successes continued at their present rate, it might suffice until the end of the war. Middle East diplomacy called for apportioning most or all of Northern Ireland's recent successes to President Siddique's strategy and support, achievements that gave the President deep personal satisfaction. A little diplomacy laced with its due share of credit goes a long way.

It was a long way too for Cork native Vincent from the south-west to Northern Ireland where he spent much of the past year. The homesickness he earlier experienced faded quickly on seeing others in more difficult circumstances, caught up in and affected by a war that appeared to be rapidly spiralling out of control. If he allowed himself time to ponder, he could acknowledge that as a freedom-fighter and terrorist he was in some small but sinister way contributing to the chaos and impasse. But, in the heat of battle there was neither the time nor the inclination to think. It was now important to score many hits and victories while arms were plentiful and thereby gain the advantage. If outright successful, he could emulate his forefathers and become a hero for evermore. He left the pondering and reflecting to another time.

He found a kind and trusting ally in Liam McCabe whom he liked and admired from the outset. Liam often confided his concerns to Vincent, revealing family secrets he should normally keep to himself. He openly confessed to having little interest during adolescence in associating with the I.R.A. or espousing its causes and ideals. 'Growing up in a family steeped in republicanism, was there any choice?' he asked ruefully. 'There was nothing more important discussed in our house than the injustices meted out to Northern Ireland Catholics, with the tacit agreement we should try our best to correct them. I still have doubts we are going the right way about it. I quickly discovered at school that intimidating or beating up one of my classmates alienates him permanently. Neither does coercing our Protestant neighbours help them to better see our point of view and encourage friendship. But I dare not mention this subject, much less express my true feelings in front of my father and my older brother Jim.'

'I can assure you it's not very different in my house - and many....many houses, south of the border,' replied Vincent. It remains an enigma of Irish politics for centuries, many doing their utmost to develop and build the country while a minority few try their damnedest to destroy it. When will it change?

Meanwhile, the war raged on with Vincent and Liam in the midst of the action. Having considerably more arms at their disposal pressurized them to achieve far greater success and, consequently, take undue risks. But, having been down this road before gave them a distinct advantage. They were glad to renew their acquaintance with Michael and Mary McCracken to whom they owed a deep debt of gratitude for their guidance and protection. Michael hadn't mellowed with age but was instead imbued with confidence that the British, under sustained pressure and bombardment, might soon capitulate and agree to an united Ireland. Vincent was astounded that a man of his years could be so naive and that history hadn't taught him the British are no quitters, even more so under provocation. Did not the brave men engaged in the 1916 Easter Rising in Dublin have similar beliefs, only to be greatly disillusioned and the leaders shot? Michael was prone to bouts of wishful thinking.

The next month brought some hair-raising experiences. Despite Liam and Vincent being adept at the hit and run attacks which proved so devastating to the enemy, they hadn't fully reckoned with the heightened surveillance and security which were beginning to nip some of these raids in the bud. When trying to attack an army barracks three miles inside the border, they couldn't come within a mile of the target. Had British intelligence been alerted or was it part of a wider plan to seal off and patrol the border? The war of attrition meant there were calculated risks associated with every border incursion.

It reached crisis point two weeks later. Preparations were never more calculated and meticulous. The plan Liam and Vincent had painfully rehearsed all but backfired. A group of British soldiers routinely travelled in two military vehicles from their barracks to the border post each evening sometime between 21:30 and 22:00 hours. Operating from a "safe house" not far from the main road, along which the vehicles travelled, gave Liam and Vincent the time and latitude to wire the bomb that was neatly camouflaged beneath the road surface. All the preparatory work was done by night and all that remained was to detonate the bomb by remote control. How it all went horribly wrong is not easy to explain. Vincent, who nine times out of ten would have hit the target, miscalculated and the bomb exploded almost ten seconds before the first vehicle arrived, sending pieces of concrete and debris into the air in front of them.

For one split second death stared Vincent in the face. He ran from near the scene as fast as his legs could support him, knowing the British soldiers were in hot pursuit and firing indiscriminately. He was within one hundred yards of his "safe house" when a bullet pierced his left calf muscle, causing him to shriek with anguish and shout for help. Fortunately, Liam was on hand within seconds and, throwing him over his shoulder, rushed him to the house and to a concealed basement where his bleeding wound was quickly washed and dressed. Realising that the police would cordon off and search the surrounding area called for the greatest care and vigilance. They had no choice but to bide their time until the cordon was lifted or relaxed and Vincent's wound had healed enough to enable him to travel unaided. It took all of seven days before Vincent felt comfortable and it was safe to move.

A thought occurred to Liam that appealed to them both. 'What we need right now is a well-deserved rest away from the hustle and bustle of this war zone. I suggest you come with me to my home where you'll receive all the care and attention an injured man needs. That's if we can escape the clutches of the security forces. We can "recharge our batteries", review what successes we've had and constructively plan for the next series of strikes. What's more, I need to meet my family, of whom I've seen far too little of late. And, lest I forget, you are assured of a warm and affectionate welcome from my sister Jane.'

It was Liam's last remark that soothed much of the aching pain in Vincent's calf muscle. However long it was since Liam last saw his family, Vincent hadn't met Jane in what seemed ages.

Not that she was ever far from his mind and heart. Since their very first chance meeting he conjured plans for regular get-togethers, not the casual kind but those allowing their friendship to develop along the steady lines he wished it could. But the call of duty and logistical problems stood in the way. Was the time gap too long to revive a friendship that initially seemed to promise so much? The answer was not far off and he was excited at the prospect.

They were relieved to avoid detection and be safely south of the border. A number of lifts in passing cars quickly brought them to Liscorley and to home comforts all too rarely enjoyed in recent weeks. For reasons not easy to identify or explain, Vincent felt more at ease at McCabes than in his own home. Whether it was the sheer novelty, the friendship meted out to him or his growing maturity on a one-to-one basis, he could not find the answer. Perhaps, he hadn't yet fully taken account of his interest in Jane and how it might inevitably lure him even further from ties to his own family. Jane qualified only last month as a fully-fledged nurse and was shortly to take up a post in a nearby hospital. She was glad to be home to help restore to full fitness her first love of whom she saw too little. Emotions were sure to run high.

It took Vincent all next week to improve to the point where he could leave for home. It was without doubt one of the most relaxing, enjoyable and fulfilling weeks he could remember. As he watched Jane wash, disinfect and dress his leg wound twice daily, he marvelled at how she carried out her work so methodically and delicately. He accepted this was a simple task compared to the many arduous and complex jobs nurses were called upon to do each long working day. The cheerful way she went about her work convinced Vincent she was enjoying every minute of it. Vincent wondered if there were many other more noble causes than to tend to the sick and infirm, with the same enthusiasm and gusto Jane now displayed. It was not so much a job as a vocation.

That week provided the cement for a relationship that appeared destined to endure. Vincent recalled reading a book about the Second World War in which an Irish soldier, who was wounded shortly after D-Day on the French coastline, was admitted to a nearby hospital. There he met, and was attended by, a young French nurse who later became his wife. Were there not many other similar tales throughout that infamous war and several other wars? Was there a special bond established and reinforced between patient and nurse that few could sever? Or did a nurse's selfless devotion to healing raise her esteem, in the eyes of the patient, to an admirable level? Whatever the reason, there was that indefinable chemistry helping to synchronize Vincent's and Jane's emotions.

The eve of Vincent's departure was full of joy and romance. The McCabe family described how much they had treasured Vincent's friendship and were loathe to see him go. With friends and neighbours in attendance, they entertained him with music and song as well as plenty of food and drink to liven the spirits. Vincent celebrated his near return to full fitness by inviting Jane for a slow waltz, to the cheers and guffaws of his admirers. He whispered sweet endearments in her ear and suggested they should have a special moment together before the night was out. He lost no time in thanking all the McCabe family for making the entire week a home away from home.

The special moment Vincent had awaited came as he was just about to retire for the night. He heard a faint knock on his bedroom door with a tender voice saying 'may I come in?' Almost immediately Jane entered, clad in her dressing gown and exuding all the fragrances that sent Vincent's pulses racing. Sitting beside her on the edge of the bed, Vincent put his arm around her, kissed her on the cheek and said, 'I cannot thank you enough for all you did for me this week.'

'It was a pleasure to treat a patient and handsome man like you,' she replied, 'and besides, it was my first opportunity to practise many of the skills I've learned over the past three years!'

The joke was not lost on Vincent. He pulled her tightly towards him, feeling almost every contour of her soft and tender body. Lying beside her on the bed, he slid his hand inside her dressing gown and fondled her firm but soft breasts. He proceeded to explore all parts of her back and tummy, stopping short of touching her more private parts. All the while, she was visibly aroused and it sent aches of pleasure through his loins. They were eager for more but each knew full well they were on a slippery slope, from which very soon there may be no escape. Or, as Vincent mused, having miraculously escaped so often in the past, was this the one time he dare not?

His deep respect and feeling for Jane won out in the end. He displayed nerves of steel so often in the past but, this once, he did not have the courage to violate Jane's dignity and self-esteem. This was the beginning of something special and, if patience and self-control were called for, he was prepared to do whatever was needed.

*

Religion and politics make strange bedfellows and in Northern Ireland's context they border on the bizarre. To use religion as a springboard to further political aims, and in so doing subvert the minds of the innocent, produces a cancerous growth from which few completely recover. When strong and respected religious leaders, through their beliefs and pronouncements, elect to sow seeds of hate within the wider community, they set in motion a train of events having devastating consequences. To hide under the "cloak" of religion makes it even more grotesque and despicable.

For more than a decade before 1969 the province of Northern Ireland enjoyed relative calm and was at peace with itself. It might have continued so were it not for the rash and sudden outburst of the Presbyterian minister, Reverend Trevor MacMichael. Little did he realise on that March Sunday morning in front of his faithful community how his poor choice of words would polarise Protestants and Catholics. By encouraging and exhorting Protestants to dissociate themselves from their Catholic brethren, he was preaching a type of heresy no religious creed can justify. It causes outrage coming from a layman and, when it emerges from the lips of a minister, it should be unequivocally condemned by the Protestant Church. Instead, apart from the odd murmur of discontent few Protestants voiced their open disapproval. Only in Northern

Ireland's sectarian divide could a 'wound' of this magnitude be ignored and go untreated.

But then Reverend MacMichael was merely giving expression to the beliefs and silent feelings of many Protestants, too timid or cunning to say so publicly. It was the way Protestants regarded and treated Catholics ever since Protestant King William defeated Catholic King James in the year 1690, staking their rightful claim to the province of Ulster. That was almost 300 years ago, more than sufficient time to have healed the deep wounds dividing Protestants and Catholics. Reverend MacMichael made sure he kept on stoking the fires that maintained the gulf and rivalries and, thereby, guaranteed Protestant supremacy. Was he not taking a calculated risk of inflaming hostilities even further and a danger of outright war? Trouble was, he never knew how to act or behave any different.

As a young child of six he had his first encounter with a Catholic boy. Trevor came off second best but it left a scar that never healed. That boy epitomised all that was wrong with the mixed society in which he lived. His hate for Catholics accelerated through his teens and he longed for an opportunity to express it more forcefully. He didn't have long to wait. Looking upon a religious life as a means of gaining a position of power and prestige, he pressed right ahead not altogether sure where it might ultimately lead. As luck would have it, window after window of opportunity came his way. His father's encouragement and influence in high places catapulted him along his chosen religious career. On the day following his appointment as minister of the Presbyterian Church his photograph, surrounded by his beaming and proud parents, appeared in all of the daily newspapers. Reverend Trevor MacMichael had come of age, was sitting on top of the world and was willing to bide his time before influencing the course of political developments in a corner of Ireland he intensely loved.

The timing of his maiden outburst for March 1969 was seen as a knee-jerk reaction to the republican demonstrations and riots of the previous six months. He had witnessed too much of what he regarded as "Catholic hooliganism" directed against the law-abiding Protestant majority. He premeditated and stage-managed his response with the maximum media exposure, ensuring that reverberations reached many corners of the world. At last, his long-sought revenge on his Catholic brethren was taking root and he vowed not to relent in the years ahead. He would show to the world that "Rome rule" did not dominate his corner of Ireland and be a direct threat to his own church. He knew he had an uphill fight on his hands but he vowed to fight with all the energy his Creator had given him.

Nineteen years had since elapsed and, now in the cold reality of 1988, there was no sign of a let-up. That fact alone astonished both his admirers and detractors. The intervening years bore witness to thousands of deaths and several-fold injuries but Reverend MacMichael stood steadfast and resolute. Not once did he show even the slightest sign of remorse at having ignited the fuse that sparked Northern Ireland's most turbulent years. At least in public he could not be seen to relent or 'lose face' but, according to close friends, his private life was a virtual hell and he constantly feared for his own safety.

Ever since his March 1969 diatribe he was the symbol of hate for Catholics, and with some justification. Many Catholics were insulted and hurt and what compounded the injury was knowing there was little or nothing they could do to redress the balance. The fact that Reverend MacMichael was also a political representative meant he was doing his utmost to put his provocative words into everyday practice. That he was rarely if ever a serious target for I.R.A. assassins is indeed perplexing, considering the number of less outspoken opponents who at one time or another met untimely deaths. Perhaps, in a sinister way, he was the sustenance for the I.R.A. - the more he ranted and raved, the greater legitimacy it gave to their quest for an united Ireland.

For all of Reverend MacMichael's outward show of *bravado*, he was privately affected by his celebrity status. There was scarcely a day or night during the past 19 years when he was able to relax and enjoy life as he once did. It was as if he was constantly looking over his shoulder to protect himself. When leaving his house, he did so only after taking all necessary precautions that nobody, who should not be there, was lurking within earshot. Though security police weren't intrusive, they were seldom far away and ever alert to any suspicious personnel or movement in the vicinity. But Trevor wasn't so naive as to believe he was in no danger of being gunned down by a would-be assassin. Had he the chance to relive his life, he would seriously question the extremist stance he took on Northern Ireland. The whole episode caused him untold personal anguish and he was the butt of some of the severest criticism - and even hostile ridicule.

Even during the still of nights on end, when he should be sleeping peacefully, he was awake for long periods brooding over his turbulent past. When sleep eventually came it was often almost time to get up and start his daily routine. Worse still, he occasionally had some horrible nightmares involving the ghosts of his perceived enemies only too ready and willing to strike him down. Whether or not he was willing to admit it, Reverend MacMichael had become a prisoner of his past and there were few really good opportunities for him to escape.

Age had begun to mellow him and, moreover, he didn't possess the vitality and enthusiasm of even a decade ago. He still looked forward to his Sunday service and meeting all his parishioners and friends. His congregation hadn't changed drastically over the years except it diminished significantly in number but still had a hard core of trustworthy and loyal followers. Most of the others were devout churchgoers who did not fully subscribe to Reverend MacMichael's views and beliefs. His sermons were also much lower key, preferring to concentrate more on his Church's teachings and less on politics. Judged by post-service conversations among moderates, they would have been pleased were it always so. Sundays were gradually becoming more normal and sociable once again.

One Sunday about three weeks ago he decided to hold an informal post-service news conference. It took place in the nearby social hall where they had their weekly get-together over tea and biscuits. It signalled a departure from the regular routine and was Trevor's way of sampling the views and mood of his congregation. In simple terms, 'the shepherd was trying to keep more in touch with his flock.' At the same time he feared it might raise issues with which he wouldn't be entirely comfortable. If this was the case, he decided to reply objectively and not impose his own views, as was his custom in the past. The opening few questions were simple and straightforward and were dispensed with amicably and through friendly exchanges. A couple of impetuously-raised hands towards the back forewarned Trevor of likely controversial issues.

It was now Malcolm MacVeigh's golden opportunity to unload his long-troubled conscience, revealing a problem that plagued him for years but never found the opportune moment to express himself. 'Reverend MacMichael, I can well appreciate how concerned you and our entire congregation are for the chaotic political situation in which we now find ourselves. There is a consensus that we have reached an *impasse* from which there is no honourable retreat. Each of us here must ask ourselves the stark questions: to what extent have we contributed to this bottleneck, how much of the responsibility do we together share for going down a one-way street and, more importantly, has our Presbyterian church stance including its pronouncements poisoned the hearts and minds of our perceived adversaries, our Catholic neighbours with whom we ought to live in peace and harmony? I honestly plead with you, Reverend MacMichael, to answer these questions as clearly and conscientiously as you can, seek the views of others here present and, if we have done wrong in the past, start the reparation process herewith by issuing a statement indicating how and to what extent we propose to correct our past wrongs. This gesture, more so than all the prayers we collectively recited here earlier, will start the healing process with our Catholic neighbours and help to build a new and more secure future for all the people of this province.'

There was a hushed silence in the hall and a look of disbelief in Reverend MacMichael's blue eyes, that one of his parishioners could not only raise such a topic but phrase it so eloquently. It took him all of two minutes to gain his composure and prepare his reply. Meanwhile, the scattered group formed into a more tightly-knit unit and moved forward with attentive ears to hear the minister's reply. 'I am extremely glad, Mr MacVeigh, you raised the most pertinent and provocative questions ever heard within this small community. Had you done so 15 or more years ago, I might have been rash enough to ask you to retract your statements and seek forgiveness, such was the mood within our church community. It is a measure, perhaps, of our maturity, of the different ways we look at a given problem and of acknowledging our past mistakes. I admit to being too outspoken, insensitive to the feelings of others and even inciting to violence one third of our population. I've had to live with the repercussions which plagued me daily for many years.'

He went on 'But, did I have any alternative? We as Protestants and Unionists have to protect our rights and future from a minority bent on wrecking all we hold dear. We have to ensure we remain part of the United Kingdom, enjoying all the rights and privileges which that bestows on us.' He was now in belligerent mood once again but, before he could spew more poison, a second raised hand from the back interrupted the minister and insisted on having his say.

'Let me state, Reverend MacMichael, that your views are not representative of the majority here present. It's about time we stand up and be counted. Let me emphasise further that we must consider and take on board the ideas and aspirations of the third you so casually dismiss. All Catholics are not party to the evil minority you project them to be and I happen to have many as trusted and loyal friends. If we had spent more time in understanding and assisting, than in denouncing and ridiculing, them, then we would not now be in the horrible situation we find ourselves. The sooner we show the maturity you alluded to, but show no signs of practising, the faster we'll move forward.'

It was obvious Reverend MacMichael and his small band of faithful supporters were calling the shots - and getting away with it. Even they had serious reservations about the wisdom of their ways but would not dare say so publicly. Unreserved admission would certainly hasten the day they were desperately trying to forestall. Nobody had enough courage to remind them it was precisely how an ostrich deals with such a problem!

*

There are times in life's journey to stop and reflect and now it was Shane McCabe's turn. Not that he was often given to brooding over what might have been but the pace of recent events was more than he could assimilate. In March he celebrated his 58th birthday and was only two years away from the magic figure of 60 when, as he had long promised, he would quit teaching and begin the rest of his life. Also, earlier this year he and Brenda celebrated their 30th wedding anniversary and were just as much in love as when they exchanged vows on that bright sunny day in 1958. Not only had Brenda borne him three handsome sons and two beautiful daughters, she worked tirelessly to run a home any husband would be justifiably proud of. In every sense, Shane was continuing to enjoy married and domestic bliss.

Nonetheless, all hadn't gone as he would have wished it. His entire family, save his youngest daughter Eileen, were involved one way or another with the republican movement about which he had a deep sense of pride tempered with a few misgivings. From a young age Eileen let it be known she had no desire to follow the route of her elders and Brenda was able to prevail on Shane to respect her wishes. It was a brave and rare move for the youngest who often aspires to emulate her older brothers and sisters. In hindsight, Shane relished the benefits it brought him. The disproportionate love Brenda and Shane showered on their young daughter was less likely to be endangered or lost amid the tensions and upheavals gripping the province.

Shane's contacts with the Dowlings of Inistogue were less frequent and more business-like than previously. Each family was too busy with day-to-day chores and concerns about current trends and an uncertain future that left them with little time or inclination to get in touch, exchange views and enquire about each other's wellbeing. Invariably, meetings to discuss guerrilla war tactics and progress brought Gerald Dowling and Jim McCabe face to face but Seamus and Shane were more and more leaving it to the younger men to carry the torch. During the rare times they spoke over the telephone, they rambled on and on about what might have been and in wishful thinking that redemption for beleaguered Northern Ireland may be near at hand. It was this "end of the rainbow" quest that had sustained them through good times and bad.

On average the bad greatly outnumbered the good but wasn't that what the struggle was all about? Shane took immense satisfaction from Jim's relationship with Deirdre Dowling, two young people very much in love and on the threshold of marriage. Now his daughter, Jane, was increasingly seeing more of another southern freedom fighter, Vincent Tuohy, who had from the start made his interest and intentions known. Shane was not altogether happy having a second daughter attracted to a republican support group and pleas from Brenda to discourage her were of little avail. When it came to affairs of the heart, they both knew it was unlikely anything they did or said would change the *status quo*.

Many of their recent worries concerned the misadventures of their son Frank, now in a west German prison and awaiting possible extradition to England. He was a member of a group taking the war effort to the heart of Germany and killing English troops engaged in NATO exercises. An academic through and through, his sole qualification for the job was his proficiency in the German language, a skill he didn't remotely consider could land him in such awful trouble. A novice though he may be, he outmanoeuvred and outwitted German security for days on end and it was only the greed of a paid informer that led to his eventual capture close to the Dutch border. As he witnessed the dawn of yet another day in a long drawn-out saga, he prayed for the patience and perseverance that would help him through his present ordeal and ultimately to the freedom he desperately craved.

Shane, and even more so Brenda, constantly empathised with Frank's sad plight. Why, they asked, does the ultimate penalty fall on the shoulders of those least involved while the die-hard terrorists causing death and destruction often escape and are seldom apprehended? In Northern Ireland's conundrum, it was a question they often posed but to which they couldn't find a satisfactory answer. But, wasn't it a fact of life in the present conflict - very many questions and too few answers! Some English, frustrated with the Irish *impasse* down through the years, summed up the situation thus: 'As soon as we provide the answers, the Irish keep on changing the questions!' It was symptomatic of the mistrust and lack of understanding that plagued these two near neighbours for centuries.

Despite Frank's fair treatment by German prison staff, the threat of extradition to England, where he would certainly be regarded less benignly, constantly hung over him. Although the German media didn't portray the I.R.A's tactics in the best possible light, the public generally were *au fait* with what goaded them to action. After all, weren't Frank's captors living in a divided country for which there was little or no rationale? They must likewise wish to be reunited with their long-separated relatives and friends in eastern Germany. He appreciated that close political ties between Germany and the United Kingdom could work against him and he might become a mere pawn in big power politics. While the routine and monotony of prison life was beginning to frustrate him, he appreciated that each rising sun temporarily lifted his spirits and also bought him valuable time. He knew from experience that the impact of atrocities diminished steadily over the weeks and months.

A deep relief came from being able to write to his Mam and Dad who awaited the postman's visit as never before. He took care not to mention the circumstances surrounding the bombings, his arrest and imprisonment. There was more than a hint at being 'hard done by,' awaiting judgment on crimes in which he played a small role. But he had confidence in the fairness of the British legal system and the sentence would surely fit his crime. He phrased it in such a way that it evoked the utmost sympathy from his parents who were reduced to tears on reading each heart-rending account of his feelings and hopes. He ended his last letter by saying 'There is a reasonable possibility that extradition requests may not be approved. The British are patently aware I am a small player and are furiously in pursuit of the others. The vibes I'm getting within the prison are that the German resolve to turn me in may be weakening.

But, I'm bracing myself for the worst and I promise not to do anything which might bring dishonour on our family.' It was this last sentence that caused tears to well up in Brenda's eyes as she slowly closed the letter and tried to muster up the energy to go about her daily work.

Frank's arrest and imprisonment cast a shadow and strained relations within the McCabe family. While Brenda was careful not to say anything that might damage their thirty-year-old marital happiness, she left Shane in no doubt about her growing concern with the family's brush with danger. The war had taken a new and more dangerous twist and anyone caught in the wrong place at the wrong time, including the countless innocent, suffered the consequences. She wished she could be more explicit and outright condemn what was happening but she knew it would simply fall on deaf ears. She reluctantly decided to assume a passive role without hiding her true feelings. Shane's genetic make-up conditioned him to pursue the republican route, come what may, even if it meant imminent danger to his next of kin.

Neither did Shane get the expected support from his brother, Michael, who was becoming more vociferous from distant Johannesburg. This was not an overnight development, as from the very start Michael was openly opposed to violence in any shape or form. He had advanced his South African car business to the point where he was a rich and influential man in the community. Shane reckoned that his opposition to violence grew proportionately to his wealth accumulation, said with more than a hint of jealousy. He also wondered whether it was the influence of his English-born wife that steered him along this path.

And from what had once been a close friendship between brothers noticeably soured in the past few years. During his bi-annual holidays at home, Michael stayed with Shane and Brenda and never once contemplated doing otherwise. Michael also intended making the trip this year until an unfortunate set of circumstances shattered his plans. One evening a few months earlier, Jim showed his Dad a letter he had received from Michael, urging him strongly to give up his life of violence. He said he had earlier written to Paul Dowling who shared his dream of a peaceful approach to Irish reunification.

The repercussions were stark and instantaneous. Shane didn't wait to draft a letter but lifted the telephone and spoke directly to Michael who had just returned to his beautiful north Johannesburg home after another hard day. He needed no reminding from the tone and urgency of Shane's voice that something was amiss. There were few preliminaries before Shane unloaded his concerns. 'I have known for many years your views on Northern Ireland and on what side of the fence you stand. You are entitled to your opinions which are personal and private. You can be excused for trying to influence others to your way of thinking. It is quite another matter to impose your political doctrine on my son Jim and I believe you tried to do likewise with one of the Dowlings of Inistogue. At the risk of tarnishing our long-standing friendship, I respectfully urge you to keep members of my family outside your sphere of influence. In other words, mind your own damn business.'

The phone suddenly went silent, confirming that Shane had hung up. After a long day exposed to the hot Johannesburg sun, it was the kind of 'welcome home' Michael could have done without. It took him several minutes to recover from the shock whereupon he decided to 'switch off' and spend the rest of the evening with his family. There was plenty of time to respond and, when he did, he would be fully composed and able to logically explain to his fiery brother his Northern Ireland stance and the reasons therefor. As he had done so many evenings before eating dinner, he threw off his shoes, sat in the west-facing veranda and sipped his favourite Scotch and soda as the red sun gradually disappeared beyond the picturesque horizon.

Michael typed and mailed his letter exactly a week later. The first few paragraphs contained no reference to their telephone conversation and dealt mainly with brother-to-brother news of general interest. The last paragraph revealed his reaction and intimate feelings:

'I would be untruthful if I said I wasn't shocked by what you emotionally stated on the telephone last week. It certainly took me by surprise. I hate to think that different political views might come in the way of our long uninterrupted friendship. Let me categorically state it was never my intention to interfere in your own family affairs. Far from me to impose my views on others. What I was merely implying (but by no means *imposing*) is that the way forward in Northern Ireland must surely be a peaceful one and, if I'm given the chance, I will spare no effort working towards this end. I realise you don't agree and I respect, if not accept, your opinion. Although I had looked forward to holidaying with you again later this year, I feel it is prudent to postpone it to a later date. We beg to differ politically but let's work on maintaining, and even cementing, our hard-won friendship.'

*

Recent successes exceeded the I.R.A.'s wildest expectations, using it's own special measurement criterion. Frequency times intensity of hits gave a verifiable measure of damage inflicted, including material loss, injuries and deaths. Not how normal mortals judge progress, but the I.R.A. used little else over the past two decades. Like boxers in a ring: it is only when an opponent is on the ropes, and virtually clamouring for mercy, that he is likely to give up. So too might the British grow weary, relent and make significant concessions when their backs are to the wall. It was the philosophy of the I.R.A. and it worked hard at implementing it. At home, throughout England and on mainland Europe it was justifiably satisfied with what it had achieved.

Complacency, however, was never an option as history taught the Irish many lessons well worth heeding. Foremost was the British reluctance to give up even when severely intimidated or rocked. They were often at their best when backed into a corner and in danger of collapsing. Many pages of the history books testify to this fact and, sadly, too often the Irish were at the receiving end. But the I.R.A., like many others engaged in guerilla warfare, was ever hopeful this one last attack would do the trick, after which the British finally gave in and said enough is enough, we want to get out. These were sweet words that, unfortunately, never fell on I.R.A. ears.

President Kemal Siddique of Syria was, as expected, keeping a close watch on things. Not only was he the "engine" behind recent successes but he staked his very reputation and possible future on securing a comprehensive victory that for long eluded him nearer home. The Palestinians had become disillusioned with the slow progress in obtaining concessions from the Israelis in terms of extra land, let alone the prospect of a Palestinian homeland to which they had a God-given right. They were forced to protest and engage the Israelis in constant skirmishes in both urban and rural settings in a new wave of attacks, known as the *Intifada*. In providing Syrian support troops, President Kemal was trying to advance a cause dear to his heart but one he intuitively knew would take many.. many more years to resolve. He was, therefore, more optimistic about a 'quick fix' to the Irish conflict.

Behind the scenes, President Al-Madhi of Libya kept the pressure on Syria not to let-up on its support for Ireland, something he himself originally started and subsequently promoted for many years. Although slightly envious of Kemal's successes, he was prepared to overlook these for the broader good of oppressed peoples. Al-Madhi encouraged Kemal to do all within his power to gain the long-awaited and ultimate victory. Al-Madhi was still smarting terribly from the bombing raids on Tripoli two years earlier, instigated by the U.S. and supported by Britain. He was deeply involved in his own private agenda. If everything goes as planned, he would soon deliver a retaliatory strike on both the U.S. and Britain, the scale and ferocity of which hadn't yet been experienced in the western world.

It was review and regrouping time for the I.R.A. There was general agreement that bombings across England and parts of mainland Europe had fulfilled their objectives. It awakened those, who were still ignorant or apathetic, to the stark injustices which were simultaneously given important international publicity and exposure. Increasingly, the I.R.A. was regarded not as mere terrorists but genuine people with serious grievances to which they would like the world at large to listen and, if possible, help solve. In other words, the point was forcibly made and, hopefully, heeded and respected. It was time once again to concentrate on Northern Ireland.

If the I.R.A. was determined to pressurise England into relinquishing its claim to and hold on Northern Ireland, it needed the same resolve to convince its Protestant and Unionist rivals in its midst of the fallacy of their ways i.e. continuing to remain loyal to Britain while living in a region of Ireland. The I.R.A. was applying the self-same strategy here: continuing to harass, intimidate, oppress and physically harm them to the point where they too will question the wisdom of their ways. The chances of their giving up are in direct relationship to the pressure applied. So far, there were signs it was only partially successful but, over sufficient time, might not the sum of all the successful 'parts' achieve its ultimate ambition? It was the dream fuelling the I.R.A. and was set to continue. The job was yet unfinished.

The next major I.R.A. attack in Northern Ireland surpassed all previous in scale, intensity and callousness of execution. It was one last throw of the dice, using all the firepower at its disposal to vent the pent-up anger and seek revenge for not been granted vital concessions from the British and their loyal northern supporters. It was planned over many months while the attacks were proceeding across England and mainland Europe. Now, with the scaling back of these operations, more experienced senior personnel were employed at home. Because of its delicate nature, it called for meticulous preparation and thorough rehearsal including the survey of routes and intended targets, personnel assignments, approach and escape options and numerous other details too crucial to be left to chance. There were serious risks factored in but, if it was executed with all due precautions, it should be as successful as previous attacks.

The target was Ballysorley, a predominantly Protestant town in the centre of County Fermanagh. Its elected representatives regularly and vehemently attacked the motives and tactics of the I.R.A. And with a good deal of justification because the townspeople were intimidated and attacked at one time or another in the past. It epitomised all that was so wrong - and even sad - about two communities living in close proximity but not mixing and socialising as normal human beings should. The further and longer they stood apart, the deeper grew the mistrust and misunderstanding, making it well-nigh impossible to nurture a healthy society. Enter the I.R.A., to add insult to injury and hell-bent on bombing and blasting them into submission. Nobody was ready to predict how seriously it would damage relations, if some still existed, in this rural town.

The project's importance was highlighted by the full involvement of some of the McCabe and Dowling families, either as members of the vanguard or support groups. Their experience was invaluable and their dedication and loyalty unquestionable. The plan called for the following: all staff, vehicles, materials and supplies are in the vicinity of Ballysorley for at least two weeks beforehand, giving ample time to research the locality, observe the movements of people and security forces at pre-determined times, decide on the most appropriate time to strike and rehearse each stage thoroughly. Two separate cars loaded with explosives, and timed to go off at exactly the same time, are driven to two different parts of the town. Each site is selected with the maximum strike capability and destruction in mind. Gerald Dowling and Jim McCabe are joint coordinators.

It wasn't altogether a male affair as Vincent Tuohy was joined by Jane McCabe and Deirdre Dowling insisted on coming along to help Jim McCabe. In between the work and rehearsals there was enough free time to let their hair down and enjoy themselves.

Everything had worked splendidly so far. Their research taught them to plan the attack for precisely 5 p.m. on a Friday evening, coinciding with the mass exodus of people from offices and businesses and greatest traffic congestion. Not only would the explosions cause untold havoc but the slow flow of traffic would result in pandemonium. It also reduces the chances of capturing the getaway groups.

The first car, driven by Gerald in the company of Vincent and Jane, arrived at its chosen site in good time at precisely 4:37 p.m. To any shoppers or passers-by, they could be any threesome starting their long weekend. When nobody was near, Gerald finally checked all the gear and timing devices and satisfied himself it would go off on the hour. By 4:45 p.m. they had begun in a second car their exit to a safe house about two miles out of town. Later they would rendezvous with Jim and Deirdre before taking the back roads and heading well away from the scene of the crime.

For Jim and Deirdre, it was much less straightforward. Although they had set out at the same time as Gerald, they incurred a delay nobody could have anticipated. Approaching the edge of town they saw a police car immediately ahead with flashing red lights in the midst of a traffic pile-up. It was enough to send shivers down their spines. Police were called to what appeared to be a head-on crash between a car and a large truck. It happened just minutes earlier and they were in the process of cutting through the mangled car and trying to extricate the occupants. The thoughts going through Jim's head boggles the mind. His first reaction was one of shock - and more so fear - at not being able to reach their destination on time, the repercussions of which didn't dare contemplating. To Deirdre seated beside him, he looked, and had just begun to behave, like a cornered fox. It was another spine-tingling 20 minutes before a policeman waved the traffic backlog through the narrowed street. Not to arouse any suspicion, Jim nudged his car carefully and slowly along.

It was now a question of life or death, trying to reach his selected location before 5 p.m. and not exceed unduly the town speed limit of 30 m.p.h., lest he attract police attention. As time was not on his side, he chose the happy medium. As there were few people around at that time, he went virtually unnoticed on screeching his car to a halt with only thirty seconds to spare. 'Let's get out and run,' he shouted to Deirdre who was in the front passenger seat. Slamming the car doors shut and with beads of perspiration on their foreheads, they scampered towards the street corner with Jim about 50 yards ahead of Deirdre. Before they reached it, a deafening explosion shattered the afternoon air followed by falling concrete all about them, with human cries of pain and anguish. Jim narrowly escaped death by a falling slab that instead struck his left thigh, pinning him to the ground and leaving him gasping for air.

After he regained a little of his composure his first concern was for Deirdre. Limping on one leg, he edged his way backwards and after 30 yards found Deirdre almost entirely submerged by rubble, with only her head and shoulders and her right hand protruding. It was a sight that would perpetually haunt him for however long God spared him. Almost overcome by his own pain, he caught hold of her hand, tried to free her from all the surrounding concrete and gently eased her to the surface, not yet fully aware of the lacerations, bruising and permanent damage to her lower body. Holding her in his arms, he soon realised her breathing was laboured and spasmodic and he said 'Deirdre, Deirdre, I love you and you are going to be alright.' His sixth sense was telling him otherwise. He kissed her gently on the left cheek that was rapidly losing its colour. She motioned to him with her index finger and when Jim put his ear close to hear what she wanted to tell him, she said ever so faintly 'Jim... Jim, I... did... it... for... you.' With that, she slumped heavily in his arms, closed her lovely blue eyes and took her last breath.

CHAPTER 9
Ireland (North and South) - Late 1988

Fate dealt a cruel blow to the usually serene village of Inistogue, a quiet rural backdrop of county Kerry where little of note disrupts the daily monotony and routine. Only a death brings an inordinate solidarity and togetherness not experienced elsewhere. The passing of an elder, of whom the village had more than its share, is always an occasion for people to assemble and pay their last respects. Several years elapsed since anybody under thirty fell ill and died and the grief enveloping the community lingered interminably. Youth is admired and treasured and evokes a deep sense of pride.

None of the young adults were more loved than the beautiful and vibrant Deirdre. Twenty-one months younger than Gerald, she took on a mother's role from an early age helping her younger sister, Joan, with everything from school work to protecting her adolescent innocence from the prying eyes and growing attention of the precocious young males. She was equally attentive to the needs of her baby brother, Paul, not yet exposed to life's harsh realities. By the time Deirdre said her farewells to Inistogue she had left an indelible mark on village minds and hearts.

And more than a few male hearts were broken in 1981 when, at the young age of 23, she suddenly decided to accept a teaching post in Libya and carve out her own future. It was a move that at once saddened and bewildered many, evoking questions and stirring gossip in a village having its due share. One of the local newsmongers spread the malicious rumour that she was pregnant and in fleeing spared the family this atrocious embarrassment and indignity. Those who understood and trusted her knew otherwise. Sure, her natural beauty and pleasant personality guaranteed an almost steady queue of boyfriends but her exemplary upbringing conditioned her to always choose right over wrong. The real reason for leaving home remained strictly private, a secret she took with her to the grave.

In her republican home she saw little to inspire hope and confidence. Just as her baby brother Paul would later eschew violence, Deirdre too was convinced that remaining close to her roots was certain to immerse her in activities alien to her nature. Could she try explaining or even mentioning it to her father bent on following the path preordained by his ancestors? She had long since known better than to attempt it and the quiet way was the only option. Had she chosen to go elsewhere, than to Al-Madhi's republican bastion, he could easily have discouraged or even prevented her leaving. He lived the dream of her sharing and practising Al-Madhi's ideals and philosophy, something that couldn't be further from the truth. She loved and adored her father and in no way wanted to upset or offend him and the escape route to Libya could preserve that relationship. Serendipity and good fortune simultaneously strengthened and cemented the bond between father and daughter.

The catalyst came in the person of Jim McCabe. It was as if God predestined them to occupy adjacent seats on a London-Tripoli-bound plane on that sunny spring morning in 1981. Ironically, it drew her ever closer to a man whose views and aspirations were diametrically opposed to hers. Here was a young lady trying to distance herself from her father, and much of what he espoused, only to come face-to-face with another younger male specimen of the same ilk. It developed into a relationship as much of the heart as the mind and ideals. In the end it was their hearts drew them together but Deirdre also steadily became a greater player in the dangerous games Jim pursued. As she grew into the role, she mused about how proud her father would be to see her follow the route of his dreams. She knew her heart was overriding her innate feelings of righteousness but she was prepared to go along with it for now. After all, it was only after careful consideration she decided to assist Jim and to take on the associated risks. Nobody was around to forewarn her of the possible dire consequences.

Now the outcome was real and stark and a pall of gloom hung over the village of Inistogue. This small rural community was numbed with shock and disbelief and it would take months, or even years, to come to terms with what happened. Seamus and Nora were in a temporary daze, buoyed by their undiscovered strength and resolve to proceed as best they could with funeral arrangements. It was not the time to pose questions as to why their young daughter was taken from them so tragically and the circumstances surrounding it. That must wait for later and, despite all the words and conversation that will surely follow, nothing can assuage the deep sorrow that will torment them during many sleepless nights yet to come. They - and they *alone* - must suffer this terrible cross in silence.

Deirdre's body was brought on the long journey from Northern Ireland to her home where the open coffin lay for a full 24 hours. Neighbours and friends came, prayed and tried to console the distraught relatives, many stifling tears. The menfolk were offered a variety of alcoholic drinks while the women were content sipping tea and snacks amid the cacophony of intense conversation and bouts of wailing. Paul, entrusted with dispensing draught beer from a keg mounted on a wooden bench, felt eerie sensations enveloping him. One of the neighbours who drank more than his due share approached Paul for another pint and remarked incoherently 'they tell me you are the black sheep of the family, with not a single drop of republican blood running through your veins. You are betraying the Dowling name.' The words so enraged Paul it brought his own blood to near boiling point. As he reluctantly handed him the glass full of beer he stopped short of splashing it all over his evil-boding face.

The psychological scar was never to leave Paul's young mind.

It prompted Paul to question the real motives of those attending under the assumed guise of sympathizers. True, there was a small core who strongly empathized with the Dowling family and shared their grief. Even for one so innocent and inexperienced about bereavements as Paul, it seemed that a goodly proportion came for two main reasons: 'to be seen' and to share in the alcoholic beverages that flowed freely. Just as it was unnatural for Paul to engage in violence, so too did he lose respect for those whose raucous laughter and loud conversation rose in tune with their blood alcohol levels. Why, he wondered, had his father debased his position in the family by asking him to serve beer to the unconcerned, when his own grief and sorrow for his beloved sister were uncontrollable? Was it his Dad's way of punishing him for not following the path he desperately wanted him to pursue? He dared not think evil of a man with whom he still craved reconciliation. Besides, Deirdre's death caused his Dad much pain and might change him irrevocably.

At next morning's funeral mass parking spaces were at a premium outside the small church. Not only had Inistogue never yet witnessed such an influx of cars to their sleepy village but the number of Northern Ireland registrations were particularly noticeable. For Shane and Brenda McCabe, who had travelled independently of Jim and to whom they were giving their full support, it was a poignant sojourn. Why, they agonised, had they not driven south earlier to visit their in-laws in happier times instead of when a tragic death obliged them? Had fate not dealt Deirdre an untimely blow, they would certainly be following a similar route, perhaps within a matter of months, to attend Jim and Deirdre's wedding. It was with a heavy heart and an unsteady gait they slowly made their way up the church's centre aisle and took their places in the second pew. The altar was lavishly decorated with flowers and the organ music had just begun. The last few of the congregation were shuffling into the all-too-few seats. An enormous crowd, which flooded both the side aisles and the back of the church, snaked through the open doors and out towards the road.

Fr. Michael Finucane P.P. made it his duty to get to know nearly all his parishioners to whom he administered during the last five years. He nurtured a rapport with his "flock" not enjoyed to the same extent in his three previous parishes. The people of Inistogue have distinctive not easily definable qualities that make a stranger feel immediately at home and among friends. It is part of the overt hospitality seen throughout all of

Co. Kerry and even more pronounced in this small community. According to the Catholic church's unwritten rule of not permitting a priest to stay too long in a parish or become overly familiar with its people, he intuitively knew that his remaining time among the Inistogue congregation he had increasingly grown to love was certainly limited. His early move to another, perhaps less hospitable, parish seemed inevitable. These thoughts going through his head, as he took the podium to deliver his sermon, made the task before him all the harder. Apart from occasional muffled coughs, mostly from the elders, Fr. Finucane faced a captive audience that was emotionally shaken.

'My dear brethren,' he began, as he customarily did each Sunday and a few special weekdays of his long tenure at Inistogue, 'as you all know I am rarely lost for words but today happens to be one of the very few. We come together under one of the most tragic and bizarre of circumstances. One of our beautiful and talented parishioners, who attended mass in this church from her infant days, returns to us prematurely in a coffin that's before the altar for all of you to see. Of our beloved parishioners, the Dowling family is second to none in its devotion to Sunday mass and all the sacraments. Fr. Finucane went on.

One of the old folk seated in the back pew quipped, 'Isn't it strange that only at funeral masses is praise dished out in this parish.' 'I came to know the late Deirdre during her short but regular visits home and she epitomised all that made the Dowlings such a respected family in our midst. She practised her Christian beliefs right up till the end, even to the extent of reciting a short prayer before meeting her Creator on one of Northern Ireland's inhospitable streets. She loved and lived life as only she knew how and died for a cause she neither sufficiently understood nor totally believed in. She did it selflessly so that those deprived the freedom and rights she took for granted might one day too be liberated.' Willie Joe Kissane nudged his wife Noreen seated beside him in the second last pew and whispered 'I hope he steers clear of north-south politics,' acknowledging his propensity to digress from the main topic.

The priest then invited a special friend of the family to complete the homily. 'We gather here this morning to mourn and commemorate one of Inistogue's most distinguished daughters. The Dowling family deserve all our sympathy and support and we join in prayer that God will sustain them through this great loss and grief. She devoted her life trying to correct injustices and her noble deeds will forever be remembered and venerated. Though the Dowling family will find it hard to come to terms with Deirdre's untimely and, to a great extent, senseless death, all her great achievements will help to assuage their grief. There are numerous casualties of the acrimonious Northern Ireland conflict over almost two decades, many of whom like Deirdre gave their lives seeking equal rights for all citizens. Lamentably, we are still greatly distant from that honourable target. I know that many in the congregation harbour strong republican views but I'm not allowed to express mine.' The many nervous shuffles and loud whispers left few doubts about where he stood on this issue. That brought the soeeches to a timely end.

It only remained for Fr. Finucane to express, albeit in a more friendly and personal way, sympathy to family, relatives and many friends, something he had regularly done since he first arrived in Inistogue. To Paul Dowling seated in the first pew, the whole proceedings appeared almost as incongruous as the previous evening's events at his home. Why, he wondered, was Fr. Finucane "sitting on the fence" and not more forthright about the circumstances of his sister's death? It was nice to hear his sweet and kindly words but were these mere platitudes and spoken without any real conviction or sincerity? Did many of those present have too ambivalent an attitude to the events up north to express a view and, even if they did, could it be relied upon to be true? Paul sensed this from an early age and was loath to express his own views both to strangers and members of his own family. It was this uncomfortable situation that propelled him along the path of peace, a course that had distanced him from family and friends alike. Many of the same reasons encouraged Deirdre to leave home and indirectly to her early and tragic death.

It was now time for private grief in the Dowling household. But it would shortly lead to a lot of soul-searching, question's long-left unasked and an equal number without realistic or practical answers. Did it need the trauma of a loved one's death to hasten the process? Irish history is a continuum of tragedies and many lessons are left unlearned. Hearts and minds change with difficulty, and all too slowly, and people suffer the consequences. Henceforth all that can be relied upon is an abundance of hope mingled with all-too-little confidence.

*

Front page pictures in the following day's newspapers told their own horrific stories. Deirdre Dowling was one of 23 killed with more than 150 injured, seven of whom died within 48 hours and another five more slowly and painfully over the next two weeks. Mayhem suddenly descended on a town long known for its peace and tranquillity. In times of distress the willingness of fellow citizens and passers-by to attend to the needs of the dying and injured knows no bounds and Ballysorley on that fateful night was yet another shining example. Ambulances staffed with paramedics and nurses, and with sirens blaring and lights flashing, whizzed through the narrow streets at breakneck speed rushing the casualties to hospitals. Medical doctors and hospital staff worked frantically through the night performing emergency operations and administering to the seriously injured. The town's services were stretched to their limits and police activity and security were all-intrusive. While saving lives was of paramount importance, no time was lost in trying to bring the culprits of this hideous crime to justice. The sense of outrage was palpable both near and far.

The carnage was captured on amateur video and later shown on national and international television. It brought into sharp focus the anguish and pain of families losing one or more of their loved ones, many of whom had no political affiliations or ambitions. They were simply innocent victims who happened to be in the wrong place and going about their daily business. One particular horror story was a virtual tear-jerker: a father extricating himself from the rubble and in deep shock heard a short distance away his daughter's cry for help, whose right hand was the only part of her body visible through the mass of concrete and debris. As he strained to free her, she died holding his hand and saying her immortal words 'Take care of Mam and yourself.' Her father was left a broken but forgiving man for the remaining decade of his life, exuding understanding and compassion rarely seen in the emotionally-scarred. Those who died were the more fortunate. It was the maimed, disfigured and brain-damaged who suffered interminably, unable to live normal lives and a burden on their families and friends. Material reconstruction was steady and swift, buoyed by the financial aid coming voluntarily, but it took a generation or more to regenerate the minds and spirits. Was Ballysorley the atrocity to end all atrocities in this war-torn province? How was the recovery process to begin, with nothing short of a miracle needed to heal the deep physical and mental wounds?

Newspaper reports tried to piece together the events leading up to the two separate bombs which bore the hallmarks of the I.R.A.'s evil intention to cause maximum destruction. Some 45 minutes before the two bombs exploded, the police received and acted immediately upon a coded I.R.A. message. What Jim and Deirdre perceived to be a traffic accident delaying them en route was something more than that. The police were also using it as an opportunity to stop at random cars they suspected to be carrying weapons or explosives. Why they were able to get through the cordon remains a mystery. With Deirdre next to Jim in the front passenger seat, it appeared to the police the couple were going about their normal business. It was just a cursory road check as the main thrust of the security forces' efforts was in searching for suspect packages and abandoned vehicles and in evacuating people from buildings. But, as happened so often before, time was too short and the explosions wreaked havoc before the work had scarcely begun. It was a tactical I.R.A. ploy to drive home to its enemy how powerful and unpredictable an organisation it had become.

On that fateful evening Jim McCabe faced the greatest dilemma of his entire life. Should he leave his just-deceased loved one or stay by her side and risk almost immediate arrest? As he pondered the question an ambulance arrived to collect the fatally wounded. Jim made the heart-rending instantaneous decision to pose non-involvement and nonchalantly moved away from the scene. At a safe distance he could observe Deirdre's draped body being loaded into the back of an ambulance which immediately sped towards a nearby hospital. In the midst of trying to force back his tears, he was painfully aware of the dangers that lay ahead. He had to get out of Ballysorley and do so quickly.

A couple of streets away he hailed a taxi and asked the driver to drop him at McDaid's bar, a safe half mile away from where he arranged to meet Gerald, Vincent and his sister Jane. He chose to walk - or secretly run - the final stretch lest the police linked the taxi run to Jim's disappearance from town to meet his accomplices. As he approached the house, he broke into a cold sweat. What is he to say when Gerald asks him about the whereabouts of his sister Deirdre? Must he tell the truth or concoct a lie saying she was injured in the blast and taken for treatment to a local hospital? He would opt for the latter and do the explaining later. It was very important to leave Ballysorley with all due haste.

They could see from Jim's limp, which he hitherto tried to conceal, that he was physically scarred. He said Deirdre was recovering in hospital from a similar-type injury and would likely be released within a couple of days, though the tone of his remarks was less than convincing. Gerald was equally sceptical of getting the full story but, even for somebody of his own flesh and blood, he knew there was little he could do to help due to the risk of being apprehended. In all their previous escapades, never once did they reach this enormous dilemma or impasse. But freedom-fighters usually have one or two last options to rely on, such as a willing accomplice appearing and whisking them to safety.

Ironically, it was Gerald's close and trusted friend travelling the long journey from Inistogue that saved the day. Driving along minor roads through the dead of night they snaked their way to the safe refuge of the Irish Republic, affording them a well-earned sigh of relief. From there on it was plain sailing to a virtual heroes' welcome at Inistogue. If the hard work seemed to be over, it really had only just begun.

Police investigations were zeroing in on the perpetrators but apprehending those responsible would be difficult and protracted. The republican exploits of the McCabes and Dowlings were legendary but how could Deirdre's death be adequately explained? For one thing the police had no file on her but could she be a willing accomplice to this despicable act? They certainly must not rule it out. Jim's bombed-out car left little concrete evidence and his quick disappearance from the scene further confounded fact-finding procedures. Police were painfully aware that the greater the atrocity, the less prepared were witnesses to come forward and assist them. Ballysorley was yet another typical example.

So immersed were the two families in republicanism that the task of extricating Deirdre's remains from Ballysorley's general hospital fell to none other than Paul or "Mr. Clean". It rankled with Seamus having to plead with his "prodigal" son to do what he himself ought to have taken on. Paul was both elated and honoured, seeing it as, perhaps, the first small step towards reconciliation with a Dad from whom he was drifting further and further away. Paul knew he could move freely into Northern Ireland and do what was required to get his beloved sister's body home without the risk of being questioned or apprehended. He wondered aloud whether he was seen as a hero or an outcast. For the youngest son it was a lonely journey but he fought back the tears and anxiety in the hope it might serve as an example to other families. He vowed to be always guided by his conscience and to act as he saw right and just. He felt justifiably proud when Fr. Finucane, during the funeral homily, singled him out for special praise for all he did to lessen the family's burden and sorrow.

Much of what happened before, during and immediately after the Ballysorley bombing was forever to remain a mystery. Some say the security forces underestimated the I.R.A's. ability to strike with such ferocity and, when it did, they were unprepared and caught off guard. The I.R.A. members involved were quick to point out that small but important last-minute hitches reduced the potential carnage, an admission that both scared all responsible citizens and hardened the police' resolve to step up its vigilance. It was the type of fear and hysteria the I.R.A. had expected to generate.

The horror confronting Jim on that dreadful evening in Ballysorley would continue to torment him for years to come. His guilt-complex consumed him during the day and prevented him from his usual restful night's sleep. He craved for open discussions of what happened which might alleviate his own culpability and save him from near suicide. His first big opportunity came at Deirdre's own home on the night of the funeral. It was shortly after midnight when Joe Moriarty interrupted the eerie silence and tried to console his long-time friend and neighbour, Seamus. It was no coincidence that Jim, seated next to Seamus and also in need of a few kind words, lent an attentive ear. One by one, others soon joined the discussion and gave moral support. Apolitical Joe was quick in his analysis and both wise and practical with his advice.

'My dear friend, Seamus, I wish there was something I could say or do to lessen your intense grief. In the almost three decades of Northern Ireland's strife, never once did anyone imagine it might come to this. We were inured into thinking that all the casualties were on the enemy's side, mere numbers briefly mentioned on TV and reported in the newspapers. Not once did we stop to think that they too were human, many with wives, children and numerous friends. Those killed came from many towns and villages, not too dissimilar to Inistogue, leaving sorrow and heartbreak in its wake. Now, for the first time, it has struck at the very heart of Inistogue and we must try to come to terms with it as only the resolute villagers know best.'

A small group of close friends in discussion believed they should firstly grieve for Deirdre and, through all their combined prayers, hope she will attain her eternal reward in Heaven. They were adamant that, sad though Deirdre's tragic and untimely death is, she can do more than any of the living among us to start healing the deep divisions and wounds in Anglo-Irish relations.' A sideways glance from Seamus was enough to reveal his scepticism of the words spoken. He knew that they were only trying to put a brave face on things and as always were doing their utmost to help.

A long-time friend looked towards the sad and dispirited Jim and prayed he could find a few uplifting words. He reminded him that Deirdre's death was a freak accident that could neither be foreseen nor prevented and nobody, including Jim, was in any way responsible. She went there of her own free will because she wanted to. That she and Jim were in love with each other also happened accidentally. He said that of all the mourning taking place here tonight, Jim's grief is particularly poignant and he should remember he is the focus of everybody's thoughts and prayers. He shouldn't have any guilt complex and be aware he has the moral strength and resilience to bounce back. Fully supporting him in his struggle to normality will be his close family as well as numerous friends and admirers. The strong message he sent to Jim is to look to your his own promising future and banish all negative thoughts. Those in the room knew from Jim's changed complexion that the healing process had already begun. A few of the more experienced were convinced it would all pass quickly and easily.

It was now Jim's turn to bare his mind and heart, although somewhat at a loss of how to begin. 'Despite all the kind and consoling words, I - and I alone - am prepared to take the major share of the blame for Deidre's death.' By opening thus, he at once was facing up to his responsibilities for what had happened and was bridging the gulf, albeit ever so slightly, in Dowling-McCabe relations. It was a drowning man's attempt to extricate himself from the depths and regain consciousness, and Jim was making a superhuman effort.

'Right now I've never felt so sad and remorseful in my entire life. My foremost thoughts and worries on reaching Inistogue were how could I meet Seamus and Nora, look them squarely in the eye and expect an iota of forgiveness for their lovely daughter's death. What God-given right did I have to influence and cajole Deirdre into dangerous acts of terrorism? Why did I not discourage her from taking any part in the Ballysorley fiasco? Questions ... questions ... questions that have tortured me since the disaster first struck! It will be a small consolation for the Dowlings to know that, however great was their love for Deirdre, my love for her was many times stronger. In less than six months, we were to be happily married.' The grief, that had consumed Jim of late, was again returning and he took a couple of minutes to compose himself before resuming.

'When Deirdre breathed her last something too died in me. My one regret since then is leaving her under the hard concrete and debris that claimed her life. Was I overly concerned about my own safety, fleeing from the scene lest I'd be arrested and charged? I beg the Dowling family's understanding and forgiveness for my indiscretion. I realise it was a cowardly act and not in keeping with the bravery associated with freedom fighters. It was a split-second decision the responsibility for which will last a lifetime. But, with the help of family and friends, I want to gradually leave the past behind me and make a new beginning, the precise nature of which still requires much thought and consideration. Tonight signals the start of part two of my life.'

It was about all he could utter before reaching for a tissue to dry the free-flowing tears of a drained and heart-broken man. There was an eerie post-midnight silence which was punctuated only by occasional sobs and sniffles. It fell to kind neighbour Nora O'Connor to lift the tangible gloom and depression. 'It seems to me that light refreshments will not be out of place.' She breezed through the room, placed a trayful of sandwiches, cake and a pot of tea on a small table before exiting just as quickly. 'Begorrah, there's a woman that would brighten any home,' remarked bachelor Joe. It was enough to divert attention, however momentarily, from the subject of death and allow conversation to recommence on local topics. The hitherto quiet and subdued Seamus felt the need to have a heart-to-heart talk with Jim and clear up any misunderstandings.

He admitted to Jim that it would take months - and even years - before coming to terms with and accepting the death of his loving daughter. Since the bad news broke he has been in a constant daze and asking questions such as...why...why... why did this have to happen to us, without getting a rational or meaningful answer. Nor will there ever be any, adding to the frustration and sense of loss. Odd as it may appear, our first reaction, as well as many in Inistogue, was one of anger directed at you, Jim. Angry that you allowed Deirdre to get involved in a life or death situation. He confirmed that at times like these it is normal to look for scapegoats, people to blame and be held responsible. That early phase has passed and he now looks more objectively at what happened. Jim can rest assured that neither Nora nor himself - and indeed all the family - hold him responsible. They were both equal players in a game that, unfortunately, went tragically wrong for Deirdre. It is therapeutic to mourn, and continue mourning, her loss but we would like to exonerate you, Jim, from all responsibility so that you can rid yourself of that all-consuming guilt-complex.

Some moments later there was fire in Seamus' eyes when he resumed. 'The British occupation forces in Northern Ireland, indirectly responsible for Deirdre's death, should hear my message loud and clear. The Dowling family will do everything within its power to avenge Deirdre's death. The Ballysorley bombs killed and maimed people, many of whom were innocent. They achieved the desired objective of maximising havoc and devastation and of sending a clear signal to the British of the I.R.A.'s capacity and intent. The next time, British soldiers themselves will be the sole target. Only when many of them meet horrible and untimely deaths, will I rest peacefully knowing that Deirdre's death was not in vain. We expected that the Ballysorley bombs would signal the end but there is still much unfinished business.'

Nobody had the audacity to question Seamus or doubt his resolve. With a firm and quick farewell to all present, he took his leave. With his head full of sorrow and a desperate urgency for revenge, sleep didn't come easily that night.

*

The Ballysorley attack was not only structurally devastating but morally destructive and weakened the long-existing bonds between the Dowling and McCabe families. The repercussions strained human relations as never before. Try though they did, the senior Dowlings and McCabes were too ready to blame and counterblame each other for what happened. At times of low morale, they even began questioning the relevance of what they were trying to achieve. The seeds of doubt were taking root and, if allowed to grow and mature, could seriously damage cross-border communication and cooperation.

The degree of cooperation took a temporary knock due to the heightened police security in trying to track down the bombers. They were dogged and relentless and vowed to work long and hard in pursuit of the culprits. Little helpful information was forthcoming, drastically slowing the rate of progress. But experience had taught them that 'patience' was the key to success and would eventually help in putting pieces of the jigsaw together. Of the atrocities committed over the past two decades, only a fraction of those responsible were apprehended. Wasn't this the pattern of Anglo-Irish history since day one? Most were patently aware of the barbarity of the crime but, of all those law-abiding nationalists on both sides of the border, few or any of those with incriminating information were ready to come forward. It was this ambivalence that guaranteed the prolongation of the independence struggle. The threat of reprisals, including possible executions by the I.R.A., against those divulging information limited the flow of evidence to the police. Irish nationalists espousing the ideals of an united Ireland, but who simultaneously abhorred violence, were equally slow in coming forward. This policy played into the hands of the I.R.A., at once antagonising and frustrating the British.

During Seamus' sleepless nights and long bouts of solitude and introspection, he began to ask questions never before contemplated. He appreciated that in the aftermath of Jim losing the greatest love of his life, he must be seen to be big-hearted in his forgiveness towards him. He didn't wish to exacerbate Jim's already uncontrollable grief and agony, even if that loss is part of his own flesh and blood. He was anxious that this magnanimous gesture would be interpreted by his longtime friend Shane as a continuation of their cordial relations. Even though Shane hadn't expressed so personally, Seamus was ready to give him the benefit of the doubt.

But it was Jim's bizarre or unorthodox behaviour on that night that threw up many unanswered questions. Two, in particular, perplexed and worried him. If he was the brave republican he proclaimed himself to be, why did he react like a scared cat, with his only concern being to get to safety at all costs without fear of capture? Why did he abandon his dying fiancee, the one person he often proclaimed to love more than life itself? He instead acted selfishly and cowardly, traits not in keeping with accepted behaviour of normal, much less military, people. Besides, from most accounts, he botched his side of the operation, the one big test he was charged with since joining the I.R.A. At the funeral I did not want to be judge and jury on his technical ability but rather be a consoling and forgiving influence to help heal his troubled mind and soul. Hard though it is for me to accept Deirdre's terrible loss, had I Jim's problems and anxiety I'd be heading for a mental institution.

It was crunch time too for Jane. Before getting actively involved in the Ballysorley escapade her life was happy and carefree. In Vincent she found a sincere and trusted friend and the "chemistry" was there from day one. Together, they radiated happiness for all to see. There was an implicit understanding that sooner rather than later they would marry. More than once Jane dropped gentle hints but Vincent was in no hurry. He always cited pressure of work as a credible alibi and, with his furious pace, who could disagree? She intuitively knew that when his 'unfinished business in the north' was put to rest, they would quickly settle down and start a family. It was the subject of her thoughts by day and infiltrated her night-time dreams. Life was comfortable and rosy.

Or so it seemed until serious politics came in the way. Vincent's increasing profile in the I.R.A., and with it more work and responsibilities, excited him but unnerved Jane. He looked to a future giving him greater powers and commanding much more respect, something he had always aspired to. Moreover, he was confident of effectively using those powers to achieve justice and equal rights for the disadvantaged nationalist community in the north. At first Jane was an innocent bystander but, whether it was born of admiration for him or his subtle influence, she gradually assisted him. It started with simple tasks and culminated, with serious repercussions, at Ballysorley. She often questioned her sanity but, buoyed by more hope than confidence, prayed that one day there would be an end to it all. She hadn't fully learned the lessons of recent Irish history.

In the immediate aftermath of Ballysorley, long-established friendships were never again the same. The great devastation begged many questions for which there were no meaningful answers, no matter how long and intense the post mortems. Even for those directly implicated, whose motives could not be entirely condemned, it called into question their inhumanity to innocents in order to justify a cause. Jane also had reservations about continuing her relationship with Vincent, a man who privately expressed his love for her but at the same time showed little remorse for taking the lives of others. Could she ever feel entirely happy sharing her life with him and entrust the upbringing of a family? Would he apply the same principles in promoting his children's education and choosing their careers? Because of her own intense remorse for Ballysorley victims, it was time for Jane to act.

The opportunity came exactly a week later, coinciding with one of the all-too-rare dates they had time for lately. For once, it was Jane who took the initiative saying they should meet to discuss matters of mutual interest after Vincent detected a tone of anxiety over the telephone. He didn't want any rift between them and was prepared to do his utmost to allay her doubts and fears. Above all, he wished to steer clear of any reference to the developing strains between the McCabes and Dowlings.

It was after dinner, in a small hotel ten miles from her home town of Liscorley, that Jane got round to broaching the subject concerning her most. Holding Vincent's hand, she began.

'Not once since we first met did I ever doubt your feelings and intentions and I can vouch they are mutual. Ever since I began helping you in Northern Ireland, I felt ill at ease, sensing that what I was doing ran contrary to my principles and beliefs. To a greater or lesser degree I've been personally responsible for the loss of innocent lives, reaching a crisis at Ballysorley, and I'm filled with sadness and remorse. My brother Jim is presently suffering his own private hell, having seen his fiancee die from a bomb they both helped to detonate. He indirectly killed the one person he loved and was soon to marry. Picture what intense agony he's going through! It raises questions in many of our minds, those who hold human life sacred and want it protected, not desecrated. The carnage at Ballysorley changed me as I'd never anticipated.'

Vincent interrupted, 'Never did I anticipate having to meet under these circumstances and hurting your feelings so profoundly.'

After a short pause, she went on to explain that what happeded at Ballysorley could also change their feelings for each other but that was entirely in their ownn hands. Vincent was totally committed to the cause he pursued and she had no wish to influence him. Should she try and succeed, he may never forgive her and she didn't relish the prospect of living with the possible consequences. After much deliberation she had her mind made up and that means opting out of all activities connected with the liberation movement. By implication, she was unable to continue a relationship with someone upholding ideals she'd decided to abandon.

She knew from Vincent's jerky movements he was visibly shaken at what he'd just heard, whereupon he placed a tender arm around her waist and began his own confession.

'May I begin by saying that my love for you, Jane, is unwavering and it never was any different. All the time we've been together, it was nothing short of special. I take the blame for involving you in work you'd never have chosen of your own free will. For that I ask your understanding and beg your forgiveness. We are lucky to have escaped several life-threatening moments but not so fortunate was our good friend, Deirdre, who your brother Jim will mourn for many a day. My heart goes out to him and I pray daily that God will give him the strength and courage to carry on.'

Vincent, then took a few minutes to explain that he too didn't chart his own career because republicanism and his surname

"Tuohy" are virtually synonymous. From as early as he cares to remember, the topics of conversation in his house alternated between the numerous Irish martyrs and the urgency to avenge their deaths on the British who carried out such despicable crimes. At home and in school he was taught to believe that many British acted unfairly and brutally and retribution was obligatory to even the score. His grandfather had such a philosophy, who imparted it to his son and now Vincent has inherited the mantle. Did he have a choice? It was an unsavoury one, either to follow suit and risk his life in folk-hero style or abscond and be an outcast from the family. So far he has followed the first alternative but, in the light of what occurred at Ballysorley, he's leaning more and more towards the second.

'Whatever form my life takes, I want you, Jane, to be at the centre of it.' He paused momentarily to observe her widening smile of satisfaction, before continuing. 'Long before reaching my teenage years, when boyhood dreams and ambition were gnawing at me, I wanted to build my future in the United States. It was the hope of many youngsters but my case received an added impetus from uncle Jim in New York. During his biennial holidays in his native Cork he saw from the myriad questions posed my extraordinary interest in job opportunities in the United States.

'In your republican home, was it not an uphill battle to get away?' enquired Jane.

'It certainly was' said Vincent, before continuing. 'My father did his utmost to dampen my enthusiasm, preferring instead to channel my boundless young energy towards a cause he cherished. I acquiesced and decided to do my father's bidding, at least for a few years. I soon discovered there was no backing down or opting out without grave consequences. Each year took its toll and I was becoming increasingly uneasy and Dad, meanwhile, succeeded in discouraging Jim from luring me to the land of opportunity. Now, with the benefit of hindsight, it was a tactical error but it's not too late Jane to reinvent ourselves and make a new beginning. I suggest we both work hard towards making it possible and we shall take whatever route is best for us.'

Vincent couldn't have uttered those reassuring words a few months earlier when his mind appeared bent on the dangerous path he was then pursuing. Had her decision to quit been an ultimatum or an artificial 'gun to his head' saying that, unless he 'comes in from the cold,' there is no way forward for both of them? Was he becoming weary of a struggle yielding nothing tangible or did his love for her cause a change of heart? It may well be some of both but Jane did not think beyond his recent expressions of love which were now beginning to take on a new meaning.

Mental attitudes among the elderly, however, change slowly or not at all. Seamus' natural wit and usual outgoing personality were in decline, as if Deirdre's passing damaged his brain's concentration centre and zest for life. He was seen by neighbours walking the narrow twisting roads he had known and grown to love since childhood. He made a point of starting out as the evening light was fading and trekked for almost two hours to allow his mind ample time to wander before returning exhausted to an anxious Nora. He feigned excuses of having to count the number of cattle in a remote field or to rescue a calf from a barbed wire fence and the alibis were becoming flimsier by the day. Nora knew well it was his own peculiar way of exorcising the demons plaguing him, his mind needing time to heal and she dared interfere. He sat up long after Nora had gone to sleep, lay awake in bed for long stretches and, when he finally closed his heavy eyes, was prone to turbulent dreams and even frightening nightmares during which he screamed for help. It took all of Nora's years of understanding and patience to calm and sedate him. He withdrew into himself and needed time and space before he could return to some semblance of normality.

During the few private moments he confided in Nora, she knew there was a rare mixture of grief and hate gnawing at his inner being. His great burden of sorrow from Deirdre's death was balanced by an equal degree of hate for those responsible. He wished he was twenty years younger, with all the vigour of his former self, to resume the fight against his arch enemy - the British forces and establishment occupying what he considered to be a legitimate province of his country. It was this desire to get even, a goal he might never attain in his lifetime, that caused him so much pain and anxiety. He felt like an athlete in the throes of retirement, ever eager to continue an exacting and rigorous exercise that his body can no longer deliver. He was all too aware of being genetically programmed to pursue ideals to which he was not wholeheartedly committed.

*

The first two weeks after Deirdre's death was Jim's living hell, a time of recrimination and remorse, the 'what might have beens' and the 'if onlys'. What if they hadn't met on that Tripoli-bound plane, a young girl trying to escape the day-in day-out humdrum republicanism of home life only to fall unexpectedly into the arms of another hell-bent on a similar course. It was only after deep thought and meditation, often during bouts of interrupted sleep, did the full impact of his guilt and responsibility hit him. The one consoling feature - if there could be any - was he never applied pressure on Deirdre to engage in activities alien to her wishes. But did he influence her? Of that, he wasn't absolutely sure and a source of his greatest concern. He vividly remembers that day in Tripoli and the long delay before giving her definitive response of support. She likely agonized for days on end before reaching her decision and, then, what did love have to do with it? Judged by the pace of subsequent events, Jim was sure it contributed handsomely.

He was now in reflective mode, brooding upon how blindly he followed his paternal instincts. Were it not for Shane's constant reminders of one's patriotic obligations, he might have continued his full-time teaching career. When he decided to take leave-of-absence, it wasn't intended to last more than three years. He gave too little consideration to the I.R.A's long-term goal and how difficult it would be to leave early and so the years rolled by. He gained ample experience on strategies to kill and maim people, sadly not all enemies, during two years of intensive training and precious little about developing young children's minds. It may not yet be too late to return to his first-choice career which satisfied him as he never thought possible.

Could he still do so and not be discredited by his father and the I.R.A? It was high time for him to decide and not be swayed.

Soundings from Syria boded poorly for the I.R.A.'s military operations, another reason prompting Jim to reconsider his future. He didn't have all the facts but heard from close colleagues about President Kemal Siddique's growing disillusionment with the slow rate of progress. On assuming the mantle from Libya's Al-Madhi, he held great expectations of quick military strikes leading to an early victory for the I.R.A. He would then emerge as the master tactician and claim fame for Ireland's reunification, a task attempted by so many that met with only one defeat after another. His own continuous support and training for the Palestinians hadn't taught him the hard lesson that guerrilla war successes are painstakingly difficult and slow. The Palestinians are still mired in their new *Intifada* struggle against the Israelis and it's taking much of his time and attention. His first flush of elation at being entrusted with the Irish job was beginning to wear thin. He wanted to accelerate military strikes beyond the I.R.A.'s capacity to deliver, had little knowledge of the involved logistics and was further strained by cultural and language barriers. His present contribution was whittled down to little more than impassioned, and often empty, rhetoric. President Siddique's fading involvement and interest tilted the balance in favour of Jim moving away from a lifestyle that had taken the most valuable years of his youth. He had a clear idea of what he wanted to do but didn't yet quite know how to overcome the obstacles confronting him.

Luckily, Shane as always was very supportive. Jim recalled with pleasure his Dad encouraging him from an early age, saying there was but one short life and it should be lived to the full. He sacrificed much for Jim's education and was extremely proud when he qualified as a teacher. But, did his Dad's republican zeal unduly influence him to join the I.R.A., something that constantly worried the elder and all the more since Deirdre's untimely death? Jim could be excused for taking an unforgiving stance but he wasn't a man to bear grudges, especially for an accident nobody could have foreseen. His Dad and himself always enjoyed open and friendly relations, with an implicit understanding to discuss problems as they arose and not bottle them up. Jim was very grateful for this mature approach, being ever mindful of how little of it existed between Seamus and Gerald Dowling. Seamus made it known to all his children that he was in charge, how he wanted things done and rarely encouraged or welcomed dialogue. Not even Nora's occasional hints to adjust to changing times were much heeded. There was no doubting Seamus' allegiance to the 'old school' and it was very likely to continue.

Jim's first major obstacle along a new life's path he was convinced of pursuing was to leave the I.R.A. He did not underestimate the challenge as he knew many friends and colleagues who tried and failed. There was an implicit understanding that once you passed the strict criteria and was accepted into that noble organisation, nobody with even a trace of national blood in his/her veins would ever contemplate leaving. For those who did, they were constantly encouraged - or even coerced - to rejoin, with life made distinctly unpleasant for those not conforming. And there was very good reason for this behaviour. Former I.R.A. members were seen as "valuable merchandise" for Britain's security service, some often providing strategic information on the inner workings of the I.R.A. and, above all, it's strategy and future operations. Little wonder the I.R.A. tried to do everything within its power to 'hijack' classified information before falling into enemy hands. The ultimate penalty of death awaited those accused, or even suspected, of passing such vital information.

He took comfort from what might be interpreted as extenuating circumstances. Firstly, due to his Dad's long membership and association with the I.R.A. he had good friends and contacts within the Army Council or Supreme Command. His Dad was in a strong position to discuss with them his intention to leave and to reassure them of his continued loyalty and non-disclosure of secret information. That should be sweet music to their suspicious ears and the very least he was prepared to guarantee. Secondly, members at even Army Council level were patently aware of Deirdre's death, the circumstances of same and her impending marriage to Jim. Besides, many attended her funeral and even reputed hardliners were moved to tears. Is it not reasonable, therefore, for them to empathise with Jim's loss and immense sorrow? Has he not a compelling reason to question his continued membership of an organisation which directly or indirectly took from him the one person he loved? There was still concern for the I.R.A.'s primary fear of a leakage of information but this was regarded as either slight or non-existent. Jim was confident his transition from so-called terrorist to law-abiding citizen was a virtual reality and felt justifiably elated.

He clearly envisioned the course of his new life with its primary goal being to atone for Deirdre's death. He gave it weeks of deep thought and consideration and the framework for action was beginning to emerge . Of one thing he was sure - he would return to school, constituting the core of all his future programmes and good deeds. He saw in children's young minds the enormous hunger for knowledge and their insatiable capacity to digest and retain it. As a teacher he was scrupulously attentive to imparting the truth, allowing children time to form their own ideas of right and wrong, fostering understanding and trust between those of different creeds and economic backgrounds and helping to create communities where there is justice and equality. This is no mean task but he was determined to do all he could. He realised that correctly influencing young minds does far more to change the political, economic and social life of Northern Ireland than can ever be done by other means.

Jim remembers his own school days and how a particular history teacher coloured - or rather discoloured - his views and understanding of Northern Ireland. As an avowed Nationalist he was fiercely on the Catholic minority's side and much of what he taught was indeed true. But, instead of teaching the facts and allowing us as students to form our own opinions, he presented them in his own contrived and biased way. He left us in no doubt that the British were the villains and the cause of all our present day ills. Instead of helping us to understand the injustices so that we may work to alleviate or correct them, he fostered in us a bitter hatred of the British and all things British. This influence transcended to the streets, villages, towns and cities and inevitably provoked clashes and sectarian violence. Most certainly there were many similar instances of biased instruction in Unionist/Protestant schools. The result was a lethal time bomb, whose manifestations were seen time and again in tragic deaths and many injuries.

During all those years when Jim rather innocently and blindly followed the military route, he feared it would hinder instead of solve Northern Ireland's problems. Had he learned the hard way or did it take Deirdre's death to awaken him to reality? Whatever triggered it, there was no going back and he was on a reconciliation course to which he will direct all of his energy and time. He will form an organisation to rival the I.R.A., whose members' voices and deeds will be heard and known throughout the province. It will only partially atone for Deirdre's death but it will change minds and hearts as never before contemplated.

*

Early December's minimal daylight hours around Inistogue found many in hibernation mode. Were it not for Christmas approaching and all the childhood thrills and excitement it evoked among adults, it was sure to be a long drawn-out winter. Even Paul Dowling was beginning to question the wisdom of his decision to return home only three weeks ago.

The initial exhilaration of coming to the spot holding most of his sweetest memories was quickly fading. Nevertheless, he was both expected and obliged to do so and, in addition to meeting and socialising with several friends over the holidays, there were numerous spin-off benefits.

Despite the desperate need to shed some of the extra pounds his mother's rich food had helped to notch up, he had little mind to walk the rain-soaked fields surrounding his home . That must wait until later. He glanced at a letter from Michael McCabe with his Johannesburg return address clearly stamped on the upper left-hand corner. He remembered receiving it more than a month ago and laying it aside until he fully digested its contents and found an opportune moment to reply. With the darkening clouds and enveloping mists concealing much of county Kerry's horizon, there was no better time to respond. Seeing that certain issues to be raised were private, he made sure he wrote it secretly and outside earshot of his parents. He approached the task with gusto.

Inistogue, County Kerry
December 7, 1988

Dear Michael,

Let me begin with a valid justification instead of an apology. If I'd replied promptly to your interesting and thought-provoking letter, it would have conveyed outdated news, inappropriate suggestions and inaccurate projections. Such is the pace of change in our little secluded part of the globe. Allowing more than a month to elapse before replying gives me the breathing space to ponder on what has happened, analyse its significance and how it impacts on all our lives. I'm unsure though whether I can adequately interpret and explain the recent complex events unfolding around us.

Precisely three weeks ago today I arrived home after completing my last peacekeeping mission abroad. From my perspective, all were moderately successful and entirely fulfilling. Nothing in my short life gave me greater satisfaction than lessening human confrontations, particularly those involving the loss of many lives. Working in foreign lands, where expenditure on weapons of human destruction often accounts for more than one half of the total spent, instilled in me a revulsion of these misguided policies. Imagine how much food could be bought to feed the needy starving masses! Irrespective of the differences leading to strive, it's amazing how much peacekeepers can achieve by simply being present on the ground and trying to defuse tensions. Not that it's a viable long term solution but it buys time until a more permanent truce can be negotiated. A similar programme in our troubled province of Ulster might have saved numerous lives over the last three decades, including my own beloved sister Deirdre's life.

In these times of rapid communications I guess you are well informed of developments - or rather disasters - in Northern Ireland. And what happened at Ballysorley is nothing short of a major republican fiasco, a botched attempt to score a whopping victory at an enormous cost in human suffering. It all went sadly wrong and nobody is prepared to accept the blame. Most analysts are convinced the attack was ill-conceived, inadequately staffed and supported, insufficiently rehearsed and poorly executed. It has disrupted and delayed the entire programme by at least two or three years and, at a time when Syrian arms supply is at an all time low, many doubt it will ever again regain its momentum. What is particularly poignant for all my family is that Deirdre was the unfortunate victim of this inept bungling. We are now experiencing a taste of the horror and anguish that has plagued Northern Ireland society for far too long - with no logical end in sight.

Deirdre's tragic death was the beginning and not the end of my nightmare. My Dad, with whom at the best of times I have little rapport, had the nerve to request me to travel north to formally identify and claim her body. It was the saddest and most ignominious task of my whole life. Neither my Dad nor Gerald dared set foot in the north because their republican deeds or misdeeds left them easy prey for security police. I remember the long and sad trek northwards, being scrutinised and cross-examined as if I myself was a hunted terrorist, and the longer homeward trip without the support or comfort of a close relative or friend. It was the subject of horrible dreams and even nightmares for weeks on end. In many respects, I felt as though I was used as a guinea pig, to do the dirty work that nobody else was fit or prepared to undertake. And when it was all over I was still the "outcast" in my Dad's eyes, failing to heal the old deep-seated wounds.

The hitherto strong bonds of friendship between the Dowling and McCabe families also nosedived. At the funeral in Inistogue and immediately afterwards both sides agreed not to blame one another for what went wrong. These were mere words and of transient duration. No sooner had they returned to their respective locations than the era of silence began that was never to be broken. Old time close friends Shane McCabe and Seamus Dowling struggled to regain their composure. Not that they became bitter enemies but both intuitively knew they indirectly contributed to Deirdre's untimely death. Seamus had convincing reasons to be more aggrieved and, through his wilful silence, was sending strong messages to Shane. For his part, Shane had the will and inclination to befriend Seamus once again, as if nothing had occurred, but knew full well that Seamus was not yet ready nor was he ever likely to be. And so the silence continues, more through misunderstanding and lack of empathy rather than any conscious desire to remain uncommunicative.

It is this silence, Michael, that is distancing me further from my Dad and is also Mam's growing concern. His behaviour becomes more bizarre and mysterious by the day. In the fading twilight he goes for long walks through the small farm that has been his 'world' since drawing his first breath. He returns long after dark not having met or spoken to anyone, preferring to be alone with his thoughts and, more importantly, the sadness that gnaws at his very soul. After going to bed, often when my Mam is already fast asleep, he lies awake for what seems eternity, looking into the eerie darkness of his small bedroom. It is this bottling up of sorrow, and not openly trying to come to terms with Deirdre's loss, that cuts him off from close relatives and friends. Even my poor Mam is distraught and knows not how to respond or behave. When I try to confide in him and help it is usually met with a curt and frosty remark to mind my own business. Not sure why I burden you with all our family worries but it helps to put my future at Inistogue into clearer perspective.

And that future certainly looks precarious. Much as I'd dearly love to help and see my Dad through his present difficulties, I fear my presence is merely delaying the healing process.

Far from abandoning his republican zeal, he has let it be known to friend and foe alike he will not rest easily until he fully avenges Deirdre's death. What form this will take, or how he proposes to achieve it, I'm unsure if he himself is entirely clear. It may be an overreaction to a personal loss he never anticipated and only time and counselling can ease him back to reality. I fear for his health and wellbeing because what he has endured over the past couple of months would test anybody's resoluteness. After careful consideration, I've decided my situation at Inistogue is untenable and, as a young man, want to start a future elsewhere. It wasn't an easy decision but one to which I am prepared to devote all my energy.

In this context, your suggestions and proposals in the latter half of your letter greatly interest me. I accept your kind invitation to come to Johannesburg and be an employee of the car business you so successfully developed over many years. If working and living conditions in South Africa are anything approaching what I heard and read about, then I'm sure it will be a new and refreshing experience. Ever since I was knee-high I had a fascination for cars and, when my fantasies overwhelmed me, I dreamt of one day becoming a mechanical engineer as a means of living out those fantasies. But neither my brainpower nor the few opportunities that came my way made this route possible. It did not dampen my enthusiasm for a business such as yours, Michael, which has an excellent future.

I am conscious of the winds of change affecting South Africa and the delicate issue of race relations. In our modern world it is not a question of if but when these changes will become reality and we trust all races and creeds can work and live together. Perhaps, we can successfully apply many lessons from your adopted country towards alleviating Northern Ireland's problems. I know it has broadened your perspective and, if only a small proportion of your suggestions for the north are put into practice, it will considerably lessen tensions.

My first and principal goal is to be a conscientious and hard-working member of your staff and to further develop your business to which you have devoted almost your entire working life. I feel honoured to be invited to do so. I will have to carefully broach the subject of leaving with my parents but, in view of serving abroad on several previous occasions, it may lessen the impact. My father will have few qualms about my leaving, believing that this is the first time in his view I'm taking on a serious and worthwhile job. I'm in the strong position of having all the holiday time to discuss it and make all the necessary preparations and arrangements. All going well, I tentatively plan to leave Ireland for Johannesburg around the middle of January.

Your efforts towards peace and reconciliation in Northern Ireland are widely recognized and I sincerely hope you will continue this good work. One of the reasons motivating me to accept the position was the prospect of being able to assist you in this noble cause. Both our minds think alike in this respect and my youthful energy combined with your vast experience may in some small way move the peace process forward.

I will contact you again as soon as I've definite news about all the issues governing my move to South Africa, as well as details of my travel plans. I sincerely appreciate all you have done for me. I take this opportunity to wish you and all the family a very happy Christmas and a prosperous and peaceful 1989.

Sincere and kind regards,

Paul Dowling

CHAPTER 10

Ireland, U.S.A. and South Africa - 1992

Mail deliveries to Liscorley were irregular and often late. Shane, with the joyful expectation of a teenager, looked forward to the daily clatter of letters falling into the metal box, hung precariously under a flap that leaked the outside cold air. Not that many coming nowadays greatly cheered him as a goodly proportion were bills he preferred not seeing, much less paying in full. Government slogans constantly reminded him of the low rate of inflation, a fact not borne out by the bills that stretched his resources each month. There was a reasonable amount of junk mail, much of which found its way unopened into the rubbish bin. He always kept an eye out for personal letters but these were becoming fewer and fewer.

The pleasant surprise he had long awaited came shortly after 10 a.m. on a bright sunny Monday. His first reaction to the loud thud of envelopes hitting his mail-box was disappointment at the prospect of leafing through all the unsolicited paper and glossy print. Just as he was about to discard most of it he noted a rectangular-shaped white envelope at the bottom of the pile and he grabbed it excitedly, seeing it was addressed to Mr and Mrs Shane McCabe. He recognized the handwriting as being Frank's and this was confirmed by the sender's name and address in bold print on the back. It was more than a month since he last wrote, a change from the normal 10-14 day interval, and this letter would set Brenda's mind at ease. He would wait to open it until she returned from her daily run to the village to buy groceries and catch up with the local gossip.

Her eyes widened with excitement on seeing the familiar handwriting, anxiously tore open the envelope and asked Shane to come closer to hear the news. After the first few paragraphs of generalities Frank got down to specifics. He received the confidential news of his imminent release from a senior prison officer and, with typical German efficiency, they identified the hour and day i.e. 10.00 hours on the first Tuesday in May. They warned him to tell nobody but his parents. Realising it was merely six days hence, Brenda wrapped her two arms around Shane, kissed him as rarely she was accustomed to and shed tears of joy. It was the moment they long dreamed about and soon it would all happen. Frank was not allowed to give much information, lest it fell into the wrong hands, except to say he was finding his own way home and couldn't wait for the time to come. There was plenty of time to fill them in on all the details.

As the lilac began to bloom around Liscorley so too were the lengthening early summer days casting a feel-good factor around the locality. It was boosted further by Frank's late afternoon arrival home, courtesy of a neighbour's lift from Liscorley, whose disbelief in what he was witnessing all too obvious. As Shane and Brenda saw him step out of the car and approach the house, they rushed to greet and fondly embrace him. Brenda was in tears and Shane too displayed his emotions as he seldom does. Frank was in remarkably good shape and his broad smile and excited eyes epitomised the joys of homecoming after more than four years of virtual solitude and deprivation. He always stressed in his letters that his basic needs were well attended to and now they were beginning to believe it. Shane and Brenda had an inbuilt fear of his extradition to England and they were delighted it did not materialise as the consequences did not bear thinking about. How he managed to avoid it, given the repeated demands, surprised everybody and intensely annoyed the British hierarchy. Perhaps, he himself will explain in his own good time.

And explain he did the rest of the evening and night until sleep overcame him at midnight. He bore no grudge against the German people as they simply and efficiently only did what was expected of them. He was arrested and imprisoned for being privy to a terrorist attack on British troops stationed in Germany. It didn't take long to establish that the main culprits had already fled Germany and were outside its jurisdiction, a matter of great import and disquiet. The man, Frank, firmly within their grasp was a mere 'guinea pig' and least involved in the terrible deaths, injuries and material destruction. Within a short space of time they were able to confirm he took no active part but, nonetheless, was pivotal to its successful execution. His German language proficiency made him an indispensable link in the chain of operations and this was patently obvious to his interrogators. Were it not for Frank's early exploratory and intelligence-gathering work, the entire mission would have been far less effective.

Shane was unable to contain his curiosity and enquired why, because of Frank's subordinate role, he was imprisoned for over four years. 'It was a battle of wits between the British and Germans,' began Frank. 'The British insisted from the beginning that the perpetrators of this hideous attack should be extradited to Britain and be tried in their courts. When, to their horror, they discovered that the principal culprits had escaped they still demanded a trial in Britain for my alleged involvement but, fortunately for me, the Germans bought valuable time. They questioned the pros and cons of extradition knowing that it was likely to take not months but years before it became reality. All the while the clamour for my indictment in Britain was sure to diminish and, perhaps, lose impetus altogether.

Shane intervened by asking whether he was aggrieved that the 'minor player' received such a long sentence.

'Yes, I was initially,' said Frank. 'But, on the positive side, during the past six to nine months the dreaded subject of extradition wasn't even mentioned, thus sending a signal that my release was imminent. The German government did not formally announce it until they were certain I was safely back in Ireland. There were noisy protests for a day or two in the British House of Commons but the matter ended there. The British never really forgave German security and the police for letting the frontline terrorists escape across its borders.'

'Despite all the bad things that have been said about Germans in the past, they were good friends to you, Frank,' countered Brenda.

'Yes, they certainly were, and, besides, there is an uncanny similarity between the Irish and German situations. Before the recent reunification, it was unthinkable for the powerful German nation to be divided right across its once-proud capital Berlin, a price it paid for its Second World War aggression. More distressing is the fact that it was its communist archrival, the Soviet Union, that imposed its ideology on their east German "cousins" for more than four decades. From the random vibes I received there was a hunger for reunification, until it became a reality in 1989, equalling or exceeding that in Ireland. I wasn't surprised, therefore, that German authorities and people at large were sympathetic to Ireland's cause, a fact that luckily worked in my favour. I couldn't dare utter such words within earshot of an English person.'

For the first week Frank was ill at ease with his new-found freedom and was even beginning to wonder if he had become too accustomed to isolation and his own company. By the time of his release he had grown to tolerate, if not relish, the strict daily routine of the prison. Within days of his internment he set himself the goal of becoming fluent in Dutch and managed to achieve it in less than two years, giving due credit to prison staff who also helped to lessen his daily boredom. He remains convinced that language proficiency fosters understanding and breaks down barriers between races. Had he not shown an interest in languages, he might not have enjoyed the preferential treatment willingly given to him. It matters little what future benefits the German and Dutch languages may bring but they certainly are a welcome bonus. He immediately set about easing himself back to normal life and erasing the black spots of the last four years.

His family get most of the credit for supporting him. Jim was at first slow to act because he wasn't sure what Frank now thought about the I.R.A.'s goals and tactics but it took only a fifteen minute private discussion to clear the air and to convince Jim he shared his own aspirations for peace. 'You know the story, Jim, why I became involved in this messy business and volunteered to help against my better judgement. You might say I was thrust into the lion's den for which I paid a high price. In this game the innocent often either get caught or are killed while the real culprits escape and the pattern rarely if ever changes.

My heart goes out to you for losing the one person you held dearest in this life.' With that, the tears welled up in Jim's eyes and he rushed towards Frank, wrapped his two arms around him and they both embraced for what seemed an eternity, instantly releasing the pent-up emotions that had overwhelmed them for so long. When they let go of each other they began to enjoy a certain calm they had never before experienced. They were now kindred spirits in pursuit of goals that up till recently were alien to them and there was clear evidence of brotherly love and understanding being taken to a far higher level.

It was Shane and Brenda's thoughtfulness that quickly 'repatriated' Frank, by arranging a surprise welcome home party with all his friends in their house for the following Saturday night. His parents felt it was the perfect way for him to quickly forget his immediate past, renew old and some lost friendships and condition him for the future, their contribution to reintegrating him into society. They were surprised it took little effort and he was so composed and relaxed few believed he ever left Liscorley. Midway through the festivities, after many had eaten and drunk more than their share, Frank availed of the opportunity to share his joy with everyone present.

He expressed his immense excitement at being reunited with all of them, his friends, who mean so much to him. Their smiling faces in front of him, which for the past four years were but a distant dream, are again a life-size reality and it was their loyalty encouraged him to be patient and persevering. Not that his captors treated him inhumanely but anybody who experienced the loneliness and boredom - and could be added ignominy - of a prison surely appreciates the joy of release, that same happiness they now saw on his face. He said a big 'thanks' to his parents for organising this surprise party and all those for making it a tremendous success. He looked forward to meeting and socialising with each of them in due course.

He stopped short of giving details of his internment, realising most knew all that was worth knowing and could form their own conclusions. From the vibes he received during the night there was considerable sympathy for his plight for which he was very appreciative. He wanted to leave all that behind him and, being a young and ambitious man, couldn't wait to plan and fully enjoy the rest of his life.

*

It was a day few New Yorkers are likely to forget. Nor will Vincent and his bride Jane fail to long savour the precious memories of their wonderful wedding. Even though they had known each other for more than five years on both sides of the Atlantic, they became formally engaged only three months ago. Vincent didn't heed a close friend's advice, quipping that 'the longer the engagement, the shorter the marriage.' He wasn't in the mood to allow any such negative thoughts enter his head.

Once he accepted the last of his uncle Jim's invitations to come and work in the U.S., everything went smoothly. He was always keenly interested in taking the quantum leap but neither knew how to convince his parents nor had he the courage to step on a plane and break his strong family ties. That was until Deirdre's death changed everything. It convinced him of the dangerous life he was leading and saw little future for himself and Jane, a young beautiful girl he wanted to protect and one day take as his bride. When he finally made up his mind his uncle Jim did the rest, in arranging an air ticket and securing his first job in the Big Apple, that of barman in an upmarket area of the Bronx not far from Jim's home. He was able to meet many Irish from whom he learned much about living and surviving in a large impersonal city. Three aspects greatly impressed him: the many and varied opportunities for work, the generous remuneration for those prepared to work long and hard and the personal freedom to do what you wanted once you remained within the law. Having stayed on the 'edge' of the law for so long in Ireland, he found the latter a refreshing experience.

It was Jane's arrival six months later that all but banished his homesickness and urged him to consider making New York his permanent abode. Even if he wasn't prepared to openly admit it, he had enough of the life he led in Ireland pursuing a cause to which he wasn't one hundred per cent committed. New York offered the ideal safe haven where few recognised him and fewer still cared. All that mattered from here on was to begin a new life, advance as best he knew how and settle down and start a family, as uncle Jim had done three decades earlier. He was sure of his uncle's wholehearted support. The fact that Jane willingly came to New York was proof positive she loved him, making his proposal to her all the easier and their engagement a virtual *fait accompli*.

Even New York's numerous opportunities and attractions didn't compensate for what he missed back home. Several times during the first two months his thoughts were riveted on his native county Cork, often awakening at night to reflect on what was then happening in his rural home community. As an avid sports fan and supporter of his local football and hurling teams, he missed the camaraderie that was part and parcel of the weekly games. Uncle Jim was quick to notice and speeded Vincent's adjustment. 'We have Gaelic Park here in the Bronx where each Sunday young Irishmen play the same games with even greater passion and, with up to 10,000 screaming fans in attendance, we have a "mini-Ireland" on our virtual doorstep. Cork are playing this coming Sunday and it will be an excellent chance to get acquainted.'

The experience was all too emotional. Within thirty minutes of Jim ushering him through the gates and introducing him to several of his longtime friends, Vincent was overawed by it all.

Not only did he meet Irishmen from many diverse counties but he fortuitously rediscovered three long-lost friends from his own small parish, whom he hadn't seen since primary school. It was a tearful but joyous reunion. He talked to others who regularly return home on holidays every few years. He was impressed by their determination to carve our a living in a strange and distant country and had set a standard for himself to emulate. He was confident of doing likewise. His day was complete when Cork hurlers narrowly beat arch-rivals Tipperary in the local championship final. He lavished praise on a far-sighted Irishman for establishing Gaelic Park back in the 1940s which has since become 'a home away from home' for thousands of Irish people.

Arranging a wedding in New York had one major drawback: due to the distance and expense, very few of the groom and bride's Irish relatives and friends were able to attend. It fell short of a traditional Irish wedding, a day when even those with limited funds manage to invite all possible to share their joy and celebration. Initially, Vincent and Jane agonised over what they should do but in the end they settled for a much smaller group, vowing to spare nothing in making it a great success. Neither was much in favour of large and ostentatious weddings and New York provided them with the perfect 'escape' to do as they pleased.

They hadn't reckoned with Jim's influence and, even more so, generosity. On hearing of their plans he insisted that no wedding, wherever it is celebrated, should go ahead without the presence and blessing of the respective parents. It was something the couple had hoped for but were afraid to ask or involve Jim in. After a short informal get-together in his house he said he was happily providing four air tickets to the couple's parents and paying other incidentals to reduce wedding costs. As customary, most expenses are borne by the bride and her parents but Vincent was ever-willing to assist in whatever way he could, jokingly saying that Cork's reputation for generosity and hospitality would not be found wanting. They didn't have long to wait for confirmation.

The wedding was at 2 p.m. in the church of Christ the King in the upper Bronx. The sixty odd well-dressed guests took their seats at least ten minutes in advance of the couple's formal march up the aisle to the front of the altar. The usual *hush* descended on proceedings before the priest appeared, welcomed everybody and started the holy ceremony. Both sets of parents flew in three days earlier, were well rested and adjusted and it was heartening to see them seated side by side in the first pew. Having never previously met in Ireland, they struck up a friendship from setting foot in the Big Apple that augured well for the couple's future. The positive feedback was evident on the couple's faces as they glanced towards the first pew.

The calm and tranquillity that belong to nuptials were much

in evidence and the church ceremony went perfectly.

It proved, however, to be the calm before the storm. For New Yorkers, it was the loud and boisterous procession of cars, with many honking their horns, that rent the afternoon air and helped them remember this not-so-ordinary wedding. This show of exuberance was more acceptable to weekend shoppers and casual strollers than might be to weekday staff going about their busy schedules. Their smiles and laughter proved they were enjoying every moment and it encouraged the 'honkers' to continue for the two mile journey to the hotel where even a louder celebration was soon to begin. 'We must demonstrate to the Yanks that Irish people really know how to enjoy themselves' said Vincent to his radiant bride. 'Perhaps, they should edge closer to the hotel about midnight to appreciate what the end of an Irish wedding is like,' replied Jane. He was more in tune with likely developments when he said 'Some of the more hardened men at our party will have only warmed up by midnight and the real shenanigans will be closer to daybreak.'

The day itself belonged to the Best Man, Barry Coughlan. Barry's friendship with the groom started in the primary school of their rural Cork village, a liaison that was never in danger of breaking. Whether at school or playing at home the two were virtually inseparable until they finished primary at fourteen years of age. Economic circumstances forced Barry to finish his formal education rather than join Vincent at the nearby secondary school. He couldn't wait to pursue his childhood dream of training as a carpenter, to give expression to the countless hours and days he fiddled and chiselled with wood pieces in his home garage. It worked a treat: he was a fully-fledged carpenter at nineteen and, while he was earning enough money to more than support himself, he realised New York offered unlimited opportunities for his trade. And he wasn't disappointed, earning more within five years than he could have imagined. His reunion with Vincent was very emotional, each fighting back tears while recalling many school incidents. Barry was still a bachelor, stressing that no young wife would tolerate the long hours he put in at his work. Vincent's choice of Best Man was ready-made because, despite having fewer years of formal eduction, he lacked nothing when it came to conversation and interjecting in his lilting Cork accent funny stories and anecdotes.

Barry worked hard to ensure that every facet of the wedding reception went smoothly, monitoring cards and e-mails of good wishes he would read after the meal. It was a wise and prudent move. Because of Vincent's republican background, the "baggage" from which can accompany him across continents, he didn't wish to read any reference to that phase of his life. He was aware that those in the I.R.A's hierarchy believe that once you are a member of the organisation, there is no easy way to turn your back on it - even from a distance of 3,000 miles. It was as if a person's past returns to haunt, and occasionally persecute, him. On a happy day like this, Barry made sure he was having none of it. On opening one of the larger cards, it carried a clear printed message from the I.R.A. stating: 'Vincent, you can run but you cannot hide. However long it takes, we will hunt you down and make you answer for your traitorous conduct.'

Barry was so taken aback he temporarily turned ashen-faced but gradually regained his composure and stuffed the card into the inner pocket of his jacket. He decided not to spoil the party by reading it and delayed alerting Vincent until after the honeymoon. Once the band played a few Irish airs it got everybody into the mood, with Vincent and Jane first taking to the dance floor and leading the way for the shyer and more timid. All the while Barry was encouraging everybody, both by word and deed (dancing with various partners), to share fully in the festivities and make it 'a day of days' for the happy couple. He was the perfect catalyst with some well into their seventies or even eighties keeping the tempo with the young and middle-aged.

Barry added variety at regular intervals by calling for volunteers to sing to which there was an instant response. County pride was called into question, with renditions from practically every county in the Irish Republic. It was appropriate to first toast the couple with a popular county Cork song entitled " On The Banks Of My Own Lovely Lee" to which Vincent listened attentively with moist eyes. But it was the last tear he shed that night as joy and exhilaration descended on all present. With the drinks flowing freely the conversation, laughter and noise wafted through the early morning air and awakened light sleepers in the neighbourhood. The wedding of the decade "stirred" people in many different ways. As the couple made their flamboyant exit, after they were encircled and hugged on the dance floor, only those with boundless stamina were able to 'stir' at all. Years later, those who celebrated agreed it was the best the Upper Bronx had ever experienced.

*

Not all who try manage to succeed and it was no different for Jim coming to terms with Deidre's death. During the first few months he was consoled and advised by next of kin, friends and neighbours but to little avail, all doing their damnedest to lessen his grief and be a genuine friend and confidant. He might have spared them the trouble as he knew in his heart and soul he wasn't yet ready to face reality. He heard his Dad's words, relating to another childhood bereavement, re-echo in his ears - 'time is a healer' - and how true were those words just now. He set himself six months to remain with his private thoughts and shut out the world and, judging by progress, he was just about on schedule. That "healing" was beneficial for body and soul but he was determined not to prolong it a single day beyond what was necessary.

He had inner strengths that surfaced more with age and why should he not exploit them? He put all his energy into teaching for a few years but, looking back, cannot explain why he suddenly decided to seek leave-of-absence and join the I.R.A. The only plausible reason lay in his ability to apply the self-same energy to rid his native Northern Ireland of the injustices and inequalities plaguing his fellow Catholics. It was the idealism of youth that lured him along this route that was laden with dangers he could not have foreseen. He was now older, a good deal wiser and burdened with regret. It is a common failure of youth to continually bash their heads against brick walls only to discover all-too-late that force often begets superior counter forces that stymie long term progress. The "enemy" becomes only more entrenched and resolute. Were it not for Deirdre's death, he might still be engaged in a struggle from which he could not easily extricate himself. He owed her a debt of gratitude and was determined to more than repay her.

Since his very first day in front of a class, he was always conscious of a teacher's enormous influence on the minds and actions of his pupils. Jim recalls his own childhood school days and the teachers he respected and admired and a few he preferred to forget. He himself tried to practise and teach excellent standards of conduct and behaviour, striving to inculcate in youngsters a respect for the law and their fellow human beings. He made every effort to impart unbiased knowledge and encourage students sift right from wrong in all walks of life. It was nothing more than responsible law-abiding citizens should possess and in turn pass on to others. He remembers a history teacher giving his own biased views on political developments in Ireland that contributed in no small way to Jim joining the I.R.A. Was he not responsible for preaching "heresy" and warping young minds or spreading an "infection" that one day could reach epidemic proportions? Jim was all too aware of teacher power and influence and he was determined to exploit these qualities. His future strategy and plans rapidly crystallised before his eyes.

Central to this strategy must be Northern Ireland's fertile fields in which to sow and propagate his seed. He identified multi-faceted segregation as fuelling most of the hatred and confrontations between Catholics and Protestants and, the extent to which this issue is tackled and resolved, determined the success rate. He lost no time before starting, setting out in a very tangible and constructive way to reduce the barriers between the two religious communities. And what better place to commence than in the primary schools with the youngest pupils. Through Jim's persistent efforts, he was instrumental in convening a series of meetings with a cadre of similarly-dedicated Catholic and Protestant teachers where problems were thoroughly aired but none were seen as too big to surmount. Soon a plan was put in place after which it was all action.

Step one concentrated on an effective information exchange programme without which subsequent actions are meaningless. 'Let's face it,' Jim confided to his fellow teachers at the very first meeting, 'Catholic teachers must explain their views and feelings to Protestant kids and invite questions so as to bridge the communications barrier and Protestant teachers can reciprocate in Catholic schools. It is seen as the beginning of a long term sustained effort during which both communities feel comfortable discussing issues with one another before searching for solutions. Let's first select a small nucleus of schools and expand according to the progress we make, calling our initiative "Programme for Understanding and Fairness" From the dozen teachers present here tonight, almost equally divided between Catholic and Protestant, we can sow the seeds of a better future.'

These clear and determined few words not only heightened interest but drew a loud and sustained applause. From the ensuing lively and friendly discussion between the participants, Jim believed he was already beginning to weaken the sectarian barriers. His immediate reaction was regret it took so long to reach this very preliminary stage but it was now time for positive thoughts and direct action. A consensus was reached to begin at a total of 12 schools the following Monday and take things from there. His morale was further boosted by the news of a recent agreement with more than the required number of schools and it only remained to confirm the dates and times.

The following week's results were unprecedented in Northern Ireland's tortured history. At Friday evening's meeting each teacher effusively summarised the significant progress in such a short time and all agreed the strategy was working. There was a gross lack of understanding and appreciation of each other's point of view and it was only slowly beginning to change, something they needed to work on for several weeks and even months. The interest of and great response from the students, and the continual feedback through questions and discussion, provided the welcome springboard. Jim kept reminding all those with attentive ears that the formula was correct and they should not flinch from their goal, but be patient and persevering. The small core group of teachers was equally motivated and enthusiastic, auguring well for the future.

Though information exchange is very necessary and effective it didn't, however, go far enough, doing little or nothing for the core problem of integration. Traditionally, Protestant and Catholic children lead separate lives both at school and at home, with few opportunities to mix, play games and socialise. Compounding this anomaly was the desire of many to remain apart, fuelled by centuries of awe, mistrust and even hatred. That presented the greatest challenge to the teachers' tact and ingenuity but Jim and his colleagues remained undaunted. Through delicate negotiations with educational authorities and school management, they arranged exchange visits between certain classes of the chosen schools, starting with simple informal discussions but quickly progressing to participation in sports. It was the perfect catalyst. Care was taken to avoid perpetuating old animosities between rival Protestant and Catholic teams and the adoption of mixed competitions worked a treat, with new previously unthinkable friendships soon springing up and blossoming. When youngsters share the same likes and dislikes and discover some common ground, religious differences are often tolerated and even appreciated. That's if bigoted parents do not attempt to stifle true friendships before they mature, as has so often happened in Northern Ireland. The 'pioneering' teachers were on the alert for this and did their best to minimise it.

Everything was going according to plan. The final phase Jim never imagined would take place in his lifetime was now being acted out in front of his eyes. Children of both denominations were exchanging home visits, going to the cinema and travelling to play sports together. Many die-hards were sceptical and some even tried without success to discourage it but the winds of change were blowing strongly and difficult to stop. And who would dare turn back the clock? The dedicated teachers were still impatient with the scale and pace of progress as only a dozen schools were involved in the programme and their thoughts turned to covering the entire province. They had a secret plan and were bent on seeing it through.

It was now time to spread the gospel. They sent letters to the principal of every school within the province describing the initiatives already taken, the success achieved and the desire to expand the programme, scheduling a provincial-level meeting for two weeks hence to discuss the plans, procedures and personnel required. A few 'pioneers' of the pilot scheme were the key speakers and they were listened to in almost hushed silence. It was unanimously agreed to push on with the programme, sensing it was the opportune time to leave the past behind, and it boosted several-fold the success already attained. Even the most cynical agreed this novel approach did more in six months to change the minds and attitudes of people in Northern Ireland than the previous three decades. Jim was equally ebullient, saying there was now no obstacle to peace and reconciliation.

Ironically, while all this good work was proceeding the counter forces of militancy too continued unabated. But then, if one cared to trawl through the history books, was it ever any different over the last few decades and even further back? That's what makes much of Irish history, and particularly its long battle against British rule, complex and sometimes inexplicable to outsiders. Adverse publicity projects many of Northern Ireland's population as trouble makers, or terrorists in the extreme, despite only a tiny, tiny minority justifying this label, an indication of bad news outpacing the good. There are many working tirelessly for peace but their massive contribution is never fully recognized and often ignored. In the end it is the triumph of good over evil that ought to be pursued and only it alone has a place among civilised and democratic societies.

The large hall of the Georgian building, situated at the north-east corner of Northchester city's main square, was packed to capacity for the unusual and surprise ceremony. It was precisely 8 p.m. when, under the glare of TV cameras, the Lord Major rose and went to the podium, immediately in front of the twelve 'pioneering' teachers to be honoured. After the normal preliminaries, he got to the business on hand. 'It is a signal honour to present awards to twelve teachers whose work for understanding and peace is nothing short of phenomenal. Not only has each done outstanding work but, through example and encouragement, they have extended the network throughout the province. It is a massive achievement in a very short space of time and the programme they started is growing and becoming stronger by the day. Not wishing to detract from each individual's contribution, I'm sure none of the eleven will mind if I single out Jim McCabe for special mention. He first conceived the idea, drew up the plan and implemented the programme with the help of a fine bunch of young dedicated people. I am proud to be asked to present their awards here tonight.' Afterwards Jim, as spokesman for the group, thanked the Lord Mayor and extended his appreciation to all who helped in one way or another.

It was early morning when Jim returned home and got to bed. Exhausted though he was, sleep did not come easily because the exhilaration of the night's events kept his mind racing. Deep down he was thrilled that his hard work was recognised and acknowledged but, as the excitement subsided and drowsiness set in, nostalgia took hold of him. His mind wandered back to an inhospitable Ballysorley street where he had lost the only girl he really loved and to whom he had made a lifelong commitment. As sad thoughts began swirling in his mind, and remembering all he had achieved in recent months, it was his turn to reciprocate his love by whispering softly at the onset of sleep 'I did it all for you, Deirdre.'

*

'Tell me more about your childhood and adolescence in county Kerry,' Sarah McCabe whispered to Paul Dowling in a fashionable north Johannesburg nightclub at the rather late hour of 4 a.m. She nestled close to him, a liberty she took more often since revealing a few months ago that Paul was the only man she had dated more than three times. It was an admission hard to comprehend judged by her radiant smile, vivacity, outgoing exuberance and sheer beauty. Why, Paul mused, did a beautiful and talented 27 year old evade the clutches of many eligible bachelors for so long? He counted himself extremely lucky she had and was quietly confident he could one day woo her into marriage. Paul was only a few months from his 30th birthday and, although he always vowed never to settle down until well into his thirties, he was not the kind to let a good opportunity slip by. As he looked straight into her lovely round eyes and wrapped his two arms tightly around her slim waist, he kissed her firmly but tenderly. She held his kiss for what seemed an eternity and purposely brushed her soft breast against his chest that visibly aroused both of them. When Paul released his grip and composed himself he took her hand and gently stroked it. 'Sarah, my love, the question you posed is long and complex but you should hear the answer another night at an earlier time.' With that, they left the club arm-in-arm and made their way home.

South Africa brought Paul luck in ways he never imagined, thanks to Michael McCabe's kindness and unstinting support. Paul's longtime fascination with cars and mechanics couldn't have found a more fertile platform than Michael's car showrooms, filling and service station. Within a few years of Michael's arrival as an immigrant in 1957 he had saved the minimum start-up capital to carve out his future in a strange but prosperous country. In the short space of five years he had paid back most of the borrowed money, after one decade he was netting well in excess of one million rand (over St£100,000) annually and is now one of the country's top five richest car businessmen. In February 1961 he met and married Jennifer Ashley from Brighton, England who bore them a son Jonathan and a daughter Sarah. Just like Paul, Jonathan grew up with a passion for cars which in his teens developed into an obsession with racing cars. By his 21st birthday he was national Formula One champion, a title he was to retain for two more years. The models he drove were designed to travel at higher and higher speeds which stretched his ability and skill to control them. His short life came to a tragic end just seven days short of his 24th birthday when his car hit a wall, overturned and caught fire on a slippery rain-washed track near Durban. His body was virtually incinerated leaving little more than ashes for his parents, relatives and friends to mourn. Not only did Michael and Jennifer lose their only son but heir to the magnificent business for which they had long groomed him.

Tragedy sometimes begets opportunity and it fell to Paul Dowling to fill the breach. It was their shared aspirations to a peaceful settlement in Northern Ireland that first prompted Paul to contact Michael McCabe. Their friendship steadily flourished and gained a new momentum after Jonathan's death when Paul did everything within his power to lessen the grief that was consuming Michael and Jennifer. It coincided with Paul's desire to leave Ireland and seek his future elsewhere far from the pressures that were straining his ability to cope. And he did not have to look beyond South Africa. Not when he had the God-given opportunity and scope to indulge his childhood passion under the tutorship and guidance of a kind and friendly fellow countryman. It promised to open up a new and fascinating world.

He took up the challenge from day one and within months showed flair and business acumen beyond his years, steadily expanding Michael's sales and business to new heights. Ever since Michael first set foot in South Africa he vowed that, should the Lord spare him his health, he would retire by the age of 60 and leave his next of kin carry on, allowing him to do all the things he loved but for which he never previously had enough time. With Jonathan's death that plan went slightly askew. He reached his 60th birthday in November 1988 just a couple of months before Paul arrived and, although he was delegating more and more since then, he was still more involved than he wished. Foremost among his priorities was to devote much of his attention to peace in Northern Ireland but wasn't yet clear how he might approach it. Observing the way Paul was successfully carrying on the business, he knew there would be ample time to make trips to Northern Ireland whenever he chose to do so.

After Jonathan's death Sarah willingly stepped in to help her

Dad, psychologically conditioning herself to stay for six months until somebody permanent was recruited. That in time wasn't necessary as she made the job her own. Her earlier secretarial course followed by a few others in computer technology empowered her to do all - and more - than she ever needed in the office. And her Dad concentrated on the outdoor work, with Sarah lending a hand when time permitted. Without saying so directly, Michael was looking forward to the day when Sarah might be able to take charge of the business and employ one man to take over from himself. Little did he then envisage Paul's arrival and how he was able to do the work of not only one but two or three men. It was all working so well Michael wondered if it were just a pleasant dream. He recently noticed that their relationship extended beyond the workplace and that was giving added substance to his dream. Right now things were never so good and they promised to get even better.

News of Jim McCabe's exemplary work spread far and wide and, on the strength of several prestigious awards, it was highlighted in newspapers, magazines, radio and TV . But, despite the extensive publicity, he was ready to admit the mammoth task had scarcely begun.

His uncle Michael in Johannesburg followed events with an inordinate interest, recognized Jim's magnificent contribution towards peace and wondered how they might expand and intensify it. Besides frequently contacting Jim, he was now travelling home three or four times per year, engaging in numerous meetings and discussions and trying to fast-forward the peace initiative. Conscious of what they might learn from South Africa, whose majority black population was in the throes of enjoying a long-deprived freedom, Michael invited interested groups from Northern Ireland to study their approach and he escorted them on visits. There were many common problems and lessons to be applied and it was generally acknowledged the whole exercise was very productive and beneficial. Michael's contribution towards peace, although starting later, was gradually gaining ground on Jim's.

'Let's have coffee in the lounge and continue our conversation' said Paul. He and Sarah just finished a sumptuous dinner in the hotel restaurant and was postponing the subject he least wanted to talk about. He knew Sarah would keep him to his promise and he began shortly after they were comfortably seated and had taken the first sips. 'Mine was a childhood full of joy and contentment. Being the youngest in a family of four - two sisters and one brother - I received the love and affection befitting the "pet" and lapped it up. It was an idyllic rural setting with so much to do and see there were too few hours in each day to achieve it. I observed the world through my young and innocent eyes and saw beauty. My home is situated in one of the most scenic and picturesque regions of county Kerry where tourists of many nationalities come in their multi-thousands each summer. And they are rarely if ever disappointed.'

'I've heard so much about Kerry scenery that I anxiously look forward to seeing it before too long' remarked Sarah. 'It's one of my promises I'm determined to keep,' said Paul.

He went on to explain that transition from childhood to adulthood is seldom smooth and it was particularly troublesome in his home. All his distant ancestors were of republican stock, fiercely proud of their heritage and bent on liberating all of Ireland from British colonisation and oppression. His father inherited more than his due share and was in no mood to see his sons and daughters think or act otherwise. Paul's views were diametrically opposed to his dad's, seeing the peaceful and non-violent route as Ireland's ultimate and lasting salvation. Paul became engaged in peacekeeping missions abroad in a couple of the most turbulent and war-torn regions which brought him intense personal satisfaction. His Dad was not impressed, letting him know his energy could better be employed at home to advance his own ideology. After a childhood of love and deep affection, that single issue was to colour - and eventually destroy - their future relationship. It reached the point of having little or no dialogue and Paul was a virtual stranger, bordering on an outcast, during his regular homecomings. His attempts at appeasement and reconciliation - and these were numerous - were of no avail. Meanwhile, his sister Deirdre was killed pursuing goals strongly espoused by his Dad, on whose life the tragedy took a heavy toll. Ironically and sadly, it did not change his Dad's mentality one iota but, if anything, increased his resolve to push on regardless. It is all so terribly sad and Paul felt powerless to do much about it.

'I hate unloading all my troubles on you Sarah but it is comforting to discuss these with an understanding person like yourself. Coming to South Africa was the tonic I needed and was doubly fortunate your Dad took me under his wing. He is more a father to me than my own ever was, a sad fact to have to admit.' He struggled to hold back the tears and looked away lest she should see a young man so broken. 'Up to now, like many Irishmen, I've been slow expressing my deep love for you but I cannot thank you enough for all you've done for me. Since coming to Johannesburg my personal life has changed no end and you deserve all the credit.' With that compliment, he leaned forward and kissed her gently on the lips.

It was now Sarah's turn. 'We are kindred spirits, Paul, and have much in common. You had the misfortune of losing your sister in the prime of life, a tragedy that brought untoward suffering to all your family, and what's most annoying is it should never have happened.'

Sarah went on to describe how her only brother's life was cut short pursuing a sport that had danger written all over it. Every time he raced, her parents and herself were on tenterhooks waiting expectantly and agonizingly until he returned home in one piece. Neither my Mam nor Dad favoured what he was doing but, the more they expressed their reservations, the more he seemed to continue regardless. Formula One was his passion, breaking record after record, but with each came added danger and risk to life. He was in the throes of breaking yet another record the day he skid uncontrollably to his horrible death. Mam was in bits and Dad lost his only son he trained and groomed to take over his thriving business. Understandably, Dad was a broken man for up to a year and only slowly recovered thereafter. When you contacted him about coming to Johannesburg, he immediately consented and it lifted his spirits enormously. Intuitively, he had great hopes you might relish the challenge and one day take over where Jonathan left off. And how fast his dreams were becaming a reality!

'You will be pleased knowing how highly you are regar[ded] by both Mam and Dad and you fill with distinction the vacu[um] created by Jonathan's death. I'm getting vibes of elation that th[e] two of us are going steady and they certainly would not stand in the way of it developing further, if you will pardon my arrogance and confidence .' Paul couldn't hide his satisfaction and delight, responding that so far in South Africa life could scarcely be better.

Paul bought two Irish coffees to round off a most enjoyable night and for the first time Sarah attempted to come to terms with her own identity. 'Given Northern Ireland's troubles and England's poor handling of the situation, many of our friends in Johannesburg consider it rather odd Dad married my English-born Mam. But it was a match made in Heaven as never once did they have a serious row - more than can be said for many marriages nowadays. Politics is seldom a topic of discussion in our house but, when it is aired, my Mam comes out strongly on the side of the Irish, saying the days of colonisation are long gone and the whole island of Ireland well deserves its freedom and independence. Seeing I'm a "mongrel", of Irish-English parents and having lived since birth in South Africa, I have an identity problem. As you're witnessing first hand, we've had racial difficulties of our own here in South Africa, are on the threshold of black majority rule and entering an uncertain future.'

Paul was aware of Sarah's concerns and wanted to allay her fears. 'Your parents have shown that love transcends many problems and are a shining example to others. We need to foster that same love and understanding so that strife and senseless killings in so many countries can be alleviated. You're blessed having such wonderful parents, and you've inherited equally laudable traits, so don't fret about identity and being "mongrel" -just be you.' A broad, happy smile radiated from her face and Paul knew her mind was at ease. He was taken by her radiant beauty, as she rose and took his arm, and Paul silently prayed that before long she would permanently be at his side.

*

nd takes great pride in its own traditions and
ʼry people, a year in which the county
ʒress beyond the provincial final is a total
to win the All Ireland, the ultimate prize, is
tory. And this coveted prize had now eluded the
for six years in a row with little sign of an early
But, as records testify, since the Gaelic Athletic
ation was founded near the end of the 19th Century,
ry had won on average two or three All-Irelands in each
decade and there were no valid reasons for any sudden change.
Their ability to recover from a few years of mediocrity, to
emerge victorious in the next, is legendary.

This year 1992 was noteworthy for a different and bizarre
reason. When on a bright May morning the people of Inistogue
and the entire county awoke to the shocking revelation that their
revered Catholic Bishop was at the centre of a sex scandal, the
news spread quickly around the globe. The ordinary devout
Inistogue parishioners were stunned into silence and it dented
their faith and trust in the clergy to whom they had long
remained loyal. To the less dedicated it was a wake-up call,
confirming what they had often suspected that Catholic priests
and the hierarchy were subject - and sometimes liable to
succumb - to the temptations that continuously test lay people.
More examples were to follow that changed the attitudes and
worshipping practices of Catholics countrywide.

Instead of stifling or muting these revelations, as they most
certainly were in Seamus Dowling's childhood, they were now
openly discussed and in the public domain. Seamus' active
involvement with the G.A.A. brought him into contact with the
bishop at occasional meetings and informal dinners and he
never once suspected anything untoward. For a devout
practising Catholic the unwelcome news hit Seamus hard and he
struggled coming to terms with it, even trying to include it
among his bad dreams. Perhaps he was having more than his
own share of unpleasant dreams because, just two weeks after
hearing what he never expected in his lifetime, his life took a
turn for the worse. Prior to the advent of new medication that
might have forestalled it, Seamus developed a stroke that he had

long been forewarned about by his local doctor.

Ironically, it was his longtime close friend and neighbour, Joe Moriarty, who first came to his assistance, only about 300 yards from Seamus' home. He was returning from one of his evening farm walks, which allowed him time to brood on subjects which had the tendency to set the heart racing and that ran counter to his doctor's advice. On closing the last of a number of gates, to guard against cattle wandering to fields yet unsuitable for grazing, he felt severe tightening chest pains extending down his left arm, causing him to stumble and fall forward on his face and stomach. It was thirty minutes later when Joe came by and raised the alarm and he was helped home by neighbours. But it wasn't for long. Doctor Michael Egan arrived almost immediately and Seamus was soon on his way by ambulance to the local hospital. His wife Nora, trying to come to terms with the trauma as best she knew how, remained at his bedside keeping vigil throughout the night, without a word being exchanged. Next day's prognosis gave her little scope for optimism.

It was shortly after 10 a.m. when coronary specialist Dr. Timothy McAuliffe made his daily rounds and, after examining Seamus' records and checking his condition, called and ushered Nora to his private office. Following the usual preliminaries and small talk, in an attempt to allay her nervousness and anxiety, he broached the subject that after even thirty one years of service he felt uneasy discussing. 'I realise, Mrs Dowling, the shock and distress of your husband's sudden illness and would like to reassure you he will receive the very best medical attention we can offer. He is a very sick man and after yesterday's severe stroke that left him paralysed down the left side and with a slight speech impairment, there is a grave risk he could have another stroke in the days and weeks ahead from which he might not recover. I sincerely hope it doesn't happen but want you to be aware of this possibility.' He enquired about her family and their whereabouts and, without wanting to cause alarm, encouraged her to contact them and describe what happened. In that way, she would have no regrets should he become terminally ill. In fact, many of them may wish to come and see him within the next couple of weeks. As there was no immediate danger - at least within the next few days and under the hospital's full care and attention - he advised Nora to return home and get some well-needed rest, after which she could visit him every other day. The hard cold facts worried her but she was pleased he was under the watchful eye of Dr. McAuliffe whose expertise was very highly regarded within the county.

Within Inistogue's small community news of any sort travels quickly and, when it comes to bad news, it approaches the speed of light. Despite doctor's advice that only close relatives should visit because of his deteriorating health, there was a virtual procession to his bedside within the first few days. It was in part a reflection of the esteem with which he was held not only in Inistogue but several surrounding parishes and in equal measure to the warm friendliness and hospitality for which Kerry people are renowned. Many that Seamus had worked with and knew in republican circles made no secret of their presence and there was a covert air of security around the hospital. Not that it bothered well-wishers who were genuinely concerned for his wellbeing and prayed fervently for his speedy recovery. Nora visited daily - and sometimes twice - and in between wrote to and phoned relatives both near and far, as well as attending to her myriad household chores.

Within three days of leaving the hospital's intensive care unit and out of imminent danger, Seamus couldn't wait to get home. Apart from a week's hospitalisation at the age of 15 for an appendicitis operation, he had never since spent a single day in hospital where the medicinal vapours and odours reminded him too much of death, a route some of his older Inistogue friends had already taken. The less pleasant odours of cows and their by-products, second nature to him since birth, were the convalescent medicines he now needed most. And he put his case forcibly to Dr. McAuliffe during his rounds next morning, a man who was in tune with the wishes and desires of his patients. The experienced doctor had lost many past battles and arguments with Seamus and knew he was even less likely to win this particular one. Nor was he prepared to try. 'I'll allow you home after tomorrow on condition that you don't lift a finger to farm work and you follow the strict procedures I prescribe.' Again, Seamus got what he wanted and he could never boast about doing exactly as he was told.

The morale boost of just a few days at home was enough to bring about a considerable improvement in his health. He was better able to sit up in bed and hold short conversations with the many relatives who had come from near and far. It was late afternoon on the fourth day when his 'baby' son Paul entered his father's bedroom, after the long exhausting air trip from Johannesburg. Within 12 hours of his mother's telephone message he had boarded a plane for the ten-hour journey to London and onwards to Dublin and Kerry airports. Hoping for the best but fearing the worst he was unable to relax, much less get even an hour's sleep on the long homeward trek. Exhausted though he was, he perked up on seeing his Dad sitting up in bed with a cheerful disposition. He took a deep breath and wondered whether the barriers that had distanced them in the past would continue or did his new job and life in South Africa win his Dad's respect and admiration he had long been deprived? He now desperately wanted to dispel this thought and, even if his Dad still harboured grudges, Paul was having none of it. After all, he had advanced his career no end, was justifiably proud of what he had achieved in a short time and so should his Dad. His sense of worth and self-esteem were at an all-time high and beginning to show.

'Welcome son' came scarcely audible from his lips, whereupon Paul wrapped his two arms gently around him and, sobbing uncontrollably, whispered 'I love you Dad.' It was merely four words he had often wanted to say to his face but could never somehow manage to muster up the courage. Why did he have to wait until his Dad's ill-health prevented him reciprocating, hopefully in a positive manner? Paul then sat on a bedside chair and went on to describe his work and lifestyle since first arriving in South Africa and it was a success story, bordering on a fairytale, from beginning to end. He excitedly revealed his intention to marry Sarah McCabe in about six months time and was to inherit and run her father's business. His Dad's face brightened on hearing the good news and said, if his health improved, he would dearly love to attend the wedding and strengthen still further the friendship bonds between the Dowling and McCabe families. Paul's non-medical expertise left him in some doubt whether his Dad's health and fitness would allow him to attend.

Before leaving his Dad's side, he heard statements he preferred were left unsaid. 'I am extremely proud of your achievements, Paul, and wish you luck in your future life. If you will forgive me reiterating old issues, I am less than happy with your stance on and contribution to Northern Ireland. Many of our brave republicans on both sides of the border continue their struggle against colonialism, some of whom lose their lives for a cause they firmly believe in. Generations of Dowlings have not been found wanting and I am both surprised and disappointed you did not answer the call. I will die happily if you pledge to uphold and honour our family tradition.' He had used up all his energy and Paul was stunned into silence. Several minutes elapsed before he was able to rise from the chair and, with tearful eyes, tried to bid farewell lovingly to a father with whom he never really empathised.

'Dad, I wish I could have been a better son to you and followed your advice. Nothing has caused me more anguish than failing you miserably and not being the son you wanted me to be, not the republican Dowling and torch-bearer. But, I promise to do all in my power to try and resolve Northern Ireland's problems, perhaps not precisely in the way you perceive things, but very constructive nonetheless. The fact we see the situation and solutions differently is not a valid reason for driving a wedge between us. All I want you to do right now is take good care of yourself and regain your full health.' Upon hearing his Mam turn the door knob and enter the room, he approached and took his Dad's hand in his, held it gently and said tearfully 'I'm sorry Dad and I love you as only a youngest son could.' With that, he left the room and allowed his parents a few precious moments together.

Later that evening Paul invited his older brother and mentor, Gerald, for a quiet drink in Inistogue's least-frequented bar. Alcoholic drink was incidental to what they had to discuss but the ambience was perfect to share ideas and concerns. Gerald was only too aware of Paul's strained relations with his Dad, the distress to both, and, at a crucial time such as this for the entire family, he would do all he could to repair the damage. At the same time, he knew there was little he could do or say to change his Dad's way of thinking nor was he convinced of Paul's inclination to give an inch or two. Two stubborn Dowlings, at opposite ends of the spectrum, staunchly believing each was acting correctly. Can some of it be put down to the generation gap? So thought Gerald in his youth, until he discovered in his maturity he was following in his father's footsteps. How much did environment contribute to this? Now he was virtually certain it meant everything. Gerald had no choice, save being expelled from home and losing his right to inherit the family farm, but to pursue his Dad's republican ways. He took the easy and only viable option.

'For you, Paul, the decision of what to do with your life is entirely in your hands. From the best medical advice we have, our Dad may not survive long beyond the end of this year and, while he has worked tirelessly for the republican movement, we must chart our own course. We possess many of his genes but it no longer obliges us to follow in his path. We are of a new generation of independently-minded human beings and perfectly capable of making our own decisions. What you have done for peace abroad is truly monumental and, if you apply the same energy in that direction here at home, you will be a worthy candidate for a Nobel peace prize.' It was a surprising admission from a man whose republican work had already earned him a notorious reputation. As there were signs he might soon escape from his Dad's clutches, was Gerald about to have second thoughts about the wisdom of his ways? Or was his baby brother's example beginning to have the desired effect? Whatever change was brewing, Paul noticed a drastic softening in Gerald's attitude. Gerald was in jovial mood and they celebrated with a final drink before returning home.

Next morning, there was no change in his Dad's health and Paul was anxious to return to Johannesburg where now his new life was firmly taking shape. He was beginning to feel equally, or more so, at home in his adopted country as his native turf and it frightened him a little. He was reluctant to admit Sarah was the primary attraction, although the thriving car business contributed immensely to his job satisfaction and, when taken together, they provided a very satisfactory mix. After all the early uncertainty in his life, God was perhaps justly rewarding him and he was relishing this turnabout.

He was less than an hour into the long flight from London to Johannesburg when Paul fell into a deep sleep, induced by the stress and emotions of the previous few days. A rare assortment of dreams forced him to move and twist in his window seat and he uttered the odd word which both alerted and amused his fellow passengers. His dreams covered events from early childhood in Inistogue to the most recent at his new abode, invoking feelings ranging from great distress to sheer exhilaration. He reckoned he was experiencing and battling against the vicissitudes that were part and parcel of every young man's life and he was emerging with a significant degree of success. In brief, he had taken the hard course and benefited from it. He awoke to the hostess' words 'in a few minutes we shall be landing at Jan Smuts international airport' which jerked him back to reality. The strong feeling of coming home at once unsettled and excited him.

It was nothing to his excitement at seeing Sarah expectantly await him outside the customs area. They hugged and kissed in view of all for a couple of minutes before proceeding to Sarah's car. Driving westwards towards the city centre, she revealed a few secrets.

'Dad would like you to take over his business right away as he intends to spend more than half of each year in Northern Ireland working more closely with Jim McCabe. He's disturbed by the continuing level of violence and wants to redouble his efforts for peace. He also told me how keen he is to see us married and settled before too long. Oh, and nearly forgot, your Mam phoned to say that following the doctor's visit earlier today, he's much more upbeat about your Dad's longer-term health prospects.'

Paul wondered whether these almost unbelievable and sweet statements were the culmination of the dream begun on the plane. For now, life could scarcely be better and he vowed not to scupper his chances of keeping it so.